ETHAN
PIERCE

The K9 Files, Books 1–2

Dale Mayer

THE K9 FILES, BOOKS 1–2
Beverly Dale Mayer
Valley Publishing Ltd.

ISBN-13: 978-1-773364-43-8
Print Edition

Books in This Series

Ethan, Book 1
Pierce, Book 2
Zane, Book 3
Blaze, Book 4
Lucas, Book 5
Parker, Book 6
Carter, Book 7
Weston, Book 8
Greyson, Book 9
Rowan, Book 10
Caleb, Book 11
Kurt, Book 12
Tucker, Book 13
Harley, Book 14
Kyron, Book 15
Jenner, Book 16
Rhys, Book 17
Landon, Book 18
Harper, Book 19
Kascius, Book 20
The K9 Files, Books 1–2
The K9 Files, Books 3–4
The K9 Files, Books 5–6
The K9 Files, Books 7–8
The K9 Files, Books 9–10
The K9 Files, Books 11–12

About This Bundle

Ethan

When one door closes … second chances open another …

Ethan was lost after a major accident abruptly shifted him from a military life to a civilian one, from working with dogs to odd jobs … In that time, he'd spent months healing from his physical injuries. When he connects with Badger and the rest of his Titanium Corp. group of former SEALs, Badger offers Ethan an opportunity he can't refuse. A chance to do the work he used to do … with a twist.

Cinnamon works from home as a project manager plus is heavily involved in global dog rescues—dogs of all kinds. When Ethan walks into the next door's vet's office with an injured shepherd in his arms, she sees another lost soul—just like the canine ones she helps.

Ethan knows he's about to take a dangerous step, but he's on the job, and no one—on the job or not—hurts animals while he's around. This poor shepherd has taken enough abuse, and Ethan fears she is only the tip of a nightmare he's determined to uncover. But he knows she's going to lead him in the right direction.

He has his sights set on saving one dog in particular, Sentry: K9 File 01.

Pierce

Just because helping out is the right thing to do doesn't make it easy …

Pierce is on the hunt for Salem, a K9 military dog that belonged to Pete, a veteran, who can no longer look after himself or the dog. So the dog has been handed from owner to owner—until she's become too much to handle—and now the law is involved. No one has Salem's best interests in mind … and they definitely don't have Pete's either. Pierce is about to change all that … whether they like it or not.

Hedi, a young deputy, has lived in Arrowhead, Colorado, all her life and knows Pete and Salem but was helpless to do much when greed overtook his friends and family. She recognizes in Pierce the same qualities that Pete has, and, by Pierce's actions alone, she knows a corner has been turned. She also understands the locals won't take it lying down, and this means war …

Pierce served his country overseas for many years, and seeing another veteran in trouble makes him realize the fight isn't over, even after life in the navy ends. In fact, this battle has just begun. But … this one … Pierce will finish. And he plans to win.

Sign up to be notified of all Dale's releases here!
https://geni.us/DaleNews

ETHAN

The K9 Files, Book 1

Dale Mayer

PROLOGUE

B ADGER WALKED INTO the office for the impromptu meeting and smiled at his friends. "I had a very unusual and cryptic conversation this morning, which is why we are all gathered here."

"You going to tell us about it?" Erick asked, lifting a fresh cup of coffee to his lips.

"No, he is," Badger said, pointing to one wall. "I have Commander Glen Cross on the line." He hit the button on the phone. "Go ahead, Commander. You're on video. What can we do for you?"

The commander's stern countenance filled the screen before them. "Who is that there with you? Identify your-selves."

One by one the men executed a roll call.

The commander, a smile in his voice, said, "Now those are some names to warm my heart. I heard you've started a new company, Titanium Corp, to employ other former SEALs in situations like your own. Is that correct?"

"Yes, that's correct." Badger glanced around the room at the waiting faces. "Is there something we can help you with?"

"Yes, possibly. But only if you have time to volunteer. This is a big-heart mission that unfortunately doesn't come with pay. ... You know how very proud the military is of our K9 program, correct?"

The men nodded.

"Absolutely," Geir said. "We personally have had good reasons to be thankful for that program."

Badger added, "It's been a huge success. We worked with the dogs in Afghanistan several times."

"We had a tracking system for those dogs that left the military," the commander continued, "to make sure they went to good homes. But, with budget cuts, we've run into a bit of a problem."

"What problem is that?" Erick asked. "Those dogs deserve the best."

"We don't want them treated like they were in the Vietnam War," Jager said, his voice hard.

"Absolutely," the commander said. "I've got a dozen K9 files here of dogs that have ended their naval careers. However, we've lost track of them. The cases were supposed to be looked into, as we want to make sure our veterans, human and K9, are well cared for. But so much work is involved, and we're constantly dealing with other aspects of the K9 program, so we have no time to investigate. I find that very difficult, and I can't ignore these dogs' plights."

"What situations are they in now?"

"Everything," the commander said. "You know we have a system for naming them, and all these dogs are tattooed in a specific sequence. I have the fact sheets in each of their files. For example, the first one graduated and was immediately sent to Afghanistan. He was active for about nine months. His owner took an IED and went home as a quadriplegic. The dog went home with him, not as injured but as no longer fit for active duty. Unfortunately the owner was involved in a severe crash within six months of getting home and was killed. His wife couldn't handle the situation, and the dog was handed over to a dog trainer, who then found a home for him, who then got rid of the dog because he had behavioral problems. And so on. His whereabouts are now unknown."

The men exchanged hard glances.

"What is it you would like us to do?" Cade asked cautiously.

"I deeply care about these animals that have served our country," the commander said in a low voice, "so I'm asking you to do anything you can to locate them, to ensure they are in a good environment. But only if you can volunteer your time because there's zero budget money. Otherwise I'd be getting my men here to do this."

"You want us to track down the dogs and make sure they are okay?" Badger asked.

"We created these dogs," the commander said. "We made them the trained soldiers they are. Society seems to think, if these K9s can't get along with people, then the only answer is to put them down. But if there is *any other* answer, I would like to think we would take that avenue first."

The men looked at each other again.

Jager said, "I'm game."

Geir nodded. "Always. One of those dogs took an IED for me over in Afghanistan. Blew up his trainer too. Those animals deserve the best care that we can possibly give them."

"And, for these twelve animals, we have failed them," the commander said. "I'm not assigning blame, and I can't accept the guilt, but, as a country, we have failed these animals. I'm asking you to find it in your hearts to help them."

"Any suggestions on how?" Laszlo asked. "We're hardly

flush with funds ourselves."

"Understood," the commander returned. "That's why I delayed contacting you. I can't pay you, but … if you ever need anything else …"

Badger smiled. Having the help of a commander was priceless. He glanced around at the others. They were all grinning. "We'll find a way," Badger said. "No promises on the time frame."

"Perfect," the commander said. "Faxing the files to you now as we speak."

The whirring of the fax machine in Badger's office confirmed the commander's words.

"As for suggestions on how to find them, … everything we have is in each of the files. Go carefully. Make sure they don't need anything. That they're safe. That the people around them are too."

The men nodded.

"That's a problem with people and dogs normally," Badger said. "And trained dogs no longer working with their trained handlers get confused and frustrated at the lack of commands—often becoming dangerous."

"Exactly," the commander said. "I don't have anybody else to dump this special project on. And I'm sorry. It really is a dump. It's only because I care that I'm even contacting you. If you get any good results, I'd love to hear back. You're my last hope." And he hung up.

Badger lifted a single sheet of paper in his hand, the topmost from the fax machine, still printing out more. "He's sending me all the files for the twelve dogs listed here."

"That's a brutal change for these animals," Geir said. "Those dogs are incredibly well-trained and thrive within that structured environment."

"They were also extremely attached to their handlers, and the bond is mutual, like any pet owner," Jager said. "So where are the trainers and handlers who worked with these animals? Isn't that the first and foremost responsibility of these initial specialists assigned to the K9s, as in most cases they become the owners after the dogs are discharged?"

"Yes, and no," Badger said. "You heard what the commander said regarding this first case. We've got a handler-turned-owner who came home already severely handicapped and then died. When you think about it, his civilian wife can't handle that service dog, particularly if it's new to her family, not to mention when dealing with her own personal loss. She's also moved now and apparently doesn't know who the trainer pawned the dog off on, as she was only too happy to get rid of a *problem*."

"Exactly, although finding where the dog is now could be a dead end," Geir said. "But I'm all for trying."

"Let's get a show of hands."

Unanimously all seven raised their hands.

Badger nodded. "That's why the commander asked us. We're very much like those dogs. We were also lost in many ways. And we've picked ourselves up and pulled together as a team. We are who we are because of each other. It's up to us to find these dogs and to make sure they are okay."

Geir said, "But none of us have K9 training."

"True," Badger said. "What about asking some of the men who work for us now? Find out who of them might have K9 training and go from there."

"Ethan," Jager said. "He's swinging a hammer on Geir's house. He's an electrician by trade in the military, a very handy guy to have around. A little bit of a loner, like the rest of us, but he moved to the K9 Unit eight or so years ago and served in that capacity in Afghanistan."

"Ethan? He was K9?" Cade asked. "I didn't know that."

"That's right. I heard something about that." Geir's fingers thrummed the table in front of him. "He's also a hell of a worker."

"Yes, he is. I've spoken to him about what happened in Afghanistan. He doesn't say much, but I gather the same accident that took his dog also took his leg," Jager said. "I highly suggest we talk to him first, see if he's willing to take the first dog file."

"The first file?" Erick asked in surprise. "Are you thinking of asking a different man to look at each file?"

"Why don't we start with Ethan? Maybe he can run this whole K9 locate-and-update division. Or at least give us some leads on other K9 personnel. It's possible Ethan knows men in the industry who are back home again who can take this on," Talon said, speaking up for the first time. "Ethan needs a purpose in his life anyway. But we can't discount the idea that these dogs could be all across the country and beyond."

"It wouldn't hurt to talk to him," Badger said with a nod. "I think he's the right man, but Ethan has to be willing."

"That's good enough for me," Laszlo said. "I like the idea of Ethan handling this completely, whether he's hands-on for each lost K9 or just managing any other men assigned to these files as needed."

Erik nodded. "Ethan is a good man. Although he's not easy to talk to. A loner by nature. And he is lost. I think what's lost is that missing K9 partner in his life. Once you're part of a K9 Unit, it's pretty hard to walk away from it." He paused, his gaze going from one to the other. "What about money though? Are we offering any? Not that we have to offer …"

"I suggest we call Ethan in the morning," Badger stated, "put the proposition before him and see what his response is."

"How about we don't give him a whole lot of choices?" Jager said. "Like most of us, he has learned to take orders and to follow directions. I say we tell him that we're looking for a dog, give him an overview, then ask him to go after it."

"Maybe during his free time. He has to make money too."

The others all agreed.

Badger smiled. "Ethan's better off financially than most, after inheriting his grandparents' estate. So that might not be as big of an issue as we're thinking. Plus this might bring back his passion for life again."

"It's all about how we approach it," Erick said with a grin. "As we well know with the women, it's all in how everything is approached." He smiled down at his wedding ring as he turned it on his finger. "Just like they surprised us, I suggest we surprise Ethan. We all know it's what he really wants to do."

"It's possible." Jager nodded. "But again, it has to be his decision."

"Agreed." Badger raised an eyebrow, looking around as everybody nodded. "Agreed by all then. Ethan is it." He picked up the topmost pages from the fax machine and laughed. "Even better, this dog was lost in Texas. Last known location was Houston."

"Perfect." Cade laughed. "At least he'd have some support there with Levi and his teams nearby."

Badger's phone rang. He picked it up and chuckled. "Guess who? Perfect timing. Let's talk to him right now."

CHAPTER 1

E THAN NEBBERLY STUDIED the desolate ground ahead of him. His gaze shifted slowly, looking for any sign of movement. He'd caught sight of a dog from the corner of his eye as he drove past. He'd turned around and gone back. He didn't have any business taking this detour, but, seeing the injured shepherd take off, away from him, his only thought had been to help.

Ever since Badger had talked to Ethan, he'd been hard-pressed to think of anything but finding the dog in the K9:01 file. Ethan was never one to leave an animal in need and wanted to get started right away. Badger had persuaded him to slow down and to give them a bit of time to gather some intel.

During training, the dog's name was Sentry, but, as he'd been handed off several times, he had likely been renamed several times. So Ethan continued to call him by a number in his head, to help distance himself from the dog's fate. The last known place for the dog was Houston, which was also convenient. Levi's Legendary Security company was in the area, close to where Ethan was now.

As soon as he realized he was heading in this direction, he'd contacted Gunner, who had been instrumental in getting Ethan into the US War Dogs Association program years ago. They'd kept in touch ever since. Gunner had never been one to leave an animal in need either and couldn't wait for Ethan to "get his ass over" to his place, as he had put it.

There. Out of the corner of Ethan's eye again, he sensed movement. The small shepherd lay still, blending in with the rock. The dog was weak enough that it couldn't keep evading Ethan. He took another step forward, hearing sounds off in the distance. But he didn't dare stop, his gaze always on the wheat-colored hide of the animal in the tall grass. Drought had taken over this area and had turned the crabgrass the same color as the dog's hair. This particular shepherd had usual dark markings up around the head and chest area but with a very light-colored back. Ethan walked several more steps, quiet in his approach.

The whisper of movement continued to his left. He did not want other people involved. He preferred to live a life on the edge of society. People asked too many questions. They assumed that politeness was friendliness, and then they dug into Ethan's life, well past the point he was prepared to share anything.

This dog called to him in a way he hadn't felt since his military K9 days. He'd seen more than his fair share of injured animals, dogs hurt beyond recognition, where a bullet had been a mercy killing. But then he'd seen men in the same condition too.

Sometimes he wondered if those people would have preferred a bullet, just like those dogs he'd worked with. Ethan himself was one of the walking wounded. He understood some of what this dog was going through. Another step and the shepherd locked its gaze on him. From the dog's size, he'd guess she was a young female. She was exhausted, angry, hurt and incredibly dangerous. A low growl erupted from the back of the dog's throat.

Ethan stilled, sending waves of loving energy toward the animal. He didn't know if it helped, but he'd always had a way with dogs, particularly the vicious ones. Then he'd rather spend his time with four-legged animals than the two-legged ones.

He'd spent a lifetime hunting down the two-legged ones. Hunting this four-legged one was out of compassion; Ethan couldn't walk away and leave it alone.

Behind him, a man called out, "Hey, can I help you?"

Ethan didn't answer. He knew that was the starting volley. More questions would follow.

He took another step toward the shepherd. The growl picked up again; this time he knew the other man could hear it too. His footsteps stopped, but Ethan didn't let his gaze slide. He crouched slowly, and the shepherd's muted growl descended an octave, but it didn't stop.

He never said a word to the animal. The animal already knew words were false. She'd heard them before. No way the injury she sported was anything but man-made. Ethan crouched lower, taking another step toward the dog.

Behind Ethan came soft running footsteps, but again he didn't dare take a chance to look. He held up a palm toward whoever approached. The footsteps stopped again. When Ethan caught the sucked-in breath of the man closing in on him, he knew he too had seen the shepherd.

The shepherd started to growl again.

"Are you sure you want to approach her?" the stranger asked softly.

Ethan gave a single head nod, keeping his hand up to stop the man from approaching. Ethan took another step, crouching even lower to appear less threatening to the injured animal.

And then again, maybe not to this poor animal, having suffered abuse at the hands of a human.

Ethan could sympathize with that mentality. It wasn't that he was antisocial, but he was antipeople. Still, he'd agreed to see Gunner, and he was on the hunt for a missing dog. Not this one unfortunately. Ethan was after a big male with different coloring.

He took two more steps toward the shepherd; her eyes had a dull glaze in them, as if she had no more fight left in her. He was only three feet away. He dropped to his knees and just sat here, studying her injuries. Blood was on her flank; her leg had an open wound—showing tendon, muscle, possibly bone—but also her front shoulder needed to be looked at closer. She was starving, on the run and hurting. She'd made her last stand, and she figured she was done.

He reached out a hand in a nonthreatening way, lowered himself farther to the ground. Her eyes tracked him, but she never made a sound. Her eyes were golden and filmed with pain but still with enough fire to cause him serious injury if she went for him. Though he was concerned about her and her injuries, he had to convince her of that. Only silence floated on the wind behind him. The grass gently wafted to the side as a breeze rolled over them, and none of it mattered to her.

Or to him.

He took another slow, cautious shuffle forward. Her muscles bunched, the corner of her lips pulled back, showing her teeth, but no heat accompanied the sound coming from her throat. He slipped closer. And then she did something that made his heart break.

She just lay her head down and gave up.

He hated to see that because he'd been there himself.

Tears burned the corners of his eyes as he watched one of the proudest, strongest, most beautiful animals in the world just roll over and say, *I'm done.* That was *so* not helping right now. He needed her to fight what was coming. It would be ugly, but, if he could coax her through it, she'd be fine on the other side. But the next hour, the next day, maybe the next several weeks, if not months, would be a painful recovery. It would be a bitch.

But, with his help, she could master her recovery.

He gently reached out a hand toward her fur.

The stranger behind him murmured, "Careful. She's not totally done yet. There's still fire in her eye."

Ethan gave a clipped nod because *that* was a good thing. Maybe she hadn't totally given up. He laid a hand on her shoulder, feeling her tremble underneath his hand, her body shaking with fear. But she was so weak, she could do nothing more than lie here, knowing the end was coming. He ran a quick hand down her back, feeling each and every rib. Her leg was broken, the skin open and crusty with infection. She had wounds on her belly, and he just wasn't sure what else.

"Was she hit by a car?" asked the man, now beside him.

Ethan nodded.

"I have an anesthetic in my hand. I'd like to administer it to the shepherd, so we can get her some help."

Slowly Ethan raised his head from the animal in front of him and took a calculated risk to turn to look at the big man at his side. He studied the bald head, the massive shoulders of a man in a muscle shirt and shorts, with a very interesting prosthetic at the end of a stump barely showing underneath the tied-up shorts. *Stone.* He held out a syringe.

"Hello, Stone. I'll take it."

Stone nodded, and the syringe slowly crossed hands. The

shepherd, her body shaking, watched, the whites of her eyes showing.

With a gentle hand Ethan slowly administered the anesthetic to take the dog's pain several levels down. He doubted it was enough to knock her out, but, if it was enough to move her, at least they could get her some help.

"A vet's around the corner," Stone said. "An animal rescue's just down the hill."

Ethan's gaze narrowed as he studied his surroundings. He hadn't realized he was so close to Anna and Flynn's place. He waited for the anesthesia to take effect and for the shepherd's eyes to slowly close. He handed the syringe back to Stone as he slowly straightened. "Kat says hi."

Stone's eyes widened, and the corner of his mouth kicked up. "Well, I'll be damned. Ethan. It is you. I wasn't sure initially, but there aren't too many humans I know who can approach a wounded animal like you just did."

Ethan's lips twitched at that response. "Not quite as smooth or as good as I used to be." He motioned to Stone's leg. "I think I'm wearing a more advanced model than you are."

Stone blustered. "No way. How could Kat not give me the latest and the best?" he asked with a huge grin. He reached out a hand and shook Ethan's. "Damn, you're a sight for sore eyes. It's been what? Three or four years since I saw you last?"

Ethan shrugged. "Maybe. It's been half that long since I was in active service."

"Levi said something about you coming but didn't expect you so soon. Neither did I hear much about the reason why you're here. Other than meeting up with Gunner."

"I'm following up on a request from up the chain of

command. Looking for a K9 dog that might or might not be okay. And, yep, Gunner is on my list of people to stop by and see."

"Gunner is a good guy. I know he's looking for a pair of security dogs. Sounds like you two should do well." Stone pointed down the hill. "I was helping out at Anna's place, building another set of dog runs, when I saw you up here." His gaze dropped to Ethan's legs. "Sorry about the accident that took your leg. Sometimes life's a bitch, isn't it?"

Ethan dropped his gaze to the dog at his feet. "And sometimes it's the bitches that are life." He turned to look at his truck parked on the side of the highway. "I don't know how badly hurt she is, but it looks bad."

"Louise will let us know," Stone said.

Ethan walked around and gently scooped his hands underneath the frail dog. He motioned toward his truck. "I can hold her, if you can drive."

Surprise lit Stone's gaze again. He judged the distance and said, "You'll ride in the bed or in the front?"

"In the bed."

Stone nodded once, and the two men, not saying another word, strode over to Ethan's big black Dodge Ram 3500 pickup. It took a little bit of scrambling to get into the bed of the truck, while holding the shepherd, but Ethan managed it.

"Nice wheels," Stone said as he shut the tailgate and then hopped into the driver's side and turned the key, starting the engine. With Stone driving carefully, they headed down the road.

In the distance Ethan could see other people watching the two of them. He ignored them, keeping his focus on the shepherd in his arms. He shifted her weight and caught sight of the tattoo number on her leg. Not a navy number but from a breeder or the owner. She could have a chip too. He'd need a vet to look for that. He noted it. Someone had cared about her once.

He'd find out soon enough.

Not even ten minutes later they pulled into a large parking lot to an even larger animal clinic. Stone hopped out, came around and opened the tailgate, so Ethan could slide out with his precious cargo. Then they walked inside.

By the time Ethan made it through the double glass doors, a gurney was already pushed toward him. Very gently he laid the shepherd on it.

A woman stepped in front of him, took one look at the shepherd and said, "Do you know what happened?"

Ethan shook his head. "I saw her an hour or so ago. I've been tracking her since."

Stone interrupted. "Louise, this is the shepherd we told you about. The one we couldn't get close to."

Her gaze went from one man to the other; then she looked at the shepherd. "Well, somebody managed to." She turned, pushing the gurney toward the internal set of opaque doors, marked Surgery. "I'll let you know what I find."

Ethan followed.

She stopped at the surgery doors and faced him, shaking her head. "Medical personnel only."

He crossed his arms over his chest and glared at her.

She hesitated, looked at Stone, then back at Ethan. "So you're one of them?"

He raised one eyebrow.

She sighed. "Do you have any training?"

He tilted his head to the side. "Field style."

She groaned. "Of course you do. You're a handler."

He gave a slight shrug. "You could say that. Trainer, handler, keeper of War Dogs."

She looked torn.

"I want to remain beside her."

Louise made a quick decision and gave him a clipped nod. "Stay out of my way."

He didn't answer, just placed a hand on the shepherd and followed alongside the gurney. He walked into a large room with multiple surgical areas.

Louise snapped out orders. Staff came from several corners, and, while Ethan watched, blood was taken, X-rays were snapped, and a full physical exam was done, quickly but efficiently.

Louise said finally, "I'll be back in a minute. I want to see her X-rays."

Ethan hadn't said a word, his hand on the shepherd's head, gently stroking it to let her know she wasn't alone.

Finally Louise came back. "She's in pretty rough shape." She then ordered IVs for the dog. "We'll get some fluids and some nutrients into her and try to stabilize her. She's got a couple busted ribs. Her leg is broken. The back leg looks to have taken a severe blow. We might have to put pins in her hip," she admitted cautiously. "Someone shot her as well, a glancing blow off the right shoulder. But her broken leg, I can't say that it's looking terribly positive." She pulled her phone out and brought up a photo.

Ethan's heart sunk at the news.

"You aren't her owner. So who will pay for this?" she asked.

"I will."

Surprise lit her eyes. "Glad to hear that. Will you let us look after her?"

He patted and studied the soft fur on the dog's head. "Yes. I think her hip is okay though. It won't need pins."

"I'll see as I get further along. It looks like the animal is young and in emaciated condition when she was hit. Probably dragged herself off the road and has been trying to survive ever since."

He nodded. "Fix her up." He took a step back. "No matter the cost."

Louise hesitated, then said softly, "You know it could be expensive."

"I can easily make more money." His gaze was steady, and then he nodded. "Sometimes we all need something more than merely money." On those words, he turned and walked out of the surgery room. Instinctively he knew Louise was one of the vets who cared. And she'd do everything she could to keep that shepherd alive.

CINNAMON MICHELSON STUDIED the man standing at the surgery doors, his hands shoved deep into his pockets, a grim line on his lips, his jaw clenched. She didn't understand what was going on, but whatever it was hurt him. Even as she watched, a muscle in his jaw flexed at something happening on the other side of the frosted glass.

He stayed there for too long. She didn't think it could be good for him. Obviously an injured animal was in there, and it was one he cared about deeply. She'd brought in a friend's dog for more of a grooming-related visit, one she looked after on a regular basis. The little guy would be another half hour yet before he would be ready to go home.

She turned to look around the large sitting room, then

walked to the coffeepot. There she poured two cups. She looked at the man still standing at the door and headed to him. "I thought you could use this."

He turned to look at her with a speed that almost made her spill the coffee. Instantly his hands reached out and studied her, but he didn't grab the hot cups. He had grabbed her wrists.

Her breath released slowly. In a gentle voice she said, "I'm sorry. I didn't mean to startle you. I brought you a cup of coffee."

At the confusion in his eyes and the intent way he looked at her, she had to wonder how long it had been since anybody had done such a simple deed for him.

She smiled up at him. "You didn't look like the kind of guy who would use sugar."

He tilted his head to the side, looked down at her wrists. He dropped her hands and accepted the cup. In a low, deep voice, he said, "Thank you. And, no, no sugar."

She motioned toward the area where the coffee was set up and said, "If you need creamer, it's over there."

His lips quirked. "Black is the only way to drink coffee." He glanced at his cup and over at hers, then said, "Thank you. I'm sorry for grabbing you."

His voice seemed almost … rusty, as if maybe the apology or the polite conversation was hard for him.

She didn't know what it was about these injured animals, but she was a sucker for each and every one. She tilted her head in a gentle motion, wary of making a faster motion and scaring him. "You didn't hurt me, so it's all right." She stepped back and sat in one of the chairs against the wall. "It doesn't help to stand there and watch the animals on the other side. You know that, right?"

His eyes shuttered away something, like he took a step backward into his own little world again. She was sorry she'd brought it up.

He gave her a crooked smile and said, "Nothing wrong with doing it either."

"Don't you think it hurts you more?" she asked. "Whatever injured animal is in there is getting the best help they can get. Louise is phenomenal."

"I don't know her," he said, "but I'm hoping that shepherd gets the care she needs."

"Is she yours?"

A second curtain went down, shielding whatever else his eyes might reveal. He gave a brief shake of his head. "No, I saw her when I drove past the road. Then stopped to help her."

"Any idea what happened?" she asked curiously. She hadn't told him that most of what she did was arrange for animal adoptions, usually from other countries, but sometimes within the general area or across the country. She and Anna worked closely together. He probably didn't know Anna and probably didn't know about Anna's shelter.

"No," he said, his voice tight. "Possibly hit by a vehicle."

She felt herself recoil against that. "An all-too-common occurrence," she murmured. She dropped her gaze to the cup of coffee in her hand and lifted it, hoping it wouldn't burn her lips. She blew over the cup's edge, and, when she thought it was safe, she took a sip. "What are you doing after she's taken care of?"

He only looked at her.

"Or have you not thought that far ahead?"

He raised his gaze. "I'm not sure," he admitted. "But I couldn't leave her out there."

Cinn's heart melted a little. Any guy who would go to this much effort to save an injured shepherd couldn't be bad. Those who looked after animals the best were usually injured in some way themselves. Maybe in the hopes somebody would treat them better too. In a moment of self-clarity, she thought, *I have to stop psychoanalyzing men.* It had gotten her into trouble more than a few times. On dogs, that worked great. But men were a different story.

"Anna and Flynn's shelter is around the corner," Cinn said gently. "They might take her in."

He shook his head. "No. I'm not deserting her."

A wealth of emotion was in that word *deserting.* She sat quietly contemplating what that meant to a man who appeared to be lost in his own world.

"*Can* you look after her?" she asked suddenly, worried the shepherd would end up in a situation worse than the one this man had found her in.

"Yes."

And that was all he said. She didn't have any right to push it. But it was hard not to. "I work with animal rescues around the world. We move animals into homes from country to country. If you need somebody to look after her ..."

He gave a hard shake of his head but remained silent.

Even without words he had made that pretty clear. She settled in her chair and waited. Not another sound came out of him.

Finally the double doors opened, and Louise came out. She looked tired, but a happy smile appeared as she walked toward the man beside her and smiled at him. "You were right. No pins required. It was dislocated. I couldn't see that from the X-ray. Too much damage around it. I fixed her up as much as I could. She will need several days here with us."

He straightened slowly, towering over Louise. But Louise didn't appear to be intimidated in any way. Cinn wondered about that. Then again, Louise was with Rory and the rest of Levi's gang. And she was probably used to dealing with these hard alpha males. Though this one appeared to be a broken, dangerous one.

Cinn sighed. "I did suggest that maybe, if you didn't want to look after the shepherd, Anna might take her."

Louise turned and looked at Cinn with a smile. "Hey. I didn't see you there. You've been talking to this gentleman, have you?"

Cinn nodded. But the man in question never moved.

"Stone said your name is Ethan?" Louise asked boldly.

Ethan gave a clipped nod.

"Do you live around here?"

Ethan shrugged.

Louise appeared satisfied with that.

But, for Cinn, it raised a million more questions. Stone knew him? She knew Stone from Anna and Flynn's place. Many of Levi's men came to help out there. But she'd never seen Ethan before. Who was he? Where was he staying? She thought she knew every local male. And what kind of a man went out of his way to help a shepherd and to stay to hear her prognosis? The shepherd would need long-term care until she was fully healed. Was he ready for that?

"I want to see her," Ethan said.

Louise considered him for a long moment. "When we get her set up in the cage, I'll let you in for a minute."

The briefest of smiles crossed his face, but it was enchanting to Cinn. He sat abruptly, taking a sip of his coffee.

Louise headed back into the surgery area. Knowing the

way she worked, chances were she would deal with another half-dozen animals before her day was done.

Cinn had often wondered about getting more education, but just the thought of seven years of vet school had been enough to stop her. She was a project manager, a job she operated from home for a large company. It gave her a lot of freedom, so she could continue her volunteer work with the animals. Though sometimes it was difficult to make both of them work.

Just then Megan, the receptionist, called Cinn's name. Cinn walked over to see Mitzi, the little shih tzu she'd brought in for her friend Sandra, being led toward her.

"Her nails are taken care of," Megan said. "That one toenail was infected, but we've cleaned it out, disinfected it, and she should be good to go now."

Chuckling at the greeting Mitzi gave her, Cinn bent down, scooped her into her arms and said, "Are you okay to put this on Sandra's account, or do you want me to cover it?"

"It's all good," Megan said.

Cinn waved goodbye and left her empty coffee cup on the counter where she'd placed it. At her car, she put Mitzi into the carrier in the back, snapped it tight, making sure the seat belt was buckled, and got into the front seat.

As she looked up, she saw Ethan sitting where she'd left him, looking at her. She glanced around and saw the big black truck and knew instinctively it would be his. She frowned, wondering what she should do and why she wasn't pulling away. Because she sure as hell should be. Finally she reached for her notebook and, wondering if this was a mistake, wrote down her name, phone number and a brief note underneath. She pulled the sheet of paper from the notebook, exited the car, walked over to the truck and tucked it under his wipers. She got back into her car and drove away.

She saw black clouds forming above, and she mentally told Ethan to hurry and read her note because the rain would smear the ink. She figured what she had done was very stupid, but she couldn't help herself. That man looked like he needed a friend.

CHAPTER 2

AFTER DELIVERING MITZI to her very grateful owner—a mother with a newborn demanding most of her attention—Cinn returned to her home. She was behind on her own personal work, and then there was always the inevitable volunteer work. She parked her SUV in the driveway, got out and heard her dogs barking in the backyard. Instead of going to the front door, she walked through the gate around to the side yard, watching the dogs bound toward her. One was a basset hound missing a leg; another was a lab that thought everybody was his best friend. The two dogs got along well together and with the spares she brought home.

She bent over, giving them both a greeting. "Hey, I was only gone for a couple hours, guys. It was all good."

They kept pace with her as she walked to the back of the house and into the kitchen. There she dumped her purse and walked over to the stove, putting on the teakettle. It was a beautiful September day. She loved fall, and, once the temperatures calmed down a bit, then she would be outside every day, all day. But, for now, she had to provide a living for herself and her furry family.

After making a sandwich, she took it and her cup of tea into her home office and sat down before her computer. She opened her work email and groaned when she saw twenty-one new messages had dropped into her in-box. But this was what she did, and the paycheck was very decent. She didn't have any right to complain.

Several hours later, the dogs crazily barking had startled her out of her reverie. As the dogs reached the front door, they both fell silent and sat just inside the door, tails wagging. She studied them. Looking through the nearby window at the shadow outside the door, she knew who it was. Hesitatingly, wondering why the hell she was even thinking of doing this, she left the chain on the door and opened it the little bit the chain allowed. "Hello?"

He stared at her, his chin dropping and his eyebrows rising.

She looked at him nonplussed. That she was correct about him being behind her door wasn't necessarily good. Still, she'd left that note because she wanted to see him. But the note didn't have her address on it. "How did you know where I live?"

"The clinic."

She shook her head. "No, they wouldn't have shared that personal information."

He pulled out his phone and showed her a page he had been on. It was her license plate with her address.

"Now that makes sense," she said on a sigh. "Not too many people know how to pull up an address off a license plate."

"Let's just say, I know some people," he said smoothly.

"Levi? Stone? Flynn?"

He nodded.

"But you don't work for them?" She bit her lower lip, as she tried to figure out what to do about this. "Then why lie to me?"

"Most women would be uncomfortable with this method, so I thought saying the clinic told me would be easier."

She had given him her name and number in her note, but he hadn't followed up on that by calling. He'd taken a different route.

"I'm making you uncomfortable," he said in that low voice. "I'll leave." He turned to walk back down the front steps.

Immediately she took off the chain and pulled open the door, still not leaving her house. "Wait."

On the bottom step he turned and looked at her. "You shouldn't have opened the door to a stranger."

She raised both hands. "Yeah, I've heard that before too."

He looked at her steadily. "You can call Stone, if you know him."

She grabbed her phone and called Levi's compound. "Hey, Ice. Is Stone there?"

Ice laughed and said, "I think he just came in. Hang on."

Within minutes Stone's heavy, deep voice came into her ear, "What's up, Cinn?"

"Do you know Ethan?"

Stone sucked in breath on the other end, and he answered cautiously, "If you mean the Ethan who picked up the shepherd this morning, yes, I know him. We have friends in common."

"What friends?" she demanded.

"They're in the next state over," he said slowly. "Another group of friends of ours. Ethan's okay. He's been through a lot though."

"But you can vouch for him?"

"I can vouch he's honorable, and he's damaged, and that shepherd was very important to him."

"Well, those three things I could figure out myself," she said in exasperation. "But thanks." She hung up the phone, pocketed it, knowing, if anything happened to her, Stone would know who was responsible. She threw the door open wide for him to enter. "Come on in."

The dogs happily exited the house, greeting him as a long-lost friend.

He stood on the porch for a long moment, petting the animals. "Stone knows me but not well."

She nodded. "He said as much. He also said you're honorable but damaged."

Ethan lifted a pant leg and showed her what appeared to be a prosthetic limb.

She nodded. "That explains the gait."

"What gait?"

"You went down the stairs stiffly," she answered, walking toward her kitchen. "I'll put on coffee. Do you want a cup?"

He leaned against the entranceway to the kitchen, a safe distance away, as if giving her space. "Thank you. I'd appreciate it."

She silently put on a small pot, then felt awkward as she searched for a topic of conversation. "What's the state of the shepherd?"

"She's doing much better."

"Is she awake from the anesthesia yet?"

He gave her a glimmer of a smile and shook his head. "But she's resting easier. More at peace."

She thought about that and nodded. "I guess that's fair. Sometimes animals don't rest, even when they are under anesthesia, do they? It's more of a forced rest. But, if she's looking better, that's good."

He sat at the kitchen table, choosing the chair closest to him.

She said, "Or we can sit outside on the deck."

He stood again in a smooth motion and waited. Always silent, mostly still. She poured coffee in two cups, leading the way to the large veranda that ran along the back of her house. The dogs raced out into the backyard. A ball sat beside one of the patio chairs. With the coffee cups still in her hand, she kicked the ball across the yard. Both dogs tumbled after it. She placed the coffee cups on the patio table and took a seat. The dogs came back with the ball, eager for more. She grinned to see Burglar had won.

"You have a three-legged basset hound?"

She nodded. "Got him from Anna. His name is Burglar. He was trying to steal something from a butcher shop when the door closed on his leg, one with automatic locks, and it wouldn't open again. He lost circulation, and the leg had to be removed." Out of the corner of her eye, she watched a smile whisper across his face. "You really like animals, don't you?"

He nodded. "They're simple, straightforward, honest, clear-cut. They don't play sneaky mind games."

"Unlike humans, you mean?"

Again he nodded. He reached down, and Burglar dropped the ball into his hand. Ethan tossed it high and long into the yard. Both dogs raced after it. "What's the Lab's name?"

"Midnight," she said. "She was another foster dog of Anna's. She's way too friendly with everybody, so, the minute she escapes a fenced-in yard, she's gone looking for the next person who will give her attention."

"Do you have a securely fenced yard?" he asked, his gaze looking around the property.

"Several of them," she admitted. "I have a lot of dog runs here. Depending on what animals we're moving, if I have to get involved personally. I have ten acres here."

Appreciation lit his gaze. "I really like that idea. I'm not much for town living."

"Neither am I," she said. "Stone said something about you having mutual friends in another state."

He gave her a crooked smile. "That's true. In New Mexico—Santa Fe. Badger was in one of my units way back. And I served with Stone. But not the same unit. That was a few years ago."

"That explains the look to you," she said. "You and Stone both have that hard edge that says life hasn't been easy."

"Is life meant to be easy?" he asked with interest.

"I don't know," she admitted. "But I sure wouldn't mind if it was."

He just smiled and didn't say anything.

"So, if you're not from around here, what's the plan when the shepherd's able to move?"

"Are you worried about me or worried about the shepherd?"

"Both," she said shortly. "You both look broken."

He stared at her steadfastly, his eyes almost dark, like Midnight's, her Lab. He said in a calm, quiet voice, "I was broken. But I've put myself back together again. The shepherd will need help to do that. I hope to provide it for her."

"Any idea what happened to her?"

He shook his head, then studied her for a long moment, reached into his jeans pocket and pulled out something. He placed it on the small table in front of her.

A smashed metal piece.

She frowned at it, her throat tightening. "Somebody shot her?" She stared at him in horror, and then a realization dawned. "After she got hit by the vehicle, right? To put her out of her misery because she was so badly injured?"

He shook his head. "No. I think she was shot, was on the run, then was hit. She was very emaciated. Then she ran into traffic."

Inside, Cinn's stomach churned. "I hope not. I hate when animals get hurt unnecessarily. Animal cruelty will never sit well with me."

Just then Burglar ran toward her with the ball. She smiled, reached down, scrubbed his long ears and neck, took the ball and threw it again for him.

"Everyone here carries guns," Ethan said. "Do you know anybody who would have shot the shepherd?"

She shook her head. "No."

"How about anybody who's working with drugs?"

She frowned at him, not sure where this was going. "Well, I don't do drugs, and I don't know anybody who's involved in the drug trade, if that's what you're asking."

He nodded but stared out at the world around him, not really seeing it.

"Why do you ask?" she asked.

"Because I think she was a highly trained dog."

"*Highly trained?* Like, a police dog? A drug-sniffing dog?"

He nodded. "I think so."

"How can you tell?"

"She's tattooed, for one. I already traced it. She was police trained, but that ID isn't active. So either she didn't make the grade or was trained for something nonmilitary."

"They have a database for that?"

"If you know where to look," he said absentmindedly.

"She's lucky you found her," she said. "I hope you keep her and nurse her back to full health."

"We will," he murmured.

"*We?*"

Surprised, he gave himself almost a mental headshake and turned to look at her. "I meant, she and I will."

"Are you working?" she asked.

"You ask a lot of questions," he countered.

She sighed. "I asked because of Levi's crew around the corner. It seems he's always bringing in new men."

He shrugged. "I don't plan on working for Levi. But the opportunity is there, if I want to."

"It still doesn't make any sense that a dog would have been around drugs, get shot, hit by a vehicle, and then left to die," she cried out. "Who does that?"

He slowly turned to look at her, and the smile on his face sent chills down her spine. "I don't know who does that," he said in that voice so soft, and yet, so chilling with purpose, "yet." Then he added, "But they won't do it a second time."

"LOUISE REMOVED THE bullet that had ripped through the back of the dog's shoulder, thankfully, instead of her chest," Ethan said, "but she was so emaciated." He shook his head. "As if she'd been kept captive, starving for a long time."

"Well, I'm glad she's free then," Cinn said. "But you can't just go after whoever did this."

He looked at her steadily.

She knew that expression and sighed deeply. "If they shot the dog, what are the chances they'll shoot you, if you stick your nose in their business?"

This time he grinned, showing teeth.

She sat back. "You're going after them because of what they did to her, aren't you?"

"If you could, wouldn't you?" he asked. "Besides, if there is one abused shepherd there, maybe there are more." He sat up taller. "The reason I came here was to track down a big male shepherd cross, part of the military War Dogs unit." He explained what happened to the dog. "Making sure he's okay. It's quite possible that he is at the same place where the female came from."

Cinn's face scrunched up, making her prominent freckles come close together, giving a shadow to her cheekbones.

He didn't think he'd ever met anybody with as many freckles as she had. It was a cute look, and she seemed to come from the heart.

"Wow. I had no idea anyone cared about those K9 dogs after they were done in the military. But I'm very happy to hear they are looked after. And, yes," she said. "Many times I wished I had the means to go after some of these assholes who abuse animals. But you can't be a lone ranger. I don't know this dog you're after, but it doesn't look like you have any backup. I hate to think you're out there alone without someone to help you if things get ugly." She frowned. "And, if you're not part of Levi's crew, you're probably not protected by him or the other connections he has."

Ethan shrugged and settled back, picking up his cup of

coffee. "Doesn't matter," he said. "When you come across something that's wrong, you have to do what you can to make it right."

It was a philosophy he'd followed all his life. When he'd worked K9 Units overseas, he and his unit had been a close-knit group. Not just with the animals but with each other. He'd lost track of most of them. It crossed his mind to connect with some, but he didn't know where they were. It had also crossed his mind that Stone and maybe Levi and his group could find them, but Ethan didn't really want to spend the money on it nor did he want anybody to know what he was doing. He'd always been a private person, but, since he came out of the hospital, he'd turned hermit. Too much so.

He still couldn't understand the impulse that had led him here to Cinn's house. He'd watched her write the note and put it on his truck. Even as interest filled him, he wanted to castigate her for being such a fool to contact strange men. She couldn't know he was safe. Didn't she understand how foolish it was, how dangerous the world was? He wanted to stay and protect her from being so foolish again.

"You'll need help, if you're going after whoever shot the dog," she said. "I'm not a very brave person, but I'd do an awful lot to help save the animals."

He looked at her, not sure where this conversation was going.

"There's a property about twenty miles from here. It's a shady, ugly place, maybe twice the size my parcel is. I wouldn't be surprised if it wasn't a criminal hideout. Every time I've gone past, I see the animals there, and I put in another complaint to the city because those animals look like they're in terrible shape. But, so far, nobody's done anything.

I picked up a puppy about a mile away from there not too long ago. I didn't ask if it was theirs. The farther away I could get that puppy, the better."

"Sounds like a place to start."

She shook her head. "No, it's too far away. Your shepherd wouldn't have traveled that far."

"Dogs can do an awful lot if they are desperate."

"What purpose would that shepherd have for coming here?"

"What breed was the puppy that you picked up and how long ago?"

She looked at him in confusion. "A shepherd cross but it was six months ago I'd say. The puppy was young, maybe six weeks old at the time," she said slowly.

He nodded. "And the shepherd I found had had pups."

Her jaw dropped as he watched. "You're thinking that puppy was one of hers, and she was coming here after it?"

He shrugged. "I don't know how the time frame works, but she came here for a reason. Was the puppy staying at Anna and Flynn's place?"

She slowly nodded. "Yes. Anna took it."

"And where is it now?"

"I'd have to ask Anna. But one of Levi's crew might have adopted it. I don't know for sure."

He nodded slowly. "It would explain her need to come in this direction."

From the look on her face, she hadn't considered that, and it made her sick now. "Animals are just like people in so many ways—well, the good people," she whispered. "Steal a child from a mother, and watch her turn into a wildcat, trying to get it back again."

He nodded slowly. "People are people, and animals are

animals. Yet some instincts are universal. I can't say that's what brought the shepherd here, but I also can't say that wasn't what brought her here. She was not full of milk, so she had dried up from whatever pups she'd had, but she has given birth." He watched as she slumped in her chair and stared out at the fields around her.

"She definitely needs a chance at a better life," she murmured. "I hope she makes it."

"She'll make it," he said. But he worried too. The shepherd not only had to be strong to get through the surgery, she had to be strong to get through what it would take to get her back on her feet. "She's already been abused enough," he said. "I want to make sure that, for the rest of her natural life, she understands what love is too."

At that, Cinn shot him a sharp look. "There was a lot more human emotion in those words than I expected."

He settled back and pulled his invisible shield around him again. "I didn't mean anything by it," he said, a cool note entering his voice. "Just that the dog has had a tough life. She deserves a better one."

Cinn nodded. "But I think you've had a tough life too," she murmured. "And I think you deserve a better one as well."

He shot her a hard look. "I'm not a dog."

"No, but there are definitely similarities."

He gave a harsh laugh because she was right there. There were definite similarities. They were both junkyard dogs.

CHAPTER 3

C INN WOKE UP early and was outside in the backyard, running with the dogs as she always did. She had no style, no form. She jumped over rocks; she raced around bushes; she tossed balls for the dogs, but mostly she kept her body moving, always in a forward motion.

For some reason, Ethan slipped into her mind. He'd have a heyday with her running style. He looked like the kind who went left-right-left-right, steady for at least five miles before taking a break. Whereas she'd stop, scoop up a ball, run some more, toss the ball, keep on running, dashing around to the left, stopping to throw the dogs off the trail and then keep on going once more. She liked to have fun, and a straight jog from point A to point B wasn't enough fun for her.

The dogs stopped for a drink, while she jogged on the spot. Normally a creek flowed heavily beside her property, but it was almost dry this year. The drought had taken the creek down to just a small trickle. When she figured they'd had enough time to quench their thirst, she jumped the creek bed and carried on up the other side, the dogs at her heels. When she was about worn out, she turned and headed back toward the house. Now she'd go in a straight line home again.

By the time she hit the gate at the back of her property,

her footsteps had slowed to a walk, and she could feel her uneven breath, hot and raspy. She let herself and the dogs into the yard, walking even more slowly to the house. She had a lot of work to do today. But Ethan kept sitting in the back of her mind. She wondered what he was up to and how the shepherd was doing.

Before she realized it, her fingers dialed the clinic. They weren't open yet, but she knew Megan well and called her personal number. As soon as Megan answered, Cinn asked, "How is the shepherd doing?"

"Which one?" Megan asked in a wry tone. "This appears to be shepherd week."

Cinn chuckled. "It's so bizarre how that works."

"Hey, it's the same for all facets of life. It's like in the maternity ward. They have baby girls upon baby girls, and then, all of a sudden, it switches to baby boys."

"I meant, the shepherd Ethan brought in."

"Ah, that one," Megan said, a smile coming through the phone. "She's doing better than she deserves to be. She slept through the night. We've increased her medications for the pain, now that she's back to awareness. I expect Ethan to be on the front steps of the clinic at any moment, since we open soon."

"At least he cares."

"Right, and you can't stop thinking about him, can you?" Megan teased. "Do you want me to tell you when he gets here, so you can come around?"

"Nope. I expect he'll stop by here afterward anyway," she said. "Thanks for letting me know about the shepherd."

She hung up to avoid answering further questions and sat here for a long moment, wondering about where Ethan'd gone. But it really wasn't any of her business. It was so hard not to be curious. He was a loner, by all the things she knew about him. Everything about him made her curious. He'd arrived out of nowhere and didn't seem to have any connection to anyone or a job around here, but he knew a lot of people. She was happy he'd found the dog, or the shepherd might not have made it.

What Cinn needed to do was get back to work. She was part of a global canine rescue group. Currently they were bringing twenty dogs over from Greece. The country had hit a rough patch, and the animals, as well as the people, had suffered. The locals dumped their pets because they could no longer afford to care for them. Now starving packs of dogs ran loose in the streets, causing all kinds of mayhem.

She needed one or two shelters to take them, until they could be adopted. She was avoiding the states that had kill centers. No point in bringing a dog over here just to be killed. At the same time, she knew a lot of people were against what she was doing because so many local dogs also needed to be looked after.

That was also why she had centers in Canada and England that she worked with. Canada was always good for at least half of the animals. They had way less people but a lot more were willing to take in rescues. Considering that, she sent off an email to the three centers she worked with regularly, confirming the numbers of animals they were willing to take.

While she waited for responses, which weren't likely to come until the end of the day, she got up and made herself a shake for breakfast. She knew that Ethan's shepherd wouldn't move for quite a while, so she wondered if Ethan would stick around. Did he have a place where he could look after the dog's medical needs? She sent Louise a text, asking if the shepherd needed a home while it recovered.

Cinn could surely do something. She sent a second text, asking if Anna would be looking after the shepherd.

Surprisingly Louise answered quickly. **Ethan is taking her. But not for a few more days. She needs to be mobile and given medications.**

But that can be done at home, right?

Sure, but her bowels have to move smoothly. She doesn't leave until then.

Acknowledging that with a text back, Cinn got down to work. If Ethan would take the shepherd, that was all good.

ETHAN WAS AT the vet's office ten minutes before it opened. He got out of his vehicle, locked the truck and stood at the front door. He knew people were inside, but he didn't move from his position. They'd either let him in or not, but he wasn't budging until he had a chance to see the shepherd. He wasn't there but five more minutes when the door opened, and he saw Louise on the other side.

She smiled at him and said, "She's doing fine."

He looked at her, searching for the truth in her eyes, then asked, "May I see her?"

She nodded, let him in and then locked the door behind him.

He frowned. "Letting me in is not a good practice."

She chuckled. "Now you sound like my partner and the rest of the gang in my life."

"Who's your partner?" he asked, curious if he knew him.

"Rory. He works for Levi."

Ethan nodded. He knew many of Levi's men but not

Rory in particular.

"Are you working for Levi too?"

"I don't think so," Ethan said. "I'm not sure what I'm doing at the moment." It was the truth but sounded worse when spoken out loud. "I am on an assignment for someone else at the moment."

"Ah," Louise said with a smile. "I think all the men who work for Levi worked for someone else."

Not sure what to say to that, Ethan said nothing and followed her through to the surgery room and beyond. He studied the gleaming surgical tables, rows of instruments, cupboards, panels of parts used in surgery. They walked to a wall of cages. There were cats, dogs, bunnies, and he was surprised to see a ferret.

"She's down here," Louise said. She crouched in front of a large dog crate that had a name tag and a clipboard attached with the details of the animal inside. She opened the front so he could see the shepherd huddled in the back.

He crouched in front of her. The dog whined as in recognition. He reached out a hand and laid it on her forehead calmly. The shepherd didn't move; her eyes were glazed with pain. Louise checked her over while he gave her what comfort he could. "Any idea how long she'll be here?"

"A couple days," Louise said. "I need to make sure that she can walk and that her bodily functions work properly. And we have to confirm she's not bleeding anymore. I won't be happy until I can see her walking around the parking lot on her own steam. Animals heal much faster than people do."

"Humans make healing hard work." He could feel her odd look at his comment, but he meant it. Animals were simple. When they needed care, or they needed food, they were happy to get it. He gently stroked between the shepherd's eyes, his fingers soft, comforting.

"She recognizes you," Louise commented. "Accepts you."

"I didn't hurt her," he said. "That already marks me as one of the good guys." He heard Louise's heavy sigh.

"Unfortunately you're quite right there. Do you have much history on her?"

"Not yet," he said, stroking the soft ears as she lay here with her eyes closed, allowing him to touch her. "But I will."

"Without getting hurt yourself, I hope," she said, her tone sharp.

His only response was to stare at her.

She sighed. "No point in talking to you on this issue, is there?"

"Any point in talking to Rory or Stone or any of the other men?"

She chuckled. "No. Not about stuff like this." She straightened. "If you'd like, you can sit here. But I can't move her, so please only touch her head and keep her calm. My assistant will come in and change her dressings again later."

He nodded. "I'll stay with her for a few minutes."

Louise nodded and checked on several other animals while he watched with interest.

He dropped his gaze to the shepherd. She had her eyes closed, relaxing. His fingers stroked down her nose and back up between her eyes and over to gently caress her long silky ears. "What happened to you, girl?" he asked softly.

Her ears twitched at his tone of voice, so he kept talking to her gently, if for nothing else than to get her to remember his voice. That would be huge. Speaking calmly, he told her that he would look after her and that the worst of her life was over. But she had to heal, she had to fight and get back up on her feet. Nothing worse than an animal that gave up.

He was fully aware that Louise kept an ear and an eye on him, and that was fine until people understood who he was, what he was. Their uncertainty was expected at first. He'd be the same regardless. But he instinctively knew exactly who Louise was right from the moment he'd seen her handle the dog. She was one of those rare individuals where the animals came first. He was similar.

"I think she's sleeping now," Louise said.

With a start, he realized she was checking on the shepherd's vitals.

"She's doing very well, but we need to give her a couple days to just heal."

He nodded and stood. Louise locked the cage. With one last look at the dog, his voice slightly thicker than he liked, he said, "Thank you."

She nodded. "I've yet to find an animal that doesn't break my heart when they're in here."

"I don't think I could do your work," he said.

"It's hard for me too at times, but it's been my calling since forever. Like you but in a different way."

"I had years in the military K9 Unit," he said, his voice catching. "But I lost my K9 partner in a bad accident. I've been recovering ever since."

"Maybe it's time for a new K9 partner," she said with a nod to the sleeping shepherd. "And maybe a new line of employment."

He cracked a smile. "Yeah, that's partly the reason I'm here. I'm not sure what I want to do."

"Law enforcement can always use dog handlers."

"Don't think I could do straight police work."

"Well, I know Levi doesn't have a dog handler. Set up your own company, contract out to him. And, of course, there's always the military."

He gave her a thoughtful look. "Not sure what would be involved in setting up a company like that. Although, if I do go in that direction, Badger, from the group that sent me here, could possibly use my services too."

"That might be your first step," she said with a bright smile, ushering them forward, "to investigate what would be required."

"I also have to train dogs to have employable skills," he said with a quirk of his lips. "Not to mention a lot of K9 work would end up being voluntary. Like emergency search-and-rescue work. Not all counties or families can afford to pay."

"I guess it depends if you need the money or not," she said with a sideways look at him. "Besides, once your company is up and running, you could decide what constituted volunteer work. Maybe a portion of your business will end up being volunteer-based."

"True. I don't how I could make this work at the moment." He shrugged.

She smiled. "Then let me give you the name and number of somebody in town here who has a lot of connections."

"Who's that?"

"I was thinking of Flynn's best friend, Logan."

"Gunner's son," Ethan said with a nod. "He's on my list of people to contact anyway."

She stopped in the act of writing down Logan's name on a notepad. "You know Gunner?"

He nodded. "I know Gunner. I'm on my way to visit

him this morning."

She straightened. "Obviously you have plenty of connections on your own. In that case, say hi to him for me."

"I will. Take good care of the dog for me."

"Absolutely," she said. "When you come back, you better have a name for her. Once you've named her, she's yours because you won't be able to let her go."

He turned and walked out of the clinic. It was still early, but the front doors were now open, and a couple vehicles were pulling into the parking lot. Perfect time for him to leave.

He hopped into his truck, turned on the engine and backed out. Time to talk to Gunner. As he turned the truck around and headed toward the exit, his phone buzzed. He pulled off to the side and read the message. **If you're around, stop by**, Levi texted. **I heard from Stone and Badger that you were in town.**

Ethan thought about it for a moment, then dialed the phone. When Levi answered, he said, "It's Ethan. I'm meeting Gunner in an hour."

"Good," Levi said. "Stop by this afternoon then."

"Not sure when that'll be," Ethan said cautiously.

"Doesn't matter when it is," Levi said. "The door's always open." He hung up.

With a smile, Ethan tossed the phone on the seat beside him and turned onto the highway. It was nice to know Levi was here.

Now to meet with Gunner. That old soldier had fingers in many pots. What was the chance he knew something about that property Cinn mentioned? And would he know anything about K9:01?

CHAPTER 4

B Y THE END of the day, Cinn sat back, groaning. She'd been sitting at the edge of her seat. As she shifted in her desk chair so her lower back got support, she could feel the relief running through her spine. She checked the clock. "How did it get to be after five o'clock already?"

She shook her head when the dogs started barking. They raced to the front door, and, as she walked toward them, wondering who was out there, they both sat down and started to whine, their tails wagging like crazy. "What's gotten into you two?" she asked in amazement. She peered out the living room window.

Of course. It was Ethan. Excited and nervous, she opened the front door. "Well, this is a surprise."

He held up a bag that smelled absolutely delicious. "And maybe this is too," he said. "But I thought I'd return the favor of friendship."

She grinned. "Chinese food is a great way to return the favor, but you didn't have to do this."

"Can't I be nice?"

"Sure." She stepped back to let him in. Inside, he handed her the bag, then crouched to say hi to the dogs. As for the dog's reactions, it was as if they'd missed seeing him for weeks. In a way she felt the same. He was a curious man. One with secrets. *A loner* maybe was a better description.

Shaking her head at her dogs' antics, she walked into the kitchen. "You can sit there and play with the dogs if you want, but I'm eating."

Soon the three followed her to the kitchen. The dogs sniffed the air, weaving around her legs.

She shooed them back toward Ethan, so she could set down the containers and grab some plates. "How did you know I liked Chinese food?"

"I didn't know," he answered. "I just hoped you did."

"Well, I love it, so great choice. How was your day?" she asked as she opened each of the six containers. "I usually just order a combo," she said with a happy sigh. "This is a luxury."

"I didn't know what you would want to eat," he said sensibly. "Where are your forks?"

"Forks and chopsticks are over there." She pointed to the drawer beside the sink.

He returned with chopsticks.

She smiled and dished up a plate for herself. The dogs were on their best behavior and lay down just a few feet away. As she was about to take her first bite, she stopped and said, "Thank you. I can't remember the last time somebody did something so thoughtful."

"Should happen more often," he said. "I love to cook, but I haven't had an inclination lately." On that note he popped a bite of food into his mouth, handling the chopsticks like a master.

His comment brought up a thousand questions. "No inclination?"

He shrugged but didn't answer.

She figured that was as far as she would get in that line of questioning. "So what did you do all day?"

Another shrug.

Not sure how to break through that wall of silence, she sat quietly and ate for a few moments. "I called the clinic to see how the shepherd was doing," she confessed. "Louise said she'll probably have to stay there for a few days, but she will make a full recovery. You did a good thing bringing her in."

He nodded. But he still didn't say anything.

Together they ate in silence. The food was fabulous, so she didn't really mind the lack of conversation. As she served herself seconds, she asked, "You want more?"

He nodded. "I'm just waiting for you to get yours."

"What, and then you'll finish it?"

He shrugged again.

"Really, you can't, surely."

Ethan opened container after container and dumped the remainder on his plate.

She laughed. "So you must still be healing from your injuries if you can eat this much," she said good-naturedly. "Although you look very capable. And I'm sure you wouldn't be on this mission if you weren't in good shape."

"The accident was two years ago," he said. He cleared his throat and then, as if rusty at sharing, added, "I spent the last six months working with Badger's group. Helping out wherever needed, building Geir's house and working at security. Basically any job they had for me I took." He gave her a lopsided grin. "It helped me reassimilate into the real world."

"Hey, understood. I can't imagine." And she couldn't. It didn't bear thinking about. She was grateful for Badger's group, whoever they were. She'd have to ask Flynn sometime if he knew them. These men all seemed to have some kind of network. As she thought about such a concept, she realized, if they did, they were the lucky ones. To have a brotherhood of men? … Priceless.

"If you can't take the shepherd after Louise gives the go ahead for her to be released, Anna could probably take her until she's adopted out." She didn't know why she persisted, but she wanted to know the dog would be well taken care of.

He still didn't say a word.

"Unless you'll stick around this area," she added slowly. Just what were his plans?

"I won't be too far away," he said. "I'll be staying with a friend in Houston."

Apparently she had to be satisfied with that. "Not very talkative, are you?"

He didn't even bother shrugging.

She sighed. "A little conversation would be nice."

He looked up at her and smiled. "A little conversation is what you're getting."

She groaned and rolled her eyes. "Okay, a little *more* conversation."

He stared at her for a moment and then asked, "What do you do for a living?"

"I'm a project manager. I work for a company that does supercomputing for companies across the state. And, on the volunteer side, I arrange for the rescues of animals from other parts of the world."

He frowned. "Other parts of the world, not those that need help at home?"

"Both," she said. "But, with global conflicts, the animals suffer along with the people. Everybody is out helping the people. They forget about the animals needing assistance too."

At that, he looked interested. "Tell me more."

She launched into a tale of how they'd been bringing animals in from all over the globe and how she farmed them out to other areas of the world. "Canada takes a lot of them," she admitted. "A lot of centers here do the same."

"And yet, so many centers are here that have animal-overpopulation problems."

"Exactly, but I'm not fussy. An animal in need is an animal that I want to try and help."

A warm light came into the depth of his eyes, and he gave her a gentle smile. "I agree. I'm surprised you don't have dozens of your own here."

She chuckled. "I have to really watch myself. I'd have every one of them here if I could. I have the two dogs. I used to have two others, but a friend of mine really wanted them, so I ended up giving those two to her. Every time I go to Anna's place, I'm always afraid I'm coming home with one more."

He nodded.

"Do you have any pets?"

He shook his head. "No. I don't. Not now. Not since I left the military." He paused, then added, "I lost my K9 partner at the time. It's been hard to open myself up to that loss again."

"I'm sorry," she said quietly. "It's hard to lose a pet anytime but, when it's a working partner as well ..." her voice trailed off.

They continued to eat in companionable silence, until he said, "Today I drove past the place you were talking about."

She froze, her chopsticks in midair, a piece of broccoli perched precariously on top. She swallowed hard. "Why would you do that?"

"I wanted to see if the shepherd could have come that far."

"And could she?"

He nodded. "Quite possibly. I did track her back that far. But I want to take another look. Maybe I'll go after dinner." He glanced outside. "I've still got a couple hours of daylight today."

"But you can't track twenty miles that fast," she scoffed.

"I don't have to. I know where the possible source is, so I need to pick up the blood trail and make sure it's heading the right way," he said neutrally. "I can cover a lot of ground in a short time."

"Sure, but it's easy to lose the blood trail."

He shrugged.

"You're pretty damn sure she came from there anyway, aren't you?"

He nodded.

"What will you do?"

He didn't say anything.

She groaned. "Please don't do anything dangerous."

He moved his empty plate toward the center of the table and gave her a fat smile. "I won't. The shepherd needs somebody to look after her."

"THANKS FOR THE company," he said smoothly, "At least you won't have any dishes to do." He quickly packed up the empty containers, putting them into the bag he'd brought inside and carried it out the front door with him.

"Are you leaving already?"

He could hear the worry in her voice. Worried he would

go and do something stupid. Well, he'd done a lot of stupid things in his life. Finding the asshole who did that to the shepherd wasn't one of them.

He walked to his truck, hopped in and started the engine. It had been a long day. The meeting with Gunner had gone well. Not only had Gunner wanted to hire Ethan to provide fully trained dogs for his place but Gunner had been full of ideas as to how to help with the injured shepherd and the one Ethan was sent to find. Hearing about the possible questionable property, Gunner had become full of fire and brimstone about bringing down that place. "I know that place," he'd said. "You get the intel for me, and I'll make sure something happens."

Ethan drove away from Cinn's place, checking in the rearview mirror. Sure enough, there she was, standing on the front doorstep, leaning against the doorjamb, her arms crossed over her chest, watching him leave. A strange start to a relationship so far. But, then again, he'd been the one who had come to her house twice and had left soon afterward. She probably didn't know what to make of him.

Well, he didn't know what to make of himself either. He'd been telling himself not to go to her place, even as he bought the Chinese food, knowing he had no business there.

What was he supposed to do with that? He didn't want to be interested. He didn't want to care about anyone. He didn't want to care about anything. He'd already blown that with the shepherd. And he needed to come up with a name for her. But he sure as hell didn't know what.

And now he started to care about Cinn.

There was something about her. He loved the rescue work she did. He loved that she'd cared enough to call the vet's clinic to see about the shepherd. The attraction was there. And, because it existed, he had to deal with it—but how? He hadn't planned to get involved, but it was already too late. Apparently he had chosen the dog already. From the moment anyone suggested he give her up and let somebody else take care of her, everything inside him had revolted. She belonged with him. Now he just had to find out how.

Gunner had offered Ethan a home at reduced rent in this little town. Said it would give him a place temporarily, and, maybe if he had a home, he'd stay in the area. Gunner wanted Ethan close by to train dogs.

He drove past the rental place, checked out the property, realized it would do just fine, pulled off to the side of the road and sent Gunner a text, saying he'd take it for a week or two. At least until he figured out what he was doing. The response came back almost immediately. **It's yours free for the first month. Then we'll talk.**

Ethan smiled at that. It was so very Gunner. Then Ethan turned the vehicle back onto the highway and hit the gas.

As he drove, he considered his odd relationship with Cinn. He wasn't sure how much to tell her. This last year he'd lived more or less alone as he had healed and rejoined life. Only through Badger and the rest of the gang had Ethan slowly felt like he was back to normal.

Maybe not normal in the fullest sense but enough that being around people was more comfortable. But not so much in a relationship ... That was a new step to take.

Putting Cinn firmly out of his mind, Ethan refocused on the shepherd. He'd tracked her several miles from across the road where he found her. Once he had picked up the blood trail, it had been pretty easy to see the direction she'd come from. He used GPS and Google Maps to see what was on the other side of that long stretch of land, and what it was, was that same property Cinn was talking about. It was pretty easy to put two and two together.

But he needed proof. And, for that, Ethan needed to check out the place after dark. To think somebody was using that shepherd and other dogs as expendable tools just burned him.

He wasn't somebody to judge. Not yet. Instead he was on a fact-finding mission. And, if he found out this was the place that had hurt that dog, well, … he'd come back, and he'd be on a revenge mission. He knew revenge wasn't always right, but nobody got away with hurting a dog like that. And, if they had more dogs they were hurting, Ethan would release them too. And then he would shut down that place.

If they'd done something to K9:01 …

He stopped on the high ridge, two miles away from the property. With the truck parked behind the rise, away from plain sight, he hopped out, grabbed his cell phone and water jug, and headed toward the property.

Moving steadily, he stopped when the electric fence came into view. He crouched and studied the area. Twenty acres, Cinn had said. He did a slow perimeter search first. By the time he made it back to where he'd started, he'd seen that, although the fence was electric, still men with rifles were inside, dogs at their feet. But those dogs were healthy. Although lean, they looked to be fighting fit.

So, had the female he'd rescued not made the grade? Was she one that had failed to do her job, being distracted by something not allowed? Because that bullet said they wanted her dead and disposed of, not necessarily in that order. She hadn't even deserved the mercy of a clean kill shot. Ethan studied the sentries, who were more concerned about talking with each other and smoking cigarettes than walking the perimeter.

The main house was set about an acre in. A double gate led to and from the main residence. There were other outbuildings, but he didn't see much else on the twenty acres but drought-dried land. From the power grid and the solar panels, he figured something was going on underground. It didn't have to be very deep underground, just enough to stay hidden. He crept along the front to the main gate, studying the electric fence system there.

It would be a little harder to get through the fence than he had originally thought. He walked around until he found a section where it looked like critters had dug along the fence line. From the fur caught in the wire, this was likely where the shepherd had made her way out.

He tossed a rock against the fence and saw sparks fly. Moving quietly, he carefully scoped out the spot where the shepherd had dug out a little bit deeper, a little bit wider. Then, on his back, he scooted under the charged wires, and, just like that, he was in. He shook his head. If the guards were any good, this should have been found immediately. The dog had been shot from a distance, a shot that hit her shoulder only.

Which meant they hadn't even bothered to go outside the fence to find her, nor had they bothered to find out where she'd gone. Happy to have her all alone in the wastelands. He moved to the tree line and studied the outbuildings. The two sentries were off in a different section, and this area appeared to be deserted. He walked carefully, checking into the windows one by one on the rear of this particular building. He couldn't see anything in the half-light, and he didn't dare turn on a flashlight as he heard noises and dropped down.

A door opened—probably at the front of this building—and eventually he saw several women came out; more came behind them. They looked exhausted from a hard day's work.

Two gunmen waited for them. But they seemed to be protecting the women, not holding them prisoner. The women moved slowly forward, around another corner. He crept to the corner and peered after the women to see two vans. The women were loaded up, and the first van drove off. A gunman locked the door, walking back toward the second van. He hopped in and followed the first van down the long track to the main road. They stopped at the gates and locked them behind them.

He crouched down and headed back toward the building they'd just exited. Ethan didn't see any dogs, but the property was huge, so they could be anywhere. Including out in the miles of deserted terrain surrounding the property.

As soon as the others were out of sight, he picked the lock and crept inside the building. The upper building was empty, but the stairs descended on the right side at the back. He went downstairs and found a large drug lab, a working one it seemed. He took photos and crept back outside, locking up the building after him. Now he had proof, but he also didn't dare get caught.

He sent the photos to Gunner and made his way to the next outbuilding. Nobody was there, and it wasn't locked. He went inside, did a quick sweep of the room, didn't see anything important.

Just as he was about to exit, he heard voices.

"We need a couple new gunmen for this next shipment."

"Why?"

"We'll be moving a double load this time. We have a new network, and it needs to be secret. But, because we'll be moving so much product, they want a couple more guys on it."

The other man said, "We can grab some of the men we've used before."

"They have to be expendable," said the first man said, his breath catching in the back of his throat.

"Damn. We use them off and on because they're good."

"Yeah, we need a couple who aren't so good. Or else we sacrifice these."

"Do they *have* to be terminated afterward?"

"Yes. The boss doesn't want any loose ends."

"Sure, but it's probably not a one-off, so somebody will have to know."

"Maybe, but you know what this business is like."

The second man sighed. "Well, the two brothers are around."

Silence followed for a moment. "Good. They're screwups anyway. Maybe, if they do a good job this time, he'll decide not to kill them."

"Nah, he'll kill them. I don't understand that. It's like he wants to bloody the first trail every time."

"And maybe it's a ritual for good luck. I don't know, but no way I'll argue."

The two men separated, but one of the footsteps walked toward him. Ethan crouched low in the far corner behind the door, just in case the man came inside. Ethan had taped the conversation the best he could with his phone, but he couldn't guarantee the quality.

The door opened, and a flashlight shone inside. Yet the flashlight did only a quick pass. Then, with nothing to see, the door slammed shut, and a lock popped on the outside. The footsteps slowly moved away.

Under his breath Ethan whispered, "Shit, shit, shit."

The door hadn't been locked when he'd entered, so he hadn't considered that end to his escape later. He could bust down these walls, but he didn't want to let anybody know he'd been here.

He did a quick search and, at the back, found a panel of the wall was already half warped. He applied gentle pressure and ripped loose the bottom of the boards. Dropping to his belly, he managed to squeeze through, scraping his back in the process. He couldn't stick around any longer.

His back burned, and he dared not leave blood behind. With a hand holding his shirt tight around his waist, he stayed close to the trees, following the tree line back to where he'd gained entrance under the electric fence. This time he went down on his belly to avoid leaving blood on the ground, being extra careful not to touch the wires either. As soon as he was on the other side, he stood again and shoved a bunch of rocks in the hole under the fence. It would be easy enough to find next time. But, just in case, he took a GPS reading, tracking the exact spot where he'd entered, and then he ran away from the property. He could hear voices behind him, but there wasn't anything for them to see now.

And nobody shouted. No lights were turned on. So Ethan figured, if there was some security alert, it had nothing to do with him.

Back in his vehicle, he put the transmission in neutral and let his truck roll back down the hill, the way he'd come. He was miles down the highway before he turned on the engine and lights. He pulled to the shoulder, stopping so he could call Gunner.

"Did you get the pictures I sent?"

He was spitting mad. "Yeah, I did," Gunner said. "I've already talked to a couple cops. They'll set up a raid on the property."

"Good. I managed to get in through a spot in the fence. Looks like the shepherd dug a low-lying spot under the fence. It's a little hard to get in and out, but I made it."

"Are you sure nobody saw you?"

"I'm sure. My back is bleeding, but I don't think I left any blood behind. Yet there's always that possibility. I'll get that bandaged."

"Get yourself fixed up. The police are on this. I'll light a fire under them to make sure it happens fast."

"They're moving product. I've got audio of it. I hope it's audible. Let me send it to you."

He clicked off from Gunner and listened to the information he'd recorded, then forwarded the audio file to Gunner and called him back.

"I sent you the audio file. Make sure you listen to it. Not a ton of detailed information is there, but it will help explain what's going on."

He ended the call and sat here. His back still burned. He could feel wetness along his spine as sharp pains dug at him. He was afraid he'd gotten a good splinter in there under his skin. If it had been anywhere else but his back, he could take care of it himself. Given where it was, chances were he would need help.

With that thought uppermost in his mind, he picked up his phone and called Cinn.

When she answered, her voice was slightly distracted, as if she'd been doing something. He asked, "Am I disturbing you?"

Her voice turned brisk when she heard his. "No, I was almost asleep. What's up?"

He hesitated, then said, "I don't want to disturb you. I'll talk to you in the morning." He ended the call.

Almost immediately his phone rang. It was her.

"Don't do that," she snapped. "You had a reason for calling me. Now what is it?"

He hesitated again, then said, "How are you with first aid?"

She gasped. "Are you hurt?"

"Not badly but I think there are splinters are in my back."

"Then get your ass over here." And she hung up.

He grinned. He really loved that temper. It was very refreshing and honest. And he had had very little honesty in his life. With that thought in mind, he turned on the truck and headed toward her place.

CHAPTER 5

C INN GOT UP and dressed. She had just gotten into bed and was relaxing when Ethan called, but sleep was the last thing on her mind now. Downstairs she went to the first aid cabinet. She kept a fairly extensive one because of the animals. Taking out her field kit to the kitchen table, where the light was the brightest, she located tweezers, antiseptic and sterile gauze. She didn't know how far away he was; she should have asked him. But, if she called him now, he'd be driving. She didn't want him to talk and drive, particularly not if he was already injured.

She put on coffee, sat at the table and waited. She had one cup half gone when she saw the lights coming up her driveway. She poured him a cup and brought out a bottle of whiskey she kept in the back of the pantry. She opened the door, relieved to see him walking mostly normally. As he approached, she could see the pain on his face.

She ushered him in, closed the door behind him, turned and cried out at the blood on his back.

"How bad is it?" he asked.

"I won't know until I get that shirt off you. That's a lot of blood though."

"Damn. I was trying to avoid leaving a blood trail."

"How did you even drive like that?" she asked, walking around him.

He spotted the whiskey, and his face lit up. Then he looked at the coffee.

As his gaze bounced between the two liquids, she shrugged. "If you drink some of the coffee, you can always top it up with whiskey."

He grabbed the chair, flipped it around and sat backward, undoing his shirt buttons as soon as he was seated. Ever-so-gently he extricated his arms from the sleeves. Some of the blood had dried, making his shirt stick to his back.

"Before you pull that off, let me soak it. We don't need any more damage done."

She walked to the bathroom, grabbed several washcloths, soaked them under the faucet, then returned to the kitchen and laid them across his shirt, soaking the dried blood, so it would release the shirt. It took several attempts; finally the wet shirt pulled away. She placed it in the sink and ran cold water on it, went back to the kitchen table and gently cleaned his back with a wet sponge.

Finally she saw the splinters of wood in his back. "What did you do? How did you manage to get these splinters?"

"I got locked into a building," he explained drily. "At the back wall were a couple busted boards, so, rather than making a big exit—telling them I had been there—I tried to sneak out and got caught on some of the jagged edges."

"I'll say. You'll need some of that whiskey," she warned.

Obediently he took a big slug of his coffee, reached for the bottle of whiskey and filled his cup. She grabbed the tweezers and went to work.

"I'll start with the little ones. I'm placing the slivers on a paper towel."

She set the paper towel on the table beside him. Carefully she pulled at the wood splinters until she had the easier ones out. But two were big ones, one of which was jagged. Using the tweezers, she gently got the smaller of the two out, feeling his back muscles stiffen.

"I've got the easiest ones out," she said gently.

She grabbed the gauze, put some antiseptic on it and cleansed all the areas she had cleared of splinters. His back muscles tensed at the pain, but he never said a word.

She sat on a chair next to him. "You've got a bigger one, but it's jagged. I'll have to cut the skin to get it out."

"Then you have to cut the skin," he said, his tone neutral. He discussed this like it was nothing unusual.

She sighed. She walked over to a kitchen drawer, grabbed one of her sharp paring knives, poured some antiseptic on it and came back to him again. She studied the splinter for a long moment, seeing where it was hooked in and wouldn't pull out. She sliced the skin from that hook forward. His muscles bunched underneath her hands, but he never said a word.

Amazed, she murmured, "Always got to be the strong guy, don't you?"

"I am what I am," he said quietly.

She nodded to herself, then realized he couldn't see that. "You are indeed."

She reached for the tweezers and grabbed hold of the splinter embedded in his skin. She pulled it out, all three inches of the jagged wood, and laid it on the paper towel in front of him.

He took a look and then nodded. "No wonder that hurt."

She cleaned his wounds once more, then studied the rest of his back. "Just abrasions from here on, I think." She took a long moment to clean the area thoroughly, then, grabbing the antiseptic ointment, she carefully covered the area. "That's a pretty big area to cover with gauze."

He shook his head. "I'll be fine."

"You won't be fine if it continues to bleed," she warned.

He frowned when she held up a large sheet of gauze.

"I suggest for the night we at least cover this. I can tape it down, and then you won't get any more blood on whatever clothing or bed you're sleeping in."

He nodded.

"And then tomorrow morning," she said, "you can come back, and I'll change it."

"Thank you," he said quietly.

"While you were out there playing cops and robbers, did you find anything?"

He grabbed his phone, flicked through it and held up a photo for her to see.

She peered over his shoulder and gasped. "Is that a drug lab?"

He explained what he'd seen, about the women, and when he went into the building itself.

"That was dangerous," she scolded. "Cops are around for that reason, you know?"

He chuckled. "The work I used to do was way the hell more dangerous than this," he assured her.

"That doesn't make me feel better," she snapped.

She sprayed his scrapes with an antibiotic spray, for extra prevention, then placed the gauze on top and taped down the corners. She'd have to tape the edges too. Otherwise, every time he turned while he slept, it would tug and pull.

As soon as she was done, she said, "That'll hold for the night." She motioned at the photos. "What will you do about it?"

"I've already contacted Gunner," he said. "He's contacted the police. I believe they're pulling something together now."

She sat down hard in the chair across from him. "Oh, thank God."

He looked up at her in surprise.

"I was afraid you'd go in after them yourself."

The corners of his eyes crinkled up with laughter. "If I wasn't alone, I might," he admitted. "But I don't know how many men are out there. I heard at least four."

"And all armed?"

"All armed and dangerous, and two, possibly more, highly trained dogs."

"Shepherds?"

He nodded. "But these were in better shape."

She looked at him for a long moment. "Do you think she was fired from her job?"

He shrugged. "If she was fired, it was a long time ago because she's pretty skinny."

"Or she could have been sick. No way to know."

"Not yet," he said. "We should get to the bottom of it soon enough."

She nodded. "Do you want to stay here for the night?"

His face showed his surprise.

It mirrored the surprise in her heart. She shrugged. "I meant on the couch," she said drily.

He shook his head. "Thanks, but no thanks. I have a bed for the night." He stood. In a smooth move, he straightened as if it was no big deal.

She groaned as she watched him. "You don't always have to be a big tough guy, you know?"

He smiled and repeated, "I am what I am."

"We are all what we are. But we can change."

He leaned down, and, in a surprise move, kissed her gently on the forehead. "Thanks for the first aid, Doc." And he walked back out into the night.

She looked around her kitchen. The bloody shirt was still in the sink. She wished she'd had some painkillers for him, but, by the time she thought of it, he was already in the truck and backing out. She swore softly and cleaned up. She'd been wishing for something exciting to happen, but she hadn't really expected anything like this.

"Just goes to show you that you should watch what you wish for."

THE NEXT MORNING when he woke up, it was hard to move. His back was stiff and sore. He half stumbled, half hopped toward the shower and let the hot water run down his back. Only belatedly did he remember a bandage was all across his back. He reached around and tugged at the corners. The water had loosened the tape, and the gauze was, of course, soaked to his skin, but it had, in effect, loosened from the scabbing on his back. With one corner free, he loosened the other, and then it dropped down, the water hitting his sore flesh.

He stood like that for a long moment, rotating his shoulders and neck, easing the pain. He checked the time as soon as he got out. It was almost 8:00 a.m. Normally he didn't sleep that long. But he'd taken painkillers before bed, and that seemed to have knocked him out.

As he walked to the bed, a towel wrapped around his waist, his phone rang. "Gunner, what's up?"

"They'll go in today," Gunner answered.

"I want to be with them," Ethan said.

"No. You can't. They were very specific about that. But I did try."

He swore softly. "I don't want them shooting those dogs," he said.

"I know you're trying to save every animal on the planet, but those are trained attack dogs."

"We don't know that," Ethan said with irritation. "They're trained, yes, but that doesn't mean they will attack. They aren't responsible for their training. I'm pretty sure I could get them to follow my commands. I'm after one in particular. You know that, but I'd save them all if I could."

Gunner hesitated.

"Call whoever back and tell him that I can pull the dogs off of his men. No need to kill those animals. I'm all for him taking out the bad guys, but let's not hurt any more animals."

"I know K9s have been your life," Gunner said, "but I'm not sure we can do anything to help these."

"If the police are going in without somebody to work with the dogs, the dogs will attack because they won't have any choice," Ethan said forcefully. "They'll be ordered to attack. Somebody has to be there to counter those orders."

"But those dogs don't know you," Gunner said. "Why would they listen to you?"

Ethan shrugged, then winced at the movement in his back. "I can only tell you that they will."

"I doubt the police will listen to that. They're probably more than happy to shoot the dogs."

"Sure, but the dogs have been well trained. Most likely we can use them. I don't know what their skills will be, and it'll take some time to sort it out, but you and I both know how valuable well-trained dogs are. You're looking for a couple yourself."

He could almost see Gunner nodding and thinking about it.

"At least call them," Ethan said. "It's what I do. You know that." At least it was what he did—before his accident set his life on a difference course.

"I'll call you back." Gunner hung up.

Taking the opportunity, Ethan called Louise at the clinic. "How is she?"

"Doing remarkably well," Louise said cheerfully. "It's amazing what food and water and some medical care can do for an animal. She's bouncing back nicely."

"When will she be ready to be picked up?"

"I'm not sure. I think you need to see her again and note her reaction to you, when she's not so drugged."

He thought about it and said, "Maybe this morning. I'm waiting on a phone call that could change my schedule."

"Come when you can," she said. "I've got to go. I'm heading into surgery."

He heard the *click* in his ear that said she had ended the call.

He was getting dressed, when his phone rang again. He answered it, surprised to see Cinn on the caller ID.

"Do you need me to put a clean dressing on your back?" she asked without preamble.

He froze, reached around to his back to check, and his fingers came away wet with blood. "Yes."

"Then I'll see you here in twenty then." She ended the call.

He frowned but appreciated her no-nonsense attitude.

He dressed his bottom half and left off his shirt. He would need something to protect his truck seat and something to wear temporarily. He'd already left his bloody shirt with her at her place.

With a towel for the back of the seat, wearing a disposable white T-shirt and bringing another to don afterward, he packed a bag for the day, including water and some granola bars, and walked out to his truck.

His house was about fifteen minutes away from Cinn's house, and he'd just pulled into her driveway when Gunner called him back.

"They could be leaving in a couple hours," he said cautiously. "No guarantees, but, if you're on the spot, and if you follow orders, they might let you get to the dogs first."

"Where do I meet them?"

Gunner gave him the GPS location where the meeting was taking place and a time frame.

Ethan checked his watch. "I'll be there." Disconnecting from Gunner's call, he hopped out of the truck and walked in to find Cinn taking several pancakes off the griddle, placing them on two plates.

She set them on the table, next to butter and maple syrup, and said, "You might as well eat while you're here."

He frowned at her.

She frowned right back. "Sit down."

He sat, pulling off his bloodied T-shirt. He sniffed appreciatively. "Thank you."

"You're welcome," she said, and that was the end of their conversation. She quickly dropped his T-shirt in the sink and ran cold water on it, then redressed his back.

He grinned.

She looked at him suspiciously, as she sat down to eat.

"What are you smiling about?"

"You," he said. "Who'd have thought anybody out there was as short on talking as I am."

She shrugged. "There's a time for talking, and there's a time for eating." She motioned with her fork at the stack of pancakes in front of him. "Eat."

He dug in and moaned in delight. "These are wonderful," he said enthusiastically and polished off the stack. When it was all gone, she got up, reached into the oven and pulled out a plate with more, then put it down in front of him. When he looked at her empty plate, she shook her head.

"I'm full."

He didn't need a second urging. He moved the stack onto his plate, mopping up the spare syrup, and, at a much slower pace, ate the second stack. When he was done, he pushed both plates away and said, "That was excellent. Thank you."

She carried the dishes to the sink, where she put them in hot soapy water, then poured two cups of coffee.

He was stunned to think she had gone to that much effort for him. As much as he had loved the pancakes, the fresh coffee was just as nice. He looked at his cell phone and said, "I'm heading to the clinic to see the shepherd."

She sat across from him and smiled. "Say hi to her for me."

He nodded.

"Have you got a name yet?"

He shook his head. "Hard to come up with a name. I don't really know who she is yet." He could see the understanding in her gaze; at the same time he knew just what a strange thing it was he'd just said. Most people picked a name because they liked the name. They didn't match it to the animal. He motioned at her medical supplies and asked, "Can I replace what you've used?"

"I'm not worried about it," she answered. "But, if you'll be hanging around, and you'll be doing this a lot, you might want to pick up some more bandages and gauze," she said, tapping a box of Band-Aids. "Those too."

He nodded. "Next time I'll hit a drugstore." He finished his coffee, stood, walked to the sink and, before she could stop him, he washed the dishes. He stacked them on the rack, grabbed his cell phone and keys, and said, "Thank you." And he left.

He stood out on the veranda on the top step, knowing he should say something else but not sure what. He heard footsteps across the floor, and she came to stand in the doorway behind him.

"Will I see you again?" she asked.

He turned to look at her. "Do you want to?"

Her lips quirked. "Yes."

He could feel that sense of satisfaction roiling through his stomach. "Then, yes." He smiled and walked over to his truck. She was still watching him as he turned onto the highway. He wasn't sure what was going on, but it was nice to find somebody who didn't ask too many questions.

He'd been a loner for a long time, and it felt right. But he'd known he needed to get back to civilization, around people. His social skills were still rusty, his sense of humor still off. Interaction with anyone other than at work didn't come easy anymore. That was why he always related better to the animals. He preferred them over people any day.

When he drove into the vet clinic parking lot, a couple vehicles were here already, but it wasn't too busy yet. He imagined Louise ran a pretty decent business, considering the scope of the ranching and farming in the area. He didn't know if she did large animals as well, but she probably wouldn't have a lack of business in that corner either.

As he walked into the clinic, Megan smiled. "She's really doing much better."

"Is she walking?"

Megan nodded. "With help."

He frowned at that.

She let him into the back, where the shepherd was still in the cage. "If you wait here," she said, "it's time for us to take her out. You can come with us."

The shepherd had yet to see him. He walked outside to the designated area and waited, loving the fresh air versus being inside the surgery area, with its chemical super-clean smell.

When he turned around again, the door opened, and Megan and a vet assistant walked out with a band under the shepherd's belly, supporting her.

He pointed at the shepherd, frowning. If she couldn't walk on her own, he wasn't sure he could take her with him today.

"She *is* walking. We're keeping her from putting too much weight on that hip yet."

He nodded with understanding.

The vet assistant stepped back, so Megan walked with the dog. The shepherd took several hesitant steps, then a few more. She still hadn't seen Ethan. Megan walked her to the grass, where she very carefully managed to pee.

He smiled. "She's doing so much better."

The dog, hearing his voice, turned to look at him. Something in her gaze he didn't quite understand. But she was still weak. Her tail wagged, and her ears went down, not in an offensive manner but in compliance. He crouched in front of her, giving her a chance to get used to him. She moved closer, one step at a time. When she reached him, she gave him the gentlest of licks on his cheeks. He could feel his heart melting.

He scratched her under the chin. "You'll be fine now, little one. I don't know who did this to you, but you'll be much better off now."

She nudged his hand when he stopped scratching. He chuckled and, with both hands, gave her a good head scratch. When he looked up, he saw Megan beaming, the vet assistant standing off to the side and watching the interaction.

"How has she been with everybody in the clinic?" he asked. He was pretty sure he knew the answer. The shepherd was just too damn grateful for having been taken away from that horrible life and all the pain she'd been in.

The assistant walked closer, exclaiming, "She's a sweetheart. She's never barked or snarled at any of us, even when we were hurting her, which we had to do to change her needles and her dressings," she admitted. "But she's been incredibly patient with us."

Ethan nodded. "What will we call you, girl?"

"We've all been searching for names too," Megan said. "But we haven't found anything that's perfect. If you're taking her with you, then you get to name her anyway."

"Sally," he said suddenly. "Her name is Sally."

At the name, Sally's ears perked up. She reached up and nudged his chin with her nose. He chuckled. "Sally it is then."

"It's not a very heroic name," Louise said from behind

him.

He turned to look at her. "Actually, it is."

Megan handed over the leash attached to the belt around Sally's underbelly, showing Ethan how to walk her with gentle support.

He took her around, so he could get used to helping her. When he came back to Louise, he said, "How much longer does she need assistance?"

"Animals heal incredibly quickly," she said. "The issue will be that we don't want her to overdo it. So maybe another day, two days maximum."

He smiled. "I'd be happy to take her now, if I thought she would be okay without you."

"Let's give it another day," she restated. "And how is the name Sally heroic?"

He watched Sally being led back into the interior of the clinic. At the doorway she turned and looked at him. "It's all right, Sally. I'll come back and get you tomorrow."

She gave a bark and then went inside the clinic, as if fully understanding.

He turned to look at Louise. "It's short for something."

She raised an eyebrow but waited patiently.

He smiled. "It's short for Salvation."

CHAPTER 6

C INN COULDN'T HELP it. She reached for her phone and called Louise. "Has he been there?"

"He has indeed," Louise said warmly. "He's a man of hidden depths."

"Why is that?"

"Do you know what he's named the dog?"

"No. What?"

"Sally."

Cinn sat back and thought about that. "Well, it's not a bad name," she said cautiously.

"If you know what it's short for, it's a fantastic name," Louise said. "And he did tell me."

"Oh, do share."

"He named her Sally, short for Salvation."

Cinn gave a happy sigh. "He really is a good guy, isn't he?"

"I think you'll find he's exactly the same as the rest of the men we have around here. Rory, Flynn, Stone," Louise explained. "I've talked to several of them about Ethan. They all know *about* him, but they don't *know* him. He was in the US Navy K9 Unit, had an accident, recovered, but slowly. In the meantime he lost both parents and slipped into a major depression. When he came out of that, he was lost for a while. He's part of a group, the same people who sent him here, but they are back in Santa Fe. He knows Gunner and some of Levi's men too."

"Great! They seem to know each other all across the country. Which is good because they probably need that family connection. Brothers, so to speak."

"Very true," Louise said. "Anyway, he's coming to get Sally this afternoon, providing she's good enough to go."

"Wow, that'll be interesting. Man and dog do travel, I guess," Cinn quoted badly.

"I think he's looking for a reason to stop traveling," Louise said simply. "He just doesn't know what it is and probably won't know until he finds it. Maybe not even then."

Silence filled the air for a few moments.

"Have you dropped a hint in there?" Cinn asked drily.

Laughter peeled through the phone. "Not necessarily," Louise said. "But, if something's there that you want to explore in greater detail, don't let him walk away. You don't know where he'll stop next."

"He's heading into a whole lot more trouble and probably won't be leaving except in a body bag, so don't count on Sally having a home just yet," Cinn said.

"What?" Louise asked, the confusion evident in her tone. "What is he doing?"

"He's tracked down whoever did this to Sally. And I know he's contacted Gunner to do something about it, and Gunner called the police. Ethan will make sure he stops this, and he doesn't really care if he gets hurt in the process."

"Well, maybe Sally is a good thing then. Maybe she'll encourage him to be safer, so he can look after her," Louise said. "Otherwise he could be biting off more than he can handle."

After she got off the phone, Cinn chewed on her bottom lip for a moment, wondering what she could do to help Ethan. But she didn't really have any options. She walked back into her office and stopped, looking out at the road. She saw a vehicle parked on the side of the highway. People didn't stop there, unless they were broken down. Her driveway came off the highway to her place down below, so she didn't hear or see much of the traffic—unless they parked on her side of the road. She watched and waited. Finally it turned and headed off again.

She forgot about it until a couple hours later, when she looked up, and possibly the same damn truck was parked once more on the roadside, facing the opposite direction this time. She got up with her cell phone and took a picture. It was too far away to show any details. Even if something funny was going on, who would she call? There was no reason for anybody to be watching her. The only thing different in her life right now was Ethan. And the dog.

Her breath caught in the back of her throat. She walked to a different window and peered out. It was just past noon, and she hadn't seen Ethan for hours. What if these men were looking for him? What if they'd seen him come to her house?

Unnerved, she went to call him, then stopped. Should she call him or not? She didn't know what he was doing. Not second-guessing herself, she hit the Dial button. When he answered, his voice sounded distracted.

"Any chance somebody followed you here?" she asked.

"What?" His voice was sharp. "Why would you ask that?"

"About an hour after you left, a truck parked out on the road. I thought I saw somebody looking down here at me. I didn't think anything of it because the truck started up and drove away. But, a few hours later, the same truck, or what appears to be the same truck, has parked up there again. I tried to take a picture of it, but it's pretty far away."

"Send me the picture, and I'll call you back."

She shrugged and sent him the picture with a note. **I told you it was far away.**

She went in the kitchen and put on a pot of coffee, hating the tension coiling inside. She didn't want to think he'd brought trouble to her door, but then she knew she couldn't blame him. Not only was he the kind to walk into trouble, he was the kind to deal with trouble nobody else wanted. And he had gone looking for it. He'd gone to help save Sally.

Just as the coffee was done, her phone rang.

"Stay in the house. Lock it up. I'll come back this afternoon." He disconnected.

She glared at her phone and tossed it on the kitchen counter. The last thing she wanted was to be given orders.

She looked outside and saw the truck moving away again. She smiled, grabbed her phone and sent Ethan a text. **False alarm. Truck's leaving.**

Order still stands came the instant response. **Let me know if it comes back.**

"Like hell I will," she said aloud good-naturedly.

She headed back to her office and her work. She had tons to do, and, if she was lucky, she would get something accomplished. She had another mess of emails and phone calls to make. She wanted to get through her business work and get back to her dog rescues. Just because Ethan was focused on saving Sally didn't mean other animals weren't desperately in need of her assistance.

STARING AT THE property, two cops at his side, more stationed close by, a dozen in all, Ethan hated to think somebody might have followed him to Cinn's place. He'd kept a careful eye out the night before and hadn't seen anyone. But it was possible the owners had a lookout. Once at the property, he'd been so focused on the sentries there that he'd forgotten more could be higher up.

He froze, thinking about that and then swore softly. The two cops beside him turned to look at him. "When I was here last night," he said softly, "I think a lookout might have been up on that peak." He turned to look at the hill where he'd been parked. "I parked up there and came down here. If somebody up on the top saw me ..." He let his voice trail off, looking at the text on his phone.

"Why are you thinking about that now?"

"Because a truck is parked on the highway, watching a friend's house where I'd been last evening. It disappeared, then it came back. I want to make sure nobody from here followed me to her."

"Then go look after her," urged Matthew, one of the two officers.

"She says it's gone now, and she will stay inside locked up." At least he hoped she would. He motioned at the property in front of them. "I need a chance to help these dogs."

"Not if she's in danger, you don't."

He shook his head. "I don't think she's in danger. But it could mean somebody's out there looking for me."

The signal came just then. The men moved out. Ethan's military training kicked in, and he already knew where he was due to be. As he approached the front, he kept behind the policemen. His best defense was getting those dogs on his side. He just had to get to them before the place exploded in chaos.

Just then one of the armed sentries called out, "Stop. This is private property. You're trespassing."

Ethan's gaze zoomed in on the dog at his side. Her hackles were raised, and she snarled. She wore a prong collar, and it was all the guy could do to hold her back. Ethan knew, with a minimal touch, she'd go at the first intruder. Quickly using his fingers, he whistled a high-pitched tone that he'd used on his own dogs in the military—a tone that animals could hear much better than humans.

Silence followed.

The dog's barking stopped as if cut off with a knife. Her ears went up, and she turned, looking toward Ethan, her gaze intent. The handler was so focused on the men at the front gate that he didn't notice the change in the dog's behavior.

Good. Because they would need every advantage they could get.

Darkness dropped as heavy clouds moved overhead. It added a somberness to the situation. His focus was on the dogs, but he knew the other men were focused on not getting shot as they took down the operation. Not part of the inner workings of the police team, Ethan watched as they all moved into position.

On the other side of the fence, two more men arrived with two more dogs. One a big male. Was that K9:01?

The dog he had whistled to no longer pulled on her leash. She looked around, confusion in her eyes. He let out a light whistle, easing the tension in her system. She gave a headshake, as if not quite sure what was going on. Her lips curled, and she snarled again. Her handler pulled back on her leash. Ethan watched as her neck was jerked to the side with more force than necessary. Her lips curled harder, and the snarls could easily be heard from where Ethan hid.

Matthew, still beside him, asked, "Why don't we just pop a bullet in her? It'd be easier. She looks like she's ready to eat one of us."

Ethan shook his head. "Her collar has metal spikes that are digging into her neck, probably cutting her throat right now. She's been trained on torture and mishandling. It's not her fault."

"It might not be her fault," the guy said sarcastically, "but I sure as hell don't want to be at the receiving end of those teeth."

Shots fired from the left. After that, chaos ensued inside the compound. There were shouts, sirens, and the dog lunged in a frantic frenzy. Ethan knew, once the attack dogs hit that blood rage, it would be hard to control them. He had to get them away from their handlers.

One of the men lost control of his dog. It jerked hard, jumping at the fence. Instead of going after the dog, he pulled his rifle from over his shoulder and fired at the police team.

Ethan crouched below the hillock. He didn't think this was the way it was supposed to go down. For some reason he'd expected this to be a simpler operation. But, once they'd been sighted, instead of more talking, the compound had fired at them.

As quickly as it started, it stopped.

Silence hushed over his ears. He looked at the man at his side. He talked on his walkie-talkie.

Matthew bounced up, nudged Ethan and said, "All clear. One dog is injured. I don't know about the other two. We've got six shooters down and secured. You stay behind me the whole way."

Ethan did as instructed, happy to be in the background on this one. As they forced open the gates, another alarm went off, causing the dogs to howl. Ethan pulled the ropes and leads he had brought with him out of his backpack, and, with his hands well-gloved and his forearms wrapped, he headed in to the left, as all the men went to the right.

One of the dogs headed toward the policemen. The officer turned, lowered his rifle and called out at Ethan, "She's got one chance. Then I shoot."

Ethan stepped in front of the rifle. The dog jumped at him, her mouth wide, teeth shining bright. He twisted at the last moment, shoving his padded forearm in her mouth. He gravitated as her weight hit him. He went down with her, flipping her to the ground, putting his foot on her neck and grabbing control of her leash. The dog released her chokehold on his arm and lay on the ground, quivering.

He looked at the officer, still pointing a gun at him. "She'll be fine."

The officer stared at the dog and then at Ethan with disbelief. He shook his head and said, "Better you than me. Watch out for the other two."

Ethan nodded as two more dogs approached. They were confused with their teammate on the ground. Ethan released his gentle but effective hold on her neck, waited for her to get up. With a special training collar firmly in place, he tied her to the open gate so she had no choice but to stay down. With her neck at an angle, she couldn't lunge at anybody. It was temporary until he could get the other two dogs under control.

He pulled out another lead and approached the two dogs. Two was harder than one because they would double-team him if they were well trained. He went down into a nonthreatening crouch. He whistled a high piercing sound. The dogs started to howl. And, with that, their bodies relaxed just slightly.

The dog behind him howled too. He glanced at her, but she was fine.

Instincts told Ethan to lunge and to hook on the collars so this pair couldn't turn on him. But he knew that any heavy-handed approach would bring them instantly into the red zone.

He took several steps toward the closest one. It turned its gaze on him and curled its lip, dragging its leash with each movement. All Ethan had to do was get a hold of that leash himself.

He yelled out commands, but the dogs wouldn't listen. He walked forward, his body ready for the attack he knew was coming. He needed to successfully repeat the first scenario. But this was a big male, and it didn't look like he would go down easily. Ethan braced himself, but the dog suddenly broke to the left and circled around behind him. Then it barked in front of the female, already down and tied up. Ethan couldn't keep an eye on both loose dogs, now split up.

"Very smart," he said, admiration in his tone as he backed up slightly so he could get a wider view of each one. "Are you also trying to protect her?"

He knew the officers kept an eye on what was happening. Most of them would agree that a bullet was the only answer in this situation, but Ethan didn't agree. It wasn't the animals' fault they were defending something the good guys needed to stop.

The big male, still standing in front of the captured female, barked and barked. Ethan studied him, trying to understand what his weakness was. The other male on his right lunged. Ethan deliberately kept his gaze on the second male as he went for him. Still crouched, he raised his arm to give him something to bite on. As soon as he bit, his jaw locked down, he grabbed the leash dragging behind him. With that done, Ethan put another one of his restraining collars on the second male and dropped him until he was flat on the ground. He still had a grip on him and fought. Once he released his jaws, and it would take some time, he could pull free from him. But he surprised him, unlocking his hold before he went down.

He gave him a moment, safely behind him with his hand on his throat. He talked to him in a calm, quiet voice. "Take it easy. You'll be fine."

When he stopped snarling, he gave him the command to lie down. He did.

He smiled. "I knew you were well trained."

He ordered him to stand and to heel. He stood and took his position just behind Ethan's right leg. All the while the first male, now even more confused, showed signs of attacking. Ethan was surprised he hadn't attacked at the same time as the earlier one had. Ethan wondered how much of that was due to the female behind him. Maybe the male dog felt he was the defender of all of them. Animals stayed in packs, and the first male was the alpha male obviously. Now his pack was being split and taken down, but, as long as Ethan held the leash of this second male dog, Ethan had to make sure he kept the other male contained too.

He looked around for a place to tie him up, but there was only the fence. Using commands, he moved slowly toward it. With the short leash hooked so his head, neck and chest were against the fence, he couldn't move. After securing him, he headed for the first male, wondering if this was the K9 he was looking for.

"Hey, boy. I know you don't understand this, and you're just fighting for your life. I have no intention of hurting you."

He spoke in the same tone he used to work with dogs all the time. Usually he worked with dogs delighted to be working, dogs that loved to learn, dogs that loved to have a job to do every day. But, every once in a while, he came up against animals either wild or badly abused, and those needed the same loving care he'd given his own.

This one was missing great big chunks of hair along its back and sides. Ethan didn't know if it was from mange or abuse. Scars and definitely some blood were on his shoulder. Again, who was to say where that came from? There was nothing wrong with the breadth of his jaws. The male looked like it was a good forty pounds heavier than the females, also the norm. But he also had something else about him. He wasn't a purebred shepherd from the looks of him. Ethan wasn't sure just what he was though.

He kept his gaze on the dog, knowing every action would show in the dog's eyes first. Ethan just had to be ready. He had another restraining leash in his hand and, just in case, a big choke chain. He figured the male would be the hardest to take down.

He risked a glance up and found he was surrounded by officers. "Is everything else under control?" he asked.

"Yes. By the way, this is the one that got shot."

"Hopefully it's not bad," he said. "That explains the blood on his shoulder."

"Are you sure you don't want us to give him a second

bullet?"

Ethan shook his head. "No. Just like the two others, he's only doing his job."

"And how the hell will you win this fight?" Matthew asked. "It looks like he'll go for your throat."

"He will, if I give him that chance. But there can only be one boss. And he has to understand that I mean to be that boss."

One of the men snorted.

That sound set off the big male dog in front of him. Ethan backed up several steps, giving the dog room to run, and he took advantage, seeing his prey as weaker. He lunged for Ethan's throat. As soon as that jaw opened, Ethan thrust his left arm forward into the dog's open jaws, as far as he could, forcing the dog's jaws wide, then flipped him to the ground onto his sore shoulder. The dog yelped but was already locked in place on Ethan's padded arm.

One-handed, Ethan calmly disengaged the spikes on the dog's collar he currently wore and pulled it a bit tighter so the dog wouldn't completely slip from it. Then Ethan let the dog roll over to his other side, onto his good shoulder, and stepped on the chain leash, all while the big male chomped down firmly on Ethan's padded arm. In a bold move, Ethan's free hand removed the glove from his other hand, then shoved his glove into the dog's mouth, forcing his jaws to open wider. This pushed it past the point where it could apply force to bite down, freeing Ethan's arm finally. With the dog already weakened, it couldn't do much. Nor did it try.

And, just like that, Ethan had the third one secured. While it was down, Ethan used his other leg to hold the jaw and the head firmly on the ground without hurting it and checked out the bullet wound, but it was more of a burn. Ethan studied him. His markings were close to the picture he had of Sentry, the K9:01 dog. He'd have to wait to check his tattoo to confirm his identity. The dog was already stressed; now wasn't the time to add to it.

"I don't know who shot him," he called out, "but all you did was piss him off."

The uniformed men stared at him.

Ethan looked at the three dogs and then at the policemen and asked, "What's wrong?"

They shook their heads. None were apparently concerned about more unfriendlies on the compound, so presumably the place was secure.

"Damn it. I'd rather take down six gunmen than face one of these dogs," Matthew snapped. "That was crazy."

Ethan smiled. "I used to train these guys to do just what they did. They're well trained. They did their jobs. They don't know the difference between good guys and bad guys in this case," he said. "They don't deserve a bullet for having had no choice."

"Yeah, but now what will you do with them?"

"It depends what the law will allow me to do," he said. "I have a place I can take them. I have a vet to get this one treated. I'd like to rehabilitate them, so they're good protective animals."

The officer in charge, Sergeant Mendelsson, walked toward him, his hands on his hips. The male shepherd growled.

Ethan applied gentle pressure on the dog's jaw to let him know what was acceptable and what wasn't. "If you just stand your ground there," he said to the sergeant, "the dog will understand that, A, I'm the boss, and, B, he's not in any danger."

The sergeant nodded. "I think I can arrange that. I don't know what will happen to them long-term."

"Destroyed, I would imagine," said another officer, approaching. "But, if you think you can rehabilitate them— and, after what we've seen here today, I think maybe you can—we'll do our best to give you that chance. But you need a place to move them."

Ethan nodded, his mind spinning rapidly. "I have a house at the moment. It is fenced. But I'll need a better way to train them. Still, I can arrange that."

"You got your chance then. What about your truck? You'll need a canopy or something for them."

He considered the options and shook his head. "The canopy would be better, yes, but I can secure them in the back so they're not going anywhere."

The men nodded.

Matthew said, "As much as I don't want to get close to them, do you need a hand moving them?"

Ethan shook his head. "I'll take them one at a time."

He lifted his foot and ordered the male to stand. Struggling with his bad shoulder, the male shepherd rose. Ethan commanded it to heel, and he walked the dog just like that out of the compound. He knew the men were watching, and he knew they didn't understand. And that was okay because it was what Ethan did. Only he had to stop and think about that because it was not what he did now. What he used to do was train these animals for military scenarios—to sniff out bombs, chemicals and weapons.

Potentially, in this case, he could rehabilitate these dogs to be used as guard dogs or maybe, once again, chemicals- and weapons-sniffing dogs. He had no clue where this was taking him.

What he did know was it felt right. What he did was worth it for the animals.

At his truck, he opened the tailgate and ordered the dog to jump. Instantly he jumped into the back. With the dog in the bed, Ethan secured it to one of the hooks. He couldn't take it very far like this; it wasn't safe, but he had limited options at the moment.

With one dog secured, he walked back to the fence and snagged the other two dogs waiting. With one on either side, he walked them to where the big male was. As soon as they realized where they were going, they were happy to follow. They jumped into the truck without any problem. He secured one across from the big male and then secured the third along the tailgate with it closed. None of them had enough leash that they could jump free, and, short of somebody throwing them over the side of the truck bed, no way they would get hurt.

He walked back to the sergeant and said, "Here's my address and phone number. I'll be there until I find better lodging for all the dogs, a place with kennels."

The sergeant shook his hand. "That was a nice job today. How well trained do you think they are?"

"Very well trained," he said. "I'll have to test them further to confirm, but I used to train dogs for bombs, weapons and chemicals missions. I'll run these dogs through the tests and see what they've been trained for."

The sergeant nodded and said, "I can't guarantee it, but you know what? If we can arrange it for you to keep them, and you think you can train them, we can always use dogs on specific jobs. We have almost no K9 Units here. And certainly none as well under control as you have those."

"I'll keep that in mind," Ethan said with a smile. "I've also got a female that came from this property as well. She's at the vet right now, recovering from surgery. Theoretically that's four good dogs that could be put to work."

"You might need another handler," one of the men called out.

Ethan nodded. "I might. First let me see how we do with these dogs."

With all the niceties taken care of, Ethan walked back to the truck. With a gloved hand, he reached down and gently stroked the back of the female, then the smaller male. As he approached the alpha male, he could hear the growl in the back of his throat, but he gently touched the dog on the back of his neck, letting him know Ethan was not an enemy. Then he hopped into the truck, turned on the engine and headed home.

CHAPTER 7

W HEN CINN DIDN'T hear from Ethan, and she saw no sign of him, she couldn't settle. She wandered around the house, unable to do much as she waited for news. Dark clouds had moved in overhead, and the atmosphere had an ugly feel about it. The humid static in the air made her sticky at the same time as it made her edgy. What she really wanted was for the storm to break to release all that tension. Instead, it just seemed to sit heavily above the property.

Finally her phone rang. She picked it up to hear Ethan's voice on the other end. Overwhelmed with relief, she snapped at him. "Is this really the earliest you could contact me to let me know you are okay?"

Silence hung like the heavy, dark clouds above her.

"No," he said thoughtfully. "I might have called while I was in the middle of gunfire. Or I might have called when I was facing three extremely angry dogs, who were ready to rip out my throat. Or maybe when I was explaining to the sergeant afterward that the dogs were worth saving. Or maybe when I was driving with all three shepherds tied down tight in the bed of my truck."

"Okay, so now I feel like a piece of shit," she said jokingly. "Please tell me all that happened calmly and quietly, and that none of you were hurt."

"I have a big male shepherd cross here that's got a burn

on his shoulder from a bullet. But that appears to be the only injury, which is rather remarkable considering a lot of dead bad guys are at that place."

She gasped. "Seriously?"

"They opened fire on the cops." His tone said he didn't give a damn about the dead men. "I was more concerned about saving the animals."

"So was it a drug lab?"

"As far as I know it was," he said. "Did you hear that part about I cared more about the animals? Once I had them calmed down and secured, I didn't want to leave them there for the cops to change their minds. If Animal Control becomes involved, I figured the animals would be taken to a cage and probably put down as soon as possible. I wanted a chance to rehabilitate them, to see just what they were trained to do."

"So now you have four dogs to look after?" she asked incredulously.

"Apparently four vicious dogs," he said cheerfully.

She stared out the window. "Why?"

His voice gentled as he answered, "Because I can."

She sagged into the kitchen chair and thought about that. "It won't be an easy job," she warned. "I thought you were looking for something different or some sort of new start."

"Can you really think of any better start than helping some animal with no future? Or, in this case, four?"

She sighed. "You know who you're talking to. I'm the one who moves hell on earth to get animals in desperate situations moved to new countries where they can have a chance."

"Exactly." His voice was quiet and pensive. "I saw those

dogs and the guns pointed at their heads, and I realized how much I could do to help them. They have really good useful lives ahead of them. They were doing a job. It's not their fault that job has now been taken away from them."

"Do you think you can retrain them to do what you want them to do?"

"Absolutely," he said. "That process is already in progress. Whether they like it or not, they now see me as their new leader. We'll have to do some heavy training and come to an agreement of sorts. But I'm pretty sure we're well in hand."

"But you need a place suited for these animals," she stated.

"Yes. That's a bit of an issue. I'm at the house I rented here in town where I'm staying," he said thoughtfully. "I might look for a place with kennels, or at least a big enough spot for kennels I can pull together fast for them."

"That won't be cheap," she warned. "You don't just need kennels but you also need a training space." She could almost see him nod in agreement. "This is rather sudden, isn't it?"

"Sure, but necessity is what drives a lot in our lives," he said. "I have to try."

She nodded. "I understand. The thought of having three killer dogs at your place is enough to terrify almost anybody. And a fourth to join them soon."

"What if I said they follow my commands and listen to the orders I give?"

"Seriously?"

"Yeah, absolutely. Give us a few days, and we'll have a completely different relationship."

"But how will they view the rest of the world?" she

asked. "You don't live on an island. You look after dogs ready to kill at a moment's notice. That won't sit easy with the townsfolk in general."

"No, but it's not that bad," he said. "It's not about dogs that will kill at a moment's notice because every animal has that potential. But it's knowing a dog will attack when instructed. And not just attack but attack properly. These dogs need some more training. No doubt about it. That male would go for my throat. He needs to learn to disable, not to kill."

All the horrible scenarios ran through her head, and she couldn't believe what she had heard. "This is so much above what most of us deal with."

"Which is why I have to do this," he exclaimed. "And I get it if that makes me something you don't want to be around …"

"No, that's not what I meant at all." She groaned. "I guess I'm shocked at how fast this all happened. You went up there to hopefully help these dogs, but I didn't expect you to take them away with you."

"I did," he said calmly. "There really wasn't much else in the way of options. They could have been put down on the spot, or Animal Control might have come and taken them, but the end would have probably been the same. But did Animal Control have the ability to remove these dogs safely? I doubt it. I was the best option."

"That is often how it is," she admitted. "If the dogs are a problem, they take them out."

"Exactly," he said. "So I stepped in. Now the question is whether I can make them do the job they need to do and have a decent life or whether I'll have to make a difficult decision down the road and put them down myself."

She winced. "Ouch."

"No," he said. "That would be almost impossible for me to do."

She smiled. "So when do I get to meet them?"

"Not for several days," Ethan said quietly. "As much as I would like to think they would allow strangers into their space, for the first few days, if not a week, it will need to be just them and me."

"That makes sense," she said lightly. What did she expect? It wasn't like the dogs would accept Ethan into their world easily, and they sure as hell wouldn't accept her, a complete stranger, either. "Can you add the injured shepherd to this group?"

"I think she was part of this group to begin with. I'm pretty sure she belongs with them," he said. "I have to see what kind of reaction I get when I reintroduce her. She's still weak and needs care for quite a while. If the other dogs won't accept her, I can't keep them together."

She winced. "If those dogs are vicious to Sally …"

"I know," he said. "Which is why it needs to be just us for a while."

She nodded and smiled.

"Any sign of that truck again?"

Startled she remembered the truck she'd seen up on the highway. "I never did see it again. I'm taking a look now." She walked over to the window but saw no sign of anything. "I think I was just being supersensitive," she said. "With you going after this group, I don't know, I guess for some reason it made me nervous."

"Of course it did," he said in reassurance. "That's normal, and it's not an issue. I'm glad you at least thought to let me know it was there."

"Why?" She laughed. "It's not like you were close enough to do anything about it."

"That's true," he said. "But I could have been there within a few minutes, and I would have called somebody closer to help."

She smiled. "Well, if I see it again, I'll let you know."

"Let me know if you see *anything* odd again," he urged. "Just because the raid went off successfully doesn't mean the police got everyone."

"Thanks," she said. "I really needed to think like that."

"Yes, you do," he said as if not understanding her sarcasm. "One should always be aware."

Sure enough, as soon as she clicked off her phone, instead of feeling better about what he'd said, the reminder that the truck had been there on the highway made her feel worse.

She needed an outlet for her nervous energy, so she changed into her running gear. With the dogs barking happily at her side, she grabbed a water bottle and headed out the back door. It was late in the afternoon, almost evening, and the worst heat had started to settle back.

She opened up the back gate to the state land and took off at a fast run. With the dogs running happily at her side, she crisscrossed over the terrain, checking out some of her favorite spots, shaking off the tension of the day and her added worries about Ethan. She hadn't realized just how much she had been focused on Ethan. You had to love a man who would go in after the dogs.

But she wasn't sure his particular project would be worth his time and trouble. And that felt awful coming from her. After all, she loved animals, and she spent so much of her time trying to save animals in need. What was it about these particular ones that scared her? Of course it was the viciousness to them. But, if Ethan could tame them, or at least keep them as well-controlled animals, then she was all for it. It would also likely keep him close by, and that made her happy.

She had no business looking at a relationship with somebody who was such a loner, someone without roots, especially when she was such a homebody. She did take trips around the world for these animals, but so much of it nowadays was communication on the Internet and phone. It was easier to send photos and vet reports back and forth than to fly over and look at the animals.

With the sun going behind the clouds, she dashed into the trees. Racing through them, her heart felt lighter with every step she took. Such interesting weather, a day full of light and shadows, not hot, not cold. By the time she burst through the other side, she was sprinting all-out. She could feel the tension inside desperately needing the outlet. Her feet pounded the ground as she ran faster and farther.

And then her energy seemed to wane, and she slowed her steps, laughing, and stumbled.

Crack.

She cried out as her shoulder exploded with pain, and she fell to the ground. She instinctively reached a hand to her shoulder and rolled over. Panic set in, but she was a good ten or twelve feet from the next set of trees. She pulled her hand away, seeing the blood pumping sluggishly from the wound.

She'd been shot!

She pulled out her cell phone while she lay here, panicked somebody would come closer for a killing shot, and dialed Ethan's phone. The dogs whimpered at her side, unsure of what happened but knowing something had.

"I've been shot," she said baldly. "I'm about two miles from the house, on the state land behind my place. Parallel to the highway. There's a large wooded area. I've gone through that, and I'm on the field between it and the next set of woods."

"I'm on my way," he said, his voice unnaturally calm. "How bad is the wound? Did you call 9-1-1?"

"Not arterial and, no, not yet. I called you and will call Flynn next." Her voice was shaky. "It's in the shoulder."

"I'll be there in a few minutes," he repeated.

"I want to run for the trees and try to hide." She peered through the long grass. "But I'm worried about taking a second hit."

"Can you see anyone?" he asked, his voice sharp.

In the background she heard Ethan slam a door, then turn on the engine. He was already on his way. Thank God. "Where are you? How long until you get here?"

"Make that eight." His voice was even and controlled. "Put pressure on that wound. And you stay alive until I get there. Do you hear me?"

She groaned, tears pouring down her face as the pain really set in. "I'm not planning on going anywhere. But I'm a sitting duck, if somebody comes after me."

"Don't move around," he cautioned. "Just lie there and don't make a sound. There's a good chance they'll assume they caught you with the first shot."

"And the dogs? They're milling around me."

"Can you get them to lie down? That's a common behavior for a dog, or at least have them sit at your side as they wait for help to come."

She instructed both dogs to sit and lie down beside her. Whining, their noses nestling against her, they obeyed. "Is it common for dogs to stay here like this?"

"Yes. They won't leave an injured owner."

"What about a dead one?" she whispered, trying to keep her tone light as panic threatened to choke her and as her heart slammed to get out of her chest. "I keep thinking somebody's coming toward me."

"Watch the dogs for that kind of a reaction," he said quietly. "I'm already on the highway."

"Good." Her voice was still shaky, the tears easily sounding in her tone. "The dogs are sitting here, whining, but they don't act like anybody's around."

"Good. Don't run for the trees because that will let somebody know you're still alive."

"Hopefully you'll see them before I will," she joked. "If you're coming from the opposite direction as the vet's, it should only be minutes after that bad corner until you see the first copse of trees."

"Can you give me any better directions as to where you are?"

She tried explaining where the turnoff was to one of the side streets and that she was just past it. She gasped from the effort, lying quiet for a moment, then she continued, "When you get to Cotton Road Drive, I'm probably another fifty to one hundred yards past the trees right there at that turnoff."

"Coming up to the turnoff now."

"The shot came from that direction."

"Good. I'm pulling over here. You stay where you are. I'll be there in a few minutes."

She wanted to look around to search for him, but she couldn't hear any sound of a truck engine. The traffic should be audible from where she was, but she heard nothing. She held the palm of her hand flat against her wound, part of her

T-shirt balled up against it, trying to press down hard on it. She stared at the cloudy sky and focused on breathing deeply.

But surely they'd know if they caught her in the shoulder, not in the head.

This was a shitty end to a rough day. She had to think it was related to Ethan because nobody out here hated her. At least she didn't think so. She hadn't spent a lifetime creating enemies. She was one of those charity workers, and few people even knew where she lived.

She took several more deep breaths, trying to force back that panicked edge. The pain, if she thought about it, was crippling. To calm down she made a quick call to Flynn. He swore and demanded answers. "Can't talk," she said. "Just come." And she hung up.

Her ears were on overdrive for any sound, good or bad, coming toward her. But Ethan was right about one thing: watch the dogs. They were both relaxed but worried. Their noses pushed eagerly into her hand as she tried to calm them. But they weren't growling or jumping to their feet or racing toward anyone or away from anything. So, as far as she could tell, nobody was out here.

And then a dog barked. She twisted but couldn't see anything for the tall grass around her.

Soon she heard a high-pitched sound and a man's hard voice snapping orders. She couldn't confirm if that was Ethan or not. She wanted to sit up but knew she shouldn't.

Then a whistle, several barks and another whistle. And she now realized what she'd heard. *Ethan*. He'd come with one of the new dogs. She frowned. "Is that a good idea, Ethan?"

She slid to a half-sitting position, holding her shoulder,

and she could see him at the tree line, and the dog was free, tracking somebody.

She could hear shouting, as if somebody else was countering the orders.

Another shot was fired and then another. She flattened against the ground, grateful none were directed at her. But had the dog been shot? Ethan?

What the hell had Ethan done? What the hell had she gotten into?

She waited with bated breath as she tried to understand what else was going on. The dogs were no longer lying at her side but stood, studying the area, barking at the other dog, easily giving away Cinn's position. So who would find her first?

And then, in her heart and mind, she knew there was no competition. It would be Ethan all the way. And suddenly she heard footsteps coming toward her. She froze. Her dogs growled. And then a strange dog barked and raced toward her. It loomed over her, and she curled protectively into a ball, until she heard Ethan issue a command. Immediately its butt hit the ground, and its nose went out, ears up.

She let out her pent-up breath as she watched this huge shepherd stare down at her. It wasn't growling at her; it wasn't attacking her. It was as if giving a command to its owner, saying, *I found her.*

And suddenly there was Ethan.

She burst into tears. She would have thrown her arms around him, but her shoulder was killing her. He crouched at her side and stroked her face gently.

"It's all right. You're safe."

He pulled her hand off her shoulder. "Let me take a look." Then he nodded. "It could be much worse." He eased her into a sitting position and checked the back of her shoulder. "It went through, and that's good."

She shook her head. "I don't know how you can think that's good. I've been *shot*."

"Yes, you have," he said and, taking out his pocketknife, dug something out of the dirt behind her. Then he exchanged the knife for a sheet of paper from his notepad in his pocket and pulled up the slug.

She stared at it. "I really was shot?" she said in disbelief. It was one thing to assume she'd been shot; it was another thing to see the proof in his hand. She glanced around. "How do you know it's safe? Is he gone?"

"He's gone," Ethan said.

"Gone? I heard more shooting."

Ethan nodded. "He tried to countermand the dog. This, by the way, is Bella."

She looked at the shepherd, still in her position, not having been released from the command given. "Is she safe?" Cinn asked tentatively. "She's pretty ferocious looking."

"The big collar doesn't help, but it does give her name," he said. He turned to Bella and gave her a hand signal and said, "Relax."

Bella, her tail wagging, leaned over and sniffed Cinn. She reached up a tentative hand. Bella placed her nose in her hand and nudged it.

Cinn smiled and scratched Bella's head. "Did she find me?"

"Yes, she did. Not that you would have been hard to find with the other dogs here."

Both her dogs milled around Bella. The three were getting to know each other. Bella showed no signs of aggression. "How did you know she was the one you should bring?"

Cinn asked, dazed. "That was taking a hell of a chance."

"The only chance I took was if your shooter might have had better control over Bella. But I don't think she has any loyalty to the abusive men who kept her before."

"How sad is that?" Cinn murmured. "You didn't explain what the shots were I heard."

"He tried to shoot her," Ethan said quietly. "But Bella dodged and managed to miss the bullets, and, when he realized she was still coming after him, and then he saw me too, he turned the gun on himself."

"What?" Her jaw dropped. "Are you serious?"

Grim-faced, Ethan nodded. "I'm serious. We need to get the cops here now, before anybody else finds out what's happened."

He helped her stand, then led her to a large rock to sit down. He called Bella over and ordered her to guard. She stood, facing out to the world around her, her attention focused around them.

Cinn, who had a lot of experience with dogs, but none with actual working dogs of this nature, watched in amazement as Bella appeared to keep a close eye on everything going on. "What happens if I get up and walk away?"

Ethan chuckled. "Well, I guess we'll find out if you try it, won't we?"

She frowned up at him. "That's not funny."

But he was already calling somebody on his phone.

"Who are you calling?"

"The team I joined on the raid this morning."

He walked away a few steps to have his conversation. She heard bits and pieces, enough to know he was explaining the circumstances.

She reached down to pet her beautiful dogs, giving them

each a cuddle. They were not Bella by any means. They were nervous and worried and staying very close. Yet they weren't intimidated by Bella. On the contrary, they were doing their best to make friends. But Bella would have nothing to do with it. She was on guard, and the dogs were completely not there as far as she was concerned. It was fascinating to watch. And, if Cinn hadn't been in so much damn pain, she'd have appreciated it a whole lot more.

When Ethan turned to look at her, putting away his phone, she asked, "How long?"

"He figures about thirty minutes. He'll get here faster if he can. He wanted to know if you wanted an ambulance."

She shook her head. "Hell no."

"You still have to go to the hospital and get stitched up." He stood with his legs slightly apart, his hands fisted on his hips, as if ready for a fight.

She nodded. "I know. But no reason you can't drive me there." She glanced at her shoulder and said, "Hell, I can probably drive myself. It's my left shoulder."

"No, you're not driving yourself," he stated firmly. "Of course I can drive you. I told him that you wouldn't want an ambulance because you'd try to drive yourself."

She went quiet. "You don't know me well enough to be sure I'd react that way," she said but realized she was arguing futilely over nothing. The pain had kicked in heavily.

He picked up her water bottle and handed it to her. When she tried to unscrew the top, he pulled it back, unscrewed the top for her and held it out again.

She took a long drink. "That feels better," she whispered. "You don't know just how rough things are until you realize you're arguing over nothing, and it's all you can do to sit upright."

He crouched at her side and checked her over. "Did you hit your head when you went down?" he asked, his fingers gently searching her temple and the back of her head.

"No," she said, closing her eyes and leaning into the gentle massage. "But that does feel good."

His fingers deepened the pressure slightly, moving down her neck, then to her good shoulder and back. "If that's the only wound, we'll put this down to pain and shock," he said. "Not to mention you were probably running flat-out before you were struck, so you're dealing with exertion and probably a lack of water at the same time."

On that note, she drank most of the rest of her bottle, then handed it back to him. "I'm worried about the dogs too."

"Why?"

"Because I don't want to leave them alone when I go to the hospital."

"You leave them alone all the time, don't you?"

"I do, but they're pretty upset right now." She turned to look at her three-legged dog. He lay right beside Bella. She smiled. "It's almost as if he's decided Bella will protect him too."

"Animals know who and what they all are. They won't argue with Bella."

"But you haven't explained how you knew Bella was safe to bring."

"I was out back working with them, and, when I issued orders, Bella followed them instantly. She hasn't been at that place very long, and, wherever she came from, she was well trained. A couple commands she didn't know because they're very unique to the military work I did. But she's certainly been trained as a guard dog. And as an attack dog."

At the word attack, Bella slipped him a half look, and her ears went up.

He smiled and said, "No, Bella, just guard."

She relaxed but continued to stare out around the area, her head moving from side to side ever-so-slowly, as if she were keeping up a full 180-degree search. At one point, she got up and walked around several times, looking out into the trees around them.

"Is she not happy about the trees?"

"She's aware of the body over there."

At that reminder, Cinn winced. "Right."

"And death does affect the animals."

"Maybe, but in this case, he tried to kill her too."

He pointed to Bella's shoulder, where it had a bit of a burn mark. Cinn hadn't even seen it. She'd been so focused on her own pain. She gasped and leaned forward. "He almost did kill her," she exclaimed.

"Well, he tried. But he missed, and, when she got around behind him, and he saw me coming at him too, I think he realized he wouldn't have much of a hope. Before she got him, he decided to take the easy way out."

"Does that mean they've used these dogs to kill people?"

Silence was his only reply.

She turned to look up at him. "Seriously?"

His face was grim. "It's a possibility."

"That's not the dog's fault though," she said. "They can't put her down because of that."

"I don't know that we can prove that's what those guys did. But he certainly took an easy way out, and he took it fast."

"You should find out who he is," she urged. "Before the cops get here."

He looked at her in surprise.

She shrugged. "I don't know how much the police will tell us after the fact."

"Glad to know we both think alike."

Her thoughts still fuzzy, she gazed up at him in confusion. "How is that?"

"Because I already checked. His name is Gary Foster."

She frowned, rattling through her brain to see if that name meant anything, but then she shook her head. "I don't know him."

"Neither do I," he said, "but I have a photo of his driver's license and credit cards."

"Do you have anybody who can track down who he is?"

He shrugged, but, in a cheerful voice, he said, "Maybe."

She'd take that to mean a definite yes. She smiled. "This is something you know how to handle, don't you?"

"Wherever there are assholes in the world, there needs to be people who protect the innocent from them. I've always been one of the protectors." He gave her a gentle smile.

She nodded. "I figured as much. I thought at first maybe you were a new recruit for Levi's team. But now, you know something? I think you need to have your own team. A canine team."

He studied her face in surprise. "I'm beginning to think so too. And fits in with the rest of today."

"Why is that?" she asked.

In the distance she could hear sirens. She sure hoped they were for them. She didn't want to deal with the cops, but she really wanted to go to the hospital, if only to get some pain meds, to get her shoulder taken care of and then to get back home to bed, where she planned on staying for a hell of a long time.

"I told the police team I was with today at the drug-manufacturing property that's what I was looking to do."

When his words sank in, she stared at him in astonishment. "Wow. Still, if you can make Bella do what Bella's doing, I think there'd be all kinds of work for you."

"It's not as if I'll be running down killers," he said, "but, if Bella has other training, … or I can enhance her existing training—for all the dogs, not just her—then we could work for many agencies."

"I think there'll always be work for well-trained dogs."

"I guess we'll see, won't we?"

ETHAN WASN'T READY to make any plans yet. In the distance he could hear sirens and other vehicles approaching. He smiled down at her and said, "The cavalry is coming."

Instead of looking pleased, she'd winced. "I'd rather go straight home."

He studied the level of pain evident on her face. "We'll get you out of here as soon as possible."

"No ambulance though," she warned.

"I told you that I'd drive you," he said quietly. "But I may have to deal with the police first."

"So that's the trade-off," she said quietly.

He crouched in front of her. "You hang in there." He could see her pain-fogged gaze deepening. Worried, he said, "Forget it. I'll tell the cops I have to take you to the hospital first. Then I'll come back and talk to them."

She gave a strangled laugh. "It's not that bad. Besides, the cops won't let you leave the crime scene."

"Well, they won't leave you here either," he warned. "So

it's me or the ambulance."

Suddenly Bella growled, a sound that raised the hairs on the back of Cinn's neck.

"Not quite," a stranger called over.

Ethan spun, squatting low, until he saw Flynn standing a safe distance away.

Ethan glanced at Cinn.

She nodded. "I sent out a distress call to him too."

Slowly Ethan rose on his feet, standing protectively at Cinn's side. "Bella, stand down."

The dog relaxed, but her gaze never left Flynn.

Flynn nodded and approached. "The cops are here. We'll let them talk to her, and then I'll take her to the hospital."

Ethan was of two minds, but she needed to go to the hospital, and he needed to stay here with the cops. He glanced again at her, but she was smiling up at Flynn.

"Thank you. I'd love the assistance." She reached up with her good arm to Flynn. He carefully helped her to stand on her feet, staying right beside her in case she fell.

Ethan watched the color drain from her face with the movement. But he deliberately didn't take a step closer. Independence was fine, but it was also a good gauge to see a person's will to live. And, in her case, she was doing just fine. He nodded at Flynn and said, "If you don't mind …"

Flynn gave a clipped nod. "I know Cinn well. She'll be fine with Anna and me."

Ethan realized he was not being butted out but being reassured that Cinn would be okay. And then it didn't matter how reassuring Flynn was because they were suddenly surrounded by police. Bella didn't like being crowded. She growled and moved back slightly.

Two of the men appeared to know Flynn. But nobody knew Ethan. They weren't the cops he'd worked with earlier, so they must have called a detachment closer to the scene. He stayed quiet as discussions about what happened went on. And finally the men turned to him. He stared back, his gaze flat.

One of the men frowned at him. "Where's the dog?"

He pointed twenty feet off, where Bella still lay on his command.

"How dangerous is she?"

"In the wrong hands she's a killer," he said calmly. "In the right hands she's a savior."

The officers didn't like hearing that.

Flynn spoke up, "It's like anything." His voice was quiet but authoritative. "Dogs and guns are both weapons if they are used that way. The fact of the matter is, she's been standing guard over Cinn to make sure nobody else comes after her. And that is priceless."

Ethan wasn't so sure that was the case, but he had brought Bella on purpose. He looked at the leader of the police group and said, "I was working with law enforcement out of Houston earlier today." He mentioned Sergeant Mendelsson's name. Several men nodded. "You can verify with him that I'm the real deal."

The commander motioned to one of the men. He stepped back and pulled out his phone. "I'm calling to confirm Ethan Nebberly's identity."

Ethan stood, his stance casual but alert, his arms crossed over his chest, but he would go from zero to sixty in two seconds flat if he had to. In the meantime, he glanced at Bella. Her ears were up, her shoulders hunched, and, though she was in a lie-down position, she watched every move

Ethan made. He had to remind himself that she was watching his hand signals. If he made the wrong one, there could be a disaster. He looked at the commander and said, "We can stand here and wait for confirmation, or I can show you the body, and we can go from there."

"What body?" the commander asked sharply.

Ethan motioned at Cinn. "The man who shot her."

"Did you kill him?"

Ethan shook his head. "I didn't have to. The dog went after him. He tried to countermand my orders on the dog. When she wouldn't listen to him, he turned the gun on himself."

The officers studied Ethan, as if trying to figure that out. Ethan shrugged and waited. It didn't matter to him what they said. If they were any good at their jobs, the evidence would prove his story to be true. He looked over at Cinn and said, "I'll see you at the hospital in a bit."

The men looked at her, and the commander asked, "Are you okay to go on your own? Do you need an ambulance?"

She took several steps with Flynn beside her all the way. "I'm heading there now. I'm ambulatory, so no need to waste anybody else's time."

The commander said, "I'll meet you at the hospital later then. I need your statement."

"I can tell you right now. I was hunted down, shot and stayed flat. I called for help. Both these men came to my assistance. Ethan arrived a good forty minutes ahead of Flynn. Ethan went after the shooter. Just as he said, I could see them in the trees, and then there were gunshots. Once Ethan knew I was no longer in danger, he came to me. But now I have to admit, I'm feeling pretty shitty. So if you'll excuse me ..." She gave everyone a wan smile and then grabbed Flynn's forearm.

Gently he led her away from the group.

Ethan watched them go.

When she was a good ten to twenty feet away, she turned to look back at him and whispered, "I'm fine."

Seeing that, hearing her voice, something inside him relaxed. He turned to look at the policemen and said, "Shall we? You may want to mark this spot," he added, pulling the paper-wrapped slug from his pocket, "where I found this."

One of the officer's had gone back to the police cars and arrived now with cones and markers. They staked out the spot where Cinn had been shot.

Ethan pointed where his vehicle was parked up on the other side of the tree line on the highway. "You can walk up there and confirm that's my vehicle. I headed here from that spot right into the tree line. Now I'll take you where the body is."

He stepped forward and snapped his finger, bringing Bella to his side. He reached down a hand, and she nudged his fingers with her nose. Gently he stroked her forehead. He wondered at anybody who could abuse such a beautiful, obedient, well-trained animal who was just looking for somebody to love.

The commander stepped up beside Ethan, but his gaze was on Bella. "The sergeant confirmed your identity. He also said that you subdued three dogs, even though the officers were all ready to shoot them, and that you appeared to have good control over them."

"It's what I do," he said simply. "Over eight years in the military working with dogs. I wasn't about to let them be shot just because they had shitty owners."

The commander fell silent at that. "We do the best we

can," he said, "but, if we can't get a dog to not attack us …" and he left his words hanging.

Ethan nodded. "Understood. But I was there. And Bella, as you can see, although I didn't train her, is extremely obedient."

"Don't different trainers have different commands?"

"Yes, but some commands are universal. I don't know all she can do yet," he admitted. "I'm hoping to find out more about her and the others. She is by far the most amiable. I have the other two dogs back at my place. Plus an injured one currently at the vet that was badly abused and shot."

The sergeant whistled. "Asshats."

Ethan agreed, but he had a lot harsher words for them.

It took another few minutes to walk into the trees. He reached down, caught Bella's attention and ordered her to find the man who shot himself, then unhooked her leash. Bella bounded forward. She headed farther into the trees, stopped for a moment, took a slight adjustment in her direction and went left. Ethan followed.

The commander asked, "How can you be sure she's not tracking a squirrel?"

"I can't," he said cheerfully. "But she has no love lost for that man. She went after him instinctively and with way too much eagerness."

"You think he abused her?"

"Abused her or possibly had a hand in training her. But there was no love in the training. If anything, what I saw when she went after him was hate."

"Were you capable of calling her off?"

Ethan nodded. "It was close, but, yes, she did finally come at my command. But, when the guy saw me and the dog working together, and he realized he couldn't get Bella to do what he wanted her to do, he turned the gun on himself."

"But there was no reason for him to kill himself. He could have just shot you and Bella instead."

Ethan gave a hard laugh. "I can't be killed quite so easily as that."

Soon they were upon the body. Ethan stood at the perimeter and waited while the cops approached. The gun was still in the man's hand, but there was no way to mistake that he was dead. He'd blown the back of his head open.

Bella sat a good ten feet from the body, her gaze locked on it.

Ethan called her to him. "Good girl. Come here, Bella."

She trotted toward him and positioned herself behind his right leg.

The commander said, "Could she have killed him?"

"Yes, she definitely could have. I'm not sure she wasn't going to. I think he preferred a bullet over the dog."

"But you said you called her back, correct?" the commander asked. "We can't have killer dogs running around loose."

"Killer dogs, in this case, would be dogs trained to kill," he said gently. "And Bella is not running around loose. As you can see, the victim has no dog bite marks. I wouldn't let her attack him, but he didn't know that. He had already panicked, trying to get the gun into position before she reached him. As it was, she listened to my command just before she got to him."

The men looked at the body, reassured no bite marks were on the man himself. They relaxed. With her at his side, Ethan stepped back another few feet, making more room for the men to maneuver.

"We'll have to take your statement," the commander said, "and verify what you say is exactly what you did."

Ethan didn't say anything.

"Do you live around here?" one of the officers asked.

Ethan shook his head. "No. I'm renting a property close by. It belongs to Gunner Redding."

At Gunner's name, all the officers looked up.

"You know Gunner?"

He gave a slow nod. "And Flynn and Levi and Stone and Logan …" He named a bunch of the other men who lived locally. He could see the relief on the commander's face. He understood. It was one thing to have a complete stranger tell you a story, but quite another thing entirely to tell a story like this and have a half-dozen good men to back him up. If they gave Ethan a good reference, chances were this would go a lot easier. "Feel free to call Gunner if you want."

"And the others?"

He inclined his head. "Of course."

At that, the men turned and studied the dead body, while one of them stepped back and made phone calls.

Ethan shoved his hands into his pockets. "Are you okay if I leave now?"

"Where are you going?"

"Home to check on the animals. I want to drop off Bella there, then go to the hospital."

The commander nodded. "We want your cell phone number and the address where you're staying."

Ethan pulled out a notepad, quickly wrote down his cell phone number, the address where he was staying, and then underneath he added Gunner's name and phone number. He tore off the page and handed it to the sergeant.

The man noted the numbers, folded up the sheet of paper and placed it in his pocket. "We'll be down at the hospital soon too." Then he stopped, turned to one of the men at his side and said, "Daniel, you go with him."

Daniel looked at him in surprise. "You mean, meet him at the hospital?"

The commander shook his head. "Go with him back to his place, check out the address, see what state the dogs are in and then head to the hospital with him."

That made Ethan respect the commander all the more. He was making it clear he didn't trust Ethan, but, at the same time, the commander was willing to give Ethan a chance. He'd contact Gunner and probably Levi, question them whether they knew who Ethan was and what kind of man he was, but the commander was also very concerned about the dogs, whether that was because he didn't want them loose and killing everybody else around them or he was concerned for the dogs' sakes.

Daniel pushed his hat back on his head, studied the commander's face for a moment, then gave a shrug and said to Ethan, "Lead the way."

With Bella at his side, Ethan walked back to his vehicle. "Do you have a cruiser with you?"

Daniel nodded. "But I came with somebody else, so they can take it back."

Ethan led Bella into the truck bed, opened the passenger side for Daniel and said, "Hop in then." He went around to the driver's side, got in and headed up the road.

CHAPTER 8

THERE WAS JUST something about hospitals that Cinn hated. Maybe it was the antiseptic smell. Maybe it was the misery of everybody in the crowded emergency room, with crying children and an old couple who looked like their world had just been decimated.

She looked at Flynn. "I don't need to be here, you know? Isn't there a clinic I can go to?"

He gave a shout of laughter. "If you were an animal, I could take you to Louise. But you're not."

She sagged into her chair. "You know we could die in the waiting room?"

He nodded. "And it's happened," he admitted. "But I'll make sure I get you attention well before that happens."

The trouble was that, although she'd been shot, she wasn't dying. Enough people were here who needed attention ahead of her.

Then her name was called. With Flynn's help, she got up again and was led into a small cubicle. She sank onto the bed with relief. A nurse came in almost immediately. With Flynn explaining what had happened, the nurse cut off her T-shirt, leaving her yoga top underneath unharmed, and took a good look at the wound.

"We'll have to phone the cops," she said. "All bullet wounds must be reported. I'll get the doctor, and he'll examine you."

Leaning against the raised upper portion of the hospital bed, she suddenly felt more tired than she could believe. "Where are my dogs?" she asked.

"I called them before I reached you," he said. "When I saw you with Ethan, I took them back and locked them up in your yard."

She sighed with relief. "I can't believe I didn't even notice."

"The dogs know me," he said. "It wasn't a problem. We needed to get as many variables out of that scene as possible."

She looked up at him and asked, "Did Anna come with you?"

"She went to your place after I told her the dogs were there and stayed to make sure the dogs had food and water and to calm them down."

Cinn nodded. "Thank you."

"I'm sorry I didn't get there sooner," Flynn said. "I was on my way back from town when you called. I started freaking out and called Anna. By the time I got to you, Ethan had everything under control."

"Not only was he there quickly, he went after the shooter," she said in wonder. "I mean, I guess it's not a great outcome for the shooter, but it's the best outcome I could have wished for myself."

"Understood," Flynn said. "At least this way you don't have to look behind you in the dark anymore."

"Exactly. What I don't know is why they targeted me."

Flynn stepped forward, tilted her chin up and glared at her. "Why do you say you were targeted?"

She filled him in on the vehicle parked on the side of the road that came back later in the day. "I don't know if it had something to do with the job Ethan went to help out the cops with."

"Explain," Flynn barked.

She rolled her eyes and gave him as much information as she knew. "I wondered if it had to do with his presence at my place. It's the only reason I can think of for why they went after me."

"But you went for a run. Do you think they followed you?"

She shrugged. "Honestly, I was pretty near the highway for a lot of the run anyway. It wouldn't take much to keep track of me. And I was headed for the tree line, so, if they got there ahead of me, it was pretty easy to take a clean shot."

"Yet they missed."

She wrinkled her nose at him. "I don't think they missed as much as I tripped at the right moment. I had just come over a patch of really uneven ground and caught my foot on a rock and went down. As it was, it caught me in the shoulder instead of higher up, maybe. I don't know. I twisted as I fell, and I didn't move again." She laughed. "He didn't shoot my dogs. They came to me and just stayed there."

"Which is normal behavior for dogs. They'll often stay with a dying owner until either they are rescued or they die themselves."

"That's a terrible thought," she said. "I'd hate to think of the animals sitting beside my cold body, waiting for me to get back up again."

"Dogs are special animals that way. Cats on the other hand …"

She chuckled. "I love cats, but I have absolutely no illusions. They're very much all about themselves."

He grinned at that.

Just then the doctor walked in. "What's this, young lady? You've been shot?" He poked and prodded her shoulder.

She tried desperately not to cry out, but his touch was not gentle.

"I have to get this X-rayed for any bone breaks," he said. "It looks like it's a fairly clean through-and-through shot. But I can't be sure how much damage might have been done on the way. It looks like you've had a lucky escape though."

He ordered her X-rays and said as he was about to step out, "We have to call the cops."

Flynn was prepared. He handed over a card and told him about Sergeant Mendelsson and the commander they'd met at the crime scene.

The doctor nodded. "Good to know. I'll give these men a call." And he left.

The nurse came in with a wheelchair. They assisted Cinn into the chair, where she was wheeled up to X-ray.

Flynn stayed with her the whole time.

"You can leave, you know?" Cinn said.

He shook his head. "Anna would never let me live it down if I did."

"I'm here. I'm not dying. I'm fine," Cinn stated.

"You aren't fixed up. You haven't been cleared to leave. We don't know if they'll keep you overnight,"

She stayed silent after that. The X-rays were painful but livable. She was wheeled back to the little room in the emergency department, and they waited for the pictures.

Finally the doctor came in and said, "Good news. We'll just stitch you up, give you some shots for the pain and a prescription for more painkillers. You should be good to go home. If you have more bleeding or any problems moving your arm or your fingers, you need to come back in immediately. Do you hear me?"

She nodded. But then she would have said anything to leave. Hospitals were definitely not her favorite place. After she was finally fixed up, stitches in place, the shoulder bandaged and her arm in a sling, it was all she could do to stand up.

Flynn held her other arm. "Are you sure you're good to go home?"

She gave him a tired smile. "I won't rest here. Home sounds much better."

But he didn't appear to be convinced.

"I'll be fine."

"I don't know about that," he said.

Just then another voice entered the room. "She won't be alone, so it's all good."

She turned to see Ethan smiling at her, releasing her hold on Flynn.

He came in, gently put an arm around her good side and gave her a hug. "How are you feeling?" he asked.

"Like I've been shot," she said with a heavy sigh. "The painkiller is kicking in, but it's making me woozy."

"In that case, home to bed with you." He looked at Flynn. "I can take her from here, if you're okay with that."

Flynn glanced at Cinn, then back at Ethan.

Cinn chuckled. "I'm fine, Flynn. It's okay."

"Are you sure?" Flynn asked.

She reached out, gripped his fingers and whispered, "Yes, I'm sure. Feel free to check on me later today or tomorrow morning," she said.

Flynn gave a clipped nod and said, "Count on it." Then he turned and walked away.

With Ethan at her side, she made her way to the front reception area, where she took care of the insurance details, and afterward went outside to the parking lot. There she was helped into Ethan's truck.

As she got in, she looked around, found no sign of Bella. "Where's Bella?"

"She's with the other dogs," Ethan said. He stopped as an officer walked over. She wondered why he was there, but Ethan appeared comfortable with him. As long as nothing else had gone wrong …

The officer went around to Cinn's side. "I came in with Ethan. Are you okay?"

She smiled and nodded. "I will be."

He looked at her, assessing how healthy she was, and then said, "I do need to ask you some questions."

Her heart sank. "Any chance you can do that tomorrow? The doctor gave me a heavy-duty pain shot, and I'm about to fall asleep."

He smiled and said, "I'll be there tomorrow morning." He looked over at Ethan. "Okay, you're good to take her back home."

Ethan hopped in, then turned his head toward the officer. "Do you want us to give you a lift somewhere?"

The officer laughed and shook his head. "No. My ride is on the way."

To Cinn's relief, there were no other delays. Ethan backed up the big truck in the hospital parking lot and took her home.

IT HURT HIM to see her in so much pain. She'd been given a

pain shot, but it either hadn't taken effect yet or wasn't strong enough. That just added to his guilt. It had to be his arrival into her world that got her into trouble. Which meant someone from the drug property had seen him parked close to the property and had followed him back here. That just pissed him off even more. Now he had to find them and stop them. They could not be allowed to get away with shooting an innocent woman. If they wanted to pick a fight with him, then he was all for it. But it needed to be with him and not those he knew.

Especially not someone he was starting to care for. That alone made her special, as his heart had been empty for a long time. When he'd finally found a woman who made him stop in his tracks, like hell he would let anyone else take her away from him.

The question now was, was this over? Had the last man died? Or were there more to take his place?

His vote was, more men would be coming …

So he had to get to them first. The police had already raided the drug base but had obviously missed someone or many someones …

Ethan drove to her house and turned his truck so she was closest to the front door. He put the truck into park, shut off the engine and raced around to her side, opening up the passenger door and helping her out. They could hear the dogs barking inside the house; then suddenly they raced out the doggy door and barked at the side of the house behind the fence.

As soon as they opened the front door, the dogs came barreling inside to greet them. Ethan brushed them back, giving the commands to calm down, but they were as untrained as any dog he'd ever seen.

She crouched, laughing, saying hi to the dogs but keeping herself from getting injured. "Don't even bother trying. I've been gone for too long, and they know I'm hurt, so it only makes sense they need reassurance."

He agreed, and, when she reached up for his hand, he helped her into the living room. "Now do you want to sit down?" he asked quietly. "Or do you want to go up to bed?"

"I'll just sit in the living room for a moment," she said, her voice faint. He watched as she stumbled to the couch. She collapsed and groaned as her shoulder was jolted hard. He gently reached a hand to the side of her cheek. "Take it easy. You're home now."

She nodded. "And damn glad of it too. I'll need painkillers soon."

"Not for a while," he said. "They gave you a shot in the hospital."

She speared him with a look that made him grin. He loved her spunk. She had a temper, and he could appreciate that. She also wasn't shy about letting him know how she felt. Either happy or sad. Also good. She seemed to be balanced, honest and comfortable in her own skin. All good things in his book too. But he really liked the fact that she was full of life and doing something about the injustices in the world. Like her rescue work for the dogs. Sure, she took a lot of criticism for rescuing dogs in other parts of the world, but he'd been there, seen firsthand how bad the dogs had it in war-torn countries. He was happy someone was doing something to help.

Of course, she was easy on the eyes too. Her eyes were not quite a chocolate brown, not quite caramel in color either, but something like a toffee tone with gold flecks. Her lashes were long in a small pixie face, almost a heart shape.

Which made him a fool for noticing. No, just lonely …

It had been a long time since he'd had a relationship or had even sat down with anybody he cared about. It seemed like he'd become a loner years ago, before he'd started working with the dogs. … But that had gotten worse after his accident, then losing his parents during his recovery … Losing Shep, his K9 partner he'd raised and trained for seven years, had been hard and had added a layer of loss. He'd worked with many other dogs, but Shep had been his partner. And they'd both gone into that mission, expecting the worst, and unfortunately this time they got it.

Shep hadn't survived; Ethan had barely survived. Maybe he shouldn't have …

Still, he had to deal with this nightmare and the woman slowly bringing him back to life.

"How about a cup of tea?" he asked.

She looked up at him gratefully. "That sounds great." She patted the couch beside her, and Burglar hopped up. He snuggled close into her lap, while Midnight jumped up farther down. With both dogs now on the couch beside her, Ethan walked into the kitchen, filled the teakettle with water and put it on. He returned to the living room and said, "I'll take the dogs out in a minute too. They likely need to go."

She made a half murmur, and he took that as an agreement. He whistled for the dogs. They didn't look too eager to leave her, but, when he opened the kitchen door, they came running. He stepped outside and walked them around the yard. She had fenced several acres, so there was lots of space for everyone. He could see the gates where she could have gone out for her run and was torn with the idea of returning to where she'd been shot.

Only he didn't want to leave her alone. He walked

around with the dogs, giving them a few minutes to play and to just calm down and relax after being boxed up for so long. When he found a ball on the ground, he picked it up and tossed it. Burglar took off after it. Midnight followed, so Ethan spent a good ten minutes, just throwing the ball and giving the dogs a chance to run. When he figured the teakettle was ready, he walked back inside to make a cup of tea. He carried the tea to Cinn, surprised to find she was still awake.

"Thank you," she said with a smile. "How are the dogs?"

"They're doing just fine," he said as he held up the cup, still with the tea bag in it. "I couldn't find a teapot. How do you like your tea?"

"A little bit of milk please," she said, "and, if you bring me a saucer, I'll take out the teabag when I'm done."

He put the cup down, went into the kitchen to get the milk. Following her instructions, he added milk to her tea, then returned it to the fridge. Walking back, he placed the saucer within easy reach and sat beside her. "How are you feeling?"

She gave him a lopsided grin that was endearing itself to his heart very quickly. She was small yet valiant. He knew a lot of women would have completely freaked out after getting shot. "I hope it doesn't stop you from wanting to run anymore," he said.

She shook her head. "No, I've always loved to run. I just hadn't expected to get attacked like that."

"Well, I'm glad I got here as fast as I could," he commented. "The last thing I wanted was for you to be a casualty in this war."

"That's what it feels like, doesn't it?"

"It does," he admitted. "The only way they could have

connected you to me is either at the vet or by following me here. And that's only possible if they saw me parked up above their place."

"It's a sad world when we have to worry about being followed."

"Agreed," he said with a faint smile. "And we still have to consider that someone might come after you again."

She stood, and he went to help her, but she waved him away. "I'm going to the bathroom. I'll be fine."

He watched as she slowly shuffled down the hall to the bathroom, the dogs milling around her feet. That was the part of the canine relationship he missed, having the dogs always there, always concerned, always ready for every movement you make. Shep had been the same. Took a step for every step Ethan had taken. They'd been partners all the time, even when at home. A lot of people didn't see who he was on the inside, and he didn't take much time to show anyone. He would only open up with somebody who was special. Cinn had surprised him. Right from the beginning … He remembered the night he'd dropped by with Chinese food. Maybe he should do that again. She certainly shouldn't be cooking for a few days. "Are you hungry?"

She shook her head as she stood at the bathroom doorway. "No, I'm not. All I need right now is rest." She smiled, adding, "If you're hungry, go ahead and find something. I doubt there's much here, but you can have anything you find."

CHAPTER 9

O N HER WAY back to the couch, much of her bravado slipped away. She managed a few more steps into the living room, where she collapsed onto the cushions. Her two dogs joined her again. She cuddled them the best she could, trying to calm them down, so they didn't jump up and hurt her arm. With the painkillers, she felt better, but, at the same time, she felt weepy and exhausted.

She sat on the couch, her feet tucked under her, so she curled into the corner again, finding that position the most comfortable. One of the dogs stretched out beside her, his head on her legs; the other one lay at her feet. Her sore shoulder was propped up with a pillow, and she just closed her eyes for a moment.

Only a moment ended up being several moments. When she opened them again, Ethan stood in front of her, setting a cup of tea on the small coffee table at her side. She smiled at him. "Is that a second cup? You don't have to look after me."

"No, I don't," he said calmly. "But I want to. And, yes, it's a second cup. Your first went cold."

Warmth flooded through her, filling all the lonely spots inside, something she hadn't felt in a long time. "You're a very nice man."

He gave her a startled look and then chuckled. "You have no idea," he teased. "I could have completely rummaged through your place and stolen all your money, while you were out cold."

"Good luck with that," she said with a smile. "I don't have anything worth stealing."

His gaze warmed in understanding. He looked around at her house. "Is this place yours?"

She nodded. "Yes."

"It's comfy," he said. "I really like that. Coziness is something you miss when you don't have a home base. This is a home, not just a house."

"It is," she said. "You'll find your home base again."

He nodded and sat on the couch at the far side from where she sat. "I will," he said in agreement.

"Where are your dogs?"

"They're all back at the house," he said. He glanced at his watch. "After I have tea and get you something to eat, I'll head out to look after them."

"I don't think I could eat anything," she confessed. "My stomach is pretty queasy."

He frowned and studied her face. "Headache?"

She shook her head, then shuddered as pain racked up and down her spine. "Okay, so there hadn't been a headache," she said starkly, "but that movement may have changed things."

"How about just a little bit of soup and a piece of toast?"

She winced. "Honestly, I don't think I could eat anything." When he continued to frown at her, she smiled and said, "No point in adding food to a queasy stomach."

"Unless it calms down the stomach and gives the painkiller something to work on," he said. "I can make you a sandwich."

She lay here, thinking about it, and then said, "Well, if

you made one and left it on the coffee table, then I could have it when I am hungry."

On that note he stood and walked the few steps into the kitchen. She could hear him puttering around, but, since he didn't ask her any questions about what she wanted, she knew it would be whatever came her way. Not that she minded being looked after. It was a novelty she could get used to. She tucked a little deeper into the couch and let the painkillers work.

When she surfaced again, her house was empty. She straightened painfully and saw a note on the coffee table beside a platter of sandwiches. She laughed. "Unless he's joining me, that's way too many sandwiches," she said out loud.

The dogs looked at her and wagged their tails.

"Oh, no you don't," she said with a smile. "Sandwiches are people food, not for dogs."

She reached for the note to see it was from Ethan. She read it out loud. "*I didn't want to awaken you. Sandwiches until morning. I'll call you later.*"

She smiled, made her way to the bathroom, and, after she awkwardly washed her hands, she walked into the kitchen, awkwardly putting on the teakettle. What she really wanted was a cup of comforting tea to have with the sandwiches.

Cinn turned and checked the clock, surprised to see how late it was. She must have slept for several hours.

As she poured milk into her cup of tea, her phone rang. She carefully maneuvered the phone and the teacup out to the living room where she sat on the couch again. "Hello?"

"Hey, you're awake. I was afraid to call earlier, in case I woke you up."

She smiled. "I'm definitely awake. Thanks for the plate of sandwiches."

"Have you eaten?"

"Just sitting down to a cup of tea and having my first bite." She hesitated for a moment, then said, "You made enough for two. Are you coming back?"

"I wasn't sure if you would go to bed and sleep for the night."

"I'm thinking about it," she said, "but maybe, once I get some food in me, I'll be in decent shape for a little while."

"In that case, I might pop by again."

"I'll save you a sandwich."

She carefully placed the phone down and picked up a sandwich. It looked to be ham and cheese. At her first bite, she deemed it excellent. She lifted the corner of the bread to see what gave it the extra special flavor and found a touch of sauce. As she tasted it, she realized it was a mix of mustard, horseradish and mayonnaise. It was really good.

She settled back, happy to relax without crying out in pain. At the hospital, she'd been devastated by the shoulder injury. At the moment though, the painkiller was still taking off the edge, and it wasn't too bad. Of course, if she jerked it or moved it too much, then that was a different story. But, in the sling like it was, she was doing quite well with one hand.

She sipped her tea and waited for Ethan to arrive.

Something about him just made them almost instant friends. It was a little disconcerting. She wasn't the kind of person to step into a relationship as fast as she had stepped into this friendship. Was it a good thing? She trusted him, but she wasn't sure that was smart. She really liked him as a person. It was obvious he had a big heart.

As the headlights turned off the highway and came down her long driveway, she watched uneasily, not sure if it was Ethan or somebody else.

Instinctively she wanted to get up and turn off all the lights in the living room, but it was too late. The truck was only two hundred yards away. Anybody coming down the highway would have caught sight of her well-lit house. With much relief, she watched Ethan hop out of his truck. When he went to lower the tailgate, and a dog hopped down, she thought he'd brought Bella with him.

No. This one was bigger. Darker fur but missing in spots. Scarred?

With the dog on a leash, which was a surprise, he approached the front door, knocked and then stepped in. Instantly her dogs went crazy. She tried to call them back, but they weren't having anything to do with that. Finally Ethan made a sharp whistling sound, and both dogs glared at him, then came back to sit beside her.

She turned to look at the newcomer. It was not Bella. Cinn frowned and shifted back in the couch. "And who's this?"

"His collar says Bart," Ethan said quietly. "He's one of the dogs I rescued from the drug center."

At that, the shepherd swiveled his head to look at Ethan. Then tilted his head to the side.

"Hey, Bart. It will be okay, boy."

The dog slowly lay down on the floor. She wasn't sure he understood what had happened to him, but he was understanding something, … an absence of abuse probably. "So there were two females and two males, including Sally?"

"Appears to be, yes."

She couldn't take her eyes off the new arrival. The dog

didn't scare her, but a calculating look in his eye made her ever-so-slightly worried. She was used to dogs, but these dogs Ethan kept bringing by were not the kind that made her comfortable to be around. They didn't laze about on the floor like any normal dog.

Bart tracked her movements as if she had something he wanted. And then she realized she was holding a sandwich. In fact, she really did have something he wanted. She carefully replaced the sandwich on the plate, watching as the dog tracked her hand movements there. She grinned. "Did you feed him?"

"Oh, he's been fed," Ethan said. He walked forward, ordering the dog to heel. The dog fell into step behind him.

Surprised, she looked at Ethan, at the dog, and then back at Ethan again. "They're very well trained."

"They *are* very well trained. I just don't know the extent of their training or their loyalty," he said. "I'm still figuring that out."

"I'm not sure how you would do that."

"I'm putting them through their paces. But it's taking some time. I'm working with them one-on-one, so I hope it's okay that I brought this guy." He walked over to the easy chair and sat himself down with Bart at his side. But Bart kept his eyes on the sandwiches.

"Sure." She motioned at the platter and said, "Help yourself."

He leaned forward, picked up a sandwich, and, as he pulled it toward him, Bart made a snap toward it. Instantly Ethan corrected him on it and had the dog lay down until he was calm.

She watched in fascination. Ethan did everything in a controlled, ready manner, as if he was expecting it. "You knew he would lunge for that, didn't you?"

"They were given just enough mistreatment that I figured he had to fight for what he wanted, especially food. A sandwich is an easy test."

"How do you deal with that?"

"He just needs to be corrected every time he steps out of line," Ethan said.

She nodded and continued to watch as Bart tracked the sandwich. With every bite it seemed like Ethan made exaggerated hand movements, moving the sandwich out to where it was obviously visible to the dog; then he would pick it up in a slow motion and take a bite. "Are you teasing him?"

"No," Ethan said. "I'm giving him lots of chances to go for it again."

"He seems to have learned quickly," she said when Bart made no move for the sandwich.

Ethan nodded. "If we were past this kind of training, then I could give him the last bite. But, as it is, I won't take that chance. It's pretty easy to ruin a good dog's training with treats."

She glanced at her two dogs and shrugged. "Mine are spoiled, not that they don't have some training, as they do, but I tend to get lax. Still, they aren't that bad."

"Most dogs are spoiled," Ethan said. "But there's spoiling, and then there's training. You don't dare mix the two."

She wasn't sure she agreed with that, but he was the one dealing with dangerous dogs. She had gentle house pets. She reached for the rest of her sandwich, and Bart's head turned to track her hand. A little unnerved, she settled back and took a bite. "He's not taking his gaze off me."

Ethan nodded and gave a small self-correction on Bart's

leash, and Bart turned his gaze toward Ethan.

She was stunned. "He really is well trained."

"He is," Ethan confirmed. "Almost too well trained. My dogs in the military were this way. Makes me wonder if they've ever had any downtime or playtime. Like people, you can't work all day without repercussions."

She ate quietly for several long moments, studying the dog. "I don't get a sense of animosity from him."

"No," Ethan said quietly. "Attentiveness. He's unsure. He's unsure of me. He's unsure of you."

She smiled. "And maybe that's a good thing."

He reached for another sandwich. His phone rang just then. Instead of picking up another sandwich, he pulled his phone from his pocket.

She listened quietly while he answered.

It was Gunner. It was obvious from the conversation that Gunner had heard about today's events. Ethan looked at her and said, "I'm with her right now, and she's fine. I have one of the dogs with me too."

She could hear an exclamation coming out of the phone.

He just chuckled. "It's fine, Gunner. I know what I'm doing."

They spoke for a few more moments, and he pocketed the phone.

"I gather news traveled fast?"

Ethan nodded, took the sandwich and scarfed it down in several bites. He looked at her and said, "You should be heading to bed soon."

She wanted to shrug, a movement she was only now realizing how often she did by the pain that poked her every time. "I will, after time for the next painkillers." She checked her watch and made a face. "Essentially that's now."

"Do you need help getting undressed?"

She frowned, sat up and thought about it. "No, I think I'm fine. I won't attempt to shower tonight."

"If you want to in the morning, I can come by and change the dressing."

"I think I'm supposed to leave it for a day and then go into the clinic and have them take a look at it."

He nodded and stayed quiet. Finally he stood, ordered the dog to walk with him and said, "Call me in the morning. If you hear anything around the place tonight, you let me know."

She turned to him, accidentally jerking her shoulder. She cried out and clapped a hand on her injury. After a few moments of deep breathing, the greasy waves of pain settled down into her stomach. "Why would you even say that?"

He stared at her with a steady gaze. "You're the one who got shot. And we never did track down the truck."

"Shit. Shit, shit, shit. I forgot about that truck."

"And maybe you should keep forgetting about it," he said. "Enough has gone on today. I doubt any more danger is coming your direction."

"But you don't know that, do you?"

He tilted his head to the side and crossed his arms over his chest. "Are you worried?"

She chewed on her bottom lip as she considered the question. "I wasn't until you brought it up."

"As soon as you lay down, that truck would have popped back into your mind," he said.

She groaned. "Yes, you're right. It would have." She walked carefully to the window and stared up at the highway. She pointed where she'd seen the truck. Of course it wasn't there. "I didn't see it close up, so I couldn't give you details about the driver. It seems like it was the same truck that was back later in the day."

He stood, frowning, thinking for a long moment. "If you want, I can go home, grab a few things, work with the dogs a little bit and then come back. I don't want to be away from the animals too long."

"Not necessary." She smiled. "I'll be fine."

But he wasn't convinced. "I don't like the idea of leaving you here alone."

"It's what we have to do," she said, "because I'm sure as hell not coming to your house. So I'll stay here. You stay there, and it'll be fine."

He thought about it for a moment and said, "I'll come back and check on you tonight."

"I'll be asleep," she warned. "Don't wake me up."

He grinned. "You'll never know I was here."

"If you come into my house, I sure as hell better," she said, "because that would really freak me out. I don't want to wake up with you wandering through my house, scaring the bejesus out of me."

He watched as she headed to the stairs. "I'll take a walk around and check your security."

She made a face at him as she stepped up on the fourth and then the fifth step. "Now you're really scaring me."

"Go take your painkillers, get ready for bed. Have a good night's sleep. I'll make sure you're safe."

With that, she had to be satisfied. She trusted him. No point in second-guessing herself now. He'd been there for her so far. She wasn't about to let nerves change anything. She still had her dogs. They might not be trained guard dogs, but they were great early warning systems.

Upstairs she could hear him walking through the house.

She took off her jeans, leaving on her yoga top, and managed to pull on a clean T-shirt. She did a quick job with a toothbrush, a face wash, and then gratefully sagged into her bed. She took her painkillers and turned out the light. One of the dogs hopped up on the bed beside her, and the other lay on the floor. She didn't hear another sound. She just closed her eyes, rolled over and fell asleep.

ETHAN CHECKED OVER the security on her house. There was only one word to call it—dismal. He didn't like the look of any of it. He pulled a couple windows closed. That would not stop a professional break-in, but it would stop most people. He checked the back door and realized it, too, was Mickey Mouse. He propped up a kitchen chair under the door handle. If nothing else, she'd wake up and would have a chance to escape, if she heard a commotion downstairs.

After doing the best he could, he walked out the front door, locking it shut behind him, and stood on the step for a long moment.

Bart stood at his side, never making a sound, but matched his step pace for pace. He reached out a hand and held it in front of Bart's nose. Bart sniffed it several times, then stared at him. He eased a hand on Bart's forehead, feeling the dog tense at the contact. "It's all right, boy. Your days of being abused are over," he said gently.

He didn't know if the dog understood or not, but he'd like to think that the tone of his voice and his reassuring hand giving pleasure and not pain would go a long way to helping the dog understand. They stood like that for a long moment, as Ethan gently scratched the dog behind the ears and then down the neck.

It would be a long time before he could clip their claws or take the matted hair off their coats. But he'd take every step in the right direction he could. He motioned toward the truck, and the dog hopped into the bed on his own. Ethan closed the tailgate, got into the driver's side, reversed the truck and headed up to the highway.

Once there he parked and got out with the dog and took a look to see if he could spot any tracks. Darkness was settling in, and he had to use the flashlight on his cell phone to check.

There were definitely tracks. The problem was, there were too many of them. Giving up that idea, he hopped back into the truck, allowing the dog in the front of the cab this time. The dog walked over to the far passenger side and stared out the window, but he obediently sat while Ethan drove back to the house.

He didn't like leaving Cinn alone. He figured he'd give himself a couple hours to sleep and then do a quick sweep again of her property, making sure all was well. This way he could change the dogs out at the same time.

Back at his rental house, Ethan let Bart into the house and proceeded to dish out dog food for all four of them. He had Sally segregated. She needed a lot more care.

He still wasn't sure what the relationship was between them. He had her in a spare bedroom down on the main floor. With food in his hand, he walked in, keeping the door closed behind him, and gently checked her dressings. Her tail wagged when she saw him. He crouched in front of her and gently stroked her head. He helped her to straighten up slightly so she could eat. Once she plowed into her food, he realized she was definitely improving.

Nothing like seeing a growing appetite in an injured dog to realize she was well on her way to mending. He sat with her for a long moment.

A dog barked outside the door to the spare room. Opening it, Ethan found Bart looking up at him expectantly. Ethan put a leash on him, then let him inside the room, so he could meet Sally. Her tail went crazy, and she whimpered. The two dogs brushed their noses back and forth. Bart stuck his head into her food and had a few bites, and she didn't seem to care. But then he wanted to sniff her all over. The problem was, she was ill and definitely had that medicine-sick smell. But Bart didn't seem to mind. As soon as he was done sniffing, he found a corner of the blanket and lay down beside her.

Crouching between them, Ethan smiled. "Well, you obviously know each other."

Sally was still tired, and, outside of tail wagging, she kept her movements to a minimum. He needed to get her outside so she could do her business. But that would be a little harder. It was one of the reasons for being in the spare room, because it was closest to the front door.

He dropped Bart's leash and put the sling back on Sally. "Come on. Let's get you out front."

He helped her to the front door, but Bart wanted to come too. So he took Bart's leash dragging behind him, opened the front door and carefully let the two dogs out. Bart wanted to dance and bark around, but, with Sally in the sling, Ethan's hands were already more than full. It was hard to give hand signals.

Carefully, Ethan let Sally walk a few steps in the grass. He was taking the bulk of the weight of her body off her injured leg, while he let her go to the bathroom. He didn't even have bags to collect anything yet. But it was good to see her body functioning normally. After she was done, he helped her walk around the yard once. It was important for her to exercise as much as she could.

He could see she was tiring because he was carrying more and more of her body weight as they made their way back to the front steps. Bart obviously wanted to stay longer. But the front yard wasn't fenced.

Ethan managed to get both dogs back into the house. As soon as he had the front door shut, he dropped Bart's leash and maneuvered Sally back into her bedroom. He helped her lie down again, gave her another blanket to lie on, and then closed the door, leaving her alone. Bart stood in front of the door and whined. But Ethan wasn't sure about leaving Bart with her. He didn't want him to hurt her at this stage of her healing.

"You can see Sally in a little bit, buddy. When we go back in, I'll make sure you get to come and visit too."

Bart barked several times, then lay down in front of the closed door. He just wanted to be close. Ethan figured that was close enough.

Bella was out back. He fed her and gave her several moments of cuddles then brought Bart out to join her. The two appeared to be good friends. Bella had taken to his presence the easiest. He was still a long way from brushing her, but at least she was amiable to having a new owner.

And that was more than he could say for Boris. His name was written in the spikes around his collar. *This* was Ethan's K9:01 dog. His real name was *Sentry*. Ethan quickly sent Badger a text, confirming he had found him.

Sentry still refused to eat. Even with the offer of food, he wouldn't trust Ethan. Sentry didn't bark or snarl when

Ethan approached, but he did back up, and his tail poofed. That was enough warning for Ethan to realize he'd already crossed the line. If he wanted to keep his head intact, he needed to give Sentry lots of reach. He figured, by the time Sentry understood what was going on, he'd already have him where he wanted him. As long as he had the other three dogs' cooperation, it wouldn't take long for Sentry to fall into line. Sentry just had to know it was his idea first.

Ethan walked out to the backyard and stood on the deck, a cup of coffee in his hand as he pondered the night ahead. He hadn't liked the idea of leaving Cinn alone. But he also had the dogs to look after. What he should have done was taken Bella there and left her to guard Cinn. But Ethan didn't know Bella well enough to trust her yet. That she got along with everyone and appeared to listen to the commands as he gave them was one thing, but he couldn't put her in a position where he had to trust her to do the right thing without him being there. He couldn't test her in that way too soon.

Bella was still an animal. That was first and foremost. She'd also been extremely well trained and wasn't as badly abused as the others. Sentry looked to have been systematically beaten into being an aggressive dog. He was the only one that worried Ethan. It could take a long time for him to come around.

As for Sally, well, she looked in pain right now, but Ethan hoped eventually she'd be just as grateful to be with her new clan, safe away from where she'd been.

Ethan checked his watch and found it had been an hour already. He'd planned to go by Cinn's house every two hours. But, once at her place, Ethan figured he'd stick around, see if he noted any suspicious activity, maybe walk the place with the dogs, give them a good run in the dark, do some practice drills and see how they reacted.

As he contemplated the idea more and more, he grabbed Bella and Sentry, leaving the other two behind, putting his selected pair in the truck. Although Sentry was eager to get into the truck, every time Ethan approached, Sentry's lips curled. He would certainly put Ethan to the test.

It was pitch-black outside. Ten minutes later he pulled onto the shoulder of the highway near the edge of Cinn's driveway, just taking a quick look before approaching closer. Then he pulled halfway down her drive and parked. He opened the tailgate, letting both dogs out and hooked Bella up to a leash. Sentry just looked at him. There was almost a dare-you-to attitude in his gaze. Calling him to his side, Ethan closed up the tailgate and walked down the driveway. He surveyed the lack of security on the place and frowned. There wasn't even a gate crossing her driveway. And sure, a gate wouldn't keep the trash out. But it did keep a surprising number of people away.

No lights were on inside Cinn's house. He could hear one of her dogs barking. He let out a gentle whistle to it in reassurance. He walked the perimeter of her yard, getting an idea of what passed for nightlife at her place. With his truck parked halfway up the driveway, he doubted anybody would approach.

He walked out the back gate, where Cinn had gone for her run, took Bella off her leash and told her to run. He picked up the pace, noting the faint path in front of him. The trail was treacherous, particularly when the ground was wet. But Bella appeared to be having a fun time racing ahead, back and forth, and finally Sentry even seemed to relax enough to jump and run around with her.

When Ethan whistled for them, they both came running. Only the look in Sentry's eyes read *What? I wasn't coming because you asked me to.*

Bella fell into step beside Ethan at his command. At that point he put her through several of his regular training paces to see what she knew and what she didn't know. She understood so many commands that he wondered if she was a police dog—or military trained. How likely would that be?

Then Ethan turned to look at Sentry, who shot him another look, this one saying, *Don't even bother.* Ethan ran to the tree line, coming up close to the spot where they'd found the body of the man who killed himself. There he slowed his steps and walked, enjoying the freedom of being out in the moonlight. The moon was high, and it cast a beautiful wide glow across the earth. It gave him a surprising amount of freedom to check out the lay of the land.

How had the shooter known she was out running? Were more drug-house guys watching Cinn's house? Ethan walked out to the highway and turned to look at her house. It was easy to see it off in the distance. If they'd been tracking her, she would have been right there in the open, coming toward them. In fact, she probably ran right into this shooter's range, so he could take her out. But he'd missed.

After Ethan watched for a few minutes, he sauntered back down onto the open fields, looking to see if it was just a lucky position or if this had been planned.

But that also implied forethought. As if the bad guys were hoping she'd come toward them, and the shooter was prepared on the off chance she did. The opportunity had presented itself. He'd have to find out from her if she ran this way on a regular basis. Routine made it much easier to pick off somebody.

He slowly walked back toward her house. As he did, he ran Bella through a few more tasks. She could jump; she was good at walking on her back legs, which really surprised him.

She knew all the basic commands. She knew *go, stop, heel, sit, shake a paw*. And *guard* was a good one because he really liked to see her snap into protective mode with her ears alert. What she had trouble with was relaxing her guard. She did seem to understand *okay*. The command should have been *relax guard*, but Bella didn't understand that command either.

During this testing of Bella's training, Sentry sat and ignored the two of them. Whenever Ethan walked closer, Sentry curled up a lip, but he didn't growl, and he didn't attack. Ethan would take that as progress. He kept walking closer, backing away, and walking closer again, but in casual movements as he worked with Bella, who was all too eager to please. She enjoyed working. She enjoyed the challenges and the physicality of the training.

Ethan could get her to jump up on logs, jump over logs, run flat-out. He hadn't worked on any of the attack signals because he wasn't dressed for it. And he needed to be in a safe surrounding before she went kamikaze on him. She had the ability to take down a man in a heartbeat. He didn't want to be the one who hit the ground with nobody there to help him. And he was a little concerned that Sentry might just jump on that attack bandwagon with a whole lot more glee. At the moment the male dog seemed content to be with them. Or maybe he was content to be with Bella. There was obviously affection between the two of them.

It was good to see that Sentry considered himself the alpha dog here, possibly only because Bart had been injured, but that was where the problem lay because Ethan needed

Sentry to follow Ethan's commands. Still, tonight showed progress. Both dogs responded to commands of *come*, and that was good. Bella responded to *stay* perfectly. Ethan had yet to try it on Sentry.

They sauntered back toward Cinn's house. He knew she was sound asleep, and that was the best thing for her. He had already been out walking for two hours himself.

As he came through the garden and around to the front of the yard, the front door opened, and Cinn stepped out. In a longish T-shirt with some slippers on her feet, rubbing the sleep out of her eyes, she looked absolutely adorable. He took the steps to stand over her.

"I'm sorry if I woke you," he apologized. But inside, he wasn't terribly sorry. He was delighted to see the vision before him.

"I needed to get painkillers anyway," she whispered. She looked down at Bella and smiled. "This is the one you had earlier, isn't it?"

He snapped his fingers and brought Bella toward him. She came over, sat at his feet and looked up at Cinn.

Cinn asked, "May I touch her?"

"Put your hand out, so she can smell you." And then he gave the command to Bella. "*Friend.*"

Bella didn't seem to change her mannerism. But neither was she being difficult. She sniffed Cinn's hand and then unconcerned, stretched out on the porch floor in front of them.

"Well, I guess that's acceptance," Cinn said with a chuckle. She glanced around her front yard. "It's been a long time since I've been outside at this hour of the night."

"It's gorgeous," he said. "We were just out running in the fields where you were shot."

She spun to look at him, her eyebrows rising. "Yes, but I don't have a regular route—nor even make a regular practice of it. I just love to run sometimes. Besides it's good for the dogs. Why?"

He shrugged. "Looking for ways to put Bella through some exercises, and I wanted to keep an eye on the house for a bit, see if any traffic ran along here," he said. "But there's been nothing. It's quieter than I expected, but that's because you are below the highway, so the noise coasts over you."

"That's normal, particularly at this hour. It's really a quiet area," she said. "That's partly why I like it."

He could understand that.

She turned to look at him. "Do you want to come in and have a cup of tea?"

"You should go back to bed," he said gently.

She wrinkled her face up at him and nodded. "I know. But you're here."

"No," he said with a laugh, hopping down the front steps. "I *was* here. But I'm going home now. Go to bed."

"Did you really come just to check on me? I thought you would drive past to make sure nobody parked there."

He smiled. "Nobody has been here recently. And it's already well past two in the morning. I'm pretty sure you'll be fine for the rest of the night."

She nodded. "I'm sure I will." Her dogs swarmed around her ankles, wagging their tails and being generally friendly idiots. Sentry sat on the walkway, ignoring them. She motioned at him. "He doesn't look very friendly."

"He's not," Ethan said. "But that's okay because he's been forced to be a lot of things. Right now it's all about him finding his own way."

Surprised, she looked at Ethan. "I've heard of people

putting all kinds of human attributes on dogs, but I haven't heard any New Age metaphysical ones like you just spouted."

He chuckled. "Hey, my methodologies are hardly New Age. It's all about common sense." He walked toward the truck parked halfway down the driveway, turning to wave at her. "Now go to bed."

She beamed at him. "Thanks for stopping by."

He motioned for Sentry to follow and gave a whistle. Bella came running to his side, and the three walked away.

CHAPTER 10

S HE WATCHED AS Ethan disappeared down the highway. When she had seen him walking around the yard earlier, happy and content, he seemed completely unconcerned about the time of night or where he was. Then why shouldn't he be? He knew he was welcome here. Besides, he *was* part of the night.

Not that he was a predator. More that he was a hunter. And now he had two capable sidekicks to work with him. Although she wasn't at all that sure about Sentry, who looked like he was a whole lot of untamed wolf. Kind of like Ethan. Loners, dangerous, keeping to themselves, and yet, likely to be there when you needed them. At least she hoped Sentry would be that for Ethan.

She slowly made her way back upstairs, grabbed two pain pills from inside the drawer at the side of her bed and swallowed them with water from the glass on the bedside table. On impulse, she got up and walked to the window to take a last look at the night. She wouldn't put it past Ethan to sleep in the truck close by, in which case he might as well have slept on the couch. She had no compunction about keeping him close. He had the protective gene as bad as any male she knew.

That was nice to see in a guy. It had been a couple years since her last relationship. When Jason had walked out, it had been painful and difficult for both of them, but they knew they'd grown as far as they could together. It was time for a change.

She had girlfriends who complained about boyfriends who cheated, boyfriends who lied, and boyfriends who ditched them. It wasn't like that with Jason. They'd sat down, taken a close look at where they were going, what each wanted from life and realized they wanted different things, and really they needed different lives. It had been hard and painful. When he'd walked, he'd walked permanently, and she'd closed the door on that part of her life.

For a while she'd dated, but her heart hadn't been in it. She found that the longer she stayed at home with the dogs, the happier she was. She wasn't antisocial, but neither was she an extrovert who needed people all the time.

As she turned to walk back toward her bed, lights shone into her window. She frowned and watched as a truck took up the same spot where Ethan's truck had been. Instantly her heart hammered against her chest. Would that be Ethan again? Did he just do a circle around and then park again?

She dashed to her night table and grabbed her phone. She sent him a text, asking if that was him again at the top of the driveway.

When she didn't get an immediate response, she walked back over to the window and realized the truck lights were out.

Her phone rang.

"What are you talking about?" he asked without preamble.

"Where are you?"

"Almost home."

"Then you better get your ass back here," she said boldly, "because now a truck is parked at the top of my driveway. And its lights are off."

"Make sure those damn doors are locked," he ordered, his voice terse. "I'll be back in five."

Petrified now, she ran downstairs, holding her injured arm, and found she had indeed left the front door unlocked. She threw the bolt, raced to the back door in the kitchen, saw a chair there and frowned. He must have had a reason for doing that. The garage door was locked.

Nervous, her knees shaking, knowing that, injured as she was, she couldn't fight as hard as she might need to, she made her way back upstairs, where she locked herself in the master bedroom with the dogs and stared out the window from the safety of the curtains, seeing if anybody approached.

She couldn't see anybody, and that worried her too. While she'd been locking the doors, maybe they had made their way down the drive and were outside the house even now. It was an old house with lots of little funky levels and decks and porches. It'd be pretty easy to break in. "Why did I never secure any of that?"

But she answered herself. "Because it's never been an issue before, idiot."

She shook her head as she argued with herself. She had to be really scared to be doing that again. She had talked to herself as a child growing up, and usually only when she was really frustrated. This wasn't frustration. This was something much worse.

Her shoulder throbbed. She wanted to sit down, but she didn't dare leave the window and miss seeing anybody who might be walking toward her.

What she really wanted to witness was Ethan's arrival,

but she saw no sign of another truck approaching. She stood motionless for a good ten minutes, waiting. Nothing.

That's when she heard somebody outside at her kitchen door. She raced to the other window, revealing the back of the house, but couldn't see anything.

With her hand to her throat, her injured arm firmly pressed against her chest, she stood behind her master bedroom door and tried to work on deep breathing. When her phone buzzed in her hand, she opened it to see Ethan was calling. "Somebody's downstairs."

"I know," Ethan said quietly. "I can see him."

"Where are you?" she cried out softly.

"I parked a little farther out and came in the back way. I want to make sure you don't move, okay? Are you in the master bedroom?"

"Yes, I am," she said.

"Good. Stay there. Make sure the door is locked. If somebody comes upstairs or even inside, let me know. Otherwise I only see one person, trying to get into your kitchen door."

"I left your chair there."

"Good," he said, "but it looks like he just went in the window anyway."

She gasped, her heart slamming against her chest. "You'll take him out, right?" Her voice quavered, and she hated that. But the thought of fighting off an intruder terrified her. Already being injured made her feel more unprotected than ever.

"You'll be fine," he said, his voice soothing. "I'm almost there now. Like I said, stay in the bedroom. If you can stop him from coming in, do that. He might ram the door with a shoulder or kick it in with a foot, so don't scream out in surprise."

She glanced around, taking the chair from her small writing table and propped it underneath the bedroom doorknob. If nothing else, the intruder would make a hell of a racket trying to come through. Then she sank to the floor by the door. "Hurry," she whispered. "I've propped a chair underneath the doorknob."

"Good," he said. "Keep thinking. The minute you stop thinking, and fear takes over, you become numb to opportunities you really can't afford to be without."

Her knees tight against her chest, avoiding her injured arm, and her good arm wrapped around her, she sat motionless, waiting. It seemed like forever as she sat curled in a ball, the dogs at her side. But the phone was against her ear just in case Ethan said something. She could hear his breathing. "You've still got the phone line open?"

"Of course," he whispered. "But don't talk if you don't have to. I'm on the way."

Even the dogs appeared frozen. Neither barked nor whimpered. Like her, they understood something was wrong.

She thought she heard something and froze, her breath catching in the back of her throat. Both her dogs were curled up at her side, only the large one bounded to the door, dropped his nose to the edge and sniffed. Instantly Cinn heard heavy sniffing on the other side. She lifted her head, tilted it sideways and wondered.

A knock came. "Cinn, it's me. Ethan."

She bounded to her feet, crying out in pain as her shoulder was wrenched in her quick movement.

"Are you okay?" he asked sharply.

"I'm fine," she said, stumbling to unlock the door.

When she got it unlocked, she pulled it open. Bella jumped into the room, her nose to the ground, and she completely circled the room and came back. Sentry stood at the doorway as if on guard as she checked the place out. Then watched as she played with the other dogs happily.

Ethan wrapped Cinn in his arms and held her close, gently swaying back and forth.

"Did you see him?" she asked. "Did he get away?"

"Yes." He turned and pointed up the highway.

She could see the vehicle was gone. She shook her head. "He was that fast?"

"Maybe he heard me coming," Ethan said. "And he slipped out the front door and took off."

"Really?"

"Or it could have been the dogs. Bella gave a sharp bark, as we came into the house. It might have been in warning, or it might have been in greeting. I don't know."

Cinn turned to look at Bella, who seemed to be happy lying on the floor. Senty still hadn't relaxed. She shook her head. "They're a marvel. But I sure wish we understood them better."

He rubbed her good arm gently, his hand holding her shoulder carefully. "Can you sleep now?"

She shook her head. "No, not now. I'm too wired. When I heard noises inside, I thought it was him coming up the stairs."

He nodded. "I didn't want to give too much warning, just in case he circled back around the house. But he's gone now."

She gave him a wide smile. "Do me a favor? Can you search very, very thoroughly?"

He dropped a light kiss on her forehead and said, "Yes.

And, just to make sure, you come with me, so you can see what I'm doing."

They started with the other bedroom on the top floor. He went through the closets, checked under the bed, behind the door, then led her downstairs so she could check every room with him.

By the time he was done, she was laughing. "Okay, so I made too much out of it."

He stopped in front of her. "Absolutely you did not. That asshat was climbing in the kitchen window. I saw him."

She took a deep breath and let it out slowly. "Right. I keep trying to forget that part."

"Don't," he said, giving her a gentle shake. "Remember he was here. I saw him. It was real. We need to make sure he didn't come with a partner."

"Now that's not a thought I want to contemplate."

"That is definitely a consideration," he said.

She nodded. "It's a grim concept. But I don't know what else to believe."

"I'll stay the rest of the night," he said. "But I want you to get into bed, and I want you to sleep. That shoulder of yours needs to heal."

She grimaced. "It's got to be … What? … Five o'clock in the morning now?"

He checked his watch. "It's not quite quarter to five yet."

She was tired. She leaned against the kitchen counter and brushed the tendrils of hair off her face. Her body was achy and sore. "It feels like I need another painkiller," she muttered.

"That's why you should get into bed and rest. Even getting four hours is huge."

She tried to assess how she felt, but the fatigue was definitely coming on now. "Are you sure you'll stay?"

She hated the fear in her voice. But, after what had just happened, she wondered if she'd ever be comfortable alone again.

"Yes, absolutely I'm staying. Come on. Let's get you back to bed." He walked at her side as she slowly made her way up the stairs. In her room, he pulled back the bedcovers and motioned at her. "Get back in."

She kicked off her slippers and slowly eased herself down.

He covered her up, leaned over, gave her a quick kiss and said, "Now four hours of sleep, nothing less. Do you hear me?"

"Why does it feel so good to finally lie down?"

"Because your body needs it," he said sternly. "I know you can see that highway from where you are, but that's not an issue now. My truck is not up there, and nobody else will be coming back tonight. Understand?"

She gave him a tired smile and waved at him. "Go. I'm fine. I'll be asleep in a few minutes." So saying, she rolled over onto her good side, tucked the pillow up underneath her head and closed her eyes.

He walked across the bedroom and whispered, "Good night."

She listened to his footsteps as he headed down the stairs. She hadn't even realized Bella was with him. But now it was like she was his ghost. Cinn could hear the light padding of Bella's nails as she crossed the top hallway and skittered down the stairs followed by Sentry's more sedate walk. Her own dogs appeared to have accepted Bella like none other. Although they were still wary of Sentry. But then they were used to rescues too. Cinn wondered if she had so easily accepted Ethan for the same reason. Was he a rescue as well? Bella was lost and homeless, a bit of a renegade. No, that was Sentry. Ethan, well, it was hard to find any description for him. But, in a way, he suited the dogs, and the dogs suited him.

The question that occupied her mind as she slowly drifted off to sleep was whether she suited Ethan and whether his whole gang suited hers.

They had something going on between them. She just didn't know what.

As sleep finally overtook her, she realized it didn't matter because she was willing to take the journey and to find out how far they would go. If it entailed two people getting together with a messy load of dogs, well, there were worse ways to live. And, with that, sleep claimed her with a smile on her face.

BACK DOWNSTAIRS, ETHAN stretched out on the couch. He kept a wary eye on Sentry, but Bella just crashed on the floor beside him. She was happy to be with him. Cinn's two dogs were in the bedroom with her. So far, all four animals were getting along, but no doubt the two smaller, happier dogs were giving the others clearance. They were happy to have them around, but they were a little wary. And he could understand that.

He stretched out, rolled over and tried to close his eyes. But his mind buzzed, wondering at the identity of the intruder and why he came here. Ethan should have checked for a license plate. And then he considered something else.

Who would have surveillance of this area? Anyone?

He pulled up Google on his phone to see if anybody might have cameras. Farther down the road was Anna and Flynn's rescue. Did they have anything? Even though it was really early, he sent Flynn a text, asking him. Letting him know an intruder had been on Cinn's property. Following that, he said he chased him off, but he was looking for a black pickup truck, likely a half-ton that had been parked at the top of her driveway.

He fired that off and lay here, thinking about it. Was this connected to him? The only way it could be was if it was connected to the same drug lab they had taken down.

He didn't know for sure, but it was too close a coincidence to ignore. Multiply that with a spy in the sky that could track things like that … But he didn't have access to any of those anymore. That was military-grade surveillance, not something he would pull in on a favor. Cinn had no surveillance and no security to speak of. And that was something he aimed to fix. Soon.

As he lay here, his phone beeped. Surprised, he saw Flynn's name. Flynn was pissed and said he was checking cameras right now.

Ethan responded. **Sorry to wake you.**

Never a better reason than to help a friend.

At that, Ethan settled back with a smile. He wasn't sure if Flynn meant that Cinn was a friend or that Ethan was. Either way, it was good they had somebody on their side.

Suddenly Sentry bolted to his feet, his hackles rising as he stared at the kitchen. Ethan hopped to his feet and glided across the living room floor, pulling up against the wall just short of the doorway.

That had been the other concern he'd had, that there

might have been two men—one who took off in the truck and the other sticking around. Ethan's truck was parked farther up the highway, out of sight. But did anybody know he was still here? He could hear something rattling at the kitchen door. He sent Flynn another text, then pocketed his phone, crouching down low.

When people came in, they rarely looked down at floor height. Once again, Sentry growled deep in the back of his throat. Ethan studied the dog. That anger, the full fluffed-out tail and hunched shoulders. Ethan wasn't sure if it was the man arriving who was setting off Sentry or the fact that it was *any* intruder at the house.

Sentry was obviously a guard dog, but was he guarding the house, or did he know the person coming toward him and hated him?

Both were possibilities, giving Ethan lots to work from. But he couldn't count on the fact that Sentry would follow Ethan's instructions. Bella, on the other hand, was now positioned right beside him, same height as he was, nudging him, her tail wagging. He studied her for a moment, as he heard the rattling at the door. Whoever it was trying to get in was shitty with a pick. And that was something he filed away.

He reached out a hand and placed it on Bella's muzzle. She quieted, her tail stilled, and she lowered her head to her paws, ears forward. He smiled. You had to love a dog that could pick up the nuances like she did.

Suddenly the door popped open. For a moment there was nothing. Ethan watched from down low as a man dressed all in black with a hood over his head stepped into the kitchen. He glanced around, as if familiarizing himself with the layout, then quickly moved toward Ethan.

Ethan held back Bella, but Sentry wasn't being held back at all. He snarled and growled audibly.

The man froze, reached out a hand. "Boris?"

Sentry froze, his nose wrinkling, but the deep growl resumed. Instead of running away, the intruder stopped, raised his hand in a stop command for Sentry and then, in a harsh whisper, ordered him to stand down.

Sentry slowly stood down, his training taking over at a voice he recognized. Ethan watched carefully because Sentry, although he was giving way, didn't like it. He was looking for an opportunity to move on his own.

The intruder walked forward a few steps. "Good boy. I was hoping you would be around." As he crept closer, talking calmly to Sentry, the dog growled again in the back of his throat. The man held up his hand. "What's wrong with you, Boris? You know better than this." He stopped a few feet away from the open doorway as his gaze caught sight of Bella. "Bella?"

Bella didn't growl or bark. She stared at him, her ears back and her teeth showing.

That confirmed an awful lot for Ethan. They both knew him. Neither wanted anything to do with him.

The man slowly reached around behind him and pulled out a leash and a rope. He also had what appeared to be a police-issue baton. At the sight of the baton, Sentry growled louder. The man tucked it behind his back. Sentry calmed slightly but not enough.

So the baton was the intruder's weapon of choice.

And the man had come prepared for these dogs.

Well, this asshole had had his last opportunity to beat up these dogs. Ethan waited for the man, leash in his hand, as he crept closer to Bella.

"Bella, you're looking good. Can you sit up for me please?"

Bella stayed down, her head flat on her paws as Ethan had told her, her ears back. The man with the leash started to crouch, to get close, and her lips curled even higher, and in the back of her throat was her first warning sound.

The man stared at her. "What the fuck? Why are both of you being such pains in the ass right now? What the hell happened to you?"

Ethan wanted to punch him flat in the face and let the dogs have at him. But the man wasn't quite close enough yet. Ethan couldn't be sure another weapon wasn't somewhere on the asshole. But, if Ethan got a chance to grab that baton, he'd take a few good wales on the asshole.

The man reached out a hand to Bella. She didn't move, but she growled. He froze, then ordered her to obey. His voice rose, although still quiet enough not to wake anybody else in the house. His tone was sharp, getting angry.

At that, Sentry stood and approached. His ears flat, his teeth showing, he growled at the intruder.

The man froze. "What the fuck has happened to you, Boris?" He took one more step forward, and it was enough.

Ethan snapped around the corner, his right hand out, connecting hard with the man's nose and jaw. He never even saw it coming. The blow was hard enough to send him backward several flailing steps before he went down on his back.

Sentry went after him.

The man cried out, again reaching for the baton, as Sentry grabbed the intruder's arm and stood over him. He shook the man's wrist, almost as if seeing the baton as an extension of the arm.

Bella still lay here at Ethan's command.

Blood running down the intruder's arm, he screamed at Sentry, but Sentry wasn't listening. He shook the intruder's arm harder, his jaws crunching on the man's weak forearm. The baton flailed around as the man tried to use it to get at the dog.

Ethan stood, stepping on the man's other arm, and said, "Drop the baton. If you don't, I'll let him take off your arm."

The intruder stared up at him. "Who the fuck are you? If you're the asshole who ruined our dogs, I'll make you pay for that," And then he screamed again as Sentry clenched down tighter.

"Apparently somebody the dogs prefer over you." Ethan grabbed the baton carefully, so as not to let Sentry see it as an extension of *his* arm, and said, "Let go."

The man really had no choice as Sentry once again shook hard. The intruder's fingers opened, and the baton dropped to the man's chest. Sentry saw it, released the man's arm and lunged for the baton. Ethan let him have it. He let him take the baton away and start to destroy it.

Ethan crouched beside the injured man and said, "What the hell did you do to that poor dog?" He pulled off the man's face mask, exposing the intruder. Ethan didn't recognize him.

"Are you the one who ruined our dogs?" the man roared.

He tried to attack Ethan, but, with Ethan stepping on his good arm, and his injured arm bleeding profusely, there wasn't a whole lot he could do except to kick his legs. As soon as one leg came up, Ethan grabbed it and pinned it down. The man screamed again.

Bella moved closer. Ethan looked at her and said,

"Good, Bella."

She looked up at him, then looked down at the intruder, but her stance didn't release.

"The dogs really hate you," Ethan said, "if even now, when they have an opportunity to turn on me, they don't want to."

"They will," the man said. He snapped out commands at Bella to *attack* and *kill.*

Bella, confused, obviously upset at the sight, stared at Ethan.

He kept murmuring to her in a gentle voice, "Relax, Bella. Just *guard*. Nobody kills anymore."

The man on the ground lost his temper, shouting and hurling epithets at her.

At this point she looked at Ethan and sat down on guard duty. He smiled. "You see? You can't lose your temper with an animal. And you can never take it out on them with a weapon," he said in a conversational voice. "You can't rule by fear."

"It's the only way you do rule," the intruder snapped. He groaned. "He broke my arm."

"Yeah, he might have," Ethan said. "But that's not my fault. You were breaking and entering into this house."

The man glared at him.

His arm bled badly enough that Ethan knew he had to put a stop to it. He noticed a tea towel tossed against the back of a kitchen chair. He looked at Bella, looked at the tea towel, pointed and said, "Bella, fetch."

She bounded to her feet, looked at him in confusion. He pointed at the tea towel, and she wandered in that direction, sniffed, looking for something to fetch, and he said, "Higher." Her nose went up a little bit higher. She grabbed the tea towel and brought it to him but obviously was not certain of her position.

He grabbed it, smiled and gave her a gentle pat. Then he praised her. "Good girl, Bella. Good girl. Now go back and *guard*."

She returned to her position and sat down to watch the intruder.

Ethan ripped a strip off the tea towel and wrapped it around the intruder's wrist, putting pressure on it to stop the bleeding.

"I need a hospital, damn you," the man cried out. "Not some backward medicine."

"What you need is a bullet," Ethan said calmly. "And, of course, if Sentry had killed you in the meantime, I certainly wouldn't have had a problem with that."

The man glared up at him.

Ethan said, "How many people have you had these dogs kill?"

The man sneered. But the waves of pain were taking their toll on him.

"They're just animals. And Boris is my number one tracker. But he's nowhere near what my Billy was."

"What happened to this Billy?"

"He was shot after he killed a man during a fight. Another guy got out a gun and shot him, but Billy got his man anyway. Unfortunately we had to put him down."

"And how many men had Billy killed?"

The intruder shrugged. "Maybe a dozen. I don't know."

"And Boris?" Ethan asked, using the name the intruder used.

"He's attacked many, but I don't think he's got any kills under his belt yet. But he's young. By the time he's six, he'll be well seasoned."

"Not if I have any say in the matter," Ethan said cheerfully. "An animal like that, which gives you his loyalty, and all you do is turn him into a killer."

"That's why he was loyal. His predecessor loved the taste of blood. Don't kid yourself. These animals love an opportunity to take something down and tear it to shreds."

They both looked at Sentry, who even now had the baton in shreds of leather and padding. But he was still working off his temper, still growling and attacking it. As Ethan watched, Sentry calmed slightly and focused on ripping off every piece of fabric and leather on the heavy steel center.

Ethan shook his head. "It's good therapy, isn't it, Sentry?"

"Good therapy is giving him a bloody cat or a rabbit to eat, preferably still alive," the man snarled. "You're ruining these dogs. And you've got a hell of a nerve stealing these animals and changing Boris's name. We all worked them and hard to get them to be the way we wanted them, and you are messing them up."

"It's not your problem anymore," Ethan said. "You'll go away for a long time."

"For what?" the man sneered. "For breaking into my girlfriend's house because she was having a little snit fit? Obviously she changed the locks, and I didn't know about it."

"It's not that simple," Ethan said. "You're connected to the dogs. That puts you in the drug operation."

"What do you know about the drug operation?" the man asked, his voice hesitant.

"More than you do," Ethan said. He could hear a vehicle

approach. He wasn't sure who it was, but he hoped it was Flynn. He needed back up soon. This asshole, as much as Ethan didn't want to get it for him, needed medical attention. Ethan was of the opinion a six-foot-deep hole out in the back would have been a perfect answer. But rough justice had gone out of Texas a long time ago. Too damn bad.

"You can't know anything about it. That place has been operating in the shadows for a long time."

Ethan nodded. "So true. Until she told me all about it," he added with a smile. "Once I heard about it, then I couldn't leave it alone." He could see the confusion in the intruder's eyes.

"Her? What are you talking about?"

But Ethan decided not to share. "Besides, it's shut down now."

"Yeah, but it'll only grow," the guy said. "It's not like you'll hit them hard enough to stop them."

"If you want to share that information with the police, they might let you off a little lighter."

"Not likely. I'll get killed in jail anyway," he said. "The bosses went through a bad patch a while ago. They should have killed off any loose ends. It would have saved them a lot of pain and money. Now it's standard practice after that mess."

"Quite possibly," Ethan said. "And I can tell you one thing, if you ever come back here, I'll kill you myself."

The man glared up at him, then he said in a low voice, "I still don't understand what woman you're talking about."

"And I won't tell you," Ethan said. Hearing footsteps at the front door, Ethan slipped back slightly out of view. A heavy knock came at the door. "Flynn?"

"Yeah, it's me. You okay here?"

"Come on to the kitchen door. Turn on some lights. This asshole is bleeding all over the floor."

As Flynn approached, Sentry stood, growling in the back of his throat. Flynn stopped in the doorway and put up his hands.

Ethan said, "Hit the light switch."

Flynn followed his instructions. Light flooded the living room so Ethan could see Sentry with his haunches up, standing over the absolutely destroyed baton. But it also showed Ethan beside a man bleeding quite badly on the floor.

Flynn's eyebrows rose. "Is she still asleep or is she upstairs hiding?"

"Believe it or not I think she's asleep."

Flynn looked at the dog in front of him and said, "This must be one of those big rescues you took on."

"It is. This is Sentry." Ethan let out a sharp noise, then said, "Sentry, Flynn is a *friend*."

Sentry wasn't listening.

"Sentry, *stand down*."

Sentry gave a hard shake.

Ethan looked at the smirking intruder. "You think it's funny you created a dog that's a killer?" He motioned at Bella. "Bella, *stand guard*." And then Ethan slowly straightened and walked over to Sentry, who stood in front of Flynn. Ethan walked up beside Flynn and stood at his side.

Sentry looked at Ethan and then back at Flynn.

Ethan reached down a hand, put it on the dog's fur, reached out his other hand toward Flynn and said, "Give me your hand." He did so, and Ethan told Sentry in a firm voice, "*Friend. Stand down.*" His voice brooked no argument, but it was also calm and orderly.

Sentry slowly quieted, the hairs on the back of his neck easing down as he studied the new arrival.

Flynn brushed his hair off his forehead and said, "Wow."

"It should be safe for you to approach."

Flynn looked beyond them into the kitchen and said, "Good thing because your intruder's trying to escape out the door."

Ethan turned and saw the guy getting to his feet to make it to the kitchen door. "Bella, *attack*," he ordered.

Bella spun and jumped on the intruder's back, clamping down on his shoulder, bringing the man to the floor again.

Ethan walked around Sentry, who was already heading toward Bella, looking for some fun himself.

In the kitchen, Ethan ordered both dogs to stand back, which they did surprisingly enough. He grabbed the intruder, slammed him onto a chair and asked, "Do you want to go for another round?"

By now his shoulder welled up with blood too. He stared up at the two men, pain glazing his eyes.

Ethan turned to look at Flynn and said, "Do you want to call the cops for me?"

"I already did," he said. "I figured that, if you had an intruder, you probably would take them down, and we'd need the cops eventually."

Ethan checked the intruder's shoulder. "You'll be fine," he snapped.

"I'll fucking shoot the dogs," the intruder said. "You just wait. I'll get another chance, and I'll take them both out."

Sentry lunged forward as if understanding what the intruder had said.

Ethan held up his hand and ordered Sentry to stop. He didn't look like he would for a long moment. With his growling up the back of his throat and his hackles raised, Ethan stood strong. But he didn't use force.

Finally Sentry calmed down. As if giving the intruder a disgusted look, Sentry gave his head a shake and turned to join Bella sitting off to the side.

Flynn approached quietly. "Are you sure he's safe to have around?"

"He'll be the best damn guard dog anybody could want," Ethan said. "But we have to let him know most people aren't mean assholes, like this guy."

"If you say so."

Ethan laughed and sat on the floor between the dogs. He reached up to scratch them under the chin.

Flynn stared in astonishment. "You're braver than I am. How did you know they would let you do that?"

"Both dogs are good animals," he said quietly. "They will take to affection as much as they're running away from the brutality of this asshole."

"They're our dogs, and you're ruining them," the intruder roared. "I came to get them back, not sit here and watch you destroy them."

"Oh, interesting," Ethan said. "I thought you might have been here for other reasons. Regardless, you'll be disappointed on both counts." He tilted his head to the side and studied the man. And then looked at Flynn. "What am I missing?"

But Flynn's face had shifted and had locked down into a much harder, colder man than the one who had first arrived. He stepped backward, flattening against the wall as he sidled up to the window. "Did you have a chance to see if this guy came alone?"

Ethan froze. Then he hopped to his feet and moved forward. "Bella," he ordered, "with me." At the bottom of the stairs he turned to look at Sentry and said, "Sentry, *guard*."

Sentry snapped to attention, his ears up, and returned to the intruder on the chair.

Ethan ran up the stairs with Bella, wondering if this had all been a distraction, and he'd missed the main event. Knowing he would wake her and terrify her, he shouldered open the barricaded door and stepped in regardless. With his heart in his throat, he stared at the empty bed, his worst thoughts confirmed. Bella raced forward and searched, but she ended up at the window. The window beside a door that led to a deck with a nice set of stairs down the back to the bottom deck.

Somebody had kidnapped Cinn.

CHAPTER 11

THE PAIN WOKE Cinn first. She moaned. Feeling her head pound, she rolled over onto her side, curling up into a fetal position, her hands clutching her temples. When she felt something wet and sticky, she pulled her fingers away and slowly opened her eyes. Her lids were heavy, as if she'd been crying nonstop. Her body throbbed, achy, but it was her head and her bloodstained fingers that were her main concern.

Her hands were free but she was lying on the floor in what appeared to be an empty room. A ramshackle room. There was a door but no windows that she could see. The area was small, maybe a ten-by-ten-foot space. There was enough light to see she was into a new day, yet still early.

What the hell?

Not sure what had happened, she propped herself on her right elbow, then cried out at the pounding in her head. She collapsed back down, gasping for breath, shuddering as her shoulder took the force.

Her shoulder throbbed. Slowly memories filled in the blanks in her mind.

Ethan had sent her back to bed. She lay here, frowning as the memories filtered back in. If this had happened to her, what had happened to Ethan? She was pretty damn sure he'd have been a hell of a watchdog. For her to be here now, something calamitous had to have happened to him.

She rolled over gently, trying not to cry out in pain. Between her head and her shoulder, she was mess. Where was she? Was she truly alone? Or were more assholes waiting outside for her?

The door was to her right. Moving gently so as not to further jar any of her injuries, she leaned on the wall beside the door. She reached up with one hand and tried the knob. It was not locked. She frowned, wondering if it could be that easy. Using the door for support she slowly made her way upright.

Once stable, she leaned against the wall for several moments as her breathing calmed. She listened through the crack in the door but heard nothing on the other side. Frowning, she pulled the door open enough that she could stick her head out—finding herself in a shed in the middle of a large property. But she noted other sheds were here too. This made no sense at all.

A larger building stood in front of her. She didn't recognize the area. She didn't recognize the buildings. She had absolutely no clue where she was. But she hadn't come on her own. Those people had to be around somewhere. She had to get out of here, and she had to get out fast. She crept around to the back of her shed and surveyed her options. A fence was ahead of her, but it had rolled barbed wire over the top as a major deterrent. Not to mention it could be electric. She'd only find out the hard way.

The fence appeared to go all the way around on all three sides she could see of the property. She moved to the left side of the shed and still couldn't see another way out. What were the chances this was a compound, and she was caged inside with just the one escape route? Maybe, with her injured arm and head, she could climb up to the barbed wire, but she wouldn't make her way through the big coils at the top.

Moving as fast as she could, she slipped over to the next shed to get a better view of what was on the other side. She peered around the corner to see a road and a gate. She tapped on the shed behind her, wondering if anybody was there. She didn't hear anything. She found a slight hole in one of the wooden planks. She lowered to her knees and whispered. With no answer and not seeing anything through the odd knot in the wallboard, she wondered if the other sheds in the area were empty. Then she caught sight of something hanging.

She peered at different angles, trying to look up, but couldn't see what it was. It appeared to be plants drying. She straightened slowly, studied the area around her, wondering if she was on the drug property that Ethan had worked to bring down. In a twisted way it made sense. And notched her panic up that much higher. She needed to get the hell out of here. But there didn't appear to be any breaks in the fence or any spot where she could slide under. Then she reconsidered that. Directly behind her, along one of the fence posts, was a little bit of a hollow, with rocks filling the gap.

Could she stay hidden long enough to clear that hollow enough for her to get under? She wasn't very big. She crept over, crouched down flat and started removing the rocks.

As soon as she thought she had enough room, she flattened and scooted under headfirst. By the time she got her hips through on the other side, she could feel her panic choking her. Finally she'd managed to scrape her way to her feet, and then bolted as fast as she could away from the fence.

Every step made her want to cry out, but the fear of getting caught won over her pain.

There was a rise ahead of her. She climbed it, her heart pounding hard inside her chest. She crested the rise, skidding down the first few feet on the other side. There she came to a stop amid the dust. All she could see was more of the same. Sand, rocks, tumbleweeds even. There was vegetation, but it was wild, unkempt, uncultivated. All around her was miles of raw land.

She stared in awe at the vastness, wondering how the hell she was supposed to know which way to go.

The smart thing to do would be to follow the road. But it was also likely a way to bring her in contact with somebody she didn't want to see. If she could keep the road in sight, she could follow it from a distance. It had to lead somewhere.

With that thought uppermost in mind, she crept up to the next rise, so she could study the property below. It was large, fenced, secure and very private.

If it was the drug property, it was also the same property Ethan had collected the dogs from. She searched for her phone, but of course she didn't have it. Neither did she have much in the way of clothing. She was wearing a long T-shirt, of all things. And bare feet.

She stared down at her bleeding feet in bemusement. She hadn't even considered that. She was out here in the middle of nowhere in the thinnest clothing possible, with nothing to protect her feet, not even socks. "Shit. Shit. Shit."

And she had no way to contact Ethan. He was definitely the one she needed to call. She considered returning to the shed to see if anything would make her walk a little bit easier. Shoes? Water? A cell phone? But she was afraid she'd run out of luck and get caught. She turned to study the miles of rough land around her.

Once the sun rose higher, her feet would burn in the sand too.

Keeping just under the rise, so nobody could see her, she moved in the direction of the road. The rise dipped down, almost flattening up ahead as it came along the road.

Grimly she pressed on. Time was of the essence. Had these men replaced the dogs Ethan had taken? If they had, the dogs would find her in no time.

Moving as fast as she dared, she kept going until she could see the driveway turning away from the property, heading toward town.

About a half hour later she had to sit down, gasping for breath. Not only was her head booming again but the pain of her feet now added to it. With all the jerking and slipping and sliding in the rocks, her shoulder was on fire. Oh, for a sling. Even worse she'd barely covered any ground. The property was still in sight. Thankfully she saw no sign of anyone. She figured, if she did see any strangers, it had to be the men who had kidnapped her. Her head throbbed at that thought. *They must have hit me, knocked me out, then taken me here.*

Grimly she searched over the rise to see if there was any activity at the property. But she couldn't even see a vehicle, which surprised her. Had she been dumped here and left alone, not one guard on duty? If so, when were they returning?

She was just coming around to the side where the front gate was. She was tempted to go into the guard house and see if she could call for help. But who would she find there? Was it suicide contemplating doing that?

Making a sudden decision, she crossed over the rise and

skidded down the far side, swearing at the pain that rubbed against her feet and opened a million little slices along her soles. She hit the driveway and kept going until she saw what appeared to be a huge building ahead of her. But instead of going in the front, she headed around to the back.

There wasn't a sound. It was like a ghost town. But then she remembered what the cops had done here, so maybe no one was left.

There was a door. Hesitantly she reached for it. When the knob turned under her hand and the door opened, she stepped inside, loving the cool air. She crept into what appeared to be a large open room with several smaller rooms behind it. There were no lights on, no sounds. The place appeared to be empty.

She did a quick search and found no one. Then she did a closer search, looking for anything she could use. An old water bottle was on the floor. She snatched that up. Now all she needed was water. Continuing to check, she found a pair of socks tossed into a corner, a big hole at the heel of one of them. She didn't care; her feet would be only half as big as the person who had worn these socks.

She carefully placed them on her feet, almost crying out in relief at the soft padding. She put weight on her feet again. That was an improvement. Now all she needed were boots, water and a phone, but she couldn't find anything.

Back in the main room again, she checked what appeared to be a desk and found a cell phone. But it was dead. She popped out the battery and left it on the desk for a moment. Had it been left behind in the chaos with the police?

She knew, if she gave the battery a moment before putting it back in again, she might get a few seconds. Maybe enough to get a call through—if there was any cell service out here.

Hey, she'd try anything. She popped the battery back in, her mind working as to who to call. It would be tough to get 9-1-1. They asked so many questions she'd have no time. She hadn't memorized Ethan's number. How about her own? She dialed her phone and waited. When the voicemail kicked in, she gave a quick report as to where she was and what had happened. Just as she finished, the phone died.

She stared at it in her hand and then pocketed it. She didn't know who it belonged to. But, if it had anything to do with this place, maybe the police could do something with it.

She wandered the rest of the huge compound, looking for anything that could help her. She did find a small kitchen and running water in the main building. Thirstily, she drank her fill and then filled her bottle. Even if she could locate a bicycle, that would help. She did find shoes, but they were too big to keep on her feet. Other than that, she was pretty well done here.

With a final look around, she headed to the entranceway to the property. Just then she saw a plume of dust in the distance. She scampered up the side of the rise again and disappeared over the edge. Had she made it before they saw her?

The vehicle sped in and hit the brakes. As it came to a stop, she heard doors opening and then more doors opening.

She winced, picked up her feet and started to run. The socks helped a lot. Her feet were sore, but worse than that was the option of getting caught by these guys. Not again. She had very little choices of places to hide. But she'd seen where the plume of dust had come from and knew the general direction that the road would go.

She headed off cross-country toward the road. She just had to stay out of sight. She knew she didn't have much time. Five to ten minutes at the most. Then they'd be all over the place, searching for her. When that happened, she would be in deep shit.

HEARING THE PHONE ring, Ethan ran back into Cinn's bedroom. He'd been searching the top floor, looking for anything. Her phone on the night table continued to ring. Just as he got to it, it stopped. He picked it up, unlocked it and listened as the phone said he had one voicemail. *To hear the voicemail, press 11.*

He pressed 11 and heard Cinn's voice. His blood ran cold. When the message was cut off, he wasn't sure what to think. Had the phone died? Or had she been captured? Or had she been forced to say that to lure him into a trap? Not that it mattered because he was obviously going. He ran downstairs to tell Flynn. His voice terse, he explained the message.

Ethan pulled out his own phone and called Levi. "I'm heading home to get my gear and switch out the dogs," he called out, running to his truck.

"I'll track your GPS and follow you," Flynn called after him, "as soon as the cops arrive to take this asshole off my hands."

At home, Ethan freed Sentry and Bella from the truck bed, figuring out the best plan for this rescue. They all fast-walked straight through to the backyard, Sentry and Bella at his side. Sally barked inside, wanting to join them. But it was too soon for her. Bart had been outside in the fenced-in backyard all this time and came toward Ethan. He frowned, not sure he could handle all three. Sentry, of course, was the wild card. Maybe Ethan would leave him behind this time.

Grabbing Bart and Bella, securing Sentry inside the fence, Ethan returned to the truck, put both dogs into the bed, grabbed his SAR vest and turned around to see Flynn standing right behind him. "How did you get away so fast from the cops and their questioning?"

Flynn smirked. "Told them that you were nearby in state land, and I would grab you real quick for them." At that, Flynn laughed. "They didn't leave our bad guy to follow me. ... We'll explain later when we have more time."

"*Humph*," was all Ethan murmured, but his expression said, *Good job*.

"What are you going to do?" Flynn asked as he followed Ethan to enter his rental property.

"I'm going after her," Ethan said. "I know the property, where the drug bust was earlier. There's a way to get in under the electric fence, if we want to try that way in."

"I thought the police cleaned out that place?"

"They did," Ethan said tersely. "That doesn't mean the drug runners didn't move back in. Obviously she thinks that's where she is, so I have to go find out."

"If she got free, she could be anywhere around the countryside," Flynn said.

"I know. That's why I have the dogs."

"You should take Sentry too," Flynn said.

"Why is that?"

"Because these men have guns. They can take out the dogs. But the more dogs there are, the harder it will be for them to shoot them all."

Ethan considered that, then nodded. "You have a point.

Still two are enough to handle. Although Sentry might be the better tracker in this instance. Let me grab a medical kit, ropes and more water." He changed his shoes for hiking boots and then grabbed his emergency supplies vest—the one from his truck, the one he'd used on search-and-rescue so often, yet not in the last several years. Then he walked into the kitchen and filled the water bottles from his vest. There was no way to know how badly hurt she was or how dehydrated.

His mind raced through the possibilities of what he would need. He moved with the same care he was known for. He'd done this type of rescue many, many times. What he didn't have was weapons. He turned to look at Flynn. "I need a weapon."

Flynn raised an eyebrow. Then he nodded. "I have a piece in the truck." He disappeared.

Ethan packed up and loaded the rest of the gear he needed in the front of the truck. Sentry understood something was going on, and he was being excluded. He bucked like a crazy man, trying to jump up and over the fence. Ethan came back with a heavy leash and stepped out into the back door.

Sentry ran toward him. But first they had to come to a meeting of minds. Ethan stood there, arms crossed, leash in his hand as Sentry tried to get past him. Sentry growled and howled and kicked up a fuss. He really did not like to be left behind. Then Ethan held out his hand with the leash. "Sit."

Sentry stared at him, but his butt went down, and his head went up. Ethan clipped on the leash, told him to heel and then walked him through the house, out to the back of the truck. He opened the tailgate and let the dog jump in to join the others, then moved Bart into the backyard. "Not this time, boy."

Now with two dogs aboard, Ethan went to the front of the truck. He should have a big suburban to carry the dogs or at least a canopy on his truck to keep them safe.

Flynn walked toward them, talking on the phone. He handed Ethan a small handgun, service-issue, and several clips. "I'm coming behind you," he said. "Levi is on his way as well."

"Tell him to contact Sergeant Mendelsson," Ethan said. "He's the man I was with yesterday morning."

Flynn nodded. "Will do. Remember. You're not alone anymore, dude." And he turned and hopped into his truck.

While Ethan watched, Flynn did a quick turnaround, taking off to the left. Ethan drove up to the highway and took a right. He might not be alone anymore, but he sure as hell didn't understand exactly what he did have. Things had gone from slow to top speed in no time. And poor Cinn had been caught in the middle.

Just like the dogs had been.

Ethan had taken on a lot all at once. But he realized, as he headed out toward the countryside where she was probably on the run, he was the best person to find her.

Both dogs knew her scent, as Ethan had remembered to grab the jacket that she had been wearing the day before. She'd worn it to the hospital, carefully draped on her shoulders, and, even better, it had some of her blood on it. If the dogs could find her, they would.

Ethan drove to where he had parked last time. He pulled the truck into the hollows behind a rise so it couldn't be seen, or at least he thought it couldn't be seen. Considering somebody had tracked him back to Cinn's place, he wasn't so sure about that now. He hopped out as his phone rang.

"Ethan," he said, his voice terse.

"Ethan, it's Levi. We have a team of four men coming in your direction. I need you to stay in contact with them."

"I've just parked. I'm unloading the dogs now."

"Is that wise?"

"This is what I do," Ethan said. "The dogs will track her in no time."

"But will they save her, or will they take her out?" Levi asked, his voice worried.

"Good question," Ethan said. "I guess this is a good trial. If I have to, I'll kill them. But it's not what I want to do."

"You could also be going up against more of their trainee dogs."

"That could be both good and bad," Ethan said. "Don't forget. These animals were abused."

"Oh, I remember. That's why I'm worried. Go get her," Levi said, his voice calm and steady. "We'll be right behind you."

CHAPTER 12

SHE DIDN'T KNOW when the pain and the lack of oxygen took over. But she was on autopilot, just moving one step to the next step. Somewhere along the line she realized anybody driving on the road would see her now. The ridge was long gone; it was just flat cross-country terrain. She approached a bend in the road up ahead. She didn't know if that was a good or bad thing. She twisted behind her to see a vehicle driving toward her, dust billowing out behind it. There was a second plume of dust, although the vehicle creating it was hidden by the first.

She hit the ground. She wasn't sure what to do. If she kept running, they'd probably see her. She had very few places to hide. But there were enough hollows and dips that, if she lay completely still, she might not be seen. She was still several hundred yards from the road. As she glanced back, she noted the two vehicles still had a ways to go. She bounced to her feet and darted cross-country away from the road again.

A clump of trees was up ahead and several bushes. She expected, if they had seen her, they'd figure that she'd race there for cover. But she had to do anything to keep hidden.

As she tripped into a creek bed, a dry hollow, she realized this was the perfect answer. She raked the dirt on top of her, and, with a couple rocks placed carefully around her face, she left her mouth and her injured head open between them, while covering up most of her. Her auburn hair, her pale skin, her freckles, even her beige T-shirt, they were all camouflage-worthy attire for her right now. Here she lay, her breathing shallow and heavy. She drank the last of her water, then lay still.

In the distance she could hear voices. She knew they had seen her.

"Where the hell did she go? Did you see her?"

"I saw her running about a hundred yards off," one of the men called. "Just keep walking. Keep walking."

She didn't dare breathe heavily. She lay as still as she could, frozen and waiting. She could hear footsteps in the distance, men still talking. God help her if one of them stepped on her.

"Search to the left. I saw her run that way."

"No, I don't think so," one of the men said. "There's no sign of her anywhere."

"If she was smart, she went for the trees," said yet a different man.

"Yeah, but, of course, that's the first place we would look for her," another man said.

Inside, she thought to herself, *Please, just keep walking. Just keep walking.* She knew, if they found her, it would be the end. This time, if they recaptured her, she'd have a much worse time escaping. Chances were they'd kill her.

"Okay, I'll head off to the trees. You guys keep scanning this area. Just keep walking. She couldn't have gone far."

"There's no place she can hide," one of the men said. "Look at this place. It's just dirt and rocks."

"She was wily enough to get free. She could have other tricks up her sleeve."

She could hear the men grumbling, but one man's voice got fainter. Probably heading for the copse of trees she had avoided. She knew they'd head there. Any sane person would. She figured she was the last person anybody would consider sane. She kept wishing for Ethan to hurry and find her.

And then the fear crept in again that he hadn't heard her message. That was so not what she needed to think now.

All of a sudden a couple heavy crunches of booted feet on rocks came close to her. From her left, one of the men called out, "Did you see anything?"

A man, almost upon her, called back, "Nah, there's nothing out here. Besides, if she is, she might as well stay out here and die. The desert will kill her in no time."

She winced. But he was right. Just because she'd escaped, didn't mean she was safe. The footsteps crossed in front of her as the man headed over to join the other men. She didn't dare move. And, no matter how curious she was, no way could she raise her head and remain unseen. All she could do was wait. Hopefully these guys would leave, and the right man would arrive.

But she didn't know how long that would take. She listened intently as the men's voices faded into the distance, and she heard a vehicle start up and take off again. She relaxed and thought that maybe, just maybe, she was free and clear.

The sun beat down, but, under the dirt, it was not too bad. She didn't dare get up, just in case it was a trick. Some of the men could have driven off and left the others to stand watch. She lay here in the heat of the sun and could feel her eyes growing weary.

Eventually she told herself, she'd nap to regain her

strength, just for a few minutes.

And she closed her eyes and fell asleep.

ETHAN FROZE AS he watched figures in the distance. Vehicles parked, armed men running around, but Ethan didn't see a woman. He let his gaze relax, becoming accustomed to the scene in front of him. He tried not to search for anything but rather have movement jar his awareness. He couldn't guarantee she was out here, but it was likely, given the location. He knew Levi was heading toward the main part of the camp. But Ethan saw no sign of Levi's vehicle, at least not from where he stood.

He was more concerned about the men, four that he could count, combing the acres of land between him and the next rise. He couldn't hear any sounds from this distance, but just their actions, their frantic movements, were enough to get reactions from the dogs. Bella and Sentry both stood, their backs bristled, a slight growling coming from deep in their throats. Ethan judged the distance between him and the gunmen to be a couple miles. Bella stood eagerly at attention, willing for whatever was coming.

The four gunmen continued in their search for Cinn, unaware of Ethan.

On that note, Ethan drank some of his water, then clipped it onto his belt, let Sentry choose the direction and started to run. Every step caused pain in his stump, but he ignored it. Cinn was going through something so much worse. Besides, Ethan had been working hard at training his injury.

The dogs were also injured but ran eagerly at his side.

Both leashed, both running level with him. He appreciated the training that had gone into their original care. He was just damn sorry they had ended up with somebody who had turned them into killers.

From where Ethan was, he didn't think he was visible, but again any movement on the horizon like this could catch the bad guys' attention. In the distance a movement caught his eyes. He turned to see a fox running away from him. He smiled and whispered, "Go, fella. We wish you well."

He turned his attention back to the men, seeing them split, two going one way, two heading toward the copse of tress. Most people in Cinn's position would head for the trees, hoping for a hiding place that would keep them safe. But, because it was the first place the men were likely to look, it was also, in this case, probably the worst thing she could do. But she wasn't a fool.

He kept running. It took a good three minutes to get his breathing even.

The terrain was rough, unsteady, his footsteps landing, occasionally rolling ever-so-slightly. It ate up his energy, this cross-country running. But it was necessary. He kept his eyes trained on the men ahead. They stopped, checked out the surrounding trees, and just then he heard a shout. The two closest to him turned and headed toward the others, all now heading for the copse of trees.

Ethan was still at least a mile out.

He kept up the pace, jogging steadily, needing a bit of good luck getting close without them noticing his approach. Just then the four men broke from the trees, stopped and stared. He hated to, but he stopped, minimizing the dust rising up around him. Crouched, he peered just over the rocks to see the men staring in his direction. He waited, the dogs at his side panting heavily, their gazes locked on the men in front of them. Good. They should know exactly who it was they were up against.

What he couldn't count on was the dogs' reactions when they reached the men. Would they see them as friend or foe? Would they listen to Ethan's commands or to the enemy's? Surely some of the men had befriended the dogs? But he would never get a better chance than here and now to see where their loyalties lay and to see if, in any way, he could redeem them. Bella had already proven herself to be trainable and loyal to him, but she hadn't been put to the real test yet. Sentry, on the other hand, he'd been trained to kill for these men, making him the bigger problem.

Still, Sentry had listened to Ethan over the intruder they had caught at Cinn's house. Would Sentry welcome a chance to go after these men? Or would he welcome them with yips and howls of joy and jump all over them? Ethan could only guess what would happen. Sentry certainly wasn't pulling back or resisting the run. Right now he wanted to tear ahead. Ethan just didn't know for sure why.

The men seemed to turn and look toward their vehicles; then they slowly marched back. Ethan stayed where he was, watching as, every once in a while a man turned his gaze, sweeping around, probably looking for Cinn, and maybe for Ethan. The question was, where was Cinn? And would the dogs pick up her scent? Was she hurt? Had she been shot again? Was she running for her life in a completely different area? Did she have any water?

It was too easy to lose somebody in this countryside. Without helicopters, without motion sensors, without any GPS tracking, finding her, especially in time if she was injured, would be hard. He didn't know if Levi had access to any satellite imagery, but, if they would be so lucky to have the police involved with similar technology, then maybe they would catch sight of her. Deeming it safe, he got up. Instead of running, he walked slowly, as the men were now all in their vehicles. Two of them drove ahead of the other two. Ethan didn't want to push his luck, waiting until they took the first corner.

Then he picked up the pace and ran toward the area where they'd been. Another vehicle drove toward him, but he couldn't tell who it was. He wished he had a better view. It would tell him if it was Levi meeting up with that group of gunmen, or if it would be more of the foes.

Taking a chance, he bent down, unclipped Bella, gave her a sniff of Cinn's jacket and told her to search. And Bella took off. Sentry tried to jump behind her, but he was still leashed. Ethan picked up the pace, running behind Bella, who was now flat-out racing across the countryside toward the road.

And there she stopped, milling around, and started to sniff. She wasn't a bloodhound. She was an attack dog. Ethan knew it was a slim chance that she'd pick up Cinn's scent, but all dogs seemed to have a sense for tracking that completely outshone anything humans could do.

He didn't know for certain about that with Sentry or Bella.

Finally reaching Bella, he gave her another sniff of the jacket, and she walked up and down the road, whining. "I know. Where could she be? Maybe she hitched a ride from someone?" He thought about that. There were just too many unknowns. As he looked to the left of the road, he realized nobody had gone that direction. He moved forward along the road to where the men had gotten out of their vehicles.

Bella and Sentry started to whine and howl, barking as they picked up the scent of the men who'd been here. He just didn't know what their reaction meant. He led the way to the trees, with Bella now racing ahead, following the men's trails.

"Sure, Bella. But do you want to see these guys, or is it because you can also smell Cinn's scent here?"

They were a good two minutes away from the trees. He walked slowly, his gaze roaming carefully across the sand and dirt.

She had to be here somewhere. His worst fear was that she'd collapsed, had been shot and was even now bleeding out into the dry ground.

Shots split the silence. He dashed into the tree line to make sure he and the dogs were out of the firing line. He peered through the trees to see what was going on. But there was just dust and chaos where the vehicles had met, face-to-face.

"Well, that answers that question," he muttered. "I'll take that as Levi met up with the enemy." Ethan bent down and gave Sentry a good scratch as he whined. "It'll be fine, buddy. I don't know about the fate of your previous owners, but you'll be fine. We need to focus on finding Cinn." He called Bella to him, and slowly, carefully, methodically went through the trees. He looked up in the branches, just in case she'd climbed up.

Deeming they were safe enough, he called out, "Cinn? Are you here? Call out if you're hurt. It's me, Ethan. I've got the dogs."

In a gentle voice he kept calling to her. But there was no answer. As he came to the end of the trees, he thought about going back down for another run, but so much land surrounded him. He couldn't spend too much time here.

He also couldn't be sure the men hadn't seen her, shot her and left her somewhere. He hadn't heard a sound, but, depending on how close they'd been, he might not have. If the wind had been moving up the hills, sweeping away from him, it could easily have been disguised. He glanced down at Sentry and held Cinn's jacket to his nose.

Sentry barked and strained at the leash. Bella came back over, milled around the two of them, sniffing the air and sniffing the jacket.

Ethan was taking a hell of a chance to let Sentry off his leash. He could disappear on Ethan. But he made a decision to give the dog some trust and to hope the dog would trust him back. Ethan reached down, unclipped the big harness off the dog's shoulders, and Sentry bolted cross-country into the area Ethan had not searched when coming in.

There was still a good mile of land out here that the dogs ran flat out into. But this time Bella was ever-so-slightly behind, and Sentry moved with intent. Ethan picked up his feet and raced forward. He didn't call out to the dogs. For all he knew, Sentry was headed back to the compound. But Ethan had to give Sentry a chance.

And suddenly Sentry came to a complete stop and barked.

CHAPTER 13

CINN WOKE TO a horrific barking above her and a heavy weight on her chest. She shifted and then groaned. But she could hardly hear her thoughts. A dog barking outrageously stood on her torso, his head above her head. He terrified her. He was huge, looming over her, barking in her face. She wasn't sure, but she thought it was Sentry. But wasn't Sentry under Ethan's command? Or was Sentry now back under one of the assholes' control?

She knew she wouldn't have much time to make a decision. She could either bolt, and the dog would likely take her down, or she could lie here and hope the dogs didn't belong to the bad guys. Her heartbeat slammed against her chest, and the dog's drool dripped on her face. But she didn't move.

And then suddenly she heard someone call out, "Easy boy, easy boy." She strained her ears. Ethan?

"Bella! Come on, Bella."

Bella?

She smiled. "Ethan?" she called out weakly.

"Cinn?"

She managed to get her good hand under her and lifted her body. Dirt slid off her shoulders as she cried out, "Yes, it's me."

And suddenly there he was. He bent beside her, moving

Sentry off to the side, clipping him on a leash. His hand went to her head, brushing off the dirt. "Are you okay?"

She gave a broken laugh. "Yes. Bruised, my feet are killing me, but I'm alive. I buried myself in the dirt, so the assholes wouldn't find me. When the dogs arrived, I was terrified Sentry was working for the wrong team."

Ethan cleaned the dirt and rocks off of her. When he could, he reached down, grabbed her under the shoulders—careful of her injury—and helped her to a sitting position. She cried out when her bloody feet scraped along the ground. He lifted her feet, took one look at her soles and the gentlest wince whispered across his face.

"I couldn't find any shoes," she whispered, holding her feet up in pain. "The best I could do was these socks."

He gently removed the socks and held them up so she could see she had worn the soles right out of them.

She stared at them. "I really don't want to see what my feet look like."

"No," he said grimly. "You do not." He slowly lowered her feet so her calves rested sideways on his legs. "What about other injuries?"

She shook her head and shot a hand up to her head. "A headache—from those assholes knocking me out, I presume—and, of course, my shoulder," she admitted. "But everything else appears to be in good working order. I ran and walked as much as I could, following the road back out. But then I saw the vehicles coming after me, and I had to hide."

He glanced around at her hiding spot and smiled. "You did a great job."

"Not really," she said, motioning at the dirt. "Once I disturbed it and opened up a dark slash of dirt, the sun didn't have a chance to dry it out and turn the camouflage the same color as the rest of surroundings."

"But it was enough that you stayed hidden. They all headed to the trees."

"I know at least one was very close. I didn't dare look around to see where the others were," she said, her heart hitching at the reminder. "They were almost upon me. If they'd had the dogs, for sure they would have found me. And I couldn't keep my head completely buried because I had to breathe. But I was between the rocks, so it was deceptive. I was hoping they'd think some animal had disturbed this part of the dirt."

"It worked," Ethan said in an admiring tone. "You did good."

Just then she felt a wet nose against her face. She looked up to see Bella. "Hello, Bella," she murmured, gently scratching her thick neck. "Did you help find me?"

Bella nudged her, when her hand slowed down, and Cinn chuckled.

"Bella, lie down," Ethan ordered.

Bella lay down and dropped her head lower on Cinn's lap, so Cinn could scratch the rest of her.

She glanced over at Sentry and asked, "And him? Was he okay?"

"He found you," Ethan said proudly, reaching out to scratch the big male who again stared in the direction of the vehicles. "But we're still not out of danger here."

She looked in the direction Sentry was focused on. "What are you talking about?"

"Two vehicles came down and met up two of Levi's vehicles." He pointed to the other side of the trees. "I heard a lot of shooting, but I can't be sure who's left standing."

"And we're in the open," she cried out. She shook her head. "You should have left me here. I can't run anywhere right now."

He stood, looped her arms around his neck and picked her up. Moving at a steady pace, he walked back toward the trees.

"Not that I have anything against being carried," she joked, "but aren't the trees where they'll look for us?"

"Indeed it is," Ethan said. "But out here, like you said, we're sitting ducks. In the trees, we have a little more opportunity. Besides, the sun is very hot."

He walked steadily. She marveled at his strength. She wasn't a big woman, but, at the same time, it wasn't easy to hike while carrying someone else like this.

Finally they headed into the cooler shade of the trees. He found a large downed tree and sat her gently on the stump. "Now stay here, rest up against this tree. I would like very much to find out what's going on over there by the vehicles, but I don't want to leave you."

"No, please don't," she said. "Can't you stay here with me?"

"I'll leave Bella with you. I'll take Sentry and go over there." He pointed up ahead about forty feet. "I promise I'll stay in sight."

She nodded and let him go. She was too tired to protest. Her feet were killing her; her head pounded, and she wished he'd left her some water. She checked her bottle. There was just enough to wet the inside of her mouth. She hugged Bella and marveled at a dog who'd gone from being part of a killer pack to being part of a defending pack. And then she realized it really had nothing to do with choice. The dog was being swept along by the same nuances of society as Cinn herself was. There were only so many choices the dogs could make on their own, and they had to deal with the hand they were dealt. Bella was doing the best she could. At the moment she seemed happy to be with Cinn.

Cinn reached over and scratched her, pulling her ears gently, moving her hand down the side of the shepherd's face. "You're quite the beautiful girl, aren't you?"

Bella turned her head to look at her and then turned to follow Ethan's and Sentry's progress. Cinn could see the two sneaking out from behind one of the big trees, and she looked toward the vehicles. They might have been shooting at each other earlier, but she couldn't hear anything now.

And just then a cry rang out.

She almost fell off the log in surprise. She turned to see one of the men from the compound run in her direction. She swore gently, gripping Bella as she tried to get into a better position, but, as she tried to stand, her feet collapsed out from under her, and she fell onto the ground, leaning up against the log.

He was on her in an instant, his hand at her throat, closing around her windpipe, as he gave her a slap. "You little bitch," he roared. "We were looking for you."

Bella barked and launched herself forward.

"*Down*, Bella," her attacker ordered.

Bella subsided slightly, confused.

"I thought you were all shot," Cinn gasped when she could, her hand gripping his. His grip eased, and she choked and coughed.

"Not me," he said. "As soon as the shooting started, I snuck away and came back. I'm not up to face-to-face gunfire. A sneak attack is much more my style. Besides, I knew you had to be out here somewhere. But I checked here earlier, so I don't know how the hell you got here."

"I crawled," she lied. She could only hope Ethan and Sentry were well hidden from this asshat. "Besides, what do you want with me? I didn't do anything to you."

"I want that asshole boyfriend of yours," he said. "He's the one who came in with the cops, stole the dogs and blew up the entire operation at the compound."

She wanted to cheer Ethan's work but knew she would get a punch in the face for it. "Then why are you after me?"

"Because coming after you will lead to him." He sniggered. "That's the way it works. Use a piece of pretty bait, and the men just keep coming around."

She glared at him. "So you're the one who came after me? Broke into my house, terrorized my own dogs?"

"Me and Tom, yeah," he said. "Why? You didn't like that treatment? We were planning on coming back and showing you a good time. Imagine our surprise when you weren't there anymore."

She could hardly swallow for the bile rising up her throat. Just the thought of what these men would have done to her if she hadn't escaped …

He released her suddenly and said, "You didn't escape alone though, did you?"

He jumped behind the log, his hand going out to Bella, who stared at him, her lips curling. Cinn could understand Bella's confusion. He'd been aggressive but not deadly. And Bella was confused as to who to work with.

Cinn reached out and stroked Bella who whimpered and pushed her hand into her nose.

The man stared at Bella and said, "Jesus Christ, did you ruin her too?"

"Is she a killer?"

"No. She was like the other bitch, too soft. They said bitches make the best killers, but we always found they were too soft. Boris, on the other hand, now he's got the making of a killer."

"And what about this poor girl? What did you do to her?"

"We were training her to attack. She could run them down with the best of them," he said in a conversational voice. "But she held back from doing the final kill."

"It's not her nature," Cinn said, her fingers stroking and scratching Bella's neck.

The man sniggered and said, "It's every bitch's nature." He reached an arm around Cinn's neck and pulled her back, choking her.

Bella jump forward and barked.

The attacker glared at her. "Bella, *stand down*."

Bella sat back down again and started to whimper. But her whimper turned to a growl, and then she barked again. Cinn understood. So much confusion, double masters, which way should Bella go?

"You could leave her alone and let her have a decent life," Cinn gasped. She reached up and clawed her attacker's arms. If nothing else, maybe the DNA in her nails would help catch this asshole if he did kill her.

He roared, snapped her head back against the tree and let her go. Then he smacked her on the side of the head and said, "You'll be sorry you did that."

Only Bella, it seemed, had enough evidence to make her decision. But he didn't give her a chance. He reached out and smacked her hard on the side of the head, knocking her to the ground. Cinn could hear Bella crying as she landed, but she bounced back up, growling and howling, this time darting in and darting back out again, avoiding his hands, snapping at his legs.

Cinn's head pounded, throbbing, as she lay here, desperate to move. The only thing she could do was roll. She stretched out and rolled onto the main path, hoping Ethan would see her.

But her attacker stood and lunged at her. Only a huge furry body jumped over Cinn and attacked first.

The man screamed in terror and pain.

Ethan's voice roared over the din at Sentry to stand down. Cinn rolled several more times until she saw Bella snapping at her intruder and Sentry looking for an opportunity to go in for the kill. A kill they couldn't let happen. She lay there trying desperately to stay out of the way.

Ethan stepped up and ordered, "Sentry, down."

Sentry's shoulders hunched, the ridge on his back high and long, his teeth bared, growling as he argued with Ethan's command.

But Ethan straightened, laid a hand on his shoulder and said, "Good dog. We've got him."

And suddenly the man broke and turned to run away.

Ethan took command and said, "Sentry, *attack*."

Sentry took six huge jumps and threw himself eagerly in the air, landing on the man's back, face-planting him into the ground.

Ethan was on him and said, "Sentry, *stand down*."

Sentry glared at him.

And then Ethan reached out a hand, completely ignoring the fact that Sentry was in full attack mode, stroked his head and said, "We've got him. Good dog. We don't kill anymore."

Sentry slowly calmed down. Ethan had him sit at the

man's left arm while he placed Bella at the man's right arm and slowly flipped the man to his back, holding him captive with his knees on his chest.

The man glared up at him. "What did you do to my fucking dogs?"

"Saved their lives, most likely," Ethan said calmly. "Why would you try to change these animals? They're perfect as they are."

"We needed animals that would kill. If they can't do the job, they don't need to be around. Same damn thing for employees. If you can't take that step, you're too damn weak to be with us."

"Yeah? And how many men have you killed because of it?"

The guy glared up at him and said, "Who the fuck knows. We've been doing this for a long time. It's not our problem a lot of assholes are out there."

Cinn managed to get herself into a sitting position and watched the men, now a good fifteen feet away. "That's not an answer," she snapped in a hard voice. She got on her hands and knees and slowly made her way closer.

Sentry, however, was between her and the attacker. He growled as she approached. She stopped and looked at Ethan.

Ethan looked over at Sentry. "Sentry, this is Cinn. You know her. She's a friend."

Sentry gave him a look as if to say, *What the hell?* As Cinn slowly, cautiously inched forward, Sentry subsided and let her approach.

She shook her head at Ethan. "Are you sure he's safe?"

Ethan said, his voice sure, calm, "There are times when having that killer instinct is helpful."

"See?" said the man pinned to the ground. "Like I said, killers are required."

Cinn settled on her butt and looked at Ethan, wondering if he considered killer dogs as a requirement, and then she remembered his military background and what he'd trained the dogs to do. She nodded. "Just remember. We're no longer at war," she said gently.

He stared at her, his gaze hard. Then he slowly seemed to calm, and his hardness eased. He pursed his lips. "You're right, at least not a war like I used to be in."

She nodded and reached out a hand to Sentry, who sniffed and then nudged his nose into her fingers so she could pet him. "Sentry, same for you. There'll always be assholes who we need protection from, but the least amount of force is the best."

At that, voices came from behind them. She turned to see Flynn. She lifted her arm as he dropped down beside her to give her a big hug. "I'm so glad to see you," she said.

Flynn called to Ethan, "Are you okay?"

And Ethan responded, "I'm good."

Flynn rose, lifted her up to stand on her feet so fast that she didn't get a chance to tell him that she couldn't. As soon as her feet hit the ground, she cried out. Pain shot up her legs, into her body and up to her head. It was just too much between the headache, the pain in her feet, her thirst and the shock. She crumpled into his arms.

ETHAN TURNED TO see Cinn as she collapsed in Flynn's arms. But already Levi and several other men raced to her side. The dogs growled and snarled at the new arrivals. It was all Ethan could do to hold them back and to calm them down. He got the leashes on both dogs and got them to sit under order.

Levi said, "It's hard to believe you've known them only a few days."

"Less than two days to be exact," Ethan said with a crooked grin. "We're still getting to know each other."

Levi's eyebrows rose. "I wasn't so sure when we first arrived. Thought we might have a problem on our hands." He motioned toward Sentry. "But it looks like things are under control."

"They are," Ethan said, "but they're still new to being on the good side." He motioned to the man on the ground. "These assholes were training the dogs to kill."

"And did they?"

Ethan didn't really want to admit it. He shrugged and said, "Depends if you can believe what this guy says. But it's possible."

Levi nodded. "We both know dogs in the military that had to do the same thing."

Ethan felt something inside him relax at that because Levi knew. Just like Ethan knew. He nodded his head, his emotions stronger, feeling on firmer ground. "Yes. It's all about discerning when it's necessary."

"Exactly."

Levi turned and frowned at Cinn, held closely in Flynn's arms. He walked over as Ethan approached with the dogs at his side.

Ethan explained, "Her feet have run down to nothing. When Flynn stood her up, it was too much."

Flynn turned so Levi could see the soles of her feet.

Levi winced. "That's just plain hamburger stuck to the

end of her bones." He motioned toward the vehicles. "Let's get her to the hospital, where we can get her treated. Where'd you leave your vehicle?"

Ethan pointed back where he'd come from. "About three miles that direction."

Levi said, "If you want to ride in the back of the truck with the dogs, you're welcome."

Ethan grinned. "That's the perfect place for the three of us."

Together the large crew walked back out of the trees, leading Cinn's attacker to the vehicles.

"We heard gunshots," Ethan said, studying Levi. "How bad is the damage?"

"On our side, none," Levi said cheerfully. "On the other side, three dead."

Cinn's attacker roared and stopped walking to look at them. "What?"

Levi nodded. "If you'd stayed, you would be dead too. Maybe it's too bad you didn't."

But that was enough said. The man fell silent as he contemplated the fate of his friends.

Back at the truck, Ethan got the dogs into the bed, and he sat down against the cab with them. He continuously worked on their commands, letting them know they were still in working mode. Within five minutes they were at the spot where he'd parked his truck, and he transferred the dogs.

Then he got into the driver's side. He needed to take the dogs back home first. He would have to deal with the police and check on Cinn at the hospital.

So first things first, he started up the engine and headed home. He didn't know if it was all over for sure, but he could damn well hope so. He figured this mess was, but there would always be a new one out there to deal with. Still, with the dogs at his side, he wasn't against being part of the fight.

In his driveway, his phone rang. He hopped out of his truck, pulled out his phone and answered it. It was Sergeant Mendelsson.

"I hear you had fun this morning."

"I'm not sure that's what we'd call it," he said, "but the dogs found Cinn, and she's relatively unhurt, so that's what counts."

"How do you think you'll do with their training?"

Ethan wondered if he'd be plagued with those questions from now on, but, in a steady voice, he explained how well both Bella and Sentry had done, how they both needed some training, to work on *fetch, find,* search-and-rescue work, but that Sentry had been called off from taking down and killing the attacker.

"Is this something you want to stick around and work on?" the sergeant asked curiously.

"I'd like to think so," Ethan said. Gunner has asked me to train some dogs for him."

"Well, if he thinks you can do it, then that's a pretty decent referral right there. I spoke with Levi, and he backs up your story. Nice to know you had control of the animals at the scene too."

"I did. Obviously the relationship between the three of us is still young, but it's there. And Bart and Sally are great additions too."

"Good. So are you interested in doing contract work? Because, if you are, get those dogs up and running, then give me a call."

Ethan grinned and gave Bella a good stroke. She

dropped her nose to shove it into his face. "I think we could do something like that. I'll have four able-bodied dogs here pretty soon."

"Then it sounds like you might need another handler."

Ethan shrugged. "If somebody else with the skills comes my way … In the meantime, I can handle four myself."

"Good, we need someone like you," he said, "But it's not just us. Consider the airport, consider private security. I think you've got yourself quite a business right here."

After the sergeant hung up, Ethan pocketed his phone, reached for the tailgate, let the dogs out, led them around to the back, where Bart happily greeted them all. Ethan gave them all food and water and walked inside. He kneeled beside Sally and asked, "How are you doing, girl?"

And his heart smiled as she rolled over and struggled to her feet. He led her a little way outside, so she'd go to the bathroom. She walked over to him afterward and nudged his hand gently. He bent down into a squatting position and spent a few moments just loving her.

"You know what? Maybe that is a good idea. Start with rescuing dogs, then retraining. We could train in many different specialties—drug-sniffing, bomb-smelling, guard dogs. Who knows what else we could do?" he murmured into her fur. "Maybe it's a new beginning for all of us."

Sally barked gently, and the other three dogs ran over. Ethan chuckled. She barked again, nudging at his coat pocket. And he laughed because, of course, he had dog treats in his pocket. Every decent dog trainer had treats. He reached into his pocket and pulled out four and gave them each one. Maybe he was finally home. Just like for the dogs, something was here for all of them.

Now all they had to do was convince Cinn that she belonged with them too.

CHAPTER 14

C INN WOKE UP, lying on the backseat of a twin-cab truck driving at a steady pace. She listened to the conversation going on around her. She couldn't be too badly hurt because nobody was crying over her. But her feet sure hurt.

As she struggled to sit up, Flynn, who was sitting beside her, put a hand on her good arm, telling her to lie back down. She smiled up at him. "Where's Ethan?"

"He's taking the dogs home. I'm sure he'll be at the hospital soon."

She winced at the term *hospital.* "My feet?"

"I suspect so," Flynn said with a bright cheerful smile. "At least if that's what you call them. Levi said they look like hamburger on sticks."

She groaned. "Please tell me that they're not that bad. I'll be bedridden for weeks."

"They're that bad," Levi said from the driver's seat.

Soon the big hospital building rose up in front of them.

Levi parked in front, and Flynn got out. She struggled to sit up and made her way to the edge of the seat. She was not looking forward to getting down. As a matter of fact, just the thought sent waves of nausea to her stomach.

As she tried to stand, Levi arrived at Flynn's side. "No, you don't," he said. "That's what this is for."

They had a wheelchair. Levi reached up, and she put her

good arm around his neck. He scooped her off the seat and plunked her gently onto the chair. Then they did something to the footrests so her legs stuck out straight.

She said, "I don't even know what they'll do for them. They're so dirty." She looked down at herself. "I mean, I was buried in the dirt, so I guess all of me is a huge mess."

"And for that reason alone," a smiling nurse said, greeting them at the doorway, "we may just take you in the wheelchair into a special shower and see what we find underneath all that dirt." The large portly woman smiled down at Cinn. "I hear you've had a rough morning."

"Tough night and a rough morning," Cinn said with a smile. "But this is a much better-looking afternoon."

At that the woman laughed, got behind the wheelchair and pushed Cinn forward. "We'll get some information from you, but we really won't see anything until we get you cleaned up."

"Are you serious about a shower?"

"Can you tell us if you've got any other injuries?"

"My head was bashed in." Cinn thought about it and said, "I don't know how bad they are, but there's some scrapes and bruises. And, of course, a previously treated gunshot wound to my shoulder."

"In that case, yes, just to be sure. You were kidnapped, and you've got a head injury. If the doctor okays it, I think we'll get you cleaned up first, get those feet soaking, and we'll see what else might need to be done."

And that's what they did. It took a good thirty-five minutes though before she was okayed, and the nurse took her into a completely different area of the hospital, pushed open a door to let her into a series of bathrooms with a large wheel-in shower. With the nurse's help, she was undressed and, still in the wheelchair, put into the shower.

There, the nurse helped her shampoo until they could check the head wound. "I feel something running down my face," Cinn said. "Please tell me it's shampoo." She felt so much better just being clean.

"No, it's not," the nurse said. "That's blood from the head wound."

"I was hoping it wasn't that bad."

"They tend to bleed a lot. A couple stitches should put that one to rights, but the cleaner we can get it and everything else, the better it'll be. Otherwise we'll have to cut away a bit of your hair there."

Gently avoiding the head wound as much as she could, she scrubbed down, loving the water streaming down her body. As the nurse noted, several of Cinn's ribs were pretty bruised, but nothing was as bad as her feet.

When she was all cleaned up, she sat with her feet out, letting the water run over them. "I don't think this is getting the soles."

"No," the nurse said. "We'll have to soak them in hot soapy water with antiseptic. Then the doctor can take care of your head."

She was soon on a bed, wearing a hospital gown with a robe over it, sitting up with her feet in a big bucket of warm soapy water with antiseptic. The doctor sat on a stool, poking and prodding at her hairline. Needles went in for numbing, then sutures closed her scalp wound.

Finally the doctor said, "Now let me check the rest of you, see what has happened. The ribs don't appear to be broken. You're banged up. The shoulder wound, … well, it's a little worse but will hold. We can get the feet back in good shape, so you'll be just fine."

She smiled up at him, the fatigue of the day hitting her hard. "Honestly, if I could sleep for a few hours, I think I'd feel a ton better."

"And sleep is what you need. But those feet have to be cleaned up first."

She nodded. "How bad do they look?"

He lifted one up and took a look and then sighed. "Let's just say, you won't like the next hour or so."

She sat bolt upright and said, "Why not?"

"Because soaking has taken off a lot of the dirt, but rocks are embedded in the cuts, and we have to clean out lots of little bits and pieces. I'll put some numbing gel on them, and I'll give you a shot for the pain."

By the time they were done, she was in agony. The tears had flowed, and she lay on her belly, her feet elevated. The nurse finally put a soothing ointment over Cinn's soles. Just her touch made Cinn cry again.

The nurse finally said, "There, you're done."

Her muscles relaxed. She hadn't realized how tense she'd been. She lifted her head and gave the nurse a watery smile. "Thank God for that."

The nurse, obviously distressed at the pain she had put Cinn through, nodded. "It is one of the worst jobs I have to do. I'm so sorry."

Cinn shook her head. "It's not your fault. Thank you for cleaning them up."

As the nurse cleaned up the mess from the medications and the bandaging, she said, "Now you just lie there and rest. Close your eyes. When you wake up, if you're in pain, we'll give you some more medication."

On that note, the nurse walked out. Cinn lay here, wondering what had happened to Flynn and Levi. But then she didn't care because sleep dragged her under, and honestly, it was the only place she wanted to go.

ETHAN WALKED INTO the hospital and headed to the reception area. "Cinnamon Michelson was brought in this morning with damaged feet. If she's still here, may I see her?"

The receptionist nodded. "She was brought in this morning. She's still in emergency, I believe."

Frowning, Ethan made his way over to emergency and was stopped by an orderly. He explained who he was and who he was looking for.

The orderly held up a hand and said, "Now, that little girl needs sleep. Let me go take a look." He turned and peered through a curtain and studied what was probably Cinn on the bed, then he came back. "She's still sleeping."

Ethan nodded. "May I sit beside her then?"

The orderly looked at him and frowned. "Family?"

"No," Ethan admitted. "But maybe soon."

At that, the orderly chuckled. "In that case, you go right in, but don't wake her. Understand?"

Ethan nodded and stepped behind the curtain. One chair was at Cinn's bedside. He pulled it up closer and sat down but not before he took a solid look at her feet. He sucked in his breath at the lacerations and the bloody pulpy look to them. Cleaning the wounds had to have been the worst. Though they would heal, it would take time.

From his chair he reached out, sliding his fingers into hers. He sat here and waited for her to stir.

It was another ten to fifteen minutes before she lifted her eyelids and smiled. "Ethan. How's Sentry? Bella?" she asked, worry tinting her voice. "And Bart? Sally?"

He leaned over, kissed her cheek and said, "Sentry is fine. So are the others. How are you?"

"I'll be looking for a houseboy to keep me off my feet for the next week or two," she said with a chuckle and winced. "Don't think I'll be doing any walking, much less running, anytime soon."

"How's the shoulder?"

"They checked it and said it was healing," she said. "But I'm not sure the doctor wants to see me ever again."

Just then the curtain was pulled back, and the doctor stepped into the room. "I'd love to see you again but without being shot or kidnapped, okay?" He checked her feet. "You can go home, *but* you can't be alone. You're not allowed to stand on these feet at all."

She looked at him. "I have to go to the bathroom on my own."

"No, you don't," he said. "We are talking a wheelchair and lots of padding around these feet. You'll have to shift and shuffle your butt from one to the other. But no walking. You can stand for a short time, but you'll find you don't want to stand at all. If you have no one, we will see about home care visits."

She sank back into the bed. "You know I live alone, right?"

"Not for the next week or two you don't," the doctor said. "I'll write a prescription for the pain meds." He disappeared through the curtain.

She groaned. "I wonder if I can get one of my girlfriends to move in."

"Not an issue," Ethan said. "I'm not a girlfriend, and hardly a houseboy, but maybe you'll classify me as a boyfriend. I'm moving in and looking after you."

She propped herself up on her good elbow. "You don't have to do this because you feel guilty, you know?"

"How about I do this because I want to?" he said, leaning across and kissing her on the tip of her nose. "And I do feel guilty. I was supposed to look after you. And, well, I was dealing with one intruder, while the second guy came in and stole you away. Of course I feel guilty."

She frowned.

He lifted a finger, placing it against her lips. "I'm not arguing with you about it. Bottom line is, you need care, and I can give you care."

"I really don't want to think about you carrying me to the bathroom," she announced in dismay.

"You may not have a choice," he said. "Would you rather it be a stranger?"

She wrinkled up her face and shook her head.

"Good, then no arguments. I'll take care of the paperwork. Then we'll get you moved back home again."

"What about the dogs?"

He turned to look at her. "I was thinking about that. How do you feel about the five of us moving in?"

She laughed. "You know what the neighbors will say?"

"No, I don't know what they'll say, and I don't care what they'll say." He folded his arms over his chest. "Do you?"

She thought about it for a moment and shook her head. "No, I don't. But this isn't an invitation to come into my bed. You know that, right?"

"That invitation has been there right from the beginning, whether you're aware of it or not," he said, leaving her gasping in surprise. "And, when you're feeling better, I'll take you up on it, though not for the next few days. Right now you need care, and I'm the one who'll be there, ready to give you that care." He turned and walked out. He had to because he was laughing so hard.

He stopped, pushed aside the curtain and saw her struggling to sit up. He leaned in, placed a gentle hand on either side of her head and kissed her. When he tried to pull back, he found he couldn't. Instead he pulled her closer into his arms and deepened the kiss, letting her know with absolutely no doubt the direction they were headed. When he finally lifted his head and looked down at her face, he said, "See? Invitation all the way."

He dropped a kiss on her nose, turned and walked out.

CHAPTER 15

A FTER FIVE DAYS at home, she was angrier, more
frustrated and pissed off than she could imagine. Ethan
wouldn't leave her alone. He'd disappear for five minutes,
and he'd be back before she had a chance to move. Like now.
She'd asked him for a glass of water, so she could go to the
bathroom—alone—but he was already standing in front of
her, holding her water. She sat on the edge of her bed and
glared at him.

He shook his head, crossed his arms over his chest and
said, "You can try standing tomorrow. That's what the
doctor said." And with that he spun on his heels and left.

"He didn't say I couldn't try earlier," she cried out.

"Yes, he did. He said to stay off your feet."

"That means stay off my feet *most* of the time," she said
in exasperation. "Nobody in their right mind would expect
me to stay off my feet all the time."

He poked his head around the corner of the doorway.
"Absolutely not. The minute you put more pressure on those
feet, you'll damage the blood vessels, and you'll slow the
healing process. Now get your butt back down and get your
feet up."

She flung her head back on the bed and put her feet
back up on the stack of pillows he had placed there for her.
It was really humiliating. The only way she managed to get

any privacy was by crawling across the floor, getting into the bathroom on her own, using the bathtub for support in order to get to the toilet. She hadn't had a bath or shower in five days, *five days*, and she was dying for one. He had offered but also said he'd carry her there and help her get stripped down. She wasn't having anything to do with that.

But, if she made it to the bathroom, maybe she could make it into the bathtub on her own. Because one thing she did need was a damn good wash. In order to make that happen and to not get in deep trouble, she had to assure herself and him that she could do it without her feet touching the floor.

With a grin, she rolled over to lie on her belly and slid off the edge of the bed to land on her knees. She may have landed a little too heavily because instantly he was back inside her bedroom, checking up on her. She glared at him from her hands-and-knees position and said, "I'll have a bath whether you like it or not." She crawled over to the bathroom, her feet up in the air.

"You could at least ask me to run the water for you," he said, stepping ahead of her. "You don't have to be so stubborn all the time."

He walked into the bathroom, and the dogs followed. At the moment, they had Bella and Sally with them. Plus her two dogs. She was overwhelmed in K9s who all thought it was a great game having her at their level. She laughed and spent a few moments cuddling each one as she heard the water pouring in the bathtub.

She didn't know why she was being so feisty, but it was just impossible to be around him. She didn't even know what the issue was, but she hated feeling like an invalid. And she hated being catered to. He did it with such a happy-go-lucky smiling expression that she wanted to hit him half the time.

When he came back out, she said, "You can't be so nice all the time."

At that comment he squatted in front of her. "Why? You want me to be mean and nasty?"

She shrugged irritably. "You're pissing me off."

"I noticed," he said with a smirk.

She glared at him.

"There's an easy answer to it."

She frowned. "What's that?" she asked suspiciously.

"You're not ready for it yet."

And that did it again. She crawled past, ignoring him. She hadn't really been inviting him to share her bed. Well, maybe she had been, but she would put it down to the pain and the medications. He was too irritating for her to want to spend any more time with.

But inside she knew she was lying to herself. She just didn't want to feel incapable of living the life she wanted to live. It was a temporary situation, and she should stop acting like a spoiled brat and start feeling grateful. It was one thing to know that, but it was another thing to do it.

She maneuvered her way into the bathroom, shooing the dogs out as she tried to work her way past them. She shut the door, turned around and locked it. Feeling immeasurably happier, she twisted around so she sat on the floor and quickly shimmied out of her pajama bottoms. Carefully she pulled the socks off her feet, wincing at the tenderness of them, and stripped off the rest of her clothing.

Ethan knocked on the door and said, "You've got an hour. That's it."

"And then what?" she called out.

"I'm coming in to help because I'll assume you can't get out on your own," he said with a light warning.

She growled and then laughed because it was a fair time frame. It took a little more effort to maneuver herself up to rest on the bathtub edge so she could carefully maneuver herself over and into the water. Awkwardly she splashed down on her butt, her feet hanging off the side of the tub, water coming up and over the sides of the bathtub to the floor on the other side.

It felt so damn good to get into the water, she lay here with her feet dangling for a long moment, just letting her head sink into the gently rocking water.

After a few minutes she sat up and slowly lowered her feet into the water. She knew this would be the real test. Her feet had been cleaned and were definitely healing, but they were still sore and tender. She moaned in delight when they were finally submerged. She should have done this way earlier.

She reached for the shampoo and proceeded to scrub her scalp and then, with soap, scrubbed the rest of her. She tried to examine the soles of her feet, but it was hard to see in this lighting. They looked so much better. There were scabs and definitely tight pink tissue, signs of healing, but they were still puffy.

She knew that standing on them would hurt like crazy. Another couple days and they should be better. The doctor told her it would take about a week, and then she needed to walk with multiple socks on in order to give her feet the cushion they would need. And she'd also find it hard to stay on them for very long. That was all good. She was totally okay to follow *those* doctor's orders. So why was she being so bitchy?

Sure, being an invalid was part of it, but it was also having Ethan around all the time. They were dancing around in this newbie relationship of theirs, but she was in no position to move it forward. She wasn't even sure how to move it forward.

He'd taken on the role of a comfortable brother, almost. And that was very unsexy, going against where she thought they were heading. He was a really good man, she admitted. Too good a man maybe, she thought with a laugh.

But that wasn't true. He never lost his temper, but she could see the darkness in him. The pain. He'd been through some tough times. When he was asleep, she heard him cry out. She never asked him about PTSD, but she was sure that kept him up in the night. He had his secrets, and she had hers, although hers were pretty minor. They were getting to know each other. And she'd only found more to like.

Still, he was doing everything he could to help her get through this, and she appreciated it.

By the time she was done, had the water drained and sat on the bathtub's edge again, she wished she'd had a few more days of recovery time under her belt. She was wrapped up in a towel, but it would be hard to get back to the bed. There was no rush; she still had time before Ethan took over. She was sure he'd heard her get out anyway.

She pulled on pajamas again, and, now fully dressed, a towel wrapped around her head, she pulled another towel down and crawled on top of it back to the bed. It helped preserve her knees a bit.

Before she could get back in the bed, strong hands reached down, picked her up around the waist, and lifted her onto the bed. She let out a cry, not hearing him come up behind her. "You scared me," she scolded.

"Well, if you'd let me know that you could use a hand, then you wouldn't have been surprised," he said, his exasperation coming through his voice.

She flipped around and sat down on the bed, looking up at him. "I'm sorry. I'm being difficult, and I don't mean to be."

His gaze warmed. He sat on the bed beside her and said, "Have you figured out why you are?"

She waved a hand off to the side. "I don't like being an invalid. I don't like being treated like a child or being in a position of needing so much help," she said with a half smirk. "Particularly from you."

His eyebrows shot up. "What's wrong with me?"

She realized he'd taken it as an insult. She tried to get the words out correctly, but every time she tried to formulate her thoughts, she couldn't say them. Finally she raised her hands in frustration and said, "I don't want you to see me as helpless."

He stared at her for a long moment, stroked her cheek and said, "What I see is a valiant, strong woman who survived a terrible ordeal. The ordeal was brought on by me. And I'm doing everything I can to help you get back on your feet."

"I knew it," she cried out. "You feel sorry for me. You feel guilty."

"It's because of me that you're hurt. But, no, I don't feel sorry for you. I'm saddened this happened. But obviously you'll get better, and it's not a permanent injury. So I'm just helping you where I can." He stared at her for a long moment, then tapped the tip of her nose. "Is something else going on here?"

She snapped her lips closed and glared at him.

He nodded. "I'm not sure what's going on. Yet I understand a lot of it," he admitted, "because nobody likes to be treated or thought of as helpless. We all want to be independent."

She sighed and held out her hand. He covered hers with his and squeezed her fingers gently. "What are we doing here?" she asked softly.

His gaze locked on hers, and he smiled a slow, gentle smile that made her heart weep with emotion. "What is it you want to see us do here?"

She shook her head. "Oh, no you don't. You're not answering a question with a question."

He chuckled. "I'd like to get to know you better," he said. "I'd like to see where this goes."

"Are you planning on moving back to your own house?" she asked with a laugh. "Or are you planning on moving in here?"

He tilted his head to the side, his gaze twinkling. "Is the latter an option?"

She chuckled. "I hadn't planned on a house guest. But it is a big house."

"I have a place in town, as you know, but you have acres here for training exercises, plus the dog runs. But I think we're getting ahead of ourselves."

"How long do you think you need to be here looking after me?"

"You go back to the doctor in two days. If he says you can start walking around a little bit, then we'll see how it goes. Plan on maybe four days, and then I'll move back out again," he promised.

She smiled. "That sounds fair. And thank you very much for looking after me."

He shook his head. "Don't say that. I'm happy to do this. You know that." He leaned forward and kissed her gently.

She wrapped her arms around his neck and tugged him closer, turning a light kiss into a real kiss. When he straightened and pulled away, his gaze was searching, and she smiled up at him. "Why do you really think I've been snappy?"

He narrowed his gaze.

She nodded. "It wasn't an invitation," she said, referencing what he had said before, then admitted, "but in a way it was."

He smiled, then kissed her on the tip of her nose. "I know."

She pulled back slightly, changed the angle of their position and kissed him. "I guess we're not quite ready for this stage," she said, "but it would be nice if we were."

His gaze darkened. When he gave her a kiss this time, it took her to the depths of a passion she hadn't expected to see so fast. It left her gasping and surprised, wanting so much more.

When he straightened, she collapsed on the bed, just staring at him.

He grinned. "It depends on you," he said. "I've already expressed my interest."

"Oh, no you haven't," she said in astonishment. "At least not in so many words."

"I'm living in your house, looking after you," he said. "How is that not telling you that I care about you?"

She frowned. "That's just your guilt talking."

He gently picked her up, twisted her so she sat in his lap, tilted her head back and kissed her again. When he lifted his head this time, he said, "Guilt?" And he lowered his head again.

When he finally lifted his head the next time, she had all but melted in his arms. "This is not guilt," he whispered against her lips, his hand brushing her hair back once, then twice. "It's concern. It's caring. It's wanting to make sure somebody I want to spend time with is doing okay. Yes, a smidgen of guilt is in there, but it's more about wanting to spend time with you, making sure you are okay."

She nodded with a smile and said, "But that's not the same thing as wanting to take another step in a relationship. If we're just friends, then let's just stay friends."

He chuckled. "Was that kiss like a kiss between friends?"

"I have no clue," she said, confused herself at this point. She wished he'd just kiss her again and stop the talking.

As he went to put her back on the bed, she shook her head, slung her arm around his neck, grabbed hold and tugged him toward her. "My turn."

This time she kissed him. She hadn't realized how much she'd bottled up inside. This was what she wanted. It was what she'd wanted days ago, maybe longer. She didn't normally accelerate relationships, but no doubt they had something they needed to work through. She didn't know that bed was the best way to do it, but it sure would take some of the stress off. And what she wanted was a whole lot more than stress relief. She wanted to know they had something here they could build on …

He pulled back and looked at her. "It's too soon," he said, his voice thick.

"Why? What do my feet have to do with this?"

"Your shoulder …"

She glanced at her shoulder. "Well, your kisses are so distracting, I didn't even notice," she admitted. "I don't think it will be a problem."

His breathing came out in raspy breaths, and she could feel his heart pounding against her chest—both reassured her. She smiled up at him and whispered, "Unless you don't want to ..."

He lowered his head and crushed his lips against hers. She shifted as the pain shot through her shoulder, but the passion quickly caught her and dragged her back under the surface. And her shoulder ceased to exist. In fact, when she roused from his drugging kisses, she found herself completely nude, lying on the cool sheets, and somehow he was there beside her, almost stripped down. "Wow. You made that happen fast."

He placed a finger against her lips and then replaced it with his own, and she was caught up in the maelstrom of his passion igniting hers and taking her back under until she no longer knew where she started and where he took over. It was an experience like none other. It was more emotion than she was used to. It was less about bodies and more about feelings.

Time flew as they tried to learn everything they could about each other. Conversation came in bits and pieces as they explored and questioned. She found the wounds on his chest, the scars on his back, the damage to his thigh, his stump. He was so adept with his prosthetic that she often forgot he was missing a leg. Every point she reached down to kiss and caress, and then asked him about them.

He finally pulled her up to rest on top of his chest and whispered, "Maybe a little less conversation?"

She smiled, shifted on his chest, drew her knees up to either side of him, and stretched up, resting against his erection. "We can always talk later," she said in a teasing murmur.

"We can also do this again later," he said. "At least I hope we can." He ran his hands over the top of her thighs to her hips, where he held her tight against him and started to shift.

She covered his hands with her own, and, using his hands for strength, rose and fell as she started to ride. She couldn't imagine where any of this had come from. Normally sex was a fast coupling, but this was learning who he was inside, at a level she'd never experienced before. It was special. It was slow. Until it wasn't slow anymore, and suddenly she couldn't talk any longer.

She threw her head back and let the emotions and the passion take over. She moved as her body wanted to move, letting her emotions and her feelings take charge. When he gripped her hips with his hands and picked up the pace, driving into her faster and faster, she matched him thrust for thrust.

Soon her body started to splinter apart; she arched, crying out as her world exploded.

He shifted until she was underneath him, and he drove once, twice, three times, and finally his own orgasm rolled over him. He collapsed beside her and held her close.

It was a long moment later when she whispered, "I've never experienced anything like that."

"What, an orgasm?" he teased.

"No," she said, shifting onto her arm. "Making love where it was okay to talk, where it was okay to ask questions, where it was okay to show emotion. Where it wasn't just following a road map from point A to point B, so you could get there the fastest route." She reached out to stroke a scar on his chest. "That it was okay to take time to explore and to understand, to really learn who you are."

He pulled her head down, so he could kiss her thoroughly. And when he let her go, she sagged against his chest.

"That's very addictive."

"I'm glad to hear it," he said with a soft chuckle. "Maybe we can do this again."

"I sure hope so," she said, a yawn sneaking out of her mouth. "I'm really not into short-term relationships, so I hope you're in for a long one."

He stroked the hair off her forehead and whispered, "Absolutely. That's what I figured we were here for, … for a long time, not just a good time."

"How about both?" she whispered and slowly drifted off to sleep.

HE HELD HER close as she slept, until his phone rang. He shifted her to the side and sat up grabbing his pants. Pulling his phone from his jeans pocket, he answered it. "Jimbo, what's up?"

"Been hearing about you and some K9 dogs. As you know I've been working at the US War Dog Association. I'm not sure if you're setting up training or maybe a rescue, but I've got a female here. Her front leg was damaged from a mine explosion. She's being shipped stateside, but her foster family deal fell through because she has special needs."

They both went silent. Ethan could hear the rustling of papers.

"You might even know this one. Her name is Jessie, for Jezebel."

Ethan caught his breath in the back of his throat. "I saw

her as a puppy."

"Yeah, she's not quite four now. But she won't be work-ing in the field anymore."

Ethan frowned, thinking about the beautiful shepherd she'd been. Small, but she was incredibly fast and very intelligent. "You mean, because she's missing a leg?"

"Yeah, and she's lost her nerve," Jimbo said. "At least that's what the notes here say."

"I'll take her," Ethan said immediately. "I have no clue what kind of business I'll end up with here, but it seems like rescuing working dogs is part of it."

He slowly put his phone on the night table beside him and lay back down. As soon as he was stretched out, Cinn curled up at his side.

"Why do I think this will involve way more dogs than the current four—make that five—now?"

"Because it definitely will." He hugged her close and whispered, "We'll need a bigger place."

She propped up so she could cross her arms on his chest and look down at him. "*We?*"

He reached up, flicked her nose with a smile and whis-pered, "*We.* You, me and all the dogs we could possibly handle."

Tears came to her eyes. She leaned down, brushed a kiss across his chest and whispered, "I'm in."

"I'm in too," he whispered back.

And they kissed, a gentle kiss, full of promise, full of tomorrows and, with any luck, full of K9s they had yet to meet.

CHAPTER 16

WITH CINN SLEEPING gently beside him, Ethan sent a text, updating Badger. Just then his phone rang. He shifted out of bed and hopped out into the hallway, trying not to wake up Cinn.

"Hey, glad to hear you're doing okay. Sounds like it was bit rough though," Badger said. "Good news on K9:01. Are you keeping the name Sentry?"

"I haven't given you all the details yet," he said, laughing. "And yes, I've gone back to calling him Sentry. He's been called Boris for the last while, so it might be hard on him for a bit."

"Maybe, but he'll adapt. And now you've got what, four dogs?"

"Yes, although a fifth is on the way. I've got Sentry and the dogs that came with him and Jezebel is being shipped from the War Dog Association. They are all a mix of both breeds and skills. But still, I can work with them all."

"That should keep your hands full."

Ethan winced, knowing Badger was referring to the other dogs he had said he would find. "In a way, yes," he said. He added more slowly, "And I'm sorry, but I'm not sure I'll go after any of the other dogs."

"Doesn't sound like it," Badger said with a laugh. "And that's all good. We didn't expect that. If it had worked out that way, great, but, considering you just inherited four, five dogs, … and maybe a new girlfriend, … sounds like you are exactly where you belong." There was a pause on the line, then Badger added thoughtfully, "But it would help us if you had any idea who might be interested."

"Talk to Pierce Carlton. Last I heard, he was helping Jager out on a security issue, I think. Pierce has a lot of K9 experience." Ethan paused. "We haven't spoken much about it, but I know he spent five years heavily involved in the DOD's Military Working Dog Breeding Program at Lackland Air Force Base in San Antonio. He was injured, and, while in the hospital, his wife divorced him and somehow took damn near everything he owned. So he's at loose ends, trying to find a new direction. This might not be it, but it could be a step in the right direction for him."

"If you think he'd have any interest in tracking down a dog, that would be huge," Badger said. "I'll call him and see what he says. We've got eleven more dogs to find. And now, buoyed by the success of finding this first one, it would be nice to give positive reports on the others."

"You'll let the commander know about Sentry?"

"Absolutely," Badger said. "Stay in touch, you hear?"

Ethan grinned. "Will do."

PIERCE

The K9 Files, Book 2

Dale Mayer

CHAPTER 1

PIERCE CARLTON TOOK the next exit onto Highway 14, heading to Fort Collins. He wondered what he'd gotten himself into by agreeing to look for Salem, a black female German shepherd who might or might not be missing.

In theory, handlers and dogs weren't supposed to get too attached. Pierce had snorted the first time he'd heard that because how could one not?

Still, this dog was last seen in the community of Arrowhead outside of Fort Collins. Hence Pierce's stop here. If he remembered right, a small café was along this main boulevard that had absolutely the best apple pie you could buy. He pulled up to the café called Marge's. If ever a name could make you think of apple pie, it was a name like that. He went in and smiled. Right in front of him was a large glass case with lots of what looked to be homemade baked desserts.

His stomach growled.

A portly woman walked toward him. "Well, that's a sound I like to hear."

He looked at her in surprise. "Please don't tell me that you can hear my stomach from all the way over there," he joked.

She smiled and nodded. "My ears are trained for that. Come on in and take a seat. We'll get some food in that belly."

But he didn't want to leave the glass case in front of him. "What's the deal with all these treats?"

"Well, they're for sale," she said. "Is that what you mean?"

"Are they fresh-baked? Home-baked? Or brought in from a city somewhere?"

"I bake all my own pies here," she said proudly. "I'm Aunt Marge." She held out a big beefy arm and a rotund muscly hand.

He gave it a good shake and knew she did the baking herself from the strength of those arms alone. "So is there real food too, or do I just eat apple pie for the entire meal?"

"Nope, you're gonna sit down and have a good-size burger and some fries, and then we'll give you a piece of pie to top it off."

He hadn't been terribly hungry when he walked in, but just the sound of that made his mouth water. Obligingly he went to the table she pointed out and sat down. Within seconds he had a hot cup of coffee in front of him.

"What brings you into our town?" she asked.

"What makes you think I'm not a local?" he asked, looking around. "I heard you have the best pies around, but I haven't been here in many years."

"This is a small community. I know every person who lives here. The rest are mostly passing through."

"Well, if they know about all those baked goods under that glass," he said, "I wouldn't be at all surprised if everybody goes out of their way to come here."

She chuckled. "Enough that I make a fine living," she said with a smirk, and she disappeared into the kitchen in the back. He could hear her talking to somebody and wondered if this was a mom-and-pop place. She came back out soon with cutlery and a glass of water. "You never answered my question."

"I'm tracking down a dog," he said.

"Purebred? For breeding?"

Surprised by that line of questioning, he shook his head. "No, she's a War Dog, shipped home with her handler. He had to have multiple surgeries, then ended up in a rehabilitation center and wasn't able to leave. Since he couldn't live on his own, the dog got lost somewhere in all that."

"Pete Lowery," she said abruptly.

Startled, he looked up at her. "Sorry?"

"Are you looking for Pete Lowery's dog, Salem?"

Pierce frowned, pulled out his phone, checked the notes and said, "Yes, I am." He twisted to look at her. "Do you know where the dog is?"

"It attacked somebody," she said, staring at him hard.

He didn't know what she was looking for, but her gaze searched his as if to see which way he would go on the issue. His heart sank. "Seriously?"

She nodded, her face grave. "I'm not sure what happened, but she bit a man in the leg," she said. "She might still be at the police security yard, locked up. There was some talk about putting her down, but I haven't heard the outcome on that."

"Who could I talk to about it?"

"You'll have to speak to the sheriff," she said. "Give him about a half hour, and he'll probably pop in here for coffee and pie." And, with a smirk, she left again.

Pierce slowly stirred his black coffee to help it cool and wondered what would make a dog like that attack someone. Most likely a scenario where the dog was cornered and felt threatened or somebody she cared about was threatened. Pierce frowned, thinking about that until Aunt Marge returned with a heaping plateful of a burger and fries. Curious, he asked, "Do you know the story behind the dog attack?"

"Something to do with Pete's brother, I think," she said. "Ross said two guys were just talking to him, and apparently the shepherd took a dislike to one of them and attacked him."

"Dogs often see a threat we don't quite understand," Pierce said.

"I don't know all the details," she said with a shrug, walking to the counter, returning with mustard and ketchup.

He nodded his thanks, picked up a fry and crunched it. He loved crispy fries. And these were hot and tasty. He dumped ketchup on his plate and plowed through the fries. When he was almost done with them, he picked up the burger and slowly ate the beefy sandwich.

The meal was excellent. He'd come back just for the food. Aunt Marge returned once more, refilled his coffee and his water, but she didn't stop to talk this time. A couple other customers came and went, so the work was steady but not terribly busy. Pierce was about done with his burger, putting the last of it into his mouth, when a sheriff's car drove up. Pierce wondered at the timing. The sheriff was a bit early today apparently. Aunt Marge greeted him as he sat down and poured him a cup of coffee, then pointed at Pierce and said, "He needs to talk to you about Salem."

The sheriff snorted. "If there was ever a dog that deserved a bullet, it's her." He looked straight at Pierce and said, "If you come to collect her, you're too late. Somebody already stole her from the yard."

Aunt Marge gasped. "What? Now who'd do that?"

Pierce studied the sheriff's face. "Any idea who or when?"

"A couple months back," he said. "And, no, we have no clue who. Cut the fence and let her free. Hope they took her out back and put a bullet between her eyes. That's all she's good for."

Aunt Marge nodded in agreement. "So true. Last thing we need around here is dogs attacking innocent people."

Or rather people attacking dogs, Pierce thought to himself. But no use getting into that discussion here and now. Not until he knew the full story. But two things he did know: men attacked others without provocation, and dogs only attacked out of need.

Pierce highly doubted the dog would get an honest hearing with the sheriff though. That man had already made up his mind.

HEDI MILLER STEPPED into the diner, surprised at the odd silence around her. She caught Aunt Marge's gaze, whose face lit up with a beaming smile.

"There you are," she said, rushing toward her, arms open.

Her hug felt a little too effusive, her eagerness a little too grateful for her sudden arrival. Only it wasn't a sudden arrival. She'd been following the sheriff for the last ten minutes down the highway. But, when she pulled in just after him, she stopped to write down her notes. She was in a tough position. She was a deputy and loved her job, but the sheriff was getting harder to work with each and every day.

She walked to the counter and sat down on one of the stools.

"What can I get you, Hedi?" Marge asked, rushing behind the counter.

"How about a piece of that apple pie?" Hedi said with a grin. "If it wasn't for those fresh-baked pies, I don't know how often I'd make the trip."

"A lot of other good stuff is here too," the sheriff called out behind her. "And, if you weren't so uppity, you could sit at my table."

Her shoulders stiffened at his comment. Anybody else would have just let her sit wherever she wanted. But the sheriff was all about control, all about being the dominant alpha. Guess he hadn't read the most recent research that said there really was no alpha male in a pack. Still, the sheriff wouldn't share the leadership anyway. It was all about being the *one.*

She turned and glanced at him. "I was just going to have a piece of pie," she said quietly, "and then head on back to the Johanson place."

"What's going on there?" he asked. "Is there something you haven't told me?"

She shook her head. "No." She spoke in the same quiet tone. "No, I've told you lots. Same damn shit day after day."

"Well, you can't put too much worth into what that wife of his says."

"This time the kids were calling," she snapped, and she heard Aunt Marge's hard gasp. She turned to look at her. "Aunt Marge, you know what situation those kids are living in?"

Marge's eyes filled with tears, and she nodded.

"And you also know there's very little I can do about it,"

Hedi added softly.

Behind her the sheriff just snorted. "Nothing's wrong with Jed," he said. "He likes the bottle a bit too much. If he'd knock that off, it would all be fine."

"But the fact of the matter is, he doesn't knock it off," Hedi said. "And it's getting to the point that he'll do something serious that none of us can walk back from."

The sheriff waved his hand in a dismissive manner, as if to knock her nose back where it belonged. She just glared at him.

A sound on the other side of the café had her turning to see a stranger stand up. Aunt Marge rushed toward him. "Oh my, I forgot to give you the pie."

"No," he said, "you gave it to me. It's just my plate is so clean, you can't tell what I had." He picked it up and handed it to her.

Hedi watched, her gaze locked on the stranger. "Sorry, we're not usually so public with our dirty laundry."

He nodded his head but stayed quiet. He picked up his backpack, walked up to the till and dropped a twenty-dollar bill on the counter. Aunt Marge gave him change, but he just waved his hand and said, "Keep it. It was the best burger I've had in a long time." He turned to look at the apple pie in front of Hedi and smiled. "I have to admit it was pretty darn good apple pie too."

"Aunt Marge is a hell of a cook," Hedi said with a big smile. "She's got a big heart to match too."

He chuckled. "I can see that." He walked out the door, letting it slam behind him.

Behind her she heard the sheriff say, "Arrogant asshole."

"What did he do?" Hedi asked curiously.

"He was asking about the dog that escaped from the

fenced lot," the sheriff said.

She stilled, searching his face. "Why?"

"He's looking for it," Aunt Marge said hurriedly. "He didn't like that it had escaped."

"Was released, kidnapped, stolen," the sheriff snapped. "We didn't lose it, and it didn't escape. Somebody stole it, and good riddance."

Hedi glanced at Aunt Marge.

She just shrugged in a philosophical way. "I can't say I'm sorry she's gone. Obviously the dog was dangerous."

Hedi didn't say a word; she just inclined her head. She picked up a bite of apple pie and popped it in her mouth. Eating was a great excuse for not talking. She polished off her pie and then rose, throwing back the rest of her coffee. She walked to the register and left a five-dollar bill. "Thanks, Aunt Marge, as always." And, without saying another word to the sheriff, she headed for the door.

On the way out, she heard the sheriff sniff. "Damn women," he muttered.

Aunt Marge hushed him. "You know she can hear you."

"I don't give a damn if she does or not," he snapped. "We shouldn't have women deputies. You know that."

"Hey, times are changing," Aunt Marge said. "Girls have better opportunities now than just running little restaurants and baking pies."

"That's where they belong. You do what you do, and you're the best at it," he said in admiration. "And I do what I do because I'm the best at it."

"But that doesn't mean she can't be a good deputy," Aunt Marge argued. "You know she's always there for whoever needs her. She's the most conscientious of any of your deputies."

"Only because she's a woman," he said. "That's what makes her conscientious. It's a genetic thing. She should be staying home and raising babies. But she hasn't even got a damn boyfriend anymore."

Hedi stood on the front step and heard the sheriff push his chair back. She moved toward her car so he wouldn't know she had been listening. On the way she saw the stranger sitting in a big truck, the cab door open.

She walked to him. "What's this about you looking for Salem?"

At the sound of her voice he turned to study her. His eyes were a deep dark chocolate color with thick eyelashes. His face was lean and tanned, as if he worked outside.

"Is there a reason why you're looking for her?" she asked again.

"Are you asking professionally?"

"Deputy Hedi Miller, and…" She frowned at that answer. "Should I be?"

He gave a negligent shrug. "A friend is worried about the dog. I was asked to come and track it down. She was a War Dog and deserves a hell of a lot better than being locked up in a fenced yard for somebody to steal."

Inside, she felt her heart beat a bit harder. "So are you here for the dog or against the dog?"

He pushed the door open wider and twisted in his seat so he could look at her. "I'm here to save the dog."

Perfect. She gave him a smile. "In that case maybe we should talk."

He glanced back at the restaurant. "Not now. We got company."

She didn't turn around but knew it was the sheriff. "Exactly. If you give me your number, I can give you a shout later, give you the details from the case."

"We're not handing out no information no how," the sheriff said.

Hedi just smiled. "It's public knowledge. We picked up the dog. He could ask anybody, but he might as well get the truth from us."

"Don't you have something to do? Go chasing after those kids who are always whining." He got into his vehicle, turned on the engine and reversed out of the parking lot, taking off down the highway, back to his office. His tires spit out rocks behind him.

She turned toward the man, still sitting in the truck. "He's not quite as bad as he looks."

"I've met lots like him," the man said, his voice hard. "And they're a hell of a lot worse than they look."

CHAPTER 2

HEDI WINCED AT that because really the sheriff *was* worse than that. She was just trying to make light of his behavior. "Look. I don't know what happened to the dog, but she went missing about two and a half months ago. I came in one morning, and the wire had been cut. The dog was long gone."

"So somebody helped her get out of there, huh?"

She nodded but kept her face neutral. "It appears that way."

"I understand Salem bit someone."

She shoved her hands in her pockets and rocked on her heels. "Yes, she did. And, if there was a man who deserved it more, I haven't seen him."

A funny light filled the stranger's gaze. "That's what I would have expected," he said. "It's not the dog's fault then, is it?"

"In this case, I don't think it was the dog's fault," she admitted. "But you won't get anybody else to agree."

"What about Ross, Pete's brother?"

"You're free to go talk to him," she said. "It doesn't mean he'll be sober enough to give you any lucid answers though."

"How about you give me a map of how to get there."

She walked to her cruiser, pulled out a notepad she always kept close by, and he hopped out of his truck. When the door slammed, she turned to look at him. "We're here," she explained as she drew the directions. "You go up to the second set of lights down that road, take a left, another left and a right. "There's a ten-acre piece of property, no dogs, at least not now, and you'll find them there."

"Both of them?"

She shook her head. "I didn't mean Pete. I meant his brother, Ross. From what I heard, Pete is not likely coming home." She stopped writing and looked at him. "I could use some ID."

He raised an eyebrow, reached into his back pocket and pulled out his wallet, showing her his driver's license.

"*Pierce Carlton*." She nodded. "Welcome to the county, Pierce. Just remember. The sheriff doesn't like dogs. Most people around here don't like dogs that attack."

"Nobody does." His voice was calm, neutral. "But I train dogs to attack. When it's the right time, they often save your life."

"You're a dog trainer?" She frowned. "You don't look like it."

"I'm a navy veteran," he said quietly. "Trained dogs for years. Been at loose ends lately. Somebody asked me to stop by and check on Salem and make sure she was okay and in a good home."

"She was but not for very long," Hedi said simply. She reached out and shook his hand. "I'm Hedi. Here's my card. If you run into any trouble, give me a shout. Better you call me than the sheriff. He'd just as soon lock you up as not. If you're not from around here, and you're causing trouble, he'll call you a vagabond and toss you in jail for the night."

"Nice county you got here."

As she walked back to the driver's side of her vehicle, she flashed a grin his way. "It used to be. Hasn't been for a few years now."

"When did it used to be?" He studied her with an intense gaze.

"When my dad was the sheriff," she said with a wistful smile. She got back into her cruiser, turned on the engine and headed down the road. She had more than enough trouble up ahead of her to stay here and brew some more.

If Jed had found that damn bottle again, those kids would be in more danger. The last thing she wanted to do was shoot their father in front of them, but she wouldn't let him hurt those kids anymore, not while she was there and able to stop it.

In her rearview mirror she could see the dust as the black truck turned off the highway and followed her. She realized he would be behind her for at least ten or fifteen minutes because the two properties, although not side by side, were well within walking distance of each other. When she got to his destination, she honked her horn, and, with her arm out the window, pointed where he needed to go, and then she sped on past. Gratified, she watched as he slowed and turned into the driveway. She hoped, really hoped Ross would be sober and could talk today.

Somehow she doubted it. Ross was nothing if not consistent. And this whole area had a problem with alcoholics. A lot of jobs used to be in town, mostly attributed to the mill until it closed. Then things got pretty ugly a few years back, savings ran out, odd jobs were taken up. Now most people lived hand-to-mouth, and it made them an ugly bunch.

What she never understood was how they still found money for booze. And it wasn't just Jed and Ross. Two other men, twin brothers, Billy and Bobby, were not only drunks but she suspected they were making moonshine in the back of their property. She wouldn't put it past them. It was the cheapest way to get alcohol, and they didn't seem to care if they drank one hundred proof either. Their guts would rot from the inside out, but again she didn't think they gave a damn.

She drove up to the front step of Jed Johanson's place and parked. Even as she opened the door to her cruiser, she could hear kids crying inside. She hopped out, walked up the steps of the house, rapped hard and then shoved the door open. It looked like she was just in time.

With a sigh she opened her arms, and two of the little kids raced toward her. All in a day's work in this job, damn it.

PIERCE PARKED BESIDE a battered old truck. What he saw was a run-down farm with an oversize barn and an open workshop/machine shop with several other unidentified outbuildings dotting the same area. An old tractor was parked outside on the left, and an even older car was parked on the right.

With his gaze sweeping the area, not hearing the sound of a dog or seeing signs of any other animal, Pierce slowly strode up to the front door, where he stopped and listened. There was no sound of anything anywhere. He reached up and rapped a knuckle. A startled sound came from inside, as if a chair had slammed down onto all fours. He waited a few seconds until the door was opened abruptly. He studied the swollen red nose and red eyes. "Ross, by any chance?"

"Who's asking?" the man asked belligerently.

"A friend of Salem's," he said calmly.

The man just blinked at him and then blinked again. "Who?"

"The dog you got rid of," he said.

"That bitch," he snarled. "Damn near bit me several times. And she did bite someone else. The brother of a friend of mine."

Pierce couldn't help but cheer the dog on. "Well, were you going to kick it or hit it with something?" Pierce asked. "They do tend to attack when provoked."

"I didn't do nothing to her," he growled. "She always had a chip on her shoulder."

"She loved Pete very much," Pierce said, keeping his voice even. "Obviously it was hard for her when he went into the center."

"Maybe. Doesn't mean she had to take it out on me." He glared. "The dog is not here, so what the hell do you want with me?"

"I was wondering if you knew what happened to her," Pierce asked.

Ross shook his head, spittle flying from the corner of his mouth as he did so. "Nope. After she bit Chester, the cops came, took the dog away and kept her in the fenced lot. Last I heard, some crazy cut the fence and let the dog out. I hope the dog bit him in the ass for that."

"Interesting," Pierce said. "And you have no idea who would have loved the dog enough to have saved it?"

"There was nothing lovable about that dog," he snarled. "She ate me out of house and home. Didn't do nothing. We had an intruder in here, stole all kinds of dog shit, and she didn't do nothing."

"Sorry, what was that?" Pierce asked in confusion. "You're saying somebody came in here and stole the dog's stuff? Like what stuff?"

"Dog bed, leashes, harness, blankets, that kind of stuff."

"Are you sure Pete didn't send somebody to collect the dog stuff, hoping maybe he could find somebody to take the dog?"

"Don't know nothing about that." He tried to lean against the doorjamb, only missed and fell against the wall. He quickly straightened himself so he leaned properly. "And Pete didn't say nothing to me about it." He looked around the room with a frown on his face. "All I know is it was stolen."

After saying that, Ross gave Pierce a sideways glance, confirming something Pierce had already suspected. "So what were you doing with the dog that she wasn't here that day the intruder came?"

He shrugged. "Don't know what you're talking about."

"No, of course you don't," he said. "What's the chance you were out hunting and decided, when the dog was taken by the sheriff, to just ditch the rest of the dog stuff? Not like you were taking Salem back in again, were you?"

Ross straightened. "No way I would. But I got a gun. I can shoot my own damn deer. She was useless."

"Maybe, but a dog can certainly flush them out of cover so you can shoot them, can't they?"

At that, Ross had the grace to look ashamed. He looked around and said, "A man's got to eat. Times are tough around here."

"Well, you'll starve now without the dog, won't you?"

"I got a job coming up," he said. "I'll be just fine."

"Too bad the dog isn't though." Pierce stepped back,

turned to look around and said, "Is any of the dog's stuff still here?"

He shook his head. "No. Whoever it was took everything. Every last bit of it."

"Okay. Thanks for your help." Pierce walked back to his truck.

The guy stepped onto the front step and called out, "Hey, what do you want the dog for anyways?"

"She's a very expensive, well-trained dog," Pierce said. "I would have bought her off of ya, giving you some good money for her. But, of course, since you let the cops take her away, and then somebody stole her, I guess I can't do that, can I?" He started up the engine and reversed out of the guy's yard, leaving him standing there openmouthed, as if he'd just lost a gold mine.

If it had come to that, Pierce would have paid to have the dog returned to a life she was better suited to. This place would have just been terrible for her. War Dogs weren't allowed to hunt animals, unless they were the two-legged variety. At least not the dogs he trained. It wasn't fair to the deer, and it sure as hell wasn't fair to the dog.

Back out on the highway, Pierce took the same road where the deputy had gone. He wasn't sure exactly what was going on, but he'd heard enough to realize it was ugly. But the useless sheriff, of course, wouldn't help.

Seeing her car parked up at the neighbors, he pulled in behind it and hopped out. So much caterwauling was going on in the house that he didn't think anybody would have heard his arrival.

As he stepped up to the front doorstep and knocked, he was correct. Kids were screaming, and Deputy Hedi stood nose to nose with a man holding a rifle in his hand.

She yelled at him, "Jed, put that gun down!"

"You ain't taking my goddamn kids," he roared, waving the gun around.

He wasn't pointing it at her, which was a good thing. Pierce looked around to see four little kids of various sizes—one in diapers and barely standing on his own two feet; two little girls who looked to be twins with tears in their eyes, hanging on to Hedi's pant legs. The other little girl, slightly older than the rest, stood off to the side, watching.

But it wasn't shock on the eldest kid's face. Pierce knew what was coming. He'd seen it before. He just didn't know how to stop it.

Just then Jed shoved the deputy back. "Hedi, I told you to get the hell out of here. My kids are just fine." This time he did raise the weapon, and he pointed at her. Even worse, he poked her in her chest with it. "Now you just get the hell off my property."

She was spitting mad, Pierce could see that, but she also didn't want to pull her gun and get into a gunfight that no one would win.

Pierce, on the other hand, didn't have any such qualms. He took two steps inside. Just as the man realized somebody else was in the game, he turned to face the new threat. … Pierce had already pulled the rifle free of Jed's hands and slapped the butt hard across Jed's face, knocking him to the ground.

As the man struggled to turn around to see what the hell happened, Pierce pointed the rifle down at him and said, "Go ahead and move."

The ice in Pierce's voice had Jed falling back, so he was lying flat on the floor, staring up at him.

Hedi walked over and said, "Give me the gun please."

Her voice was calm but hard.

Pierce assessed her, then nodded and handed over the rifle, speaking to her but for Jed's benefit as well. "Nobody ever points a gun at a woman or uses it to push a woman backward or threatens her with it in my presence. Especially a woman in uniform, disrespecting both the woman and the office she holds." His tone was equally hard, even as he lowered his voice. "Never, ever in my presence."

She studied him for a long moment, then nodded. She opened the rifle, pulled out the two cartridges, disarming it, and placed it on the table. She pocketed the shells.

In the meantime, Jed was lying there, rubbing his hand on his head, complaining about a headache. He didn't appear to realize he had pulled a weapon on an officer. Or, if he did, he didn't give a damn.

Hedi dropped to her knees and wrapped her arms around the kids.

Pierce took in the scene, and his heart melted. He reached down and belted Jed with his boot. "What kind of a man are you that you reduced your kids to this?" he snapped.

Jed just looked at him with hate in his eyes, but then his gaze fell on his kids bawling all around Hedi.

Pierce could see the sorrow and self-condemnation in the man's eyes. He wasn't just an asshole; he was somebody on a downward spiral. Pierce stepped past and walked to the front door. Sure enough, nearby was a gun cabinet full of weapons. He whistled and spoke over his shoulder. "Hedi, does he have licenses for all of these?"

"Not likely," she said. "I've taken them away in the past, but the sheriff just hands them right back."

He turned to stare at her.

She shrugged. "It won't stop until something really ugly

happens," she said in a low voice.

"Where's the mother?"

"She works at a Laundromat in town," she said. "She'll be home in time to cook dinner. But he's supposed to be looking after these young ones."

"Yeah, right. Find upstanding citizen you got here." He walked back over and crouched beside Jed, who still lay on the ground. "So have you done anything decent for your family in the last couple years?"

Jed looked at him warily. "Who are you?"

"It doesn't matter who I am," Pierce said. "What I will be is your biggest nightmare for the next couple days until I find Salem."

Confusion clouded Jed's gaze. "Salem?"

"Yeah. The best damn dog anybody ever had that apparently this town has done nothing but treat like a piece of shit."

Something flit into Jed's gaze and had him shifting his eyes to the side.

Pierce studied him for a long moment, stood and turned toward Hedi. "I think the dog is here," he said. "I want to take a look."

"Not without his permission," Hedi said firmly. "And he ain't giving it."

He glanced down at Jed, who sneered up at him. Pierce dropped to the ground and grabbed Jed's wrist with his free hand. "You right-handed?"

Fear flared in Jed's gaze. He tried to pull away his hand, but Pierce just crunched his fingers together.

"I want to see if you got my dog," he snapped. And kept squeezing.

"She isn't here. She isn't here," he cried out. "And it

ain't your dog."

"She is now," Pierce said. "Somebody has got to give a damn about her. And, if that ain't you guys, it sure as hell is me."

CHAPTER 3

HEDI STUDIED THE man with the vicelike grip on Jed's hand, watching the hard coldness in his eyes and the panicked look on Jed's face. She stepped closer. "Hey, you need to back down."

Pierce turned slowly to look at her. "Hell no. Jed's a bully, picking on kids, and only understands one thing, and that's dominance."

Even as she watched, he tightened his hand around Jed's fingers and listened to him scream.

Urgently she rushed to his side. "But not in front of the children."

Pierce looked at the children and smiled. "Hey guys, have you seen a big dog around here?"

The oldest one nodded. "Daddy had it for a while. But it took off."

As Hedi watched, Pierce eased up the pressure on Jed's fingers, helping Jed to sit up, but kept a grip on his shoulder where he knew he could render him unconscious if need be. "Any idea where the dog went?"

The little girl shook her head slowly. "He just wasn't here one day."

"*He?*" Pierce asked. "Do you know if it was a boy or a girl dog?"

She smiled, showing the beautiful young woman in her,

if she ever had a life without fear.

"It was a girl dog," she said proudly, as if that was an association she could be a part of. "She was a nice dog too."

"Do you know why she took off?"

Her gaze slid toward her father and then back again, but she didn't say a word. Pierce gripped Jed's collarbone harder and in a low tone said, "I'll owe you for that too then, won't I? You're stacking up reasons for me to teach you a hard lesson."

Jed started blubbering.

"Go easy," Hedi said, with a motion at the children.

Pierce locked gazes with Hedi. "Is there anything you can do about this guy to keep him from scaring the kids?"

"It's hard to do if the sheriff won't back me up," she said in low tone.

Pierce nodded.

"He beats them," she said in a low voice. "Not just his kids but also his wife."

"And he also pointed an armed weapon at you," Pierce said. "In no man's law is that allowed."

"I've tried to pull him in for that before too," she said, "and the sheriff just lets him go."

"And the population around here put that sheriff in power?"

At that, she fell silent.

He looked down at Jed. "Pretty sure you voted for him, didn't you?"

"I'm sure he did," Hedi said with feeling.

Jed just glared at them.

As if not liking the look in Jed's eye—and who would, considering he looked feral—Pierce clamped down even tighter on the muscles behind Jed's collarbone, with Jed screaming like a little girl. Pierce leaned down and whispered in Jed's ear, "I've decided that I'll be around for a long time. If I even hear you have hurt these kids or their mother or even threatened to hurt them, I'll come back and pay you a visit in the dark of night." His voice was soft and deadly. "And you don't even want to think about what I'll do to you if you ever pull a gun on Hedi again."

Fear lit up Jed's eyes as he stared into the cold darkness of Pierce's. And that was one scary gaze. Hedi was stunned. She didn't know who or where Pierce had come from but, not only was this guy completely dominating Jed, Pierce was worried about the condition of the children and herself, even the absent mother. More than that was the fact that Jed was terrified of this man. And that was something she could get behind.

"Kids, can you show me where you last saw the dog?" Hedi tried to move them away from the obvious power play.

The oldest girl walked toward the door, calling to her brother and sisters. The four of them ran outside.

Outside Hedi stopped for a second and took several deep breaths. Every time she came here she knew she was taking her life in her hands. At some point, Jed would go over the line, and she would pay the price. She'd thought for sure it was today. That look in his eyes was just blood-spitting mad.

As she stood here, a little hand slipped into hers. She looked down to see Molly, her eyes still nervous as she crept close and hung on to Hedi's leg. "Is Daddy feeling better now?"

"I think Daddy will feel much better for quite a while," she said. At least she hoped so. As long as he believed Pierce's threat, Jed would behave himself, at least for a bit.

She'd tried to get their mom to leave him, but Jed was

just as much of a threat to her if she lived with him or not. In fact, he threatened to do away with her and take the kids and go visit his grandpappy somewhere in the north country. She didn't even know what that meant, but, as a threat, it was pretty effective.

Molly stepped up onto the porch again to be with her. She leaned up and said, "Do you know that man?"

"No, not particularly," Hedi said. "Why?"

Molly looked back toward the door, where the two men were still in their line of vision. "My dad is scared of him."

"Is that good or bad?" Hedi asked curiously.

"It's good," Molly said, and then she darted toward the barn. "The dog was here."

"Do you know when she came here? Or how she got here?"

"Daddy just said he would keep her for a while. She'd be good for getting meat."

Hedi nodded slowly. "You know that's not a good way to hunt animals, right?"

"There's no good way to hunt animals," Molly said. "But Daddy says we have to have meat, that he doesn't have any money and that we need to eat somehow."

"True enough," Hedi said. "Come on. Show me where she was kept."

She followed the kids toward the barn, hoping it was okay to leave Pierce and Jed alone. Maybe without any women around to see his humiliation, Jed would show a little more fire so Pierce could punch it out of him. She was all about Pierce dominating this drunken excuse for a father and a husband. The problem was, the next time he got a hold of a bottle, Jed would be pretty damn ugly. And, if he remembered this, it would just be a meaner version of pretty damn ugly.

At the barn, the kids led her to a couple dog runs. They were all empty at the moment but large enough to have kept something Salem-size.

"Do you know how long ago the dog disappeared?"

They just shrugged. Time had very little meaning for kids. But it sounded like Jed had had the dog since the dog supposedly escaped from the police yard up until Salem ran away. Which meant that either Ross or Jed was responsible for cutting the fence and letting her out. And that was interesting in itself. Then again the sheriff might have done so himself to get rid of the dog.

"Has your dad had any other dogs?"

The kids shook their heads.

"Has he ever kept any people in the barn?" She didn't know why, but she'd had to ask that question. After all, if Jed abused his wife and four kids, then abused Salem, what's to stop him from branching out, like into human trafficking? That downward spiral Jed was in could lead to all kinds of criminal activity.

The kids shook their heads again.

Hearing their answers, sheer relief washed through her. She still didn't know if Jed was evil through and through or if he was just a misguided soul who had fallen down a deep, dark well of abuse and addiction and was taking out his ills on those he should have loved the most, on those who could have loved him the most. He still had no excuse for abusing his family, then Salem.

Hedi looked around the area. "Looks like the dog would have been quite comfortable here."

"It was nice to see her," Molly said. "I didn't like the way Daddy treated her, and she didn't like Daddy at all."

"I'm sure she didn't," Hedi said.

"Is that man taking the dog away?"

"I think so," Hedi said. "I don't know who she legally belongs to, but I think he has some kind of a claim to her."

"I hope he does then. I liked the dog. I don't want anything to happen to her."

Hedi smiled at the little girl and picked her up, hating that she was out here stumbling around in bare feet. But then, as she looked at the other kids, she saw they were barefoot too. "I should have had you put your shoes on before I brought you outside," Hedi said sorrowfully. "Your feet will get all scratched up."

Molly looked at her in surprise. "Our shoes are only for going to town and for school. We're not allowed to ruin them out here."

"Ah, you only have one pair of shoes each?" she asked.

"Yes," Molly said. "Daddy said we don't have any money."

"No, I imagine it's tough times right now."

Hedi led the way back to the house, an anger burning deep inside. Although it might be tough times, these kids had no shoes, and that asshole of a father had money for booze. And that dropped her back to thinking whether they made moonshine in the proverbial back forty.

She thought they had twenty-acres out here, but it was woodland acres. You couldn't grow anything without bringing in truckloads of good dirt. So all kinds of stuff went on in these back corners that the sheriff's office or the police department never had a chance to see.

As she walked toward the front door, she could hear the two men talking. Jed now stood on his feet, and Pierce faced him, apparently reading him the riot act. But Jed's head was hunkered down, his shoulders were slanted in, and he leaned forward, taking the verbal beating Pierce dished out.

She stopped the kids from going in because she was just too damn happy to see this and didn't want to interrupt Pierce.

When Pierce fell silent, he turned and looked at her through the screen door. He motioned for her to come in. She pulled the door open and stepped in the house, putting Molly on the floor. "Jed, you need to get these kids a second pair of shoes or boots to wear outside."

He lifted his tired gaze and stared at her. "There ain't no money for shoes."

"I heard Jacky down at the gas station was looking for a hand."

Jed's lip curled.

She held up a finger and pointed it at him. "Don't you let your pride get the better of you," she snapped. "A job is a job."

"He won't pay enough to put food on my table."

"He's paying more than doing nothing but sitting here and drinking booze that could have paid for shoes." She studied his gaze to confirm her suspicions. She stepped closer. "Unless you're making it yourself out in the back illegally."

He just raised his eyebrows and stared her down. "We ain't doing nothing like that," he said stoutly.

"Right," she snapped. "Like I believe you."

He gave her an almost injured look, as if to say he was the most innocent man in the world. But no man who beat his wife and kids and a dog was innocent.

She turned to walk back to the front door, then paused and looked at Jed. "Whether Pierce is here or not, the next time you point a gun at me, you better be prepared to shoot it because I'll fire first." And she walked out, letting the door snap closed behind her.

When she heard it open again, she knew it was Pierce. She walked to her cruiser and got in. She didn't give him a chance to speak. She slammed the door shut, turned on the engine and backed out, deliberately avoiding his gaze.

She didn't know why she was being difficult. Part of it was because he'd done something she couldn't do. It was something she was supposed to do as a deputy, but some things the badge just wouldn't change. Jed would never listen to a woman.

And she headed off down the road.

PIERCE WAS IN the truck and on her tail almost immediately. He couldn't get anything else from Jed about where the dog was. The kids had spent a few minutes telling him the dog just disappeared not too long ago. But Pierce knew something was going on when he watched Hedi, the lovely deputy, get in her car and take off. He figured she was either heading back to talk to the sheriff about whatever it was or, better yet, she'd ponder over it a bit herself.

Now he had something to wonder about. It had damn-near broken his frozen solid heart when he saw Jed lift that rifle and point, and then slam it directly against her shoulder. When he found out the damn thing had been fully loaded, he was beyond furious. But she'd stared down Jed, calm and collected as could be. Pierce had seen the fine shimmer of sweat on her forehead and knew she understood just how close she'd come to getting shot today.

Was that what her life was like? Dealing with these kinds of assholes? He remembered the sheriff had just brushed it off, saying Jed was harmless. But nobody who tried to shoot a deputy or even threatened a deputy was harmless.

From the looks of it, the kids were not so much abused as neglected. Then again, some beatings were done where the damage couldn't be seen. Hedi had said Jed was hitting the kids, and Pierce trusted her. Now he had to do something about it. And about protecting the wife too.

But he was here to first follow up on Salem's fate. He wasn't too happy with what he had heard. It sounded like she'd been mistreated for a long time and had done her best to get away from her abusers, like any other animal, human or four-legged.

Up ahead he watched as the deputy pulled off on the shoulder and shut off the engine. He pulled in behind her and hopped out. She didn't get out but sat in the car, having rolled down her window.

"Are you following me?" she asked bluntly.

He grinned. "No, it's the only way back, the direction we came in."

She nodded. "It is. But you don't have to be quite so close. I'm fine, you know?"

He studied her intently for a long moment. "You shouldn't be," he said just as bluntly. "You could have died today."

"It's part of the job." There was a note of fatigue in her voice. "I'm the only one who will talk to Jed."

"None of the other deputies will? Are they men?"

She nodded. "That's one of the sheriff's big beefs. There shouldn't be women deputies. We're all supposed to sit at home and bake apple pies," she snapped, repeating the sheriff's earlier words. "It doesn't matter that female deputies are found the world over. As far as he's concerned, in *his* county, that ain't happening."

Pierce nodded. "It doesn't mean he's right, just means he's an asshole and a sexist. The thing is, guys should go out there, and they should give Jed a good shakedown every time he pulls shit like that. What happens if you tell the sheriff what happened today?"

"He'll say I handled it wrong, and what did I expect? How I couldn't possibly understand what it was like to lose my livelihood and be dependent on a wife." Her tone was dry, but she said it almost in a routine way, as if she'd said it time and time again. Then she had.

"Your sheriff really doesn't like you, does he?"

"He doesn't like very many people," she said. "The fact that I am his deputy is just adding insult to it."

"Then he's an idiot." Pierce's tone was hard. "He needs to move into the new age."

"Maybe," she said, staring out at the countryside around them. "But, just because you and I say so, won't make it happen." She glanced back up at Pierce.

He had to agree. "What do you know about the dog?" he asked.

"Why do you care so much about her?" she countered.

He hesitated, wondering how much he could tell her. Then he realized, no longer being in the military, this wasn't a secret mission. He squatted in front of her door, and she opened it to see him better.

"Salem was a War Dog. She spent a lot of time training. She saved lives in Afghanistan," he said. "We send the War Dogs home with their handlers for a better life. She'd been injured and had a terrible time recovering. Pete was also injured, as you know. Then she lost Pete. Even though he's still alive and fighting the good fight, he can't do it with her at his side. As a general rule, War Dogs are well taken care of, but somehow Salem fell through the cracks. We're not supposed to get attached to our dogs while we're over there, but it's unavoidable. I certainly loved mine, and I know most of the handlers loved theirs. In this case, I was asked to track down Salem when somebody in the division realized Pete couldn't possibly be looking after Salem. She should have been handed to another person capable of looking after her."

Hedi frowned at him. "Seriously, you're from the government?"

"I'm here on the behest of a commander from that department in the military," he said, "but the job came through Titanium Corp, which is a group of former military SEALs now trying to help people like me, and, in this case, dogs like Salem, find a new and better life."

She latched on to what he had accidently slipped out. "Like you?"

He shrugged. "I came stateside almost ready for a metal box," he said. "I spent a long time in a hospital. In the meantime, my beloved wife ..." His words carried a cynical tone. "... found somebody better, divorced me, and, in the process, somehow I lost my home and everything else. My dog was killed on the same mission that injured me." His voice halted for a moment. "So I didn't even have the comfort of knowing Trigger was at my side. And, to be honest, like Pete, I couldn't have looked after her for the first while. I was in pretty rough shape."

She nodded slowly. "You look fairly healthy now."

"I am," he said, "or at least as good as I'll get. We received a dozen files of dogs potentially in trouble that had gone missing or were in bad situations. The military didn't know what their fate was, and so they asked Titanium Corp if somebody had time to volunteer to check them out."

"Have you found any of them yet?" she asked.

"We only started a little bit ago," he said. "Ethan, a former K9 trainer, went looking for the first one. He found him guarding a drug lab and being trained to kill intruders." At her gasp he nodded grimly. "And you know what happens to dogs that kill humans." His voice was bleak. "Ethan got there in time to rescue four shepherds from that fate. He has now taken all four on. Plus I believe, from what I last heard, he adopted a fifth one, who just lost her leg and had no place to go and will need special care. He's decided to build his own group of trained dogs."

"Is that what you're looking to do, bring this one back to him?"

Pierce shrugged. "I'm not exactly sure what I'm supposed to do at the moment. The first thing is to get the dog, make sure she's safe and cared for. She saved a lot of lives and spent a lot of years in service for her country. She deserves better than being tossed into this shithole and being used to track down deer, for God's sake. Man's got guns. He should be out there with a hunting license and hunting them humanely."

"It's not even hunting season," she said. "Something else the sheriff doesn't give a damn about."

"Sounds like you need a new sheriff," Pierce snapped.

"We do. Indeed, we do," she said. "But that's not likely to happen anytime soon. Public sentiment has to be swayed."

"Is everybody for the sheriff, or are they all just afraid of him?"

She frowned. "You picked that up pretty fast. I'd say

seventy percent are afraid of him. Of the others, ten percent are for him, like Jed. And the rest just don't give a damn because they don't think it matters what they say or do."

"It sounds like politics everywhere," he said. "Still, that doesn't change the fact the sheriff isn't doing his job. People are getting away with all kinds of criminal acts, and the whole county will end up in a bad way very soon." He motioned back at the house. "Hopefully Jed will lay off the kids and the wife for a while. But nothing will stop a man for long who's hell-bent on destroying himself and the world around him."

"That's too bad," she said. "I was so hoping he would go on the straight and narrow." There was a note of humor in her voice. "You're pretty damn scary when you want to be."

His lips kicked up at the corner. "I can be," he agreed. "When the time warrants it. And I'm wondering what the hell we're supposed to do about that piece of shit sheriff you've got here."

"As soon as you figure it out, you tell me because I haven't a clue."

"How many other deputies do you have?"

"Two. And, before you ask, they're both like him."

"So how did you get the job?"

She rolled her eyes. "The mayor thought it was a good idea, a woman-initiative thing. I think they both thought I'd be stuck at a desk, making coffee for the guys when they came in from their hard work," she snapped. "But, as soon as they gave me the deputy badge, I was the first one out the door, patrolling the trouble spots. I knew what deputies did. I was raised by a sheriff. My dad isn't terribly impressed I'm a deputy, but he's even less impressed with the sheriff who replaced him."

"Why did your dad step down, or was he forced out in an election?"

"Car accident," she said succinctly. "He's better, but he's not 100 percent. He withdrew from his position, which is when they brought in our current sheriff."

"Do you think the voting was fair?"

"They put him in, but I don't think they expected what they got. They should have though. He's been in this community a long time. My father was horrified. He felt for sure the people would have understood and known better, but the sheriff was a smooth talker back then. He doesn't give a shit about being a smooth talker now. He runs this place like he's a god."

"Except he can't seem to keep you in line."

"No. I've placed a couple complaints above his head," she said, "so he's worried about me. He doesn't know how much trouble I'll be for him, so he lets me do my stuff. He rarely calls on me, only sends me out on jobs if he thinks something'll scare me away, instead of jobs he thinks I can handle. Other than that, we try to avoid each other."

"And yet, you followed him down the road coming in the café?"

She nodded. "I did," she said in surprise. "How did you know that?"

"Because I watched you," he said. "Even from where I was having coffee, I could see. But I don't know if you were following him to see what he was up to or if you needed him to see you before you went to Jed's place."

"A bit of both," she said. "I was hoping he'd go give Jed a talking to. When I realized, as usual, he wasn't, I went instead."

"Interesting that he's okay with abusing women and

children. Is he an abuser himself?"

"His wife is dead," she said slowly. "So I don't know. He has no children. I'm not sure he has any girlfriends either. If he does, they're short-term, even possibly by the hour." She laughed. "Listen to me. I'm starting to sound like a real bitch."

"No. You're trying to understand the character of the man who's supposed to be a leader. The one you're supposed to follow into battle," he snapped.

She shook her head. "That I would never do. Call me disloyal if you want, but he's just as likely to lead me into a battle and step out of the way so I take the first bullet."

Pierce stared at her for a long moment. "It's definitely time to do something about him before you do end up with a bullet. Jed looked like he was mighty happy to put one in you today."

"I'm not sure he wouldn't have done it too," she said shortly. She turned in her seat, closed the door, started up the engine and said through the open window, "Try to stay out of trouble." And she drove off.

CHAPTER 4

HEDI SHOULDN'T HAVE told him as much as she had. She didn't know what kind of a man he was, and, with information like that, … he could get her in a lot of trouble.

She didn't want to work for a man she didn't trust. She didn't want to work for a man she couldn't follow into battle, to use Pierce's term. She could understand his military background. It came out in his words every once in a while.

Her heart ached for Salem. That dog had had a shitty deal once Pete had to go into the rehab center on a permanent basis. She should have done more for Salem, but it wasn't like she had any place of her own to keep her. And, if Salem was as difficult as the sheriff said, Hedi didn't have the training or the know-how to handle her. But maybe Pierce did, and maybe the best answer yet was to have Salem somehow get back into his possession. He hadn't said his orders were official, so she didn't know if he could just take the dog. But, considering the way the dog was being handed around, maybe that was the best answer after all. In this case, she thought, possession was nine-tenths of the law. Maybe that's how Pierce should handle it too.

She finally pulled into the station, parked and walked inside. It was late already; the sheriff was long gone, and so was Roy. That only left Stephen.

He looked up and frowned at her. "Where the hell you

been? I had to do all this paperwork shit myself today."

She just raised an eyebrow. "Oh, poor baby." She left it at that.

Stephen did the least amount of work possible, avoided paperwork whenever he could, but he hated going out on rides and dealing with difficult situations even more. Why he was the deputy, she didn't get. He should have been a librarian or something equally placid.

"Hey, it's not easy sitting here, picking up the reins when everybody else doesn't do anything," he said. "You better be doing your own paperwork for whatever the hell you were up to today."

"I will." She walked to her desk and sat down, logging onto her computer. "I was at Jed's again."

At least he didn't seem to think along the sheriff's line that Jed was harmless. "You know that's just a plain bad situation, don't you?"

"Even more than you know," she said, suddenly weary. She turned to look at him. "If I end up with a bullet between my eyes, you start looking at Jed first, will you?"

Stephen raised his head over the monitors. "That bad?"

"He poked me with his loaded rifle and told me to get the hell off his property," she said, paraphrasing. To be honest she'd been so damn scared she didn't remember his words exactly.

"He pushed you?"

She nodded.

"And you're still standing? He didn't shoot you or anything?"

She could hear from the tone of disbelief in his voice that he was confused as to why she was still here, not splattered all over the front of Jed's yard.

"Yes," she said, "I am. His rifle was loaded. He was drunk. And he was screaming at the kids. They're the ones who called me."

"Well, yeah. But you gave them your direct number," Stephen said. "That's what dispatch is for, remember?"

"Yeah? And by the time dispatch gets me on the end of the phone, you know those kids will be dead one day."

Stephen winced. "Unfortunately that's all too possible," he muttered. Stephen had a wife and two kids himself.

As she thought about it, she realized he'd have been a better accountant than anything. He really liked numbers. "Anything happen here this afternoon?"

"Nothing as exciting as your afternoon apparently. The sheriff came back in a pissy mood from his apple pie trip. Don't know what that was all about."

"He met somebody in the restaurant looking for Salem, somebody not taking no for an answer."

"What do you mean?" Stephen frowned.

"Somebody was sent here by the War Dogs division to look for Salem."

Stephen pushed his chair back. "Oh, God." He looked around frantically. "Are we in shit then?"

"Oh, I imagine we're all in shit," she snapped. "Just think about how much that poor dog has been through. Just think about the damn sheriff and how he treated her."

Stephen winced. "He hated that dog."

"And he did what he could to turn her into a mean vicious bitch," Hedi said.

"Well, you couldn't stop him," Stephen said. "Did you expect me to do anything?"

And that was the problem with Stephen. He always took the easy way out.

"Jed apparently had the dog up until a month ago or so, and he was trying to teach it to track down deer out of season. Said he needed the meat so he could live. Then the dog took off one day, and no one has seen it since."

"You mean, to sell the meat so he could buy more booze," Stephen said caustically. "He should be dead from the amount of alcohol running through his veins."

She remembered the yellow tinge to Jed's eyes. "I'm not sure he's far off."

"Hopefully soon," he said, "before Jed beats one of those kids to death, shoots you or that wife of his. That woman is a bloody saint."

"I don't know about a saint," Hedi added, "but she's beaten, downtrodden, terrified of leaving him because he has threatened to come after her and kill them all."

"And he would," Stephen said in a matter-of-fact tone and promptly returned to his monitors and whatever work he was doing.

She stared at him. "And so, like the sheriff, you won't do anything about it?"

His gaze turned hard. "You want to be the cavalry, then have at it. Me? I like my safe desk job."

"You don't have a desk job," she enunciated carefully. "You're a deputy. You're supposed to be out riding with me."

"I go sometimes," he said, "but you don't like doing the paperwork any more than anybody else. Everybody is happy to dump it on me."

"You're more than happy to get out of dealing with confrontations." On that note she spun around and logged back into her computer.

She wrote up a report, once again on Jed—this time

adding in him pushing her with a loaded rifle. She decided to keep Pierce's name out of the report. She wasn't sure why, but it seemed more prudent to do so. She almost wished he'd go back during the night and haul Jed out into the middle of the woods and pound him into the ground to make him see sense. But Jed would just come back to the house and grab a bottle and upend it all at once, fueling his anger and taking it out on his family.

She did marvel at his liver's resilience. But it had to stop at some point. She'd much rather it was sooner than later.

When she finished her report, she saw Stephen had left without saying goodbye. Only her desk light was on in the main office; the rest were all turned off. "Good riddance," she groaned.

She logged off, grabbed her purse and keys, and headed to the front door. As she locked up and turned to her car, a voice spoke from the darkness. "Are you going home now?"

She turned to see Pierce leaning against his truck. "Jesus, don't do that," she said. "You scared me."

"You've been working in there alone for the last twenty minutes. What's wrong with the men in this town?"

"If you're about to make a sexist comment yourself," she snapped, "I suggest you don't. Besides, Stephen would be useless as a defender or backup. The most dangerous things in his world are paper cuts."

"Is he the admin?"

"No. He holds the same position I do," she said wearily. "He just chooses not to do anything but paperwork." She could hear Pierce swearing steadily and softly under his breath. She gave him a ghost of a smile. "I do that exact same thing many times in a week." She stared off into the distance. "Not sure how much longer I can handle this job. I admit one of the reasons I stay is because I think this town needs somebody who cares. For a little while there, I thought I could change things. But I can't. Not this way at least."

"No, but the town does need you," he said, surprising her. "I'd hate to see you killed on duty by one of those assholes like Jed, but somebody needs to care, and sometimes the only ones who can care are us."

She smiled as she walked to her car. "Where are you staying?"

"Haven't thought about it," he said absentmindedly. He studied the woods behind the sheriff's department. "Where's the compound the dog was held in?"

"It's over here." She detoured to the pen where the dog had been kept. "I used to come out here to talk to her. She accepted my voice and would let me touch her a little bit, but the minute any of the men came toward her, she would get aggressive."

"Great," he said. "That'll make my job harder."

"Yes, it will," she said. "I'm sorry about that. If you're right that Salem was a well-trained dog and came back looking for retirement and a nice dog bed by a fire, she landed in the wrong place."

"I presume the brother is responsible for that?"

"I'd say so," she said steadily. "Pretty sure he lied about the dog bite, and, even if she did bite someone, I'd believe she had good reason. Still, that report had the effect of allowing the sheriff to collect the dog, and then she was *stolen* supposedly as she disappeared from the compound," she said for emphasis. "When I think about it, I think somebody just cut that wire to make it look like she was stolen. And, of course, now all the townsfolk are terrified of her because she's supposedly dangerous."

"Who did she bite again?"

"Jed's brother," she said. "Chester was visiting at the time. He's gone back East now."

"Well, isn't that convenient?"

HE SNORTED AT that. "Doesn't really matter though, does it, because the sheriff wouldn't give a shit, neither would Ross, and I'm sure nobody told Pete anything."

"I'm sure nobody did. I don't think Ross even goes to visit him. It's Pete's house too."

"Seriously? Does Ross look after it, pay rent, anything?"

She shook her head. "Ross doesn't work any more than Jed does. I know they blame everything on the mill that closed down around here, but honestly I think they're just too lazy to find another job." She studied the back compound. "I was delighted when I heard the dog had escaped, until I saw the wires were cut. And then I figured it was some bigger asshole than Ross. He's just lazy. Jed is a mean drunk, and the Billy boys, Billy and Bobby Billy, are downright mean. When that group is together, it's bad news."

"Maybe I'll pay a visit to Pete, see what he wants to do about his house. It might be time to sell it," Pierce said. "I don't know what he can get, but it would help him with his medical expenses and care. Maybe even could get him into a better place."

She stared at him. "You know you'll open a hornet's nest, right?"

He gave her a shadow of a smile. "I hope it's a really big colony when I do." He turned to his truck and hopped in. "Are you okay to go home? Is Jed likely to come after you?"

"He hasn't yet." She got in her car, turned on her engine and headed toward the road.

He watched as she took a left. He waited for a long moment; then he followed her back to the main road. One of the things at the top of his list, besides finding the dog, was solving Pete's problem because that was part of this whole bigger issue.

He remembered what Pete's house had looked like and the land around it. It was a nice place. A small smile formed on his mouth. He picked up his phone and called Badger. "What are the real-estate prices on the outskirts of Fort Collins?"

"Um, I don't know. Let me ask my little crystal ball here," Badger said. "Why?"

"Because Salem has been badly mistreated, taken and dumped from one man to another, incurring more abuse every time. She's currently 'missing,'" he snapped. "Pete's brother has taken over the house but didn't look after the dog, isn't looking after the property, and I'm about to go talk to Pete and see if he needs a hand to maybe get his life back on track."

"You think he wants to sell?" Badger asked as the confusion cleared in his voice. "Or maybe you're looking to buy?"

"What I'm looking for is to make sure Pete is taken care of," Pierce said. "And that asshole brother of his who wouldn't look after Salem needs to be booted off the property."

"Someone will have to," Badger said, "otherwise that brother will just move back home again."

"Let me talk to Pete. I can't imagine the property around here is worth much, but Pete needs what he can get." He hung up on that note.

He headed into Fort Collins and grabbed the first hotel he could find. There he unloaded his bags and laptop and started doing more research. All his shit was in his truck, but he didn't have much. Which was why it seemed odd to all of a sudden consider maybe he should have more.

When he found the telephone number for the rehab place where Pete was, Pierce put in a phone call. Pete wasn't available, but Pierce left a message and said it was about Salem. When his phone rang a half hour later, he smiled to see the number. "Pete, is that you?"

"I got a message," the man said hesitantly. "Who am I talking to?"

"My name is Pierce Carlton of Titanium Corp. I'm here on behalf of the War Dogs Program. We're doing a welfare check on Salem."

There was a hard gasp, and he could hear tears in Pete's voice. "I'd like a welfare check on her myself," Pete said. "My brother told me that she bit somebody, and the sheriff was going to shoot her."

"Apparently she bit Jed's brother. And Ross was not taking care of her in the first place. According to Hedi, he abused her. I know Jed did too. I think Hedi believes the sheriff cut the wire so somebody else could come and get her."

"No," Pete cried out. "Please tell me that's not true. My brother swore he'd look after her."

"What was your brother like before?" Pierce's voice was stern. "Did you really think a leopard would change his spots?"

"I'd hoped so." Pete was almost crying. "I was hoping to come home, but I don't have any money. Ross looks after all of that, and he said I couldn't get the necessary modifications on the property because there just wasn't any money."

"How is he looking after your money?" Anger Pierce hadn't felt in a long time surged through him.

"He pays the bills, handles my money," he said. "It comes in to a specific bank account, and he pays for this place here."

"How long have you been at the center, buddy?"

"Too fucking long," Pete said. "I was doing well in my recovery until I heard I have to stay here."

"That's not necessarily true. I'll do some investigating into your situation."

"You'd help me?" Pete's voice brightened.

"Is your brother paying rent?"

"No, of course not. He's looking after the property for me."

"Exactly what does that mean?"

"Mowing the lawn, taking care of the animals, … just the usual. There's not much population there, so it's not like I can rent it anyway," he said.

"Do you trust him?"

Pete's voice was hesitant. "Not really but I didn't have much choice."

"Do you know how much your pension is?"

Pete named a figure that had Pierce's eyebrows rising. "Your brother said you couldn't get modifications on the house for that kind of money? And that you needed to stay where you are?"

"Yeah. If I can't have the modifications, there's no way to go home. But it's not just the house," Pete said hurriedly. "I have to do some work on the truck too. It's so expensive."

"Yeah. So expensive," Pierce said. "I can do a lot of this kind of work. How about I go to your place and see what it would cost to modify it so you can get a wheelchair in, ensure a bathroom and a bedroom are on the main floor."

There was silence, and then Pete said, "If you could do that, that would be great. But I don't even know you."

"Nope, you don't," he said. "Don't suppose you know an Ethan though, do you?"

"Ethan Nebberly? Trainer from the K9 unit?"

"Yes," Pierce said. "Give him a call and then call me back." And he hung up.

He opened the motel door and stepped out on the long veranda to see where to grab some food. A fast-food joint was across the road. Definitely not his first choice, but, given the circumstances, he had few options. He pocketed his cell phone, grabbed his wallet, locked the door and walked across the street. He ordered a couple burgers and a coffee to go and sat there eating them. They tasted like sawdust, but they were food. As he ate, he wrote notes of what he'd seen and heard. Then he sent them to Badger.

Badger called a few minutes later. "This sounds bad," he said. "It's well out of the parameters of what we asked you to do though."

"The thing is, in order to get Salem's life back on track, Pete needs to come home to look after her."

Badger chuckled. "I guess we didn't give you parameters, and you took the job and ran with it, so we can't argue that. What is it you're thinking you can do? I want to know if anybody else can help. Possibly Kat can get the medical records, see how bad Pete is, see what he needs to become independent."

"He'll talk to Ethan. Then I'll return to his house to-morrow and start measuring to see just what I think will be required."

"I like the sound of that," Badger said. "What do you want to do about his bank accounts?"

"I want them frozen," Pierce said succinctly. "I'm not sure what his brother is up to, but I bet he's been living off of Pete's pension. And probably stocking it away for himself."

"You're not allowed to go in there and beat the crap out of him for that," Badger said.

"You're too far away to stop me," Pierce said, then chuckled. "Still, I think if we were to charge this guy, Pete would have a hard time with that. But we need to find a way to get Pete home and his money back and to stop Ross from taking any more. Can somebody do a check on his bank accounts and see where the money is?"

"You're not asking for much, are you?"

"You've got connections," Pierce said. "You think I haven't been around you guys enough to know that?"

"Well, maybe," Badger said. "We do have some people. We might figure this out."

"There are a couple cops in your group, right? Maybe you could talk to them about what our options are."

"You know what? That's not a bad idea. I think I'll talk to Allison and Jager tonight, see if they have any idea what our options are going forward."

"You should see the law in this town. There's no support here from law enforcement," he said. "The sheriff is an absolute nutjob." He took a few moments to explain everything he'd seen and heard.

"This Jed guy threatened her with a loaded weapon?"

"Yep, whether she told the sheriff about it or not, I don't know. Apparently it's not the first time Jed's gone after her, and the sheriff doesn't give a shit. Jed's a friend of his. And so is Pete's brother. Ross knows there's no one around who'll stop him." Pierce's voice hardened. "Well, *now* there is." He ended the call.

CHAPTER 5

WHEN HEDI WALKED into work the next morning, a weird silence ran throughout the station. She glanced from one man to the next, but neither looked her in the eye. She frowned. "Who died?" she half joked.

Again no answer. Just this weird lack of noise, as if she'd walked in on a heavy conversation she wasn't supposed to hear, and everybody shut up when they saw her. But, in that case, they should have seen her coming because she'd parked out front. She walked to her desk and logged on to her computer. Everything appeared normal, but she couldn't get rid of the niggling sense riding her shoulders.

When the sheriff stepped out of his office and called her, she frowned. Again she looked at the other two deputies, but they kept their heads on their paperwork, studiously ignoring her. That meant something was definitely up.

She grabbed her empty coffee cup, walked to the coffeepot, filled it and headed into the sheriff's office. "Good morning, Sheriff. How are you?" she said. She deliberately kept her voice up and cheerful, sitting down opposite him. "Had a hell of a visit with Jed yesterday."

"That's what I want to talk to you about," he said, his voice thunderous.

"Oh, good. You're finally on my side and charging him for assaulting a police officer," she said in excitement. She knew it would be the opposite of what he planned on doing, but her words stopped him cold.

His mouth worked and then asked, "Did he assault you?"

"He rammed his loaded rifle into my shoulder and threatened me. He pushed me back several inches, and I refused to back down," she said with a hard nod. "I told you that he would cross the line."

"And I told you to leave him alone and to walk carefully around him."

"Sure, except I get there, and all four screaming kids are terrified, and he's running around like a crazy man with that rifle of his," she snapped. She leaned forward. "Did you talk to him?"

Put on the spot, the sheriff shifted papers on his desk. "He called me this morning. He said you crossed the line."

"Yeah? What line was that?" she asked. "Responding to a 9-1-1 call from a little girl?"

At that, the sheriff looked in the direction of dispatch on the other side of the wall. He couldn't confirm or deny what she'd said because, of course, he had no fricking clue. "You didn't mention anything about a 9-1-1 call when we were at the coffee shop," he snapped. "You said you were going up there because one of the girls had called you. Little girls do that." His voice turned snide. "They're weak and whiny, and they don't know how to suck it up."

"No child should have to see their father shooting up the house in front of them. He's done it many times—you know that." Her tone was cool, her back rigid.

She needed a solution to purge this bloody office and wasn't sure how to get it done. She had talked to her father about it last night, and he'd agreed to contact some people he knew, but the wheels turned slowly when it came to elected officials, and the sheriff had been running this town for way too long.

"What else did he say?" she asked in a conversational tone. "Or will you talk to him more about it when you bring him in?"

He glared at her. "You know you have this job only because I gave it to you, right?"

She tilted her head to the side. "Partially yes. I'm also the only one who goes out and handles anything in the field," she snapped. "Stephen is great for paperwork, but you know as well as I do that he's no good in times of trouble."

The sheriff's lip curled. "But there's nothing wrong with Roy."

"Nope, nothing wrong with him at all." In her mind she added, *There's nothing right about him either.*

Roy picked and chose where he went and what he wanted to do. Most of the time, he just wanted to hang around with pretty girls downtown. He called it citizen's watch. She had another name for it. Roy was forty, always leering at her, and there was something extremely lecherous about everything he did. But he never, as far as she knew, crossed the line, and that made a difference. It was one thing to be slime, but it was another thing to be a complete sleazebag.

"You shouldn't arrest Jed without backup."

He started to bluster.

She held her ground. And waited.

"You know I'm not arresting him," the sheriff said. "He had a bad day, that's all."

"Did he call you this morning?"

"I said he did, didn't I?" The sheriff growled. "I'll talk to him again. You stay away from him."

"I'll stay away as long as he stays away from those little girls," she said, "and his wife. And any other godforsaken animal, two-legged or four." She stood, marched to the door and turned. "Make sure you don't get caught up in his garbage because you know this town will only stand for so much. The minute he really hurts someone, and people find out you just sat by and let him get this bad …"

He rose and leaned over his desk, snapping like a turtle. "And who do you think will tell them that? You?"

She gave him a hard look. "Hell yes, me. And my father. Do you think I haven't told him what the hell's going on? And what about Roger? He might not be a deputy anymore, but he was for twenty-plus years. Do you really think they won't start telling the world just how you're running this town? And letting child abusers and wife abusers get away with that kind of shit?"

She didn't wait for an answer. She opened the door and stepped out, closed it and leaned against it for a long moment because it was the one place the other two deputies couldn't see her.

She stared down at her hands, angry that they were shaking. She shouldn't be upset from the confrontation; she should be priding herself on having had it. It was hard to deal with. This office was a pain in the ass actually. But there was only so much she could fight. She'd tried to contact as many people as she could about the abuses, but what did you do when nobody backed you up?

Taking several deep breaths, she realized she'd left her coffee cup inside. Whatever. She walked to the pot, grabbed a clean mug, filled it, then she went to her desk and sat down without saying a word to either man. She could feel their glances, but she didn't look up. She answered several emails and checked the report she'd written yesterday.

They were barely adjusting to a digital system. The sheriff still wanted handwritten notes, but she kept everything digital, just in case somebody decided to doctor her reports. A practice she'd started a long time ago when she realized only shit was going down here. Because she had no place to submit them, she sent herself a copy and a copy to her father, in case something happened to her, which, after a conversation with her father last night, she realized was a distinct possibility. It would be an accident, she was sure. She'd die in the line of duty, probably from something stupid, like shooting herself with her own gun, if the sheriff wrote up the report.

She printed off the report she had written yesterday and went over it with her pen. Nobody had seen it but her. When she was satisfied it was fine, she slipped it into Jed's file and put it away. Then she wrote herself a small note and stuck the sticky on her monitor to check that the report was still there at the end of the day because she was damn sure somebody who'd been watching her will let the sheriff know, and he was likely to destroy it.

Jed's file was awfully skinny. But she kept copies of everything she had dealt with online, just in case. She didn't want a prosecutor saying Jed was a first-time offender and just give him a slap on the wrist. It was all she could do to sleep at night these days, thinking about those little kids ending up dead, and Jed taking them out back and burying them six feet deep, telling the sheriff some asshole kidnapped them. The sheriff would probably just stand there for a long moment, chewing his gum, as if deciding whether it was worth making up a report and chasing down this unnamed person. And probably choosing it wasn't worth losing an inch off his fat ass and subsequently closing the case.

She hated that this was what she was working with—hated that this was what her badge stood for because it didn't. It wasn't what she stood for, and it was her badge, damn it.

And again she felt helpless, her mind returning to Pierce. She didn't think he'd ever felt helpless. Something about him told her that he'd deal with this, one way or another. She'd heard both hero stories and horror stories about military life.

If he'd been subjected to any of the nightmares she'd heard about, no wonder he'd learned coping skills. But he didn't seem to have any of that ingrained anger she'd seen in a lot of people. Pete himself had gone from being angry to being despondent, as if working through the various stages of grief.

He'd told her once that he was still grieving for what he used to be. He hadn't come to terms with the man he currently was. She'd hoped he would see what he could become, but he was still stuck in the here and now of broken bones and missing limbs and a life that would never be fully realized, not as far as he was concerned.

She didn't know what Pierce's story was, but she could already see the kind of man he was. She just worried he was too high-strung and would cross the line, like Jed had. There was something about men like that. You just didn't quite know when they would explode.

But whatever Pierce was doing now, he was doing from the heart, because nobody else seemed to care about this dog, and that was just wrong.

She was a huge animal lover herself. She had tried hard to get to know Salem, but Salem was already in hate mode by the time Hedi had gotten around to trying to be friends. She only hoped, given enough time, Pierce might find the dog.

Salem had been everything to Pete. Hedi had even seen him bawling as he left because the dog couldn't go with him. She wished there was a way to reunite the two, but just wishing it didn't make it happen; otherwise she would have wished that sheriff away a long time ago.

PIERCE ENTERED THE rehab center and walked to the reception area. He looked around with interest. He'd been in a couple himself but always on a short-term basis. He asked the receptionist where Pete was.

She frowned. "He's taken a turn for the worse." Her voice was quiet. "He can't have any visitors today."

Pierce winced. "I'm sorry to hear that. Maybe leave a message I came to visit."

She gave him a notepad, and he wrote down his name and number.

With a nod of thanks he turned and stepped outside. He had no doubt Pete's downturn was based on Pierce's phone call last night, and that shouldn't be. Pete had enough things in his life to deal with, just getting back on his feet, without having to worry about what happened to his brother and his dog.

Pierce hopped back into his truck and headed back the way he'd come. It had been an hour and a half one way this morning just to get here. Next he'd go to Pete's house, where Ross was effectively squatting.

When Pierce got within about ten minutes of Pete's

place, he pulled off on the side of the road and checked his messages. And, sure enough, there was one. He hit Dial, and this time Pete answered. His voice was quaking slightly. "Pete, how you doing? I heard you didn't have a great night," Pierce said, his voice calm, steady.

"I heard you came by this morning," Pete said. "I'm sorry I missed you."

"I might have a chance to get up there again," Pierce said. "Just thought I'd stop in when I was close."

"Will you do anything about my brother?"

"I'll have a talk with him," Pierce said. "Is there anything you want me to do about him?"

"I had a conversation here with a couple guys, and they think he's probably stealing from me." Pete's voice was heavy. "The doctor said there's no reason I couldn't come home if some modifications were done and if I had some help."

"I think that's a great idea," Pierce said. "The question then is whether you have the money to make that happen."

"Yeah," he said, "that's partly it. I do get a decent pension, and I have my medical expenses covered. The property doesn't have a mortgage, so I was kind of half hoping that maybe ..." His voice dropped off, and he hesitated.

"That maybe what?" Pierce asked as he looked around the area. Not another vehicle had been on the road since he had turned onto it. "Your place is a little isolated, isn't it?"

"It is," he said. "That's the way I used to like it. It'd be kind of nice to have somebody living close by now though. I do have neighbors to a certain extent," Pete added hurriedly. "But they're not necessarily the best kind."

"Meaning that, when a guy gets into trouble, they're not there for you? Not talking about Jed, are you? I haven't even met his brother."

"You're not missing much," Pete said. "They laughed at me when I said I was going into the military, that I wanted to serve my country. And they laughed when I came home in pieces too," he said.

Anger speared through Pierce. "They laughed, did they? Maybe they should have done some time overseas. You and I both know what it was like. I came back mostly in one piece, but I was still in recovery for a long time. You need to focus on getting well. I'll go talk to your brother and take a good look at your house. I just need your permission to go inside and to take some measurements and just to see what your options are."

"You have my permission," he said. "No matter what Ross tells you, that's my house. I haven't signed the title to him."

"I hope not," Pierce said. "And hopefully your brother hasn't forged signatures."

He heard Pete's gasp.

"I'm not saying he did," Pierce rushed to say. "Are there any public health nurses around here, or anybody who could come in on a whenever-needed basis?"

"No," Pete said. "Almost everybody works in Fort Collins or elsewhere."

"Or they don't work at all I gather, now that the mill shut down."

"Exactly," he said.

"Pete, did you have a girlfriend before?"

"I did, yeah." His voice brightened. "We used to call her Smelly"—he chuckled—"but her name is Smelina. It's a Ukrainian name that the kids shortened to Smelly. Now she's Lina."

"I'm sure she prefers that."

"True," Pete said with another chuckle. "We were going out before I headed into the military, but, after my accident, well, I haven't had anything to do with her."

"Because of you or because of her?" Pierce asked.

"What do you mean?"

"Meaning, did she not want to see you because of your condition, or did you stop seeing her because of your condition?"

There was a hard silence, and then Pete said, "You don't pull any punches, do you?"

"Nope. I don't, and I got no patience for it. My wife divorced me and took my house and everything I owned while I was undergoing surgery," Pierce said. "So I understand either way. But, before I meet Lina, I'd like to know."

"It was me," Pete rushed to say. "She's very active. The last thing she needs is somebody like me saddled at her side."

"I think you are supposed to give her that choice," Pierce said, "not make that decision for her."

"Sometimes we have to make decisions for others," Pete said, "because they don't know enough to make an informed choice."

"Meaning, you didn't let her see how bad it was and the modifications you'd need to have a relationship with her."

"Something like that." Pete's voice grew stronger. "I don't know what kind of physical condition you ended up in, but I'm in rough shape. I wouldn't put that on anybody."

"I know you don't believe it," Pierce said, "but the human body really can heal." And on that note he hung up.

He'd heard and seen an awful lot of guys just like Pete walk away from everything they knew because they figured they were less than a whole person, thinking it was a kindness to walk away from their former relationships. And sometimes they were just too angry, not ready to deal with the fact that their life had changed and not able to believe a partner could live with it. So much anger led to a lot of violence, harsh words said that could never be taken back. It sucked all around, but it happened.

He turned the truck engine on again, tossing the phone beside him, and drove until he saw the driveway that went to Ross's place. … Pete's place, he corrected because Ross liked to think it was his place, but it wasn't. It was Pete's.

As Pierce drove up, he took note of the driveway. Pete would need a vehicle modified so he could drive with his hands, not his feet, and to get a wheelchair in and out of. He thought of Kat when he thought of prosthetics. Pete's medical records would determine what she could do for him.

Pierce pulled up to the front of the house and parked, thinking there should be a garage. Right now there was just dirt, gravel, rocks, a bit of a garden and some steps. But there was lots of room to throw up a ramp.

He hopped out, grabbed a notebook and pen from his glove box, took his phone again and walked toward the front steps. Using his phone, he took several pictures from both angles where a ramp could be built. There was no need to make a big deal out of it; it was only four steps. A ramp wouldn't be a problem, and, once Pete got up those four steps, there was a huge wide veranda. It wasn't a narrow one, barely enough room for a chair. This one was big enough for a table and a couple chairs, which meant the wheelchair could turn around and move in and out. He studied the front door and then said out loud, "That would need to be changed."

"Hey, who are you, and what are you doing?" called out

a man from deep inside the house.

Pierce ignored him, measured off the door and took a solid look at the outside. "Definitely need to have double doors that open at the same time. Certainly couldn't do with a thirty-two-inch exterior door. Why would anyone put such a small exterior door on? Should have been a forty at least." He jotted down more notes, took pictures and measurements. A big window was to the side of the door. He figured, if the window came out, a nice big double set of doors could go in.

As he wrote down notes, the door pulled open, and Ross glared at him sleepy-eyed, his hair still tousled in all directions. Pierce looked at him and said, "Hey. Did I wake you?"

"Yeah, you woke me," Ross snapped. "What the hell are you doing back here?"

"Were you working last night? Sorry. I'm not used to people sleeping this late," Pierce said, making a point to check his watch. It was well past eleven. "But then I guess night shift really sucks, doesn't it?"

"I wasn't working. Not that it's any of your business." He looked at the notepad and pen in Pierce's hand. "What are you doing?"

"Taking notes on modifications for Pete. I'm glad you're up. I need to get in the house anyway." And he stepped inside, not giving Ross a chance to argue.

"What are you talking about? Pete is in rehab, and that's where he'll stay," Ross said. "No way he can come back home."

"Why is that?" Pierce asked as he studied the inside of the door frame. He could definitely double the size of the door by taking that window out. He stepped back and took a picture of it.

"Stop that," Ross said. "You've got no business in my house. Pete can't come home because he's too injured."

"Pete is healing." Pierce turned to look at him. "I've talked to him several times."

"So what? He ain't coming home, no way. That ain't happening." Ross snorted and picked up a pack of cigarettes. He lit one and took a deep drag on the filter end. Within seconds he blew it out.

Pierce could see almost a calm come over him. "You're pretty addicted to those, aren't you?"

Ross raised an eyebrow. "None of your business."

"Nope, not my business that you're killing yourself. Of course it is now that you're smoking inside in front of me, but hey …" Pierce turned and moved off down the hallway.

He measured the width of the hallway, happy to see it was plenty wide for a wheelchair. It might be one person at a time, but the wheelchairs these days were pretty high-end machines. He took the hall down to what appeared to be a large bedroom. He suspected Ross had come stumbling out from there and assumed he wouldn't be impressed to hear the latest plans.

"What the hell are you doing?" Ross roared. "Get out of my bedroom."

"This is the master bedroom, isn't it?" Pierce asked, feigning innocence.

Ross frowned at him. "Yeah, of course it's the master bedroom. And I'm the master of the house."

At that, Pierce straightened. "This is Pete's house."

"It is, but my brother ain't never coming back. Did you hear that? That makes me the master of the damn house," he said belligerently.

Pierce reached up and poked him in the chest. "This is

Pete's house. This is Pete's master bedroom. Pete is coming back to sleep in his master bedroom. Got that?" And he poked him with every word he said.

He had Ross stepping halfway down the hallway, and then Pierce turned back into the master bedroom.

As he stood here, he looked at the entranceway, not liking the size of the door. Somehow the hallway looked like it had narrowed slightly. Out came his trusty tape measure, and he sized up the entranceway.

In the meantime, Ross came back in. "You've got no fucking business being here," he snapped.

At that Pierce pulled out his phone and called Pete. When he answered, he said, "Hey, Pete, I'm putting you on speaker." He watched the color disappear from Ross's face. "Your brother says it's his house, and I have no business taking measurements."

Pete's voice came out of the speaker, gaining strength with every second. "Ross, you there?"

"Yeah, I'm here. What the hell's going on, man?"

Pierce was happy to hear Ross sounding like a whiny child.

"Pierce is there to take some measurements to see just what kind of money is needed to make modifications so I can come home again," Pete said happily.

"Hey, man, I know that's a dream for you, but it's a pipe dream. Remember there's just no money."

At that Pierce smiled at him. "Yeah, we'll talk more about that."

Ross looked at him, and Pierce could see a bead of sweat breaking out on his forehead. "There ain't nothing to talk about, Pete. You know that. You know there's no money."

"I'm just trying to figure out why there's no money,"

Pete said. "I know how much money was in that account, and I've got the accountants taking a look at it to see if we can make this happen."

"Yeah, but I had to fix a few things here," Ross whined. "And I can't live here for nothing."

"No, absolutely not," Pierce said. "So you're looking after this place. What's that worth? A couple hundred bucks a week?"

"At least," he said. "I gotta make sure nobody breaks into the place and causes damage," Ross blustered, then straightened, as if feeling like he was on better ground. "If we'll start looking at that, Jesus, my brother owes me a couple grand for being here."

"Just a couple grand?" Pierce asked. "How long have you lived here?"

"I don't know. It must be about, maybe not quite a year. What do you think, Pete? How long has it been since you went in there?"

"It's been just over six months," Pete said, his tone wry. "I can see you moved in quite nicely, but it's only been six months, bro."

"Feels longer," Ross said. "So six months, you know, that's like twenty-five hundred bucks."

"Sure, but if you, as a renter, look at the rental stats around here, I understand that places go for about five hundred a month, and a whole house goes for about eight hundred. Eight hundred times six is four thousand eight hundred. So by my calculations, you still owe Pete about twenty-three hundred. You only worked off half the rent."

Silence.

Finally Ross blubbered away. "Hey, Pete, what the hell is going on here?" He kept walking, pacing back and forth, sucking on a cigarette like a drowning man.

Not wanting Pete to back down, Pierce said, "Pete, I'll call you back in a few minutes." He hung up and pocketed the phone, going back to looking at the measurements of the bedroom. "This is a nice-size room," he commented out loud. "It's definitely big enough for a wheelchair."

"Man, Pete can't be out here alone," his brother said. "It's not good for him."

"Yeah? Why is that?" Pierce measured the room, just so they had the basics for when they needed them.

He walked into the en suite bath and immediately knew the door would need to come off. Thankfully there was room on either side. They could just take out the door and leave it open.

He wandered through the old-fashioned bathroom, thinking out loud, "This is where the money will go."

"I told you there's no way we can modify it enough for Pete to come home."

Pierce turned to look at Ross, who appeared to be feeling better at that news. "What's the matter? Afraid you'll find yourself out on the street?"

Ross frowned at him. "You're making yourself a lot of enemies. I want my brother home as much as the next man, but not if it'll mean another failure for him."

"It's only a failure if you don't try," Pierce snapped back at Ross. "You're sitting here, living high on the hog in your brother's place without doing anything to give back. If we find out you've taken any of his money, you can bet *out on the street* will be the least of your problems."

"What the hell are you talking about?" he asked. "You don't know nothing about my money."

Pierce just snorted. "Let me put it this way. Every *gov-*

ernment-issued penny Pete had in that bank account better have one hell of an explanation if it's not there, or you'll find yourself in jail."

"Ha. The sheriff ain't doing nothing," Ross said. "We're buddies, and he knows I need money to live."

"Yeah? Did you pay him with any of Pete's money?" He watched something cross in Ross's gaze. And he nodded to himself. "You do realize Pete is a vet, right? He gets special privileges, and, when he needs a lawyer, he gets a lawyer."

Pierce didn't know for sure that the government would provide an attorney, but he knew plenty of guys who would pitch in and help out a veteran like Pete for free if it came to that. If his brother was stealing from him while he was in a rehab center, a lot of guys would come and move Ross out and dump him several counties over, then come back and fix up Pete's place for him. "That's pension money, and, if you're stealing that …" Pierce just shook his head. "You ain't going to like jail much. And it ain't going to be down here at the county lockup. This will be big-time. Actually it'll be hard time." His voice held a word of warning. "So, before I get to checking Pete's bank account and making sure everything is kosher, you better make sure every penny is back in there."

Ross's face turned white.

Pierce looked at his watch. "You got four hours."

Ross started blustering.

"I said, *four hours*," Pierce stated, his voice hard, cold. "I've already got people looking into this, but I'll give you four hour's grace to make sure every goddamn penny is back in Pete's account."

"I can't," Ross whined. "I had to pay the utility bills."

"Yeah, you did, and maybe the taxes, depending on

when they came due. And maybe the house insurance, depending on when that was due. But there had better be an invoice and a receipt for every penny you took."

"I had to have food," he whined. "He owed me for looking after this place. I had to buy groceries. And gas …" Ross wrung his hands.

Pierce stared at him in disgust. "You heard me. Four hours. A full accounting of every penny and all the proper receipts. And there sure as hell better be an awful lot of receipts in your hands. I suggest you run along and take care of that because, in four hours I'll come knocking, and you'd better have that ready. Now, you're stopping me from doing my work. Get the hell out of here."

He waited until Ross returned to the living room, figuring Ross wouldn't do what he was told. Instead he was probably making some calls. Pierce'd bet five bucks that Ross was calling the sheriff first, then Jed next.

Pierce checked his watch and wondered how long he had before the cavalry showed up to defend Ross. Pierce figured maybe thirty minutes, possibly an hour, not more.

Pierce grabbed his tape measure and headed into the bathroom. He'd like to see this room completely gutted and start from scratch. With all the measurements down, he turned and walked back to the living room.

He wandered the space, realizing this was an older house with lots of rooms, lots of walls, whereas he preferred the open concept, which would be much easier for wheelchair adaptation too. But it was post-and-beam construction. A lot of these walls looked to have been put in afterward, which meant they could also come out.

He took more photographs, wandered around, then headed for the kitchen. In order for Pete to be independent, he needed access to the kitchen and the room to work in it. Pierce winced when he saw it. It wasn't that it was bad; it was just old, and it was tiny. Back to that *whole walls coming out* thing.

He took more measurements, and an idea started to form about how the kitchen should be. He'd always loved cabinet working and carpentry. Remodels were just part of life as far as he was concerned. He'd grown up with a father who was in real estate, and they used to buy and fix up homes and sell them. He'd learned a lot, and he was grateful for every lesson because he would need every one of them here and now. He might find a few local people to help; otherwise he would have to bring in some specialized guys to do the work, and that would get pricey.

He opened the fridge and saw three-quarters of it was full of booze. In disgust he slammed it shut and checked out the plumbing under the sink. It was still copper piping, which said an awful lot about the age of the house too.

"Well, Pete, it will take some money, but we can do a lot on a little."

From the kitchen was a single glass door that opened up onto a deck. He popped it open and looked at the glass door and wrote down another note. It had to be wider, and a ramp was needed to get in and out. The damn threshold was raised, so it would be hard to get the chair's wheels up and over it. This was a shitty job. It should have been put in flush.

He stepped out on the deck and walked the back of the house, taking pictures as he went. There was no railing, but it was wide enough, and stairs were at both ends. The stairs could come out, and ramps could go in, so that was a pretty minor job too. He headed back inside and took a look at the staircase going up. Depending on what Pete wanted to do, the stairs could stay, and an elevator could go in.

As he walked around the side, moving toward the front of the house, he heard the sounds of a vehicle coming, then another and another. He gave a grim smile, tucked his notepad and pen inside his pocket, picked up his phone and dialed. "How you doing, Pete?" he asked as soon as Pete answered.

"I'm doing okay. What do you think of the house?"

"Definitely needs some work done to accommodate you," he said. "The en suite bathroom is likely the biggest cost. The kitchen is a bit small too. But it won't be impossible to do."

"Well, that's good news," Pete said with relief. "It depends on the money then, doesn't it?"

"Depends on how much money you've got and how much help we can rustle up to make some of these changes, also on your mobility." He stood at the front door. "Your brother has called the cavalry too."

"He's what?" Pete yelled out in alarm. "What are you talking about?"

"Pretty sure he's got the sheriff and Jed and God-only-knows-who-else coming down here to have a talk with me and to try to run me off your place."

"Jesus, that's not good," Pete said, sputtering. "I'm getting off the phone, and I'll call you some help." And just like that he hung up.

Pierce laughed. He walked to his truck, pulled out his handgun from the glove box and put it in his shoulder holster he wore underneath his overshirt. Then he walked back to the front steps as the vehicles pulled up and parked. He looked at the sheriff who hopped out and walked toward him, shifting his belt up over his gut. "Sheriff, good to see you again," he said.

"What's this I hear about you running Ross off?"

Pierce raised an eyebrow. "I didn't say anything about running Ross off. I said his brother was looking for an accounting of what kind of work he'd done and how much money he'd spent in the time he's been gone because Pete is on his way back home soon and needs a certain amount of money to make changes on his property."

The sheriff frowned. "What? Pete is coming back?"

"Yeah, Pete is coming back," Pierce said. "We've been back and forth on the phone all day. I talked to him about the various changes required on his house." He launched into an explanation on how he will put a ramp in and double up the front door so the wheelchair could fit.

He turned with a big smile and said, "The bedroom is fine. The hallway is fine, of course. For whatever reason, Ross moved into Pete's bedroom." He shot the sheriff a disgusted look. "Not like there aren't bedrooms upstairs he could have used without trying to move in on his brother's property and take over like he did."

Before Ross could argue, Pierce launched straight back into an explanation of how he will change out the single glass door in the kitchen so it too was a double door and to cover up that bit of a threshold lip so Pete could get out on the deck and then put a ramp around the back.

The men just stared at him.

He looked at them all. "Aren't you guys Pete's buddies?"

Jed just kind of looked down at the ground, and the sheriff ran his hand across his mustache a couple times.

"Are you or are you not his buddies?" Pierce asked, his tone turning hard with a deadly backlash to it.

Jed looked at him and said, "Ross is my buddy."

"I see," Pierce said, crossing his arms over his chest. "So you don't want the owner of the house—who has gone to war, fought for you and your country, been injured, been in recovery all this time—to come back to what's rightfully his?"

Jed had the grace to turn a ruddy red. He backed up a couple steps and spat on the side of the driveway.

Pierce turned his gaze to the sheriff. "And what say you, Sheriff?"

The sheriff pulled the hat off his head and ran his fingers through his hair. "Well, I've known Pete a long time."

"I'm sure you'll tell me that he's a good man," Pierce said. He watched another car come down the road toward them. It was a deputy's vehicle, and he was pretty darn sure it was Hedi.

The sheriff nodded. "He is a good guy. But I understood he's a cripple."

Pierce's eyebrows shot up. "A cripple? What the hell are you calling Pete a cripple for?" He turned on Ross. "Is that your words? Would you disrespect your brother like that?"

Ross opened his mouth and then snapped it shut. "I didn't say he was a cripple."

"I'd be very unhappy to hear you call him that," Pierce said. "That man needs the help of his friends, and I'm still waiting to see it."

"What's this got to do with you anyway?" Jed said.

"I went and fought for my country too, so Pete and I are brothers-in-arms," Pierce said with a half-smile and a hard gaze. "I do a lot of remodeling. So I'm here to help Pete get back into his house. You don't want to see a man like that stuck in an institution, do you? Not when he can live comfortably in his own home."

"I mean, if he's dragging shit bags and crap like that," Jed said, "maybe that's where he belongs."

Pierce snorted. "You know what? I wouldn't be at all surprised if he doesn't come back walking on his own two feet." He kept his tone very low.

Just then the deputy's vehicle pulled up and parked.

"That'd be a fine thing to see," the sheriff said. "Pete is a good man. What happened to him was hard." He turned to look at his deputy and frowned. "What's she doing here?"

"She's here at my request," Pierce said cheerfully. He lifted a hand. "Hey, Hedi. Glad you could make it."

She flashed him a confused look, then walked closer.

He didn't give her a chance to speak. "I've been talking to Pete," he said, "and the good news is, I think we can get his house fixed up so he can get home. It'll take some money and lots of volunteer hours, but I'm pretty sure his buddies here can give us a hand." He waved a hand at the two men standing in front of him.

Hedi's eyebrows rose.

He could see the humor flash across her face before she managed to school her features. "Isn't that right, Jed?" Pierce said. "I know you said you were Ross's buddy more than Pete's, but you know Ross will be here helping out too."

"Like hell I am," Ross snapped. "I can't swing a hammer."

"Everybody can swing a hammer," Pierce said coolly. "Just not everyone can swing it well. And you're not paying Pete any rent, so living here free of charge, spending your brother's money, free and clear without his permission, so I'm sure you'll want to do something to help pay him back for his generosity." Pierce made sure he injected just the right amount of scorn so Ross would stand up and do what was right. Pierce's voice snapped across the silence. "Right?"

Ross spat on the ground and shot Pierce a disgusted look. "It ain't none of your business."

"I'm moving in," Pierce said, "with Pete's permission. So you're either staying here and helping out, or you're getting the hell off this place right now."

Silence whistled across the group.

CHAPTER 6

HEDI COULDN'T BELIEVE it when she got a garbled message from her father to *Get the hell over here*. She knew he was coming too, as well as Roger and a couple other guys. Pete had sent out a call of distress to the old guard, and they'd all taken up the call. But she was the closest and the most available, so she was here first. And just listening to Pierce set down the other men was something to see. She wished she'd been here from the beginning.

"That's great news," she said to Pierce warmly. "I can't wait to see Pete again. He's a good guy." She looked at the front door. "I guess this will all have to change."

Pierce stepped up and explained how he would take out the window and put in a double door that opened both ways.

She nodded approvingly. "He'll need a ramp, and I guess bathroom and kitchen modifications. All that takes money and manpower. And Pete has his pension, with his medical treatments paid for, so there should be lots there for him." The silence behind her got even more awkward. She spun around and looked at the three men, her gaze landing on Ross. "Right, Ross?"

He looked at her resentfully. "Costs money to live here."

She narrowed her gaze. "It might cost a *little* bit of money to live here …" Her voice was gentle and calm. "… but if a large amount of Pete's pension money disappeared, that would be theft."

Ross straightened his back and glared at her, then looked at the sheriff and back at her again. "Sheriff, you won't let her talk to me like this, are you?"

She turned and glared at the sheriff.

He stared back at her balefully.

That in itself was a shift. She wondered when that had occurred. Then she realized it was in the force of the man in a black truck.

"Ross already knows his clock is ticking away on that." Pierce's voice remained calm and cool as he crossed his arms over his chest and leaned against the front door frame. He looked down at his watch. "By the way, Ross, you're down to three hours now."

Ross spluttered, then snorted and walked back inside. He went to slam the front door, but Pierce's boot was in the way. Ross turned and said, "You're not moving in. You get the hell out of my house."

"But it's not your house," Pierce said.

"How the hell do you know?" Ross snarled. "It's my house if I want it to be my house. You get the hell out of here."

Hedi was shocked. "Hey, what are you talking about, Ross? This is Pete's house. You've been living here for a few months, but you don't just get to move in and take over like it's yours. Pete's making modifications, and he's coming home."

"You believe this snake here?" Ross sneered. "Of course you would. You're nothing but a woman. You'll probably spread your legs for smack."

She hadn't even processed his words before Ross lay flat

on the ground between her and Pierce.

Pierce reached down and, with one hand, grabbed a handful of shirt, lifted Ross up, dragged him out on the deck and plunked him down. "Don't you ever talk to a woman like that again while I'm around." His voice was hard. "The fact that she's a law enforcement officer, who you obviously have zero respect for, is a really bad sign, not to mention her boss stood here and let you treat her like that. But as for me? Nobody treats a woman like that. Now you got twenty minutes to get your shit packed up and get the hell out of here."

"Or what?" Ross said, struggling to his feet, wiping the blood off his cheek. "The sheriff is here. He'll back me up."

Just then three more vehicles pulled into the yard. The sheriff spun around, took one look and said, "Shit."

Ross sputtered, "What … what … what's the matter?" And then he saw four men hop out of the newly arrived vehicles.

Hedi walked over and said, "Good timing, Dad." Hedi studied her father. He wore a brushed cotton T-shirt that said he still worked out on a regular basis, plus dark blue jeans, cowboy boots that were cut properly, and a walk, not a swagger, that said this man had seen it all, done it all, and was comfortable doing it all over again. She loved that about him. He'd been a great father and still was her biggest supporter.

Pierce nodded his head. "Good evening. I'm Pierce."

Her father nodded. "My name's Jessie. Glad to meet you." He looked at Ross. "What's this I hear about you not wanting to vacate Pete's house?"

Ross looked to the sheriff. "Sheriff, you can't let them do this to me."

The sheriff lifted his hat again to rub his head. "Well, now this is a bit of a mess up."

"No mess up at all," Pierce said. "Sometimes, when you can't do the job yourself, your friends have to take out the trash." He turned his gaze on Ross. "I mean it. You got twenty minutes, buddy."

"That's not fair. I don't have to leave."

"If you won't help do the work and help make up for the rent money you took from Pete, you're damn right you have to leave. And you're still on a clock for that other accounting problem you have."

Ross gave him a haunted look and stormed inside.

Jessie laughed. "Nice to see you around town, Pierce. We need a few more men like you."

"We need a few more men like you too," Pierce said. "I hope you guys heard from Pete. Did you?"

"Yeah. He called not too long ago, said you were here creating a ruckus."

"You can say that again," the sheriff snarled. "Looks like you don't need me after all." He walked to his car and turned. "I'm heading back to the office." He hopped in, and he drove away.

Hearing the sound of a vehicle, Ross came back outside. When he saw the sheriff leave, he looked like he wanted to cry.

Pierce turned to him. "If you thought the sheriff would back you up, you're dead wrong. In this case, the law is on Pete's side, not yours, and you're down to twelve minutes."

Ross went back inside.

Hedi said, "You'll really make him leave?"

"Oh, yeah, I'll make him leave. And there won't be any talk about him moving back in again until we get a clean accounting of what the hell happened to Pete's money."

She was horrified to think anybody would have stolen from Pete, but to think it might have been his own brother, that made it so much worse. "Did he really steal money from him?"

"Ross has another two and a half hours to make good on the amount that's supposed to be there," he said. "And believe me, Pete is checking bank accounts, and so are the accountants. Pete got a lump sum after he got back, for lost wages and to help with medical adjustments. And every damn penny of that had better be there," he said coolly. "Or none of the law around this area will do anything to help Ross. I'll make sure he's slammed into some jail a long way away without any support system for a hell of a long time."

"As long as you leave him alive, and you don't break any bones doing it," Jessie said, his tone hard, "I won't argue."

"I might break a bone or two," Pierce said with a fat smile. "But, of course, that's only if he struggles. If he's a good boy and behaves himself, then"—Pierce shrugged—"no need to force him to do anything, is there?"

The two men exchanged knowing looks.

Just then Ross came back out with a duffel bag and another bag. "The rest of my stuff is still here," he said. "I can't take it all right now."

"That's fine. I'll have a talk with Pete and get an inventory of what belongs here and what you say is yours." He looked at the two bags. "Make sure it's just your shit in there because I'll come back after you if anything from the house is missing."

Ross shot him a look full of hatred. "It's mine." He threw the bags in the back of the pickup and walked to where Jed was.

The two men talked, glanced at Pierce, the conversation continued, then they both got into their vehicles and pulled out.

Jessie and the men with him walked up to the veranda, Jessie saying, "You just made yourself a couple enemies."

Hedi laughed. "And yet, it's you, Dad, who always said you could judge a man by the enemies he makes."

Jessie nodded. "I did, indeed. But these are especially ugly ones. They'll torch this place before they'll let you have it."

Pierce narrowed his gaze as he studied the men driving away. "In that case somebody might want to make sure Jed's wife and kids go someplace for a few days until we get this sorted out," he said, "because ugly is what ugly does."

Hedi wasn't sure what the hell that meant, but she understood the meaning. "You can't get those kids caught up in this," she warned. "They're already having a hell of a time."

"He's right though," her father said. "Things will have to get worse before they get any better."

She frowned, then turned to face Pierce again. "I talked to Jed's wife. She said there are signs of a dog out in the back here. She doesn't know if it's the same one or not. It's circling away from Jed's place, but Pete's place is also Salem's last-known source of food, outside of anything it can hunt."

Pierce smiled. "Now that's the best news I've heard all day."

"How can that be?" she said. "That dog has gone half wild."

"But it always was half wild," he said. "That's what makes them the best War Dogs. If we could get our hands on her, I can help her."

"Do you really think you can?"

He nodded. "It's a good thing I did move in here today," he said. "I'll work hard to get Salem back in line, see if we can get her rehabilitated in time for Pete to come home. That's where they both belong—with each other."

Jessie nodded. "I can swing a hammer, maybe not as good as you can, but I can certainly do a decent job." He looked at the other couple guys, and they all nodded. "If there's anything we can do to help get Pete's house ready, you just let us know."

Pierce smiled.

Hedi laughed. "Thanks, Dad."

He looked at her and smiled. "I wish you had a different job. I don't know where the sheriff will fall on this issue, but it'll get bad."

"I know." Her voice was serious and sad. "It's shitty, but it's the way it'll be."

"Maybe you should head back into town then," Pierce said.

"Why, so I don't get hurt?" she challenged. "I'm the deputy. Remember that."

"Then I hope you're carrying," he said, "because you can bet Jed's gone home to get some firepower."

She looked at him, then nodded. "You're right. He probably has. But Jed is also not the kind of guy who would blast you in the face. He'll come up behind you, shoot you in the back."

"Nice community you have here." Pierce crossed his arms over his chest again. "I might have to call in some reinforcements of my own."

Jessie nodded. "If you got them, call them fast."

"I'll move my vehicle out of sight," she said. "Just in case."

"Good idea," Jessie said.

Hedi drove her car around to the side and parked it. She hopped out and walked up to the front of the house and stepped in without warning. Pierce turned around, surprised, and took note. "You move softly."

"I'm a cop," she said.

He nodded. "Why are you here now?"

"Because you'll need help," she said. "It could get very ugly."

"It could," he said, hesitating.

She stared at him. "Unless you've got a problem with a female helping."

"I don't have a problem with a female helping," he said with a grin. "Don't suppose you can swing a hammer too, can you?"

She could feel the tension ease in her back. "I can swing a hammer pretty decently. I helped my father do enough renos and fixing up fence posts and barn repairs," she said.

"Good enough for me." Pierce motioned at the kitchen. "I'm sorting out what's here and what's been done to the place since Pete was here." Just then his phone rang. It was Pete again. "Hey, Pete. Yeah, Hedi is here."

Through the phone she could hear Pete call out, "Hey, Hedi. Hi."

She grinned, leaned forward and said, "Hey, Pete. Pierce has kicked the metaphorical shit out of your brother and moved him off your property, and now you got this big mausoleum of a house waiting for you to get your sorry ass back home again."

Pete gave a big laugh.

She grinned, looked at Pierce and smiled. "If there's one thing Pete does like, it's life."

"Pete used to like life," Pete said, still shouting into the phone. "And he's starting to like life again."

"You hit a rough spot," Pierce said, "and all of a sudden that rough spot became too much to handle. You have to get through it first. Then life is different on the other side."

"Now I'm starting to believe," he said. "You will never guess, but I got a phone call from a prosthetic designer who says she thinks she can help me out." He spoke with amazement. "I told her that I had to sort out my money first, and she agreed, said she needed permission to get my medical records to see what she could do. Of course I gave her my permission, like *Holy shit, yes.* If I could actually *walk*, as in walk on my own two legs, that would be huge."

Pierce chuckled. "That's Kat. And she's dynamite. She's also an amputee herself, so, if she says she can do something for you, she can do something for you."

"Holy shit. I'm so damn grateful. I feel like everything has flipped around now."

"But that doesn't mean you're over the hump yet," Pierce warned. "You take good care of yourself. I'll hang up and see if I can find some bloody coffee in this place. Then I'll work out some modifications for the house, and we'll sit down and talk money, once we sort out the bank account, what you have left."

"Okay, will do," Pete said, his voice slowing, hesitating. "I know this shit is expensive, so it needs to be just, you know, basics to begin with."

Pete said goodbye, and Pierce shut off the call. "Do you have any idea where the coffee might be in here?"

He turned around to see Hedi already opening cupboards. She smiled at him. "Who knows?" She pulled out an almost empty bag of coffee. "It's enough for one pot." She filled the coffeemaker and had a pot brewing quickly. She turned around, took one look at him, studying him for a long moment. "Why are you doing this?"

He'd been looking at his phone, checking for messages. At her words, he stopped and looked up at her. His gaze was open and serious. "I came to rescue a dog. But War Dogs are War Dogs, both man and animal. I've been there, done that, and, if I can give a helping hand to another veteran, I'm all in. Pete's got a bum deal here. I'm not sure what the hell is going on with Jed and Ross, and whoever else is hanging around that same crowd, but they're all bad news."

"Oh, I know they're bad news," she said quietly. "But, like I said before—you've stepped into the middle of a hornet's nest, and you've got it all stirred up."

"Good," he said. "Time to swat those little buggers." He looked out the window, his gaze caught on something.

"What do you see?"

"The shepherd is hanging around the house," he said.

She looked but couldn't see what was bothering him.

"I don't want to put food out. She needs to know she can come in and get food."

"Any time she's gotten close to men lately," Hedi said seriously, "she's gotten hurt. Maybe you should give a little to break the ice."

"I might have to," he said, pondering the issue. He got up to poke through the fridge and freezer. "If there was at least a bone or something, I could give it to her. Even dog food would help."

"There should have been some. Ross said he had an intruder who stole everything, but I figure Jed just came and took it all," Hedi said. "Let me help you look. They might have missed something."

Together they went through the cabinets. Triumphantly Hedi found the remnants of an old bag in the back corner. "I bet he forgot about this one. There's only four, maybe six cups, but it'll give the dog something to start with." She handed Pierce the bag and watched as he dumped it all into a large bowl and walked out back.

He judged the distance between him and where he'd seen the dog; then he put down several piles, one farther away, another closer, and then another one closer yet. The last one he left in the bowl itself. Then he walked back inside and poured a cup of coffee.

"What makes you think she'll come in?"

"She's hungry," he said. "She's also apparently scared and worried about getting caught. If she's been that badly abused, then she'll stay away from all men. But this is also home to her and probably has some good memories."

"Yes," she said, nodding. "How quickly can Pete get back here?"

"I'm not sure," he said, taking a sip of his coffee. "But, once we get him home, if we haven't got any modifications done, we'll find a way to make some quick and fast changes for him. The kitchen is a problem. It's open enough, but the area to sit, it's pretty small, pretty crowded."

She walked to the wall behind the island where the dining room table sat. "If this wall isn't structural, why not take it out?"

He nodded, looking up at the way the joists and the ceiling met with the walls. "I don't think it is structural." He looked from the wall to the countertop that extended far out. "That would probably give him enough access. He can work at the counters, but this outside piece here ... Yeah, you're right. That might be the best answer." He looked at it for a long moment. "It's just drywall. I could probably pop that off in no time, see just what the framing is like. If it's simple, I could take it down."

"It'll be the electrical threading through the walls that would cause trouble," she said.

"Not really," he said. "I can do almost all house wiring. I just can't do high-voltage stuff."

She looked at him in surprise. "It sounds like you're a pretty handy guy to have around."

He shrugged. "You learn to do an awful lot when you're flipping houses. I can put in sinks and do basic plumbing too, but, if you want fancy stuff, I don't know. I might need some help."

"Do you think you can modify the bathroom?"

He frowned at her. "I can. I'm just not sure I could make it look decorator pretty. He needs to have access to the toilet with handicap bars, and he needs a wheelchair-accessible sink and shower stall. Would a shower chair work? I'll have to do some research on that. Maybe talk to these friends of mine."

"Are they amputees too?"

He grinned. "Yes. Eight former SEALs began Titanium Corp, and all are missing at least an arm or a leg or both," he said, roaming the kitchen with an eye toward renovations. "Lots of back injuries too. Steel plates, all kinds of extras they weren't born with."

"What about you?" she asked. "Are you missing body parts?"

"Sure I am," he said. "Lots of tissue, muscle, a chunk of liver, gallbladder, one kidney, and"—he kicked out his leg— "I'm missing the lower leg."

"So you really do understand what Pete's going

through."

"I do," he said. "And I know, if he's over the hump, he'll be okay now. But we have to do everything we can to make it possible for him to come home."

"He's missing both legs below the knees I believe, or is one above?"

"He's missing both lower legs," Pierce said. "Lots of guys without both legs can still walk."

"So you're trying to make room for a wheelchair as a contingency while he gets better or when he's too tired or if he has an injury and needs to be in the wheelchair. But, other than that, he should be capable of walking with prosthetics?"

"Potentially down the road. It takes time for the body to heal before attaching the new limbs. Plus he's got some back injuries, so we have to strengthen that up. Let's just say he has a lot of work ahead of him."

"But it's doable?"

He looked at her in surprise. "It's absolutely doable. That's why I'm here, to help make it happen as much as we can."

"But that's not what you came for."

"No, it isn't." He looked out the window for Salem, turned and added, "That seems to bug you. Yes, I came for the dog, but then I found out what was happening at Pete's place. It's really no contest. The two dovetail together. If Pete can come home, the dog gets a home again, and then somebody just needs to keep an eye on Pete to make sure he doesn't have any setbacks and that the dog is still okay."

She laughed. "I can't tell if you care more about Pete or the dog."

"Doesn't matter," Pierce said. "They both need help,

and we've got to get both back home. In the meantime, I've apparently stirred up some angry people."

"That you have," she said.

"Is that why you're here?" he asked. "You don't think I can handle this on my own?"

"I think it's quite possible my dad's right, and they'll likely burn this place to the ground before they let you have it."

He studied her face for a long moment. "And nobody will do anything to stop them?"

"You saw the sheriff. He just backs away anytime there's a fight."

"What happens when the people are fed up with the sheriff? How do you get rid of him?"

"We have to go above him."

"What if he quits?" Pierce's voice was almost a challenge.

"Then somebody has a temporary promotion until a new election."

"Interesting," Pierce said. "I don't do politics. I'm too much of a person who likes to get things done, and screw it if people are happy or unhappy with it."

"Are you still registered at the hotel?" she asked, leaning against the counter, sipping her coffee.

He refilled his cup and faced her. "No. I checked out this morning."

"So you had already planned to move in today?"

"I was happy to have his brother stay, particularly if I thought he would give us a hand with the reno. But I don't want any more deadbeats bringing Pete down."

She nodded. "So did you bring groceries?"

"Not yet," he said cheerfully. "I can make a trip to town."

"You probably don't want to leave right now," she said. "Ross is likely to have somebody keeping a lookout to see if you do. And, once you're gone, he'll be back with company. You'll find it much harder to get back in."

"Right. Good point," he said. "I think I've got a few protein bars in the truck, and that might have to do, if there isn't anything around here." He opened the fridge and snorted. "If I'm staying here, I need to get some food. Ross obviously doesn't care about actual nutrition."

"Since it seems I'm coming back this evening, why don't I pick up some basics?"

He turned and looked at her. "Why are you coming back?"

"Same reason I'm here now," she said. "I don't like the idea of you being alone with that gang. They'll lose their tempers with you."

"Oh." He grinned. "It sounds good to me. I'm so glad you're worried about me, sweetie."

She narrowed her gaze at him. "The name is Hedi. Don't call me sweetie."

"Okay. I won't, sweetheart. Hedi's kind of a slang nickname anyway, isn't it?"

She fisted her hands on her hips and glared at him.

He chuckled, opening a cabinet, finding cereal. "Let's do a quick list. Don't know exactly what's available, but we could use some milk for this cereal, if nothing else. Some eggs, bread, and bacon for breakfast." He rummaged through some of the other cupboards. "There's really nothing here. Salad fixings, pasta, maybe a pack or two of hamburger, some buns, that type of thing. Can you handle that?"

"I can handle that," she said, "as long as you don't care about the quality and are happy with the choices I make."

"It's food," he said. "I'll be happy." He pulled his wallet from his back pocket, pulled out two hundred dollars and handed it to her. "Groceries," he said.

She looked at the money in surprise. "That's a lot of grocery money."

"I've got to eat, and I've got to work," he said. "Just make sure you pick up some dog food and not too cheap of a brand. Salem'll need real food. Thinking of which, better make that several packages of ground beef. I could always get her to eat meat too."

Hedi walked out to her car. The sun was beginning to set. "I'll be at least an hour, probably twice that."

"Not a problem," he said. "I'll cook dinner for you when you get in, depending on how late it is."

"I'm likely to pick up dinner instead."

"If there's any money left, go for it," he said. "I'll start working on ramps. That's probably the easiest thing to begin with. I saw a lot of wood in the barn, and I can certainly get something started while you're out and about."

She nodded. "You take care." And she headed back into town.

SUCH AN INTERESTING woman. And a novelty to have somebody pitch in and help. He hated the idea of her getting caught up in this mess though. Still, just the thought of her made him smile. He did have a lot of good friends, and he was concerned about giving a heads-up to Badger. Thinking of that, he stopped what he was doing, pulled out his phone and updated him.

Badger's response was immediate. "Do you want some

backup?"

"The deputy is coming back, but I'm not exactly sure when she'll make it. It's a pretty strange scenario," he admitted. "I think Jessie, her father, who's the former sheriff, would be here in a pinch, but it's not the same as having men of your own."

"Let me talk to Pete and see if anybody in town can help you out."

"Okay. He's the one who contacted Hedi's dad, the ex-sheriff. And we need to figure out what to do about the current sheriff."

"Yeah, that's a bad one," Badger said. "I'll get back to you on that." And he hung up.

Pierce put the phone on the table and something caught his eyes. He looked up to see a massive black shepherd wolfing down the bit of dog food he'd put at the farthest point out. Pierce walked to the open doorway and stepped out on the porch. She froze and stared at him. "It's all right, Salem. I know you've had a pretty shitty time, but we're getting you back here, and Pete's coming home too."

Her ears twitched, but that was all. She kept eating, her eyes focused on him. If he took one step toward her, he knew she'd bolt. He kept his voice low and steady, just talking to her, leaning against the porch railing. "Make sure you eat up. You'll need it. I've got more food coming, but it'll be a few hours yet."

She finished the pile in front of her and raised her head, still studying him, her muscles tense, ready. She glanced to the side, as if hearing a sound, then hunkered down a little lower, but her gaze never left that area.

"Is something there? Wouldn't be at all surprised. Some two-legged wolves are in this part of the country," he said.

"They might be foolish enough to attack."

Then she seemed to relax at the constant voice talking to her. She moved a step closer.

"You can do it," he said. "Come on to the next pile. You need it. That's nowhere near enough food for you yet."

She took a few more steps in. Her nose had already caught the scent of the next pile. Nervously she crept forward enough so that she could devour the second pile.

"Come on. Eat it up," he said in an encouraging tone.

She was big. Her coat was shaggy and matted. She limped, and blood was on her flank but there didn't appear to be an open wound. She moved slowly, and she was injured, but she wasn't that badly physically hurt. However, the look in her eyes was one of betrayal, one that said she didn't trust anybody anymore, and that broke his heart.

He took two slow steps down the porch, stopped and sat. She froze, her mouth full of food, but not chewing as she watched him. He stayed in place and just kept talking to her. Finally she lowered her head and ate the rest of the food.

"So what did you do? Just got loose from the police yard? How did they catch you again? Probably with food and that's why you're so nervous." He looked around the area. There should have been fences around the homestead itself. It was a nice property, and, with a little bit of care, it could be quite a nice place, depending on how much land he had here. Pete could possibly have crops that could either help him out grocery-wise or be something he could sell and make a little money.

Pierce sat here quietly, content while the dog ate. When the third pile was gone, she looked at him and backed up slightly. The bowl was just a little too close to Pierce.

"It'll be here for you. You've had three piles. That'll take the worst of the hunger off."

She continued to back up. When something crackled in the bush beside him, she spun and raced off. He was happy to see her movements were clean and powerful. She held her back leg too low to the ground for a clean run, but then she was injured. He couldn't really tell how or how badly, but at least she'd been fed.

He walked to the side of the house where he'd heard crackling in a bush. He wasn't sure what was out here, if it was another dog or a wild animal or something he was quite prepared to beat into the ground. He did a quick search but saw nothing.

As he was about to walk away, he heard a meow. He turned to see a ragtag cat walking toward him. It didn't look underfed, but it didn't look terribly healthy either. He stopped and bent down. "Hey, kitty. What are you doing here?"

"*Meow, meow.*" The cat sauntered closer. It looked like a tomcat, part of an ear torn, patch of fur missing.

He didn't know if he'd been fighting other cats or taking down prey a little too big for him. Pierce reached out a hand, scooped it up, not surprised when the cat allowed him to pick him up. With the cat in his arms, he walked to the barn. "There should be a ton of food for you in here. Barns always have mice." He scratched the guy behind the ear, listening to the great big guttural engine kick in, and smiled. "You're probably Pete's too, aren't you?"

In the barn he put the cat on a bale of hay, then stopped and stared, finally struck by what he saw before him. "Pete, why do you have hay? I don't see any horses or cows." But there was hay, a good forty, maybe sixty bales of it. He frowned, hoping Ross hadn't sold off livestock that Pete had owned.

Pierce turned to the wood supply. Found at least six good solid sheets of plywood. A full sheet would be too broad, but he took out his tape measure and marked off what he needed. What he also needed was some solid tools.

He headed into the open workshop and found a circular saw and a few power tools. He grinned when he saw those. "Thought I would have to do this the old-fashioned way."

"And just what's the old-fashioned way?"

He turned to see Ross standing stiffly in the doorway. Pierce looked at him. "By hand," he said.

"This is by hand," Ross said in exasperation as he pointed at the tools. "Who the hell even knows how to operate this old shit?"

"It's not that old," Pierce said. "I imagine almost all of it is in good working condition."

"Maybe, but it's old," Ross said in disgust.

"What's with the hay? What are you doing back here?" Pierce asked as he continued to mark and measure the board in front of him.

"I left some stuff here, remember?" Ross's tone was only half derisive. He knew he'd get his face kicked in if he didn't show enough respect. "Pete used to board some city horses here. I sent them home. Way too much work to look after."

"Sorted your money issue yet?" Pierce asked thinking how foolish he was to wipe out a source of income. Then anything that required effort appeared to be too much for Ross.

"I still got an hour," he said.

"Is that all? I hadn't realized the time had gone by so fast. I figured you were already out of time."

"You said eight," Ross said in alarm.

Pierce slowly straightened and looked at him. "I said four."

"No, you said four hours, and it's only seven now."

"The question is whether you've done the job, or will I find out you've stolen your brother's money? And, of course, that'll definitely get your ass kicked across the property."

"How would you know?" Ross asked with a laugh.

"Because Pete's got the accountants and the bookkeepers and the police on his end tracking his account."

The color drained from Ross's face. "Pete wouldn't do that to me."

"Pete has to start looking after Pete," Pierce said. "And other people should be looking after Pete, not him looking after you. You're able-bodied and not working. You should be out there pulling in a decent wage, doing something with your own life, not trying to take what's your brother's."

"Don't be so sanctimonious and righteous," Ross said. "I've been living here and kept people like Jed off the place."

"That may be," he said, "but you're also making deals with Jed too, and Jed's bad news in his own right."

"He is that," Ross said. "He's gotten a lot worse these last six months."

"What's that all about?"

Ross just shrugged. "I don't know. Something about his wife wanting a divorce."

"Of course she wants a divorce," Pierce said with a laugh of his own. "Why the hell would she want to stay and get her ass kicked every day? Watch her kids be terrorized?"

"He won't let her go," Ross said starkly.

"Are you going to help him?" Pierce asked. "You don't seem to have too much in the way of ethics or honor."

"That's not fair," Ross muttered. "I didn't see I was doing nothing wrong."

"The trouble is, when you take a half step across the line, it's pretty easy to take another half step, and, before you know it," Pierce said, "you've taken so many steps you can't even see the line anymore. At that point, in your twisted mind, you're already thinking it's all yours. And you're blowing it on booze and forgetting even about food."

"I've had a pretty rough couple months myself," he said. "So I took a few dollars. That's not a big deal. Pete would never begrudge me that."

"Well, just think, it's not Pete's deal anymore," Pierce said. "It's mine. And I'll make sure Pete gets what's his. Whether you like it or not."

CHAPTER 7

H EDI CASHED OUT at the grocery store and took her loaded bags to her deputy's car. She would go home and change vehicles. She could already feel the tension in the air. Weird discussions behind her back. People looking at her sideways but not really talking to her.

She ignored everybody and kept walking to the car. "Small-town news travels fast," she muttered under her breath.

When she got home, she planned to park around back to make sure she wasn't seen. She had one handgun with her, and she wondered about picking up more from her dad's. And hated that she was even thinking along those lines.

Just then she got a phone call. She hit Talk. "Hey, Dad. How you doing?"

"I'm doing okay, but I'm a little worried about that Pierce guy out there. I really admire what he's doing for Pete, but he might have bitten off more than he can chew. Have you got an update?"

"I just bought groceries, so he didn't have to leave the place, in case Ross came back and didn't want to give up possession again."

"Good idea," he said thoughtfully. "I can't say I'm feeling too good about this."

"I know," she said, "but I think Pierce's heart is in the

right place. I just don't know if he understands how bad Jed has gotten."

"I'm not sure I understand either. Can you explain it to me?"

She told him about Jed attacking her in his house and shoving her with his rifle and threatening her. "I guess you didn't read the emails I cc'd you on, did you?"

"No, I'm sorry. I've been avoiding the computer. As you know it's not my preferred method of communication. But this…" Her father swore up and down a blue streak. "And that damn sheriff didn't do anything?"

"Nope. He's pretty cozy with Jed, and, as long as Jed stays on this side of the law, he doesn't care."

"But that was not on *this side of the law*," her father snapped. "What has this come to?"

"Hate to say it, Dad, but, when you got in that accident, all hell went to a shithole."

"I can see that," he grumbled. "I'm not sure I could pick up the reins and be sheriff again though. I kind of like retirement. I'll talk to Fort Collins, see what our next step is in ousting our current sheriff."

"You like retirement and no need to go back. But please find out how to get rid of our sheriff. He'll get someone killed with his negligence," she admitted as she moved the last of the groceries over and locked up her deputy vehicle. "What you don't like is sitting on the sidelines. So feel free to fix this. If anyone can, it's you."

"I hear you there. Do you think somebody needs to come to the house and stand watch tonight?"

"I'm heading there now myself," she said. "The sheriff won't call it on duty, but I sure as hell am. Pierce might have taken on more than he can chew. I don't know him well enough. It's not just Jed. You know he's got the Billy boys in the back, and, if he gets them all riled up, they'll shoot that place down, and they'll torch it with him in it."

"You in it too, you mean," her father said in alarm. "Maybe I'll come over myself."

"I won't say no," she said. "But we could be jumping the gun here. It wouldn't be a bad idea to have a watch on what Jed is up to, but I don't know. Those kids and his wife, she was supposed to leave. I called her at work today, and she promised me that she would, but I just don't know. I don't have a good feeling about any of this."

"Neither do I." Her father's voice suddenly sounded brisk. "You go on over. I'll call the boys and see what we come up with." And just like that he hung up.

She frowned, staring at her phone. "But I don't need to be looking after you too, Dad. You're not the law anymore," she said slowly.

She walked back into the house and grabbed an overnight bag and stuffed it in the car. She didn't know what the hell would happen, but she wanted to be prepared. She also grabbed one of her big thick flannel shirts in case it got really cold out tonight. She didn't know how much she would be in the house or outside, so she chose her black one, just to blend in the background. She wasn't the hunter the others were, but she was no slouch when it came to hiding her tracks and staying out of sight.

The last thing she did was put out some cat food and fed her dog. She had a small Maltese that was aging and wouldn't appreciate being alone tonight, but she couldn't take him into a gunfight. He was all about curling up on her pillow and being cuddled. He didn't like loud noises or aggressive moves. He'd be fine if it was a normal visit, but tonight could get ugly.

She arranged his blanket on the couch for him and walked away, locking up behind her.

In her own vehicle, she drove toward Pete's place. The air had an electric feel to it, the atmosphere felt off, wrong in so many ways.

Following her instincts, she drove into the barn and parked. There was an old blanket, kind of a car cover there. She threw it over her car as soon as she had the groceries out. It took her two trips to get the groceries to the house, but, with everything stacked on the front veranda, she knocked on the door and then pushed it open.

A light was on in the living room, but everything else appeared quiet. Frowning, she grabbed her grocery bags and carried everything into the kitchen, setting it all on the table. Outside she could see Pierce sitting on the steps only ten feet away from Salem. Her ears were back, and her lip was curled, but she was the one approaching him.

Standing still, she watched as man and dog slowly tried to work out their differences. She could see the bowl was a good twenty feet away, and it appeared emptied and flipped over. Pierce had something in his hand, which he held out for her. Salem wanted it badly but didn't come any closer. Pierce took off a piece and threw it in front of her. It didn't land on the ground because she snatched it out of the air and gobbled it down, then turned to look at him again expectantly. But she wasn't coming any closer.

Hedi smiled as she studied Salem's large frame. She was a good fifty pounds over the normal weight of a shepherd, so some other breed was mixed in there. Her feet were huge, and her jaw was massive. Hedi had only ever seen Salem more aggressive than calm. She wondered what she was like around Pete.

Hedi walked to the open doorway as she watched Pierce toss another piece toward Salem, and she snatched it up and waited. He spoke to Hedi, his voice at the same low pitch. "Step on the porch."

Obediently she did so and quietly called out, "Hi, Salem."

Salem's ears twitched, and her gaze darted toward her, then back to Pierce again.

"Can I come closer?" Hedi asked.

"Slowly walk toward me," he said quietly.

She did as she was told. "She doesn't see me as a threat, does she?"

"Are women known to have beaten her?"

"I don't think so," she said. "I've only ever fed her and given her water."

"Which is why she's not afraid of you. She'll be cautious, just in case you are like the men she's met, but you're not one of the main threats. I am."

"It's good instincts on her part then, isn't it?" she said, a note of humor in her voice. "I'm surprised she's this close to you."

"I'm not. I've been at it since you left," he said. "I hope you brought home some food though, because I'm starved."

"I did, indeed. But I'm not cooking it," she warned. "I might have been the delivery person, but I sure as hell am not a cook."

"Did you bring fast food too?"

"I did, in the sense that I brought subs."

"Oh, yum," he said, standing up slowly, still tossing food toward the hungry dog. "Salem, sweetie, I'll go in and get some food myself." He took two steps back, and Salem's butt hit the ground. She looked up at him, her ears straight up.

"It's almost as if she understands you," Hedi said.

"She does," Pierce said quietly. "I've been working on a few of the commands she would know from Pete's training. I gave her the Sit command just now with a hand signal, and she did it without argument. So we've come a long way." He looked around. "If there was a dog bed still around, it should be something for her use on the deck. Even though she'll probably be a while getting back into the house, it would be good to know she feels like this is home again."

"I think I saw something in the barn," she said. "Give me a moment."

She took off slowly at first, so as not to spook Salem, and headed toward the barn, where she took the big car cover. It might be more of a horse blanket, but it would do the job. It was large, at least a four foot by three foot. Carrying it with great difficulty out of the barn and to the deck, she place it close to the steps. "Maybe this'll do."

He looked at it and nodded approvingly. "It probably was a horse blanket, but it's thick, so I'm not sure. As long as she thinks maybe it's for her, it'll be fine." He motioned for Hedi to back up into the kitchen, then he turned deliberately and walked inside, leaving the door open. "Now we'll see what she does."

He took one look at the subs on the counter and grinned. She smiled to see such joy on his face. It was a good thing she brought two twelve-inch subs since she was hungry herself. She unwrapped the first one and cut it in four pieces. The subs were made from whole French bread loaves.

He reached for the quarter portion closest to him and then stopped and looked at her. "Do you want me to have an end piece instead?"

"We each get an end piece," she explained, "but I'm starting with a center piece." She flashed him a grin and walked to the counter. "Damn. I did buy coffee, just didn't start any. I guess we can put some on afterward." She sat at the small rickety table and frowned. "I don't think this was Pete's table. He had a big oak one from his granddad."

"It's possible," Pierce said. "I'm not sure what Ross might have sold."

Just then she heard noises upstairs. "What's that?" she cried out in a harsh whisper.

"Ross," he said. "He came to get the rest of his stuff. This is his second trip."

"How do you know it's his stuff though?" she asked.

"Because I'm taking pictures of it and checking with Pete. If it's just personal shit, I don't think Pete cares. He was trying to take some of the electronics, and Pete says those are his. We're also having an argument about how much money he owes Pete. From the looks of it, he needs to replace close to thirty thousand dollars that he stole."

"I didn't steal it," Ross snapped from the doorway, "and I ain't paying it back." He turned and looked at her. "Hey, I mean, really I didn't steal it." His voice turned into a whine. "Pete's got no reason to say that."

"Thirty thousand dollars?" she said. "What did you do with all that money? Pete needs that to fix up the house."

Ross raise both hands, palms exposed, in obvious frustration. "Well, I didn't know he was coming back, did I?"

"That's hardly any reason to steal from your brother." She turned to look at Pierce. "Pete doesn't have much money."

"Oh, he's got money, his pension if nothing else," Pierce said. "We'll have to go through the courts, obviously, to get the money back though."

"I don't have the money," Ross said. "I told you that."

Pierce turned and looked at him, pinning him in place. "A lien has been slapped on your account," he said. "I got confirmation of that twenty minutes ago. You won't be getting any of that money out of that account until an agreement is made."

"You can't do that," he blubbered. "I don't have any money for gas."

"Isn't that just too damn bad," Pierce said, standing, towering above him. "Isn't it too damn bad you stole so much money from your brother? According to the lien, over sixty thousand dollars is in that account. And I want to know where it came from. Like, where is Pete's antique dining room table?"

Ross shook his head. "No. You can't touch that money. That's *my* money."

"I know of at least thirty thousand you took from Pete. But, for all I know, it's a lot more than that, and that's why we'll do a full investigation before you get access again."

"You can't do that."

"Too damn bad, too late. A lawsuit has been filed. A lien has been slapped. Now you should get a lawyer, and you can fight it out."

"How am I supposed to pay for a lawyer," he cried out, "if I can't get my money?"

"Stealing it from your brother doesn't make it *your* money. I guess you have a problem then, don't you?"

Hedi stepped forward and said, "Ross, did you really steal that kind of money from Pete?" She knew assholes were in this world, but to steal from your disabled brother? … That was pretty low.

He looked at her sadly. "I didn't think Pete would need it. It seems like the government paid for everything for him, so what did he need the money for? I needed it."

"What did you need it for?" she asked, puzzled. "You've been living in Pete's house free and clear, Pete's paying the bills, the taxes, according to what Pierce has said. So what did you need the money for?

"Because I don't want to stay here," he cried out. "And, even if I can't sell Pete's place, and if I want to get the hell out of here, I have to have cash."

"When were you thinking of selling Pete's place?" she asked. "Did you ask him about that?"

"Yeah, but he won't sell." Ross snorted. "Look at this place. It's falling down. I won't get much for it anyway. As much as it's nice to have free room and board, I do have to think about my own future."

"Where did you get all the money from then?" Pierce asked.

"It's mine," Ross snapped. "I was working, you know? Right up until I lost my job a few months back. I saved it."

"You saved it because you were living at Pete's place," Pierce said.

"And did you sell a bunch of stuff from Pete's home?" Hedi said, looking back at the kitchen table. "He had that wonderful antique table from your granddad. That was Pete's. Where is it?" She caught a glimpse of something in the back of Ross's eyes. She stared at him. "Did you really strip his house of everything of value and sell it?"

"Just a few things," he said. "He was my granddad too."

"But according to Pete," she said, "you got cash, and he wanted the heirlooms."

"I ran through the cash pretty damn fast. It wasn't much

anyway. Maybe five grand."

"Likely two to three times that. Pete should know. That sixty grand came from somewhere. Thirty of it came from Pete's pension account. So you sure as hell don't get to keep any of that," she said, a cool note entering her voice. "If we find any of the rest of it is Pete's inheritance from his granddad …" She let her words hang as she looked at Pierce to see him already sending a message on his phone. She figured it was probably to Pete, who likely would face even more shocks. She spun to look at Ross. "Is the rest of that money from stripping out the house and selling everything you could? Ignoring that the stuff really mattered to Pete because it was the stuff that would bring in the most money?"

"It's just garbage," Ross said, throwing up his hands. "Who gives a shit about a table and chairs anyway?"

"Pete did," Pierce said, holding up his phone. "That's a piece he loved, and apparently he's more than pissed at you. And he wants to know how much and where you sold that, so he can go buy it back."

"There's no way. It's already been sold," he said. "I made a deal with a guy in town."

"Which guy?" Hedi said, crossing her arms and staring at him with loathing. She turned to look at Pierce. "Any way to check if he's got other bank accounts too? Seems like one might be too simple for him."

Ross just shook his head. "Jesus Christ. You'll make sure I have nothing left by the time you're done," he snapped.

"You mean, like your brother?" she asked.

"But the government will take care of him until he dies," Ross roared. "Don't you guys see how unfair that is? He doesn't have to worry about nothing. He gets his medical coverage. He gets enough money every month to pay for all his needs. He never has to work again."

"It's not free," Pierce said. "He was over there fighting for his country while you were sitting here drinking beer. Now he's done his time and paid the price with heavy injuries, and you're sitting here, in *his* house, like a jealous little schoolboy, wanting what he had without having to go through the work and pain he went through."

"Whatever," Ross said as he looked at the groceries behind them. "Since you've locked up all my money"—his was voice full of sarcasm—"any chance I can have a bit of that sandwich? I haven't eaten all day."

Hedi picked up the other quarter of her half and handed it to him. "I want to make sure you don't take anything else from this place. Pierce said he will go through this next load of yours just as well as he did the others."

Ross glared at her. "It's my place too, you know?"

"No, it's not," Pierce said cheerfully. "The deed is in Pete's name. You may have tried to get him to sell, but it's his and his alone. And it's also paid for. So, if nothing else, Pete has a place to live for the rest of his life."

"Which is more than I have," Ross said bitterly.

"You *could* have," Hedi said. "You could have made arrangements to put a mobile home here or to build a small house or to even share this with him. But instead all you've done is take from him. Good riddance to you when you walk out that door."

Ross shook his head, shoving the sandwich in his mouth, bite after bite after bite. And, when it was finally gone, he gave a heavy sigh. "At least I've got a full stomach." He walked to the front door where his duffel bag was. "I don't think you guys realize what you've brought down on your heads."

"Why is that?" Pierce said. "What did you have to offer these guys so that they'll be pissed off that Pete's back at home?"

"It's not about Pete," he said. "Well, it is, but not really. I let them have access to the property for their moonshine, and, for that, they turn a blind eye when I move stuff out." He grinned and shook his head again. "Jed doesn't need an excuse. He's just got blood in his eyes, and, for any reason, it's an outlet for that anger of his," Ross added. "I kind of wish Vicky would get the hell away from him. She doesn't deserve it."

"What about the Billy boys?" Hedi said. "They're Jed's buddies too."

"Oh, yeah, they are, and you better watch yourselves. They're twins, and, when Jed says, *Jump*, they ask, *How high?* They'll be coming here tonight. Don't you worry. Why the hell do you think I'm getting all my shit out of here? I want out before this place goes up in smoke." He walked to the front door.

Pierce grabbed the duffel bag, took it to the couch where he dropped it, opening it up. He removed all the electronics that had been stacked up. "No way you're taking Pete's laptop or tablet. And this is a monitor. Stuffing it in here is hardly a good way to treat it. We'll be lucky if you didn't damage it. And where the hell is the desktop?"

"I don't think it works anymore," he said resentfully. "I need a laptop too, you know? I gotta find work now. How the hell am I supposed to do that?"

"You can try your phone," she said in a conversational tone. "Which is probably Pete's, considering it's a brand-new iPhone."

Ross shoved the phone in his pocket. "It's mine," he snapped. "You can't take that from me too."

"Guess that's more to ask Pete about, isn't it?" Pierce stepped off to the side, lifted his phone to his head and called Pete again.

Hedi smiled at Ross, who sagged on the couch. "You really have done it to yourself, haven't you? Not only is everybody here pissed at you, but everybody in town, once they hear what you did to your own brother, will be too." She shook her head.

There was a loud sound outside. Ross straightened up and said, "Shit, shit, shit. I've got to go." He pulled the rest of his stuff into the duffel bag and closed it up, racing to the front door. As he approached it, a bullet went right through the solid wood, just missing him. He hit the ground, crying out, "Shit! Look what you've done."

"Oh, yeah, I'm watching all right," Hedi said from behind the window. Sure enough, there was Jed and the Billy boys. "You didn't get out fast enough. You were too greedy. Now you're here. You know they'll make you take a side, and, if it isn't their side, they'll put a bullet in your head." The trouble was, she knew she was right. That was exactly what they would do. She pulled out her phone and sent her dad a text message. **You better come, and bring some firepower. Jed and the Billy boys are here, and they're on a rampage.**

PIERCE BARELY MANAGED to get connected to Pete when the bullet came through the door. From the corner of the living room, he stared at the three men outside.

Pete called out, "What am I hearing?"

"Someone just shot through your door," Pierce said, "barely missed your brother. He was trying to run out with another duffel bag full of electronics, like your laptop and your monitor."

Pete started swearing again. "That'll be Jed," he warned. "Something is wrong with him in the head. You better watch yourself. Somehow you'll have to disarm him, but he's got a houseful of guns."

"Yeah, well, it's not like any law enforcement will be of much help around here. Hedi is here, but she's just one against three," he said. He didn't want to discount Hedi's help, but Jed wouldn't listen to her any more today than he did the last time. Jed didn't respect authority, and he certainly didn't respect women, so Hedi was a double target.

"And he'll shoot you if he sees you," Pete said. "Hedi's dad needs to come."

"Maybe. Call the current sheriff please," Pierce asked.

"I will, but it won't do no good," Pete said. "That sheriff is useless."

"Okay, but you and I both need to call regardless." He hung up the phone from Pete and made a 9-1-1 call to dispatch, telling them exactly what was happening. "If that lousy sheriff of yours doesn't get down here with his deputies, at least this recorded call will be produced when the higher-ups appear, investigating why he didn't do anything. And he'll get charged with manslaughter himself for not stepping in."

The dispatcher gasped. "I don't know who you are, but the sheriff will obviously find out."

"Go ahead and tell him. And your dispatch call had better be recorded. If it's not, you can bet there'll be hell to pay." And he hung up.

He sent Badger a message, letting him know what was going down. This was getting ugly, and it was getting ugly very, very quickly. There was a short and hard response. Something about you do what you need to do. This needs to hit the news stations. And not a bad idea at that. He pocketed his phone and walked to the front door, opened it a crack and called out, "Well, Jed, here we are again, huh?" He shoved the door open and motioned for Ross to step out.

"I'm not walking out there. Jed will shoot me," Ross cried out.

"Jed, Ross wants to leave. You going to let him?"

"Sure enough," Jed said. "Ross, come on out here."

But Ross shook his head. "Don't make me go out there. I tell you that he'll kill me."

"What do I care?" Pierce said. "It'll save us a whole pile of legal fees."

Ross just looked at him, then walked to the couch and sat down. "I'm not leaving," he said. "Outside is crazy land. Inside you guys might be crazy too, but you just might live through this. Out there, there's no way I will."

"Sorry about that, Jed," Pierce yelled. "Ross has decided you guys are crazy, and he wants to stay inside with us."

There was a heavy snort, and a couple guns were fired in the air as Pierce watched Jed and his two buddies pull together. They were talking.

Pierce took that moment to step out on the front veranda, freeing his revolver, holding it up. "Not one of you three are welcome here," he said.

Jed saw him with the handgun and snorted. "What the hell will you do with that little peewee gun?" He raised his rifle, level with Pierce's chest, and fired.

Pierce shot him and dodged left. He knew exactly where he hit him, and, when Jed started to scream, he knew the other two boys would shoot back. But he had already lined up his second shot and warned them, "I don't care which one of you I shoot, but the next guy I'll kill. That first shot of mine was a deliberate attempt to stop Jed from doing anything really stupid. But now I'll take you down."

The two men glared at him, viciousness in their eyes. They were obviously twins, both bald, pug-faced, portly, and packing a hell of a lot of firearms.

They stared at him, and one said, "You know your days are done."

"He shot at me," Pierce said calmly. "It was self-defense. He won't be using that hand ever again though."

The two men went to Jed, who was kneeling on the ground, holding his hand. Pierce knew the bullet had gone up through the bones and pretty well shattered them, blowing apart all the tiny little finger bones. Pierce didn't feel much sympathy. The man was nothing but a renegade. He'd come here with murder on his mind.

The two brothers glared at him. "We will be back," one said, as they all headed to the twins' truck. With the current state of Jed's hand, he shouldn't be driving.

Pierce nodded. "Not a problem. Just knock and come on in. We'll be waiting for you anytime." And he turned his back on them, walking inside, shutting the door.

CHAPTER 8

H EDI WAS STUNNED at how Pierce had taken control of the confrontation. Certainly he'd had full right to shoot Jed, considering Jed was trying to kill him. She'd really like to see Jed thrown in jail for a good twenty years, until he sobered up, until his kids were grown and could safely lead normal lives. It will take them all so long to get over his abuse.

She stepped forward as Pierce closed the door behind him. "Was that wise?" she asked in a low voice.

He stared at her calmly. "I know you don't know me well. But I've seen more than my fair share of assholes like Jed. The type of work I did in the military, we came up against insurgents who would just as soon kill you flat before they even said hello. And, of course, that's the way the world is during war times. But it's not just like war, it's just like bullies. And you get your fair share of those everywhere. You can't back down. Jed won't go away. He'll have to be stopped. This is a setback for them, but now the Billy boys will want justice for Jed. They need to take Jed to the hospital so somebody can attempt to fix his hand. But I highly doubt he'll allow that to happen. He'll grab a bottle and pour some on top of his wound, scream blue murder, feed his own anger and fury, drink the rest of the bottle, and then he'll come back here, firing with his left hand."

"You're right," she said. "That's who Jed is. He won't go down easy."

"You realize that not only has his blood been shed but likely somebody will die tonight, right?"

She pinched the bridge of her nose. "This is well past what I can handle on my job. We need backup."

"Then call it in," he said as he gazed out the kitchen window.

She followed his gaze and saw the dog on the deck, watching them from the open doorway.

"Hello, Salem." His tone was modulated. Salem just looked at him.

"Is she dangerous?" Hedi asked quietly. She took two steps toward Salem. The shepherd's gaze shifted from Pierce to Hedi. "This is really bad timing to bring her into the fold. She's likely to get shot herself," Hedi warned. "Jed will see her, and that'll just spike his temper again."

"Jed has really got a problem with life, doesn't he?"

"He does in a big way," Hedi agreed, studying this man who stepped into this mess yet appeared to handle it easily, as if creating chaos was handling it. "But you could see that right off the bat."

"He's a bully who's been pushing this town around, and the sheriff not only has let him, he's supported him in doing so. I still don't understand why."

"They're family, cousins," Ross snapped. "Are you trying to get me killed?"

Pierce turned a lazy eye toward him.

Hedi almost smiled. "Nobody's trying to get you killed, Ross. You had every right to walk out there at any point in the last couple hours, except when we were going through the material you were trying to steal," she said quietly. "Feel free to go. You can still leave."

"Even if they've left," Ross said nervously, "they'll be looking for me."

"Of course they are. They're looking for supporters, and you're one of them, so they'll be looking at you to stand on their side with a weapon in your hand and to shoot at us." Pierce leaned against doorjamb, his gun still in his hand. "How do you think I'll take that?"

Resentfully Ross just stared at him. "I think you're all crazy. Life was just fine before you got here. Why don't you pack up your goddamn bags and leave again?"

"Life was only fine because you were stealing from your brother, living on his land, and taking advantage of somebody who needed your help and support. Instead all you did was kick him while he was down and grind him into the dirt, taking everything he had, hoping he'd die soon."

Hedi took a step forward, realizing she had a blood war going on here in her community too. "Just stop, both of you. Ross, you know perfectly well you're capable of leaving anytime. Jed won't shoot you. They might want you to join them, but, if you took off and didn't come back, you know they couldn't find you."

He shot her another resentful look. "Who made you boss? The sheriff says you're useless, just a pair of tits on a badge."

"You mean a badge on a pair of tits?" she said. "Do you think I haven't heard that before? Do you see the sheriff here putting a stop to this? No, of course not. He won't get involved. He'll come afterward and look at all the dead bodies, bring out a backhoe and dig a hole. You know he won't put any more effort into it than that." She smiled at him, seeing the nervousness as he understood just how much trouble he was in. "And you also know, if you're part of that ditch full of bodies, you'll get the exact same treatment. He won't go to any trouble to make sure your sorry ass is saved. As far as he's concerned, he wants it all to go away, whatever's the fastest and easiest method."

"Jed will come back here, and he'll light a fire to this place. I heard him talking about it before. He's got gas at his place."

"That's an interesting thing to say," Pierce said. "Because, of course, that's the last thing I'll allow."

"Yeah? And how will you stop it?" Ross said.

"I've got a couple options. For one, I can drain all the gas on his place."

Ross stared at him, his jaw dropping. "You're going to his place? Are you nuts?"

Pierce drew his brows together at the insult. "If I just sit here and wait for the fight to come to me, I'm just sitting here helpless. I'm not into being helpless." He turned to look at Hedi, studied her carefully for a moment while she stared calmly back at him.

"I know what you'll say," she said. "The answer is yes, but it's dangerous."

"You got any better ideas?"

She shook her head. "You'll never find it all. Anything that can cause a fire like that, hell, it doesn't take much. You can just light a match. Pete's place is pretty old, and it's wood."

"And, of course, you don't have any fire trucks here in this part of the county, do you?"

"There's a volunteer fire department," she said, "but they'll be at least half an hour, if not forty-five minutes away."

"In that case, we need to stop Jed. I should have shot out his kneecaps then." He put his hands on his hips and turned around slowly in a circle.

She could see the ideas percolating as he tried to find the best solution.

His gaze landed on Salem yet again. She had dropped into a lying position across the doorway. He smiled at her. "You're doing much better. You're half inside now."

He looked at the subs, opened the second pack, cut it in four pieces and picked up an end piece, working on it while he stood ten feet away from Salem and just talked to her.

Hedi shook her head. "How can you be so calm?"

"Finally somebody's asking questions that make sense," Ross said. "Hasn't it occurred to you that Jed's got a death wish or something? The man's berserk. We know that. It's ridiculous. Jed will come back here, and he'll kill us all."

"Yeah? So what will you do about it?" Hedi asked him. "Just what are you thinking will get you out of this? Because sure as hell nothing at the moment is coming to my mind."

"Somebody," Ross said, "you and/or the sheriff, needs to arrest Jed. Just look at what he's done."

"So now you're talking about arresting him? Are you serious? How does that work?" she asked with a snort. "As far as I'm concerned, you're as much a part of this as Jed and the Billy brothers are. And all of you will be indicted on as many charges as I can write down."

"I haven't done any of this," Ross protested.

She shook her head and stepped forward, grabbed a piece of sandwich. The stomach acids were churning as she tried to figure a way out of this nightmare. As she watched, it seem like Pierce made some kind of a decision.

He approached Salem and stopped just a couple feet

away. She bounced to her feet and backed up, so she was just on the outside of the door. As he took another step closer, Salem growled, a sound deep in the back of her throat that evoked primitive feelings of fear inside Hedi.

She took a step forward, but Salem didn't even look at her. She wasn't a threat compared to Pierce. And that was understandable. Pierce was in a class all his own. Hedi trusted him instinctively, and, because of that, she was fighting that same instinct. She knew better than to trust so easily. Just because he might have been one of those protector types didn't mean he wouldn't go off half-cocked on his own and do something that would cause this mess to blow up even more.

Hell, he already had. Shooting Jed like he had just pushed those men. She knew it instinctively, and she knew Pierce knew it too, which was why he'd done it. She just didn't know if his actions were based on a clear well-thought-out strategy, unlike Jed's.

As she watched, Pierce dropped to his knees in front of Salem, and the dog stopped growling. She looked more confused than anything. He didn't reach out a hand; he just stared at her calmly, steadily. At this point she'd eaten from the dog food bowl he'd placed outside, plus eaten several treats he'd left her.

"Are you sure she's okay, that it's safe to talk to her?"

"Talk is cheap." Pierce's voice was calm, low. "And she already knows that words lie. It's all about actions with Salem."

"That makes sense," she admitted. "But do we really have time for this?"

"Are you in a rush?" he asked. "I'm not planning on going anywhere. But, when it does come down to a fight, I'd like to know she's on my side, not theirs."

Her breath caught in the back of her throat. She hadn't even thought about that. She'd sent Stephen and Roy messages, hoping somebody was on their way out. Stephen sent back a quick message, saying he was manning the office.

She hit Dial on the phone and called him. "What do you mean, you're manning the office?" she said. "We have a hell of a situation developing here."

"Yeah, and that's why I'm manning Central Station," he said calmly. "No way I'm getting out in that shit."

She gasped in outrage. "Stephen, you're a deputy. Get in the vehicle and come out here."

"Nope. You can have my badge before I'll do that," he said. "I promised my wife and girls I'd be going home to them, not that I'll get shot by some crazy-ass nightmare called Jed. Once you said the Billy boys were there, I was out."

"Who are you waiting on to fix this then?" she yelled.

"The law, that's who," Stephen said.

"*We* are the law." She wanted to scream in frustration, but this was the shit she dealt with all the time.

Pierce raised an eyebrow, then just shook his head.

"You have no idea how much we need you."

"Well, you'll have to do without me," Stephen said quietly. "You'll probably have to do without everybody because the sheriff doesn't think he's got any part to play in this whole mess either."

"Don't tell me that he's still sitting there," she said, dread in her voice. "Please tell me that he's on his way to help calm Jed down."

"If he was coming, it would be to arrest Pierce, since he shot Jed without provocation."

"He had provocation," she snapped. "Jed was trying to shoot him."

"Not what Jed told the sheriff."

She pinched the bridge of her nose and groaned. "This is just too unbelievable."

"Not my problem," Stephen said. "As for Roy, he's on the other end of town today. You're on your own."

His tone was so cheerful, she wondered if he wasn't waiting for her to get killed. "Is that you guys' plan?" Her tone turned hard. "Leave me alone in the middle of violence so I get shot and so you don't have to worry about having your job performance upstaged by a woman?"

"If you get shot, it's your fault," Stephen said. "The sheriff told you not to go."

"No, he did not," Hedi cried out. "He told me to handle it."

"Well, then handle it," Stephen barked.

He had such a feigned innocence that she finally realized he really didn't give a shit. "I wonder how your wife will feel when she finds out you wouldn't leave the office to help a fellow officer," she snapped.

"She'll be delighted because at least she knows I'm coming home to her." And just like that he hung up.

She stared at her phone, her mind racing, wondering what the hell she was supposed to do now. And, if she called the sheriff's office one county over, what would be the repercussions for her and her job?

"Please don't tell me that was the entire sheriff's office?" Ross whined.

"Might as well have been," she said glumly. "This is beyond bad news."

"It doesn't make a damn bit of difference to this shit

going on down here." Pierce looked at her. "But it makes a hell of a lot of difference to this town. How is it the sheriff is still in office? And, by the way, I taped that on my cell phone."

She looked at him in horror. "What will you do with it?"

"I'll send it to the big news station, so they can do an investigation on your lovely sheriff's department, and the deputies who turn their back on fellow officers, and sheriffs who would rather stay in their office and spread lies and rumors," he said. He was busy on his phone again.

She stared in fascination as he hit a final button and then smiled at her.

"There. I've sent it out. We'll see how your sheriff feels in a little bit."

"Don't tell me that you did that. Oh, my God! I'll be in so much trouble," she cried out.

"You're either in trouble, or you'll be dead," Ross said. He had come up at her side. "Honestly, I think that's probably what should have happened a long time ago. This is bullshit. What kind of a sheriff is he?"

"Considering you're the one who put him in power," Pierce said, "what do you think?"

"He paid us," Ross said suddenly. "We're all broke. We didn't care either way who was sheriff, so we accepted the money and voted for him."

Pierce slowly straightened and turned to look at him— his phone recording again. "Are you serious?"

Ross nodded. "It wasn't very much, so it didn't really matter."

Hedi felt her stomach sink. "Any idea how many people accepted money to vote for him?"

Ross shrugged. "I don't know. I imagine at least a hundred of us. But maybe not. Some people would have done it for future favors—you know that."

"I do know that." Her voice sounded harsh even to her ears. "I also know he broke a lot of laws doing that."

"I don't think the law matters to your sheriff," Pierce said thoughtfully. He once again sent off several texts.

"Who are you contacting?" she asked, baffled. "Everything I say, you put into a memo and fire it off."

"We have a problem in this town, and somebody needs to clean it up. I just happen to be here."

"You're hardly going to clean it up," Ross said. "You're just here for a night. A drifter doing nothing but causing shit."

"We'll see about that," Pierce said. He turned to look at the doorway.

Her glance followed his.

"Shit," he said.

And she realized Salem had disappeared with the raised voices.

HE STEPPED OUTSIDE and looked around but saw no sign of her. "Damn, that's a setback."

"Who knew Ross would let out a bombshell like that?" Hedi said.

"Everybody knew it," Ross said. "How else would the sheriff have gotten elected?"

"But knowing something and having proof of it is a totally different thing." Hedi rubbed her forehead. "This is just unbelievable."

"Yep, sure is," Pierce said. "It'll be on the news tonight

though." He motioned at the yard, completely unkempt, that hadn't been mowed in ages. "Did you do any cleanup work around here?"

Ross looked at him but didn't answer.

Pierce nodded. "I'll go for a walk," he said, looking back at Hedi. "I wouldn't mind if there was a pot of coffee by the time I get back." And with that, he stepped off the porch steps and headed toward the tree line, one hundred yards off. Inside was an anger rippling through him that he hadn't felt in a long time. To think the sheriff had bought his votes, and his entire department had refused to help Hedi was unbelievable. Pierce didn't need her help. He figured he could handle this just fine. But he also didn't know exactly what he was up against. She did. He'd hate if anything happened to her though. He'd brought this to a head and didn't want her to be a causality of this war.

The fact that her department hadn't come to back her up in any way was just ugly. And that Stephen guy had no business wearing a badge. Pierce would make sure the last thing he did before he left town was to take that badge off him and make sure he booted his ass out of the department. He didn't know about the other guy, but, if he'd taken off in the opposite direction, that was what he'd get too. They were obviously the sheriff's cronies. And how the hell had she gotten her job? He figured maybe the old deputies might have had a hand in it.

As soon as he hit the tree area, he sat down on a log, closed his eyes and tried to calm down his inner center. He already knew he had to still his energy and thoughts in order to go on the hunt.

Silence inside helped with silence outside.

As he sat for a long moment, something cold pressed

against his fingers. His breath caught, and he held it as he waited. The nudge became a little stronger. He opened his hand, and a muzzle was gently placed inside, not moving beyond anything other than his fingers. He stroked Salem's nose and under her chin.

Slowly he opened his eyes. There were a lot of shadows in the trees, and the sun, already clouded over, was starting to go down. Salem stood at his side, so silent, weary, and yet, so proud. He smiled at her and whispered, "Hello there, girl." An ear twitched. "I'm so sorry for the last few months. We'll make sure we get Pete back here."

Her ears twitched again, and she looked up at Pierce with huge chocolate-colored orbs that were wounded and full of distrust. She'd been hurt. She'd been beaten, and the people she'd always depended upon for her very living and her daily training had deserted her. Not by Pete's own fault but by injuries that had sidelined him and, therefore, her.

He blamed Ross for letting the situation go the way it had, but then Ross appeared to be so weak that it was no wonder he couldn't deal with life. He didn't have a clue how. Every decision he made was the easy one.

Pierce's phone rang. He pulled it out, still gently stroking Salem's neck. He moved up to scratch behind her ear. "Hey, Pete. How are you doing?"

"I don't know what to say," Pete said. "Sounds like hell is breaking loose down there."

"Before we get into it, say hi to Salem. She's right here beside me. I've got the phone to her ear."

There were tears in Pete's voice as he called out to Salem. "Hey, girl. I'm coming home soon."

Salem's ears twitched, and she shook her head, looking down at the phone.

"Keep talking," Pierce encouraged. "She's looking at you."

He let the two of them have a moment as Pete gently called to her, and Salem tried to figure out what was going on.

"Any idea how quickly you can come home?" Pierce said.

"The doc said I could probably come in a couple days." There was shock in his voice. "I don't know why I didn't make this happen before."

"We can't get everything modified by then, but I'm sure we can manage something."

"Did you really shoot Jed?" Pete said abruptly.

"Who told you that?"

"My brother called."

"That would have been a lovely phone call," Pierce said, derision in his voice. "He's quite the head case, that guy."

"Yeah, I know. I'm sorry. He is still my brother, but I really don't want anything to do with him now that I know what he tried to take away from me."

"Everything," Pierce said. "He tried to take everything away from you. Don't you forget that. Not only did he try, he did for a while. You were stuck in rehab, while he lorded it over you. He considered this his home, spending your money."

"Yeah," Pete said, his tone vibrating with anger. "I'm not likely to forget that."

"Why did he call you?" Pierce asked.

"To give me an update on Jed. He said that you might get the house burned down."

"You got any insurance on this place?" Pierce asked.

"I do," he said, "but I don't know about arson."

"Don't you worry about it. As long as it's insured for fire, it can be replaced. And I imagine fire is covered because it's pretty standard coverage. I hope they don't burn it down, but I don't know what those Billy boys are like."

"Evil," Pete said. "They're bullies. They're the evilest nastiness you've ever met."

"They'd have to be pretty bad then," Pierce said, "because honestly, I've met some pretty bad men."

"These are right up there with the worst of them," Pete said. "They'll likely start along the fence line and try to burn it."

"Hmm. Interesting thought," Pierce said. "Do you have any big equipment here?"

"There's a tractor. I was trying to get a couple acres into something growable, near the creek, some nearby water source. I was looking at maybe growing some barley or some grains. There's a local distillery not too far away that was looking for some. I had a soil sample tested, and they said it was good for barley."

"Does the tractor have a blade attachment?"

"There are attachments but not sure about a blade. Rakes for sure, rotors. Why?"

"Because the best way to stop a fire is to build a firebreak," Pierce said. "Is your entire property fenced?"

"Yes, it is. There are a couple fences that start at the driveway. If you take sight of both the wooden fences on either side and follow them, you'll see everything is enclosed. I've got these ten acres. That's a lot of land for anybody to drop a match on. And they can just run up the driveway and torch the house itself."

CHAPTER 9

HEDI PUT AWAY the groceries, offered Ross another portion of a sub, which he took without gratitude and sat down at the table, chewing away morosely. She studied his face. "When did you last have a job?"

He shot her a hard look. "I'm not totally useless, you know?"

"I never thought you were," she said. "I can only see what you've done in this last little while though, so I'm looking to see another aspect to your personality."

"I worked at the mill for a few years. I worked in Fort Collins, but affording a home there was hard, so I came back to the mill. Then the mill shut down, and it seems like life from then on completely stopped."

She understood that, and it wasn't the first time she'd heard such a story. "Have you tried for other work around town?"

"Sure," he said, "but it's not like this small town can absorb so many of us when we're laid off."

"No," she said, "but a lot of people moved, and a lot of people commute."

"I didn't do either," he said. "My brother offered me a place. I knew he had been injured, and I thought he was coming back. I thought I was looking after it for him for a few months, and it gave me a place to land while I figured out what I would do. But then I got cozy, and I started to see myself doing this full-time, once I realized he wouldn't get out of that place. Then it seemed like I could start over somewhere else if I could get together enough money."

"But who said he wouldn't get out of there?" she asked, turning to look at him. "None of us ever heard Pete wouldn't come back."

"I don't know," he said, "but the idea came from somewhere. I thought for sure it was from Pete." He stared out the window. "What do you know about this Pierce guy?"

"I know he's more dangerous than Jed," she said simply. "But I believe he's honorable. He's doing this to help Pete and to help Salem."

"Nobody does this shit to help a dog."

"I think you're wrong. Like Pierce and Pete, that dog served our country, so he is trying to make sure she gets more than beaten and abused."

"Good luck to him then. That dog is a killer."

"If she is, it's something you helped make her," she snapped. Then she took a deep breath and asked, "What are your plans tonight?"

He slid a look in her direction but stayed quiet and then shrugged. "I don't know. If I wait until dark, I might be able to head back into town, drive away with my lights off. Maybe they'd let me go, and I'd be good. I won't be coming back, that's for sure."

She leaned against the stove, crossing her arms over her chest, and watched him. "Do you think they'll have a problem with you leaving?"

"If they can get me to be on their side, that's what they'd ideally like," he said. "But I don't want anything to do with them. This will go down badly. Jed is likely to come back and to just start firing through the doors. He won't give a shit who he kills."

"I'm more worried about his wife and kids."

He shook his head. "I heard her girlfriends went to the house and basically kidnapped her and the kids. They headed into town for some big special event, and they were staying overnight."

Relief swept through her. "I'm glad to hear that." She turned to stare toward the living room, her focus on the front door. "We don't want them all injured because Jed is in such an ugly mood."

"He just got his hand shot apart," Ross said sarcastically. "I hardly imagine he's feeling too good."

"He should have gone to the hospital and gotten it taken care of," she said quietly.

"You know he won't. He'll just shoot himself up with some painkillers and booze and come back to get his revenge."

"And then he won't need to worry about a hospital tomorrow," she stated firmly. "If he comes out firing, I'll be firing back, and he'll go to the morgue."

Ross sank back in the chair. "How can the world always be so black-and-white for you?"

"The world isn't always black-and-white," she said, "but you have to watch how much you let that gray line move."

"Mine just never seemed to stay anywhere," he said. "I go to bed thinking this is the right thing to do, and I wake up in the morning feeling like I made the wrong choice, and I need to change it to something else." He looked at the table where one more portion of the sub remained. "Can I have that?"

"That's mine for later," she said. "I'll need it too." She

wrapped it back in the original wrapping and cleared off the rest of the garbage. Then she offered Ross an apple.

He looked at it and frowned. "Don't know when I last had an apple," he said.

"You should try it," she said quietly. "It's better for you than more sandwich."

"And yet, the sandwich is for you, so how is that fair?"

"I bought it," she said, "so that's fair." She didn't bother telling Ross how Pierce had paid for it. She also didn't think Ross would like to hear she thought jail time was in his future. He'd done a terrible thing to his brother.

He sagged back in the chair and took a bite of the apple. "It'll be a long night," he said.

"It probably will be." Her tone was cool and even. "It doesn't matter much. The night will come whether we're here or not."

He hopped to his feet and paced. "I don't want to be here when night falls."

"Too late," she said. "It's already dark out there."

He turned to look out the kitchen window. "Where do you think he went?"

"I don't know," she said. "Probably to walk the perimeter and to see what kind of danger we're up against."

"As long as he's not stupid enough to go to Jed's on his own," he said. "Jed will shoot him as soon as he sees him."

"What makes you think he'll see him?" She highly suspected Pierce's skills were top-notch, and, if he wanted to go after Jed, then he would go after Jed. And maybe it would be better if he did. Jed was coming back after all of them tonight. This needed to end, and it needed to end tonight.

"I haven't seen him in at least thirty minutes." He shifted, walked to the other window and looked out. "Maybe he left."

"Is his truck gone?"

"I don't know." He looked at her in exasperation. "You're the deputy. You should know this stuff."

She gave a half laugh. "What is it you want from me now that you put the sheriff in power?"

He shrugged. "The sheriff caught me when I was broke," he said. "That's really no biggie."

"It is for everybody in this town."

"Well, it wasn't just me who voted him in. Otherwise he wouldn't have made it in," he snapped. "And that's obvious."

"Maybe." She was tired of the conversation and him. "But you need to decide soon if you're leaving."

"You trying to get rid of me?"

"Yes," she admitted. "You're a liability here. You'll mess things up, and we've already got enough problems without you."

"That's not fair," he blasted. He stood up. "I can go now and hopefully make it into town, and nobody will be the wiser."

She nodded, walked toward the front door and opened it. "Don't let the door hit you on your way out."

He glared at her. "You're really not very friendly."

"Nope, I'm probably not," she said. "But it is what it is."

He grabbed the bag from the living room and walked out.

With relief she watched as he got into his truck. He started it up, turned around and headed down to the highway toward town instead of heading toward Jed's.

With any luck he'd stay away, but, with him, you never knew. He could take a back road and circle around. If he was smart, he'd stay a long way away from Jed. What she needed was reinforcements. She needed Jed picked up, along with the Billy boys, but it didn't look like anybody would be around to give her a hand. It figured.

Just then her phone rang. It was her father. "How are you doing, Dad? Are you coming over here?"

"We're taking up stations all around, keeping an eye on the place. I want you to stay inside that house. We'll let you know if we see anybody coming."

"That's nice," she said, "but just remember. You're not the sheriff anymore, and I'm not your deputy."

His voice sharpened. "I get that. You're the one in charge, but we need to make sure these guys don't sneak over your way and catch you unaware."

"Appreciate the extra set of eyes," she said.

"Another thing. Pete called me again." Her father had a note of humor in his voice. "And damn it was good to hear from him. He wants to take a look at what's going on."

"Wow," she said in astonishment. "That's probably a grand idea."

"I think he can. I don't imagine he'll be in great shape, but, if he sees what he's coming back to, it might help him heal faster."

"True enough," she said. "Is somebody going to get him?"

"We're discussing it now. It depends on what happens tonight."

"Anybody talk to the sheriff?"

"That would be a waste of time, as you know," he said. "But I should give him a shout and see what he has to say for himself."

"You do that," she said. "See how the old sheriff meets

up with the new sheriff."

"It hasn't done any good up until now."

"There is one thing we accomplished. Ross said they were all paid to vote for him."

Nothing but silence came through the phone for a few moments. "Are you serious?" her father exploded in outrage.

"Yes. Pierce said something about putting it on the news. I don't know if he meant it or not. He's also got a recording of the deputy saying the sheriff said he wouldn't be bothered coming to help out, and Stephen said he was going home to his wife and kids rather than giving me backup, and Roy had gone to the other side of town so he didn't have to come this direction." She listened as her father swore and cussed up one side and down the other.

"I can't believe they're in power," he said. "That's just too unbelievable."

They talked for a few more minutes. Only as she walked back into the kitchen did she realize Ross had stolen her sandwich as he walked out the door. She snorted and turned to stare at the highway. "Good riddance," she snapped.

She turned toward the countertop and put on a pot of coffee. She didn't know when Pierce would return, but she figured the coffee would be ready when he got here.

PIERCE WORKED THE back forty with the tractor, building a large firebreak. The tractor was old and clunky, but, if nothing else, it was something they could get away in if the other exits were closed off. It would travel across country that many other machines couldn't.

He parked it along the back of the yard, pocketed the

keys and jumped the fence. He walked to where he'd last seen Salem, calling out to her. Almost instantly she approached. She stayed just off to the side, but she was close enough she could see him. He reached into his pocket and pulled out another treat and tossed it at her. She didn't miss it. Her jaws clamped shut, and she kept walking beside him as he headed toward the house.

It was pitch-black outside, and there were no signs of anybody approaching. He'd be on sentry duty all night. He needed coffee to keep himself awake. He knew this would come to a major climax, and he wanted to make sure it came to a favorable one. If Jed was stupid, he'd gone home and wrapped up his hand and was now planning his next visit.

A part of Pierce wanted to go to Jed's house and take him out. But he couldn't handle Jed and the Billy boys if they were all together, and, if they were apart, he couldn't take out one either because he wouldn't know that the other two hadn't come back to Pete's house. Pierce had no problem shooting the Billy boys, but he couldn't do it without provocation.

He could see Hedi moving around in the kitchen. There was just something so welcoming seeing her like that. He respected that she'd come back. Maybe to her it was the job pushing her, and maybe it was because she was worried. It didn't matter; he appreciated the thought. But she was somebody he had to watch out for, somebody he had to make sure didn't get shot. He didn't know if the media had gotten the message about what was going on here yet or about the lousy sheriff, but Pierce's hands were full right where he was, with no time to check whether others were doing their jobs or not.

He looked at Salem and smiled. "You're the reason I'm

here," he said gently.

Her ears twitched at the sound of his voice.

He stopped and crouched down. They were only about twenty feet from the porch, and she walked closer. He reached out a hand, and gently she stretched out her head. He stroked the underside of her chin and neck, gently scratching around her ears. "It's been a tough couple months, hasn't it, baby? That's okay. We'll get through this." And he walked up to the house.

Salem stayed just behind him, her eyes ever-watchful, her body ever-ready.

He hadn't had a chance to check her to see what the blood on her flank was from. He wasn't sure if Jed had given her a parting gift or if it was just an accident while she was out roaming around. She was still favoring one leg, but she appeared to be using it, not letting it slow her down.

He stepped into the kitchen, smelling the coffee. "Perfect timing," he said, his nose in the air.

"Maybe," she said from the shadows by the table. "Ross left."

"Good riddance," he said.

She laughed. "That's exactly what I said."

He grinned at her. "Great minds and all that." He walked to the coffeepot and poured himself a cup. He turned to look at her. "Do you want a cup?"

"Yes, please." She got up and walked toward him.

Now that it was just the two of them and no other distractions except for Salem who stood at the open doorway, he realized Hedi was at least five feet, nine or ten inches, slim, maybe a hundred twenty or twenty-five pounds. She had brown hair that hung down her back. Earlier it had been in a braid and tucked up on the back of her head.

"It's a shame to tie all that hair up in back," he said.

"My father always warned me that it was a weapon for the bad guys, and, when I'm at work, I should make sure it wasn't something that could be used against me."

"He's right," Pierce said. "And how sad that we have to think about things like that."

"Right? I went into law enforcement because I believed in it," she said. "I was raised in it with my father, and I figured for sure I would follow in his footsteps. But I don't know. This last year has been pretty shitty. The first year I was here working with the sheriff wasn't so bad, but he's only gotten worse over time."

"Again it's tough to follow a leader when you have no respect for him." Pierce leaned against the sink, staring out at the darkness beyond the window. "But, when you let guys like that get too big, it's like the rotten core of an apple. You don't really see it until you dig in a little deeper, and then you see how much damage it caused. If nothing else, I want to make sure we get rid of him. Pete needs somebody to stand by him, not somebody who'll throw him to the wolves. And that seems like what your current sheriff would be like."

"I know," she said. "And that's just sad. But I couldn't have worked as a deputy if my dad was sheriff, and I don't think he wants to resume his old job. We need somebody capable. There isn't really anybody around."

"It's not just this town though either, is it?"

"No, we have a collection of towns here, and basically it's the entire county that the sheriff looks after. Only he doesn't travel. Honestly, he goes from home to the coffee shop to the sheriff's office, and that's it."

"Damn shame," Pierce said. "He's got an opportunity to do something really good here, and instead he does absolutely nothing."

She started to open her mouth when a shot was fired through the living room window.

A gas canister.

He shoved her toward the door. "Go out the back door," he said, and he dove for the canister, a kitchen towel over his nose and mouth as he picked up the canister, opened the front door, and chucked it back out. When it landed the second time, it made a small explosion. But he was already back inside with his revolver in his hand, peering through the window. "That had to be a handmade canister," he muttered to himself.

"Yeah. That'll be a Billy boy deal," she said from across the window.

He glared at her. "I told you to go outside."

"Yep, you might have," she said, "but I don't listen to you. As a matter of fact, you're supposed to listen to me."

"Considering I probably have way more experience in this than you do, how about we just not argue about it." He studied the outside intently. "Somebody's behind my truck."

"They'll probably steal the gas from it just for a start," she said. "They do that no matter who's here."

He stared at her a moment. "Wow, this is just a lovely group of people you guys have."

"Not me," she said cheerfully. "The deputy cars are generally safe just because of the sheriff."

He snorted and turned his head. "I'll go out and make sure they don't steal any of my gas."

"And why is that? Are you really prepared to get shot over it?"

"Not at all, but I hope they are." And, just like that, he was outside.

He hoped she'd stayed inside, but he couldn't count on it. She had a mind of her own and figured that she was doing her duty. Maybe she was. He couldn't really hold her back from it. Something he admitted he admired.

He crept around the side of his vehicle, saw another shadow and waited. Then he slipped alongside the fence, keeping his body still at every chance. Finally seeing one of the Billy boys up against his truck, doing something with the gas tank, he stepped up, threw an arm around his neck, choking off his air, and pulled him to the ground.

Against his ear he whispered, "Are you stealing gas or are you pouring sugar in my gas tank?"

The trouble was, he wasn't about to release his arm around his neck to let the asshole answer. He was just way too busy keeping him down. With him flat on the ground and groaning, Pierce closed his gas tank and tied the man's hands with a zip tie he'd stuffed in his pockets earlier. He grabbed a part of the man's T-shirt, ripped it off and stuffed it in his mouth. And then, just for good measure, he gave him a hard clip on the jaw, knocking him out cold.

He had to weigh at least two-forty, if not two-eighty, and Pierce thought about the pros and cons. Then he realized the only way to make sure he would not come back after them was if he was kept inside, tied up, under guard.

Taking a chance, groaning lightly under the heavy weight, he picked up the unconscious man, threw him over his shoulder and raced around to the back.

Once he was inside, the lights all off, Hedi whispered, "Who did you bring with you?"

"One of the twins," Pierce said. "He's tied up at the moment. I'll lock him up somewhere."

"Is that wise?"

"It's wiser than leaving him out there to come back after us," he said. "I don't know about you, but, once I put these guys down, I don't want to have to do it again."

"Good point," she said. "Find me some more rope, will ya? He's not tied secure enough for my peace of mind."

Pierce dropped him on the living room floor, and, with the rope, they hogtied him with his feet up to his hands, placing a bandanna around his jaws to keep the cotton stuffed in his mouth. Pierce faced her and said, "If he wakes up, knock him out again." And he took off back out into the darkness.

CHAPTER 10

H EDI WATCHED PIERCE disappear into the shadows and shook her head. "What the hell am I doing here?"

Well, trying to uphold the law for one and to help out somebody in trouble. But Pierce was a bit of a lone ranger and appeared capable enough to handle this all on his own. So again—why was she here?

She walked back to the prisoner and bent down. "Well, Billy, this is a hell of a pickle."

She checked his bonds to make sure he wasn't going anywhere, then emptied his pockets. She wanted to make sure nothing in them could free himself. With him out cold, she took a picture of his face and sent it to the sheriff.

"One down," she snapped.

She got a response immediately as her phone rang. "What the hell are you doing?" the sheriff roared.

"After Jed and Pierce got into a shootout earlier, and you walked away, the Billy boys came back looking for trouble. Pierce caught Billy siphoning gas out of the truck."

"What? So he siphons off a couple bucks' worth of gasoline. Is that worth knocking him out cold and tying him up? You guys are the ones skirting the law now."

She gasped in disbelief at his words. "Are you serious? Ross said Jed and the Billy brothers are threatening to burn down Pete's place. And you know they're gunning for Pierce.

Do you even care?"

"Why should I care?" the sheriff said calmly. "He's a stranger. He's a nobody."

"But he's protecting somebody who's part of this community," she snapped. "Pete's coming back, and this is his place. He needs our help making sure nobody rides roughshod all over it."

"You're the one who says Pete's coming back," the sheriff snapped. "You and that lover boy of yours."

She stiffened at the reference to Pierce. "Hardly," she said sarcastically. "You're the sheriff. You should be here keeping Jed and the Billy boys back."

"According to Jed and the Billy boys, your friend attacked them without provocation. So when I come out in the morning, it'll be to arrest Pierce."

She snorted. "Well, good luck with that," she said. "He's got friends in high places."

"Sure he does. That boy is all talk. You've always been an easy mark for the men. Offer you a few flowers and a cup of coffee, and you lie down for any of them," he sneered.

She was horrified that he'd go down that path. "You are out of line." Her voice was hard. "And that's not appropriate behavior between colleagues."

"You *were* a colleague," he said. "But I've just fired you, so you're nobody now." And with that he hung up.

She stared down at her phone in disbelief. "Fired?" For some reason that had never occurred to her. He had a right to fire her, but he had to have a reason. Did he in this case? She wasn't going against his orders. He hadn't ordered her to come back. He hadn't ordered her to leave the place alone. He hadn't ordered her not to get involved. She had citizens here in trouble, and she was trying to help out.

She sent her father a text. **Apparently helping out Pierce and Pete just got me fired.**

Her father texted back. **Sorry, kiddo. Not surprised. Your sheriff doesn't like anybody who goes against his wishes.**

And yet, technically he never told me not to do this. So I'm not sure what he's firing me over. Of course he made a lot of nasty innuendos about me and Pierce.

That's the level he operates at. If he doesn't have anything specific to blame you for, he'll find something. And, in this case, it'll be an inappropriate relationship causing you to overstep your boundaries.

She ran a hand through her hair and wondered what the hell she would do now. Life had gone into an absolute spiral since she'd met Pierce.

She glared out the window, pocketing her phone. "Well, Pierce, is this what happens? Do you inspire a reign of chaos everywhere you go?"

Ross was gone; one of the Billy boys was tied up; Jed was injured, and Pierce was out there with Salem. And she was stuck inside. What the hell was she was supposed to do with that?

Not liking any of her options, she slipped out the back door and wandered down the porch to take a look into the shadows. Her car was in the barn. She needed to go home, pick up the deputy's car and take it back to the station. By now the sheriff would have told Stephen and Roy. They'd both be smirking and saying they'd told her that her actions would get her fired. Not that they had, but, of course, they'd be all about kissing up to the sheriff for firing her. A paycheck was a paycheck in this town where so many businesses had gone under. She had a little money saved, so she was good for a bit, but obviously she'd now have to consider moving. She stepped back inside and headed to the living room to peer out from behind the curtains. Still no sign of anything or anyone.

Just then a text came back from her father. **Just got a phone call from your mom. Something about this blowing up all over the news.**

She brightened. Instead of trying to text an answer, she called him. When he answered on the first ring, she said, "Pierce said he would contact the media."

"Good," he said. "I've already tried to contact the higher-ups, but everybody wants to leave the sheriff to do his job."

"You know what that's all about," she said. "But, in this instance, the sheriff is just waiting for the dust to die down. Then he'll come in and make it look like he made it all happen—or not—depending on the outcome. He doesn't let anybody take the glory away from him, and neither will he put himself in danger or get his hands dirty."

"Where are you now?"

"I'm at the back of the house," she said. "Pierce took off into the shadows, and I have no clue what he's up to. Of course, I have Billy here tied up. Ross slipped away earlier, but honestly, I don't know if we can trust him. He could just as easily have gone to Jed's."

"Your mom contacted Vicky. She and the kids are okay. They're at her mom's. Your mom is trying to convince her not to go home. I'm not sure it'll take very much convincing after this. She's pretty scared."

"The only thing is, she needs her job," Hedi said sadly. "And he'll find her there."

"Yeah, true enough. The sheriff won't arrest Jed for beating on his wife and kids. He sure as hell won't arrest Jed for going after a guy who shot him."

"No, but Jed was going to kill Pierce, and I can attest to that."

"Chances are you'll have to," her father warned.

"It was all in the line of duty. But I'm no longer an official officer of the law." Her tone had turned hard. "So I guess right now I'm just a private citizen helping a friend."

"Just a question on that," her dad asked. "Which friend?"

"At this time, both of them," she said softly. "There's a lot to like about Pierce. He's a good man. He also stood up for me against Jed, beat Jed down for hurting his kids. No doubt Pierce's one of the good guys. But he's only here for a short time, and then he's taking off again."

"Too bad," the ex-sheriff said. "Sounds to me like he'd make a great sheriff."

She laughed at that. "I don't know," she said. "He's pretty unbridled."

"What the job needs is somebody who knows when it's time to act and who knows when it's time to sit back. So far we've seen he knows when it's time to act. The question now is, is he astute enough to recognize when it's time to sit back?"

"I don't know," she said, "but, as I'm no longer here on behalf of the law, I'm feeling a bit at loose ends."

"You want to stay?"

"Yes," she said, her tone sharp. "I'll finish what I started. Besides, without me, Pierce has no backup."

"Me and the boys are out here," her father said. "You can either join us or you can stay where you are. But you do need to confirm either way with us, so we know to look for you when shadows start moving."

"I'm here at the house," she said. "I want to do a full search on the outbuildings. But remember Pierce is out in the shadows. I don't know where. Not even sure what he's after."

"If he's smart, he'll have gone to Jed's house to see if they're there."

"Maybe," she said. "But I don't know where Jed is. He should have gotten that hand looked after."

"It depends on how drunk he is. Right now he won't be feeling any pain. It'll just be that same old festering anger, only now he has a specific target," her father warned. "I'm sorry for Pete. It seems like he's the one caught in the middle of all of this."

"He is, indeed," she said. "I'd love to see him come back sooner rather than later—get his input on the renovations."

"I hear you. But that's out of my hands. If Pete calls me for a ride, I'll be the first one to go get him. Hell, maybe I'll call him and offer him one first."

On that note she hung up. She stood for a few moments, then slipped outside, listening to the silence around her. There hadn't been anything while she'd been talking, but it was so easy to miss a sound.

Taking a chance, she slipped to the fence line and crept around to the barn. As soon as she stepped inside, the air felt different, staticky with expectancy. And she knew she wasn't alone.

JED'S HOUSE LOOMED large on the left. Pierce leaned against a tree and studied it. Jed was out front beside a pickup— looked like a reject from the junkyard—swearing and cursing at something. Then that seemed to be all he did besides drinking and abusing people and Salem. Jed might have been a good man in his heyday, but circumstances and the bottle had dragged him down, way down.

There was no way to make heads or tails out of his words either, but apparently the truck wouldn't start. No surprise there. A providence that Pierce would look on with a smile. He couldn't be sure what Jed's plan was, but it likely wasn't anything decent.

Just then Jed turned and stumbled back to the house, and Pierce meant *stumbled*. Jed could barely keep himself upright. He'd obviously come home and consumed the better part of a bottle. He held a propane torch canister in his hand, which also didn't say much good about what was going on in his head. He made it inside the door, slamming it behind him. Once again words filled the air, but they were just the same repeated swear words from before.

Pierce slipped up to the corner of the house and peered in the window. Jed appeared to be alone. He was pouring a slug back from the bottle that only had a couple inches left on the bottom. When he ran out, if he did run out, then things would get ugly yet again. Jed would need a steady influx of that booze to keep him going, to fuel his anger, to numb his gunshot wound. Either that or it would knock him out. But he had a huge tolerance. So many alcoholics could function at levels that would knock out normal individuals.

Pierce studied Jed as he moved around the house, knocking papers off the table and dumping chairs to the side. He was trying to light the propane torch in his hand with a sparking fire, trying to get it to give him a few inches of flame. It was an accident waiting to happen. Jed swore again when it wouldn't light. This time Pierce sighed with relief.

When something cold nestled his hand, he jumped slightly and turned to look down. "Well, Salem, you are one sneaky dog," he whispered. He crouched lower and gently stroked her head.

She looked at him with those huge eyes, worried she was trusting the wrong man yet again.

He brushed his hand down the back of her neck, scratched her ruff and said, "How are you doing, huh? You shouldn't be over here. This is one guy who'll torture you and watch you burn alive."

She seemed to understand his words because she shot a hesitant look toward the house.

He straightened, peered in the window and saw Jed coming around to the rear kitchen door. Calling Salem to him with hand signals, Pierce raced back to the tree, the two of them blending into the fence in the woods. He watched from a distance as Jed tripped out the back door, standing there cursing the moon, shaking a fist at the sky. Pierce wondered at the anger that drove this man. And then he heard Jed speak.

"Goddammit, Vicky. Get your fucking ass back home again. I'm hungry. A man needs to eat, you know?"

Pierce's eyebrows shot up. So he was upset about Vicky. He saw a phone in Jed's hand and realized Jed was talking. Then he smashed the phone against a fence post. A shot Pierce didn't think Jed could make, except for the fact that he was drunk. And somehow drunks seemed to have the luck.

"Goddamn bitch. No way you get to leave me," he roared.

That made more sense. Vicky was gone, and here Jed was. That was the last straw for him. And just like that, he fired up that spark to get the torch to light, and, indeed, it did.

Out came a good foot-long shot of flame. And that had Jed laughing like a loon. He shut down the burner again, lit it once more to make sure it worked once more, and then walked around the house toward his junkyard truck.

Pierce knew the real trouble had just started. They were heading into a full-blown war right now, and it was one nobody would win. His first priority was to avoid loss of life. The second priority was to avoid loss of property. And the only property he gave a shit about was Pete's.

Seeing Jed get into the truck and manage to start it up, put it in gear and reverse it down the driveway had Pierce racing back toward Pete's property. With Salem running free at his side, the two matched pace for pace with the truck on the road. At least the driveway would take some twists and turns, whereas Pierce cut across the back forty and would be there, hopefully, at the same time.

CHAPTER 11

B ACK IN THE house, Hedi saw Billy lying on the floor, staring up at her, absolute hate in his gaze. She crouched and said, "Oh, I'm sorry you're awake. You're much easier to deal with when you're unconscious."

"So are you," he mumbled around the cloth in his mouth, glaring at her.

She ignored him, knowing he was very much of the opinion a woman should be available whenever a man wanted, and it didn't matter if she was willing or not. She walked to the front door and stared out. Her knees were weak from her damn fast mad dash back from the barn, but now she knew that was where the danger was. Only one handgun did not an army make.

Hating to be inside, she walked back to the kitchen and slipped out into the darkness. Instantly she felt better. She hated that she'd run away from the evil presence in the barn and wondered at the sense of going back in again. Was Bobby there? If so, she wasn't ready to take him on, not on her own. Not when she didn't know where Jed was.

She checked out the lay of the land, slipped to the right, away from the barn, caught up with the fence and crept along the side so she was between the barn and the house where she had a better vantage point. A copse of trees was there, and she could hide a little easier.

From that point she crouched down low and watched. When her phone buzzed in her hand, she took a look and read the message from Pierce. "Shit, shit, shit," she snapped. This was so not cool.

She forwarded the text to her father, adding, **Jed is liquored up and running around with a working blowtorch.**

She could only hope her father and his men stopped Jed before he got here and caused any more trouble. If ever there was a mangy dog that needed to be put down, it was Jed.

In the last two years of being a deputy her job had been pretty damn easy. She'd learned a lot from her father and less than nothing from the current sheriff. She wondered if tonight's media hype would cause a kerfuffle. Or would it garner only a brief mention and disappear like so many other incidents? She really wanted the sheriff gone but didn't know how to make that happen.

Waiting for something to happen was interminable. Five minutes became ten. Where was Jed? He should be coming any moment. And whoever was in the barn, what were they doing? Just waiting for Jed to show up?

In the distance she could hear an owl's long cry. She turned to look up but didn't see any owl.

Her eye caught a sign of movement. She twisted slightly to spot Pierce motioning at her several trees behind her. She nodded, took a careful look around and then crept low along the grass. There was no way to make it, fast or slow, and not be noticed. There just wasn't enough here for total ground cover. If she was lucky, whoever was in the barn was deep in the barn and not looking out the double doors.

When she reached Pierce's side, she hunkered down and whispered, "What the hell's going on?"

"Jed is gunning toward murder and arson," he said. "I was hoping our backup would come a little faster."

"My father, Roger, and Stew, one of his former deputies, are here," she said. "They're hoping to stop Jed before he gets here."

"Somebody has to," he said. "Jed is just a live wire. He's on a rampage. I think he got a call from his wife saying she was leaving him."

"Oh, shit. That would be really bad timing on her part," Hedi said.

"And sent Jed, who was already on the edge—or rather over the edge—completely off the cliff," Pierce said.

Her phone rang. "Dad, what's up?"

"Jed is one cagey drunk. He must have seen us without us seeing him," he said. "When he didn't show up on the roadway as soon as we expected, we went looking for him. Found his abandoned truck—that second work truck of his—parked off-road. He left it and obviously took off on foot. We checked his ride, specifically for the torch. And, yeah, he still has it."

"So he could already be here," she said, looking around the area. "I think somebody's in the barn. It's probably Bobby, waiting for Jed to show up."

"Make sure you don't go back in that barn or the house," her father ordered.

"I'm out in the trees with Pierce. He also said he heard part of a conversation with Jed about maybe Vicky leaving him."

"If that's the case," her father said, "nobody is bringing Jed in tonight. He'll take out as many as he can, including himself. But, if he doesn't get stopped here, you know he'll be going after his wife next."

"Please get her someplace safe," she told her father urgently.

"I'm sending Stew to Vicky and the kids. He'll watch over them, even move them if he has to."

Hedi nodded. "Those kids have been through enough already. We can't have Jed taking them all out just because he's pissed."

"He's been pissed for a long time," her father said. "Make sure you're not a target of Jed's rage tonight."

"Not planning on that, but someone needs to stop him. And I want to make sure we take down Bobby in the barn, if that's who's there," she said. "I just can't be sure it is." She turned to look at Pierce.

He held a finger to his lips and disappeared in front of her.

"Pierce is about to confirm who's in the barn," she said. "And, if Jed sets Pete's house on fire, he'll burn up Billy. That'll just be another shitstorm."

"Don't go back inside that house," her father repeated.

She hung up the phone, pocketed it and slipped back through the trees, around to the barn, watching Pierce creep up close. The barn had double doors on this side, and a single door and window on the back. She never understood why barns didn't come with multiple windows so you had better access and better light, but apparently they didn't. At least not during the time that this one was built.

As she watched, Pierce sneaked up to the double doors and waited. There wasn't a sound. She wanted to tell him to stop, not to even bother, that they could wait Bobby out. Then they could just watch and keep track as Bobby tried to leave. But Pierce didn't appear to be the waiting kind of guy because, even as she watched, he disappeared inside the barn.

PIERCE STUDIED THE interior of the barn. He was as low to the ground as he could get, tucked alongside the wall and hunkered under a saddle stand with a big old leather saddle on top. He listened with his eyes closed and his ears wide open, and he could hear feet shifting impatiently on the left at the back. Whether he'd been seen or not, he didn't know. The barn was too dark at the moment, and he hadn't been here long enough to have the lay of the land. Chances were good Bobby knew the interior better than Pierce did.

As he waited, the back door opened, and somebody stumbled inside. "Bobby, you there?"

Bobby whispered, "Yeah. What took you so long?"

"A roadblock was out there for me. Had to walk the last part."

"A roadblock? The sheriff? No way, man. That's what we pay him for."

"Well, we didn't pay him enough because there's at least one truck if not two or three."

"Could have just been somebody broke down," Bobby said.

"I don't know. It doesn't matter. I got the torch."

"We didn't have to have a torch. We needed gasoline. We could take it from her car but we might need that as a getaway vehicle."

"That's what Billy was supposed to get. Where is he?"

"No idea," Bobby said, his voice hard but fretting. "Last I saw he was getting gas from the truck, but I never saw him again."

"Goddamn fucking shit," Jed roared. "It's gotta be that asshole."

"Yeah, I think you're right," he said. "But I don't want to torch the house until I know if my brother is in there."

"We're torching the house," Jed said. "If your brother is in there, goddammit, he better get his ass out fast."

"I don't know if he's alive or not," Bobby said. "But I'm not killing him if he's unconscious or if he's tied up and can't leave."

"We'll run out of options pretty damn soon," Jed said. "And I'm not waiting around for the roadblock assholes to get here."

"What do you want to do?" Bobby asked.

"I want to go in. We'll start the fire between the barn and the house and do a quick run-through of the house. If Billy is there, we'll get him out. But nobody else gets to leave. We'll shoot them if they try."

CHAPTER 12

S HE WATCHED AS Pierce slipped back out the door and crept along the high grass to the back. She could only imagine what he was doing because she certainly couldn't see. Then he came back around to the front and in a move that surprised her, he closed both front double doors and threw a board across them. She raced down to meet him. "You locked the men in?"

He nodded. "Their plan is to burn the place down." He held up his phone. "I recorded it all."

"Oh, wow, that's incredible."

"Not really," he said. "In normal circumstances, the sheriff would arrest these guys for attempted arson, not to mention trespassing, breaking and entering, and any number of other nasty things. In this case, we've got calls out to the other counties' sheriffs close by. One is on his way. One contacted your sheriff, and he said he's got a madman running loose, being me I presume, and that's the way it goes," he said with a half shoulder shrug. "Fort Collins has a police department, and they've been alerted to the problems. Give me a minute, and I'll send this recording to them." He sat down with his back against the barn door and started to text.

She squatted beside him, and, just as she lowered herself down, a bullet came flying from inside the barn door right where her head had been. "Shit," she said and hit the ground flat. That had been close, too damn close.

"We can expect them to keep that up too," he said. "Let's get a safe distance away."

They made their way back to the trees, where they could watch both ends of the barn.

"They'll try to come out through the window," he said, "but it's pretty high and small, or they will open the front doors by shooting their way out."

"And then what?"

"I'd love to set a trap for them," he said, running his hand through his hair as he studied the barn. "Or I can just make it so they can't get out. That sounds like a better idea to me." And he took off across the yard toward his truck. There he started it up and drove down to the end of the lane, where Jed had dropped off his beloved truck for his previous visit, before he got shot in his gun hand.

She watched, wondering how he would start it, when all of a sudden it came trembling toward the barn. She shook her head, wondering at the madness of this night as Pierce pulled Jed's truck up sideways and parked right in front of the double doors so that he had to crawl out the passenger side in order to get out. She watched as the back door rattled, and bullets shot through it. The window was shot out, and broken glass shattered everywhere.

"Don't do that," Jed roared. "We'll get cut on the way out."

"I ain't getting out that way anyway," Bobby said. "That window ain't big enough for me."

She wanted to laugh, but it was such a bizarre night she didn't dare. She stayed hunkered low, keeping watch. Bullets flew out in all directions, as if one of them stood in the center of the room and just started shooting, hoping to hit somebody on the outside.

When the shots slowed down, Pierce called out. "You're firing into Jed's truck. It's parked at the double doors."

"What the hell?" Jed exploded. "You leave my truck alone."

"Not my fault if you shoot it," Pierce said. "When you run out of ammo, let me know, and I'll open the door for you."

Immediately a barrage of gunfire headed in the direction of his voice. But Pierce was no longer there. She shook her head and sat down to wait. Pierce was right; at some point they would run out of ammo.

But she knew these men. They came prepared for bear. They could also burn down the barn and her car with it. And just then she realized Pierce had thought of the same thing. Because without a word, he went racing behind her, flat out to the back.

She stood up. "What the hell …"

But he didn't answer.

The next thing she knew, he slowly drove the tractor toward her. She frowned as he built a massive firebreak around the barn so that, if they did light the barn on fire, it would collapse in on itself and not spread to any other buildings around it.

She looked up at the trees. A couple branches could catch fire but not many. She had no idea how much value was in that barn itself, but it was a hell of a lot better to lose that than to lose the house.

As soon as Jed and Bobby heard the tractor outside, she figured they'd start shooting again. Pierce stopped when he got close to the barn, his firebreak a good six to eight feet away, and studied the barn for a long moment. He didn't trust them, and she didn't blame him.

He got off the tractor and picked up a piece of sheet metal lying on the ground. He propped that up beside him in the tractor cab, then with a hand on the top, he slowly completed the round of firebreak closer to the barn, with that sheet metal hopefully protecting him from any bullets coming through the barn. Then he went to his truck, rummaged in the back and came up with a handsaw. Next thing she knew, he shimmied up the tree overhanging the barn, cutting down branches. Obviously he took the fire pretty damn seriously. But she grinned, loving his chutzpah.

When he joined her, huffing slightly, a bead of sweat on his forehead, she whispered, "You're a handy man to have around."

He leaned over and kissed her hard and fast. "Sweetheart, you have no idea."

She chuckled at that. "Does that line actually get you somewhere with women?" she asked, trying to ignore the kiss. She'd been right when she had told her father that Pierce was a good man to have around in time of need. She figured he was one of the good guys, period.

A hell of a lot of banked fire was in that kiss. And damn she wanted to taste his lips again.

"Since we'll need a new sheriff," she said in a conversational tone of voice, "you looking for a job?"

He looked at her in horror. "You wouldn't saddle me with that, would you?"

She raised her eyebrows. "It's an office of respect. It's men upholding the law." She motioned toward the barn. "Personally I think you'd be great."

"The position isn't open anyway," he said amiably. "So I

don't have to worry about it."

"Maybe not," she said, "but you should. Apply, at least."

"Again, no open job, remember?"

"I also believe in the law," she said, "so I have to believe this sheriff will get his ass booted out somehow or another, and there will be an open position."

"What about you?" he asked. "Do you want the job?"

She shook her head. "Nope. I'm happy as support staff. It's not that I can't do the job, but I don't have the attitude you do. At the office, as it stands now, I'm the most aggressive one there, and that's damn sad. Since I met you though, I realize you're very much like my father, so I'm a good person to back you up. But I'm not necessarily the right person to lead."

He studied her for a long moment and smiled. "I'll take your lead any day."

She groaned and shook her head. "Stop the sexual innuendoes."

"Why?" he said. "I was just getting started."

"Wow," she said. "How did this come out of the blue?"

"Hasn't been out of the blue," he said with a smirk. "I know solid gold when I see it."

She stared at him in surprise. "Me?"

It was his turn to stop and look at her. "Absolutely you. Surprised?"

She nodded.

"YOU SHOULDN'T BE," he said briskly wondering why she would be. "You can tell an awful lot about a person in a scenario like this. Look at all the characters involved, and who is it who stands up straight on the side of right?"

"Just you and me and Dad and Roger and Stew from what I can see," she said.

"Exactly. You're solid gold. You were there earlier, pushing back at Jed when he was trying to hurt those kids. You came here to help me because I was trying to help Pete," he said. "You stuck around because you knew it was the right thing to do. Solid gold. The fact that you're also a looker and have a personality that balances nicely with mine only helps."

"That is not a relationship."

He twisted, looked at her and grinned. "No. But we could try."

"Try what? A relationship?" she asked drily. "You flash into town, and next you'll be flashing out of town."

"No. Probably not. I might not be able to do all those renos for Pete, but I can sure get a handle on most of them. If I need tradesmen, we'll take a look at that cost then," he said. "Hell, I might even know enough guys to help out myself. And most of them would be happy to help a fellow vet."

"Then you know the right kind of men," she said sadly. "It seems like all I've been surrounded by is these guys." She motioned at the barn. "Or the two deputies I work with and the sheriff."

"Definitely time for housecleaning," he said. Just then he caught sight of Salem. "Don't say or do anything now, but Salem is coming up between us."

She looked at him in shock. "I forgot about her."

"I haven't. She was with me every step of the way back from Jed's, and then I told her to stay in the trees. I did not want Jed to get a chance to shoot her."

"Or burn her alive," Hedi said sadly. "He's just that kind

of guy."

"I think I told her that too," he said with a chuckle. He looked down and held out his hand. Salem walked into it. He spent a moment gently stroking her forehead and the back of her neck. She was gentle and loving, and it angered him at a deep level to see how she'd been treated.

Hedi watched the two of them. "She really likes you, doesn't she?"

"I haven't starved her. I haven't made her do something against her nature. And I treat her with respect and love. What's not to like?" Hedi looked at him for a long moment, and he wondered what she was thinking.

"It's just that easy, isn't it?" she asked. "Jed did treat her badly. He never once treated her with respect or love. Just like he never treated his wife and kids with respect or love."

"Vicky was a prisoner, an abused one at that," he said shortly. "A man has got no business beating up on a woman. You guys can't fight back the same. You don't have the meanness we have, and you don't have the strength. And, if you're in a marriage, you're there because you want to be, at least at first because there's respect, there's love, and because there's a commitment," he added gently.

"Too bad it doesn't work out that way most times," she said gently.

"Ever been married?" he asked.

"No," she said. "I came close a time or two, but, in one case, a local job fell through for him, and I realized I didn't love him enough to leave here." She gave Pierce a crooked grin. "Unfortunately it took me a little too long to figure that out."

"Better late than never," he said. "Imagine if you had gotten married and had two kids, *then* realized how unhappy you were?"

"I was also very young, two months short of my eighteenth birthday. And I just wasn't ready."

"That is young," he said. "And the other incident?"

"Somebody I thought would be the one." An evident note of bitterness filled her voice. "But apparently a half dozen other girls thought the same thing."

"Ouch," he said. "Yeah, that's the other kind of relationship. I don't do those."

"What do you mean, you don't do those?"

"Multiple partners," he said. "When I commit, I commit fully. And I demand commitment on both sides. Life is full of diversions. You choose what you'll focus on and go after what you truly want. Otherwise you can expend your energy on too many things, and you get nowhere quickly."

"Sure, but a marriage isn't exactly a goal that you have to work toward."

"I think it is," he said. "Relationships are goals. Every single day you get up, and you work on your relationships to make them the best damn relationships you can have." He stared up at the night sky. "I don't understand how people can just fall into a relationship and stay there, even though it's no good."

"You have a very unique view on life," she said slowly. "But I like it." In fact, it gave her great insight into who he was.

"Yeah, probably from being in the military, going through rehab, recovering from injuries, all that good stuff," he said.

"I can't see anything wrong with your viewpoint," she said. "It seems like honesty, integrity, morality, ethics, they're all something that's becoming old-fashioned and falling out of favor."

"No. You just had a tainted view for the last few years because the people you work with suck," he said, startling a laugh from her.

"I hear you there," she said, "but I'm really glad you don't suck."

"See? That's what I mean. We click."

"Clicking is not a relationship," she reiterated, but he was getting to her, intriguing her at the same time he was mystifying her. One of the most interesting men to come into her world.

"No, but it's a good basis for one," he said.

Just then a bullet was fired in their direction. They both hunkered lower, and Salem started to growl. Pierce placed a hand on her shoulder. "Easy, girl." He studied the darkness. "Did that come from inside the barn?"

"I'm not sure it did," she said. "They might have kicked out part of the back wall and snuck around on us."

"It's all too possible," he said almost philosophically.

Salem growled again deep in the back of her throat.

"She really doesn't like these guys, does she?" asked Pierce. "But we can't watch four sides at once."

"I know," she said. "But I really don't want to see them get out before our backup arrives."

"I'm not sure where the backup is," he said. "Chances are it'll be a little far away yet."

"Dad and Roger are out there, keeping an eye out. But we should have others coming too," she said. "We put out the call at least an hour ago."

"Maybe."

Just then more shots were fired in their direction. Salem growled yet again. Pierce put a hand on her fur to calm her down.

"She doesn't like gunfire, does she?" Hedi asked Pierce.

"No. When she was attacked with Pete, insurgents had opened fire. I'm sure she associates that gunfire with what happened to her life and to Pete."

Hedi gasped. "That's terrible."

"Unfortunately it's all too common. Dogs are almost human in many ways."

The gunfire increased, a heavy barrage that kept their heads lowered.

"We're sitting ducks," he said. Quietly he grabbed her hand. "Follow me."

And just like that they were up and racing away, Salem at his side as they went deeper into the woods. Bullets fired in their direction once more.

"We can assume they escaped the barn," she gasped.

"Yep, they're out and free, or they have backup."

"Who would that would be?"

"It could be any number of people, but I see two possibilities."

"Who?" she cried out.

"Either Billy, who we left tied up inside the house, or … Ross."

SHE HATED TO concede he had a point, but it was valid. "If it's Ross, he parked somewhere out of sight and walked."

"He probably parked at Jed's and walked in. He could have released Billy, and now we've got both of them after us."

"Shit," she said. She picked up her phone and called her father. "Did you see anyone on foot?"

"No," he said slowly. "Roger said he thought he saw a shadow, but, when he went to investigate, no one was there."

"We're under heavy gunfire," she murmured. "We had two of them pinned in the barn, Jed and Bobby, but now we're in the trees running away from the house."

"You stay hidden," her father ordered.

"You be careful, Dad," she snapped. "There's likely four now, all heavily armed. At this point, I want the bloody National Guard."

He chuckled. "You won't get that, but you will get us. And we do have word that Fort Collins is on its way. They're about ten minutes out."

At the mention of *ten minutes*, her heart gave a sigh of relief. "We can handle ten minutes, or rather I can." She turned to look around to see Pierce already gone, Salem at his side. "Pierce and Salem are heading back toward the house and the barn, so I don't know that they can."

"Get them to stay where you are," her father cried out in alarm.

"Not happening, Dad. He's already too far gone for that. Get here as soon as you can. I'm going after him." And she wasted no time pocketing her phone, racing behind Pierce. She wasn't at all sure what he was up to, but she knew he wouldn't go down without a fight, and she wouldn't let him go down alone.

Swearing silently under her breath, she came up to a copse of trees where she could see the house clearly and almost cried out in surprise when a hand smacked around her mouth.

Pierce whispered in her ear. "You should have stayed behind."

She shook her head, brushing off his hand. "What, and let you run off and have all the fun?"

His white teeth flashed in the dark. "Hardly, but at least here I don't have to worry about somebody circling around and back again."

"No," she said, "you don't. On the other hand, I'm not sure that's any help." Then she passed on her father's message.

Together the two walked to the edge of the copse where they could see the house. He looked at it and said, "I don't want Pete to lose that house."

"I don't think we have any choice," she said. "There are too many bad guys. Better the property than our lives. And definitely can't lose Salem. Pete needs her."

"I want you to stay here," he said. "There might be four of them loose now, but I can knock that number down to half. There's a good chance I can take their weapons, and that'll give us a decided advantage."

"What can I do to help?"

He leaned over and kissed her again. "See? That's what I mean. Just the right kind of attitude."

"Not quite," she said. "I don't want to get shot, and whatever you're planning on doing is likely to get us both in that condition."

"No," he said cheerfully. "That's not on my agenda. What I want you to do is stay here for five minutes. When you hear an owl call, come toward the call."

"How will I know where that is in the darkness?" she asked.

But, once again, he was gone, Salem a mere shadow at his side in the dark. Hedi hated always being left behind, but she didn't have a choice right now.

The minutes ticked by slowly. She kept checking her watch, wondering how long to give him. He'd said five minutes, but five minutes was not very long.

At the five-minute mark, she started counting mentally, making it go to six minutes, seven minutes. At the eight-minute mark, she stood, leaning against the tree. She hadn't heard anything, not a gunshot, not a crackle of a branch.

And then suddenly he was right there beside her. Salem shoved her nose into her hand. Hedi stroked and scratched the beautiful animal's neck and chin. She watched as Pierce dropped a heavy load to the ground at her feet. She could hear his heavy gasping breath now that he allowed himself to let it go. His load took the shape of a large prone male. "Which twin is it?"

"Billy. He was moving a little slower than the others, but now he won't do anything until at least morning."

"What about his weapons?"

"I stashed them back there. I want to pick off one more person," he said. "Two against two are the odds I'm looking for."

She smiled, realizing he was at least counting her as an equal, and that made her feel good. "Let me come with you," she said, "then we don't have to ditch the weapons."

He hesitated, then gave a curt nod. "Just remember," he said, "that I spent a lot of time learning how to do this."

She nodded. "And you do it damn well," she said. "But time is definitely of the essence."

He nodded once and whispered, "Come on," and he melted into the darkness.

She was amazed at how soundlessly he moved, with Salem always at his side, as if they were back in the war. And essentially they were. The two were a pair. Was Salem's relationship with Pete like that too?

Was the war ever over for these men?

It seemed to her that every step she made came with a crackle and a crunch. She kept trying to not focus on it, but it was hard because Pierce apparently moved effortlessly and silently.

Suddenly they came up against the side of the house, and she saw Jed, heard him talking. She whispered, "Can you tell if someone is with him?"

"That's Jed, but is he talking to someone on the phone? I don't see anyone else."

Off to their left was a whispered "There you are." And a rifle barrel was locked and loaded with a *clink*.

Pierce wasted no time, taking three steps and diving low. She watched as he flattened the gunman to the ground, pulling the rifle from his hands, then he turned and smacked him hard in the head with the rifle butt. Salem latched onto the stranger's ankle, growling in a most horrible way.

"Easy, girl. We got him."

Slowly he persuaded Salem to back away from the man.

Hedi stood at Pierce's side, taking the rifle as he handed it over to her. "Is that Bobby?" she asked.

"Yeah," he said. "Let's get him to his brother." He looked at her. "Can you grab his feet?"

"I can for a little way," she said, "but these guys ..."

"I know," he said. "I carried his brother. Maybe we'll drag him over there and tie him up."

And that was what they did. Back at the house, Salem standing between the two of them, Hedi handed Pierce the rifle and said, "I'd prefer to have a handgun any day."

"As long as I have a weapon, I don't care. Come on. Let's go," he said, running to the corner of the house. In the distance she thought she could hear vehicles. And then Pierce surprised her. He stepped forward, around the corner and said, "Hello, Jed." He raised the confiscated rifle, aiming for Jed's chest.

Jed turned on him, pointed his rifle in Pierce's direction and said, "Don't you fucking come any closer."

"I don't need to," Pierce said gently.

Hedi watched as Salem kept to the shadows behind her around the corner.

"I can shoot you easily from here," Pierce continued. "The fact of the matter is, I want you to get the hell off Pete's property and to leave him and his property alone."

"I don't give a fuck what you want," Jed said, "because I didn't come alone." In one hand he held his rifle, still pointed at Pierce, but, in the other hand, a well-bandaged hand, he held the propane torch. "I came prepared too. I'll burn this place to the ground."

"I can't let you do that," Hedi said, stepping out to join Pierce. "Definitely not happening." She searched the area for a second man but saw no sign of him.

All of a sudden a gun poked her in the back. "Hate to do this," Ross said, "but hands up, Hedi."

"Shit," she said, slurring the word, slowly raising her hands.

"You too, cowboy."

Pierce had absolutely no problem doing the same.

"See?" taunted Jed. "Not alone."

Ross chuckled. "Not such a smartass when a gun's pointed at you, are you, Pierce?"

"I'm enjoying the entertainment here. Thanks, Ross," Jed said, his rifle lowered to his side now, but a wild-eyed expression overtook his face, topped off by a madman's smile.

Hedi turned to look at Ross. "I'm really sorry you did that, Ross."

"I thought about it for a long time, and I figured I was running away with my tail between my legs and with nothing to show for it. Whereas, if I stayed here, I still could get it all," he said calmly.

She nodded gravely, then smiled. "But you're wrong." And she dropped, kicked out, hit him hard in his kneecap. When he buckled, she flipped, kicked him in the jaw, and down he went. She grabbed his rifle and turned, holding it on Jed.

Drunk Jed was a little slow to react—or more entertained with Hedi taking down Ross—and was caught off guard, his rifle still at his side, still pointing downward.

Pierce looked at her, then at Ross groaning on the ground and said, "Wow, nice job."

"Aikido," she said. "Ross, you should have left. But don't you worry. Now you'll for sure get free room and board again but also an awful lot of very unwelcome company."

WITH ROSS AND both Bobby and Billy taken down, that left just Jed. And, hearing the vehicles in the distance, Pierce stepped forward and said, "Jed, put down your firearm and the torch."

"Hell no," Jed snapped. "This ends here and now."

"Absolutely it does," Pierce said quietly. "Your three backups can't help you now. It's just you."

"I didn't need them anyway," he roared. And he raised his firearm.

But, instead of firing, he lit the torch. Pierce swore, took aim and said, "Put that out, or I'll shoot you down."

Without warning, Jed fired but, because of his bad hand, missed. Pierce bolted to the side and dashed behind his truck as Jed laughed like a loon. He'd obviously flipped a mental switch and was incapable of rational action or thought.

Realizing Hedi was behind him, they split and came up on either side of Jed. But he was already lighting bits of grass with the torch as he moved toward the house, laughing more and more. Flames licked up the dry overgrown grass, racing in all directions.

At the front veranda Jed howled, "You can't stop me," he said. "Even if you shoot me, I'll drop this, and it'll light up this place like nothing."

"We'll put it out before it gets anywhere," Pierce said calmly. "We have to redo that deck out back and put in a ramp anyway, just like for this veranda."

"No fucking way Pete's coming home," Jed said. "This is Ross's place, and he doesn't want no broken-person ramp." He turned the torch toward the steps.

Pierce jumped him, knocking away the rifle, but Jed sent blue flames at him. Pierce jumped back, and Jed, realizing his advantage, started to laugh again.

"Come and get me," he jeered. "You think I don't want to toast your skin alive for what you did to my hand?"

The vehicle din got louder. "This won't end well," Pierce said. He used hand signals to keep Salem behind him. If Jed saw her, he'd make her his first target. She deserved better than that. He called out to Jed, "The cops are coming. Everybody in town and even from neighboring counties who can give us a hand are headed here. You sure you want to take a bullet and die this way?"

"Why the fuck not? At least I'll see this place burn. You took away my wife and kids. You blew up my hand. You ruined my life."

"Oh, grow up," Hedi snapped beside him. "You're the one who chased away your wife and kids. You're the one who ruined your life. And no way in hell we'll let you just stand here and burn down Pete's place."

"Well, Pete ain't coming back," he snapped. "So shut the fuck up."

"Jed?" A thin but valiant voice called from the first vehicle to come up the driveway. Even in the dark the voice was recognizable. "What the hell are you doing, man?"

Pierce barely caught Salem as she went to race past him. Giving her a hard command to wait, she sat but squirmed in eagerness. She'd had no trouble recognizing Pete's voice. But the danger wasn't over. Jed had a personal hatred for the dog ...

Jed faltered. He turned to the pickup parked sideways in the drive.

Pete opened the door so everybody could see him. Jessie hopped out of the driver's side, came around to Pete, dropped his wheelchair down on the ground and helped him into it.

Pierce and Hedi exchanged a glance, both wondering how Pete got here and ended up in Jessie's vehicle.

Jed's face worked up into a big frown. "What the hell? Ross said you weren't coming back."

"Would you shut that torch off please?" Pete said quietly. "You'll burn down my house, and I need it."

"You should have stayed where you were," Jed said, moving a couple steps closer. He held the torch out in front of him, as if to burn Pete. "We don't need no broken-down pieces of sorry-ass shits here."

Pete nodded. "You know what? Ross told me that too. Not in the same words but basically telling me this was a place for only able-bodied men, and everybody else needed to stay in the rehab center. And I'm sorry to say I believed him. My belief in myself had taken so many hits already that I allowed his words to dictate my actions." He turned to look at Pierce and smiled. "Pierce here reminded me that I've been through worse and probably there'll be worse ahead of me too. But you don't need to be worried about that anymore. They'll lock you up for a long time."

"Why? I haven't done nothing," Jed said, laughing uproariously. "So what if I got a blowtorch? Big fucking deal." He turned it on the grass and lit the grass around him on fire.

Pierce watched him, wondering if Jed realized how close

he was to torching his own body. "Is that how you want to die?" he asked softly. "Do you want to burn yourself alive?"

"What do you care?"

Pierce crossed his arms over his chest. "I don't. I've seen too many people light themselves on fire over in Afghanistan and India. It's not a pretty sight. But, if that's your way to go, well, whatever, man."

"I'm not suicidal," Jed roared. "It's you who'll burn alive."

Pierce just stared at him. "I don't think so. You're the one looking pretty weak and feeble at the moment."

Jed looked around, as if seeing the ten men surrounding him for the first time. He frowned. "Who the fuck are you guys?"

"Law-abiding citizens and cops from Fort Collins," the closest police officer said. "We sure as hell aren't in our usual jurisdiction, but, if we got to step in, we got to. And you're causing trouble. Where the hell your local sheriff is, I don't know."

"He's sitting in his office, not worrying about jack shit," Jed said. "That's the way he likes it."

"Maybe," the cop said, "but that's not his job." He turned, caught sight of Hedi and nodded. "So we got one deputy, and that's it?"

"Yeah, nobody else would come," she said. "And I've been fired because I did come."

The cop raised his eyebrows. "I'm pretty sure there'll be an investigation."

"Maybe," she said. "Doesn't mean it'll make any difference. Apparently our sheriff paid everybody to vote him in."

"Wow. That'll make for some fun times coming up." The police officer looked at Jed. "You going to put that out and drop your weapon?"

"Hell no," Jed said. "You want me to do that, you'll have to shoot me."

"I can," the cop said in a bored tone of voice. "It's your choice." He pointed his revolver at Jed. "Make a decision."

"Absolutely," Jed said, and he turned on Pierce with the blowtorch and jumped him.

Shots broke out, but Jed was too close to Pierce for a good rifle shot. Jed went down, shot in the shoulder, but still fighting mad. He threw himself at Pierce.

Pierce sidestepped the man, grabbed the blowtorch from his hand, shut it off, stopping the blue flame, and stomped out the grass fire Jed had started.

Jed swore and cussed, and, as they watched, then dropped to the ground, crying like a baby.

Hedi threw herself into Pierce's arms.

He held her close and said, "It's okay. It's over."

She gave him a quick hug, looked up at him and said, "It might be over, but you damn near got torched."

"Maybe," he said, "but Jed was a little too drunk for that."

Jed was quickly secured, medical aid administered. The rest of the prisoners were taken out, and explanations were given.

Pierce didn't know how many men were here from Fort Collins, how many were locals. Or why Salem disappeared. He'd figured for sure she'd have gone right for Pete but ... He glanced around, his gaze searching the area. She'd had a rough time of it lately; so, if this many men scared her off, that was fine. She could have a private reunion with Pete a little later.

As he looked over the crowd, he found Jessie and Pete.

He walked over, squatting in front of Pete, and said, "Man, you're a sight for sore eyes."

Pete reached out to shake his hand. "Thank you. And I don't mean for saving the house. Obviously that's just property. But thank you for not taking any more lives. This isn't the war we're supposed to fight, and we're never supposed to fight one on our own soil."

Pierce understood exactly what he meant. "I hear you," he said. "I figured we could probably make some rough house renos, if you want to move in tonight, and then we'll get to work over the next couple weeks to get this place fixed up for you."

He watched as Pete's jawline worked, trying to hold back his emotions.

Hedi reached over and said, "Hey, Pete, it's so good to see you." She opened her arms and gave him a hug.

Pete clasped his arms around her and just held her tight. "You got a good guy here," he said. "Make sure you don't lose him."

"He's not mine to lose," Hedi said with a laugh. "Why would you think that?"

"That's just the way it looks on the outside," her dad said. "Honestly, I'm delighted you lost the boyfriends you did. They should stay lost too. But I agree. This one's a keeper."

Pierce snorted at that. "I'm glad y'all approve, but we got to get some people back in this house. I'm sure Pete would like to go in and take a look."

"He would," Pete said. "But there's one other thing I really want to know."

Pierce nodded. Pete wondered where Salem was. Only Pierce had no idea where Salem had snuck away to.

Just then a kerfuffle was heard at the trucks. Jed had somehow managed to get another firearm free and was holding a handgun against a cop's neck. "You guys are going to let me go," Jed yelled, anger now replacing the tears from earlier. "No fucking way I'm going to jail for the rest of my life."

"Maybe not if you're dead," Pierce said.

Backing up, dragging the cop with him, Jed said, "If you think I won't kill this guy, you're wrong."

"You might shoot him," one of the other officers said, "but you'll get a dozen bullets yourself. You won't survive."

Jed kept backing up toward the barn where his truck was. "Maybe. Or you guys can let me go. I'll take off out of here, and you'll never see me again."

Pierce didn't believe that, and he sure as hell wasn't interested in making a deal with a drunk lunatic. But Pierce caught something out of the corner of his eye and realized another element had joined the fray, looking for a revenge of her own. She hadn't snuck away. Salem had snuck *around*. Still caught up in a war not of her making, she'd kept her eye on the enemy, even when the others had relaxed.

Pierce swore gently under his breath. This wouldn't be good.

Pete asked, "What's the matter?"

"There'll be bloodshed," Pierce said. "I just don't know how severe it'll be."

"It's already pretty damn bad," Hedi said. "So, if you've got a way to save that cop, I don't really give a shit about Jed."

Pierce nodded. "The trouble is, somebody has already got her own plan of action. On a target she can't see past."

Pete's breath sucked in hard. "Salem? Are you talking

about Salem?"

"I think so," Pierce said. He bolted off to the side.

Jed roared, "Get your ass back here."

Jed fired in Pierce's direction, but Pierce was already out of range and hiding behind the closest vehicle. Where he was, he could see Salem. It was the hidden element they needed, but it would be damn hard to stop her from killing Jed. She shifted, and Pierce lost sight of her. Frantic, he peered around the edge of the vehicle looking for her. Suddenly a harsh growl came, and the dog shot through the air and attached itself to Jed's shoulder.

Jed screamed. The gun went off harmlessly into the air as the dog ripped him backward, flat onto the ground. She released her grip and came in at another angle, looking for his throat. Jed screamed and rolled his arms over his head, trying to protect himself.

Pierce raced forward and kicked the gun out of Jed's hand as the cop backed away.

"Salem," Pierce cried out. "Stop."

Salem growled harder.

"Good girl," Pierce said. "We got him, and you're right. He was going to hurt this man. Good girl."

The growling eased slightly, but the dog didn't let go of Jed. Salem was obviously confused and unsure.

Pete in his wheelchair, struggling in the rough ground, came up behind Pierce. "Salem?" he asked, his voice almost broken.

Salem's ears pointed skyward. Her gaze lifted until she caught sight of Pete.

Pierce watched as recognition slammed into her. She released Jed from her jaws and bounded forward. And into Pete's lap, almost knocking him and the wheelchair over.

Pete wrapped his arms around her, his tears evident.

He hugged the dog tight. "Oh, my God. Salem!"

The cops had Jed under guard now. Pierce looked at them. "Do you think you can keep him this time?"

The man, grim faced, nodded. "He's a slippery bugger."

They handcuffed Jed, ignoring the screams as his shoulder was wrenched backward into the steel bracelets.

"He'll need medical treatment," one of the cops said, "though I'd just as soon put a bullet in his head than do that."

"If he has an accident on the way to the hospital, I won't complain," Pierce said. He looked at Jed with a hard glance. "If you ever come back on this property, you can bet there's a bullet that'll hit you right here." He poked Jed between the eyes. "So you're warned."

But Jed was in too much pain to bluster. Instead he blubbered like a child. The alcoholic haze was dimming, and the reality was setting in.

"On top of that," Pierce said, "your property now belongs to your wife and the kids. You will not fight it. Do you hear me?"

Jed glared at him. "Or what?"

"Or else ..." Pierce snapped, "I won't be leaving Pete alone for a while. I will make sure your wife and kids get what they deserve too. You'll go to jail for a hell of a long time. Don't be such an asshole as to take a roof away from over their heads."

Jed's gaze dropped to his feet. "I won't fight it," he muttered. "She won't stick around for me anyway, for when I come out of jail."

"Why would she?" Hedi said. "You beat her. You beat the kids. You terrorized them all."

Jed appeared to crumble in front of everyone. "I took a wrong step somewhere," he said. "And I couldn't find my way back."

"Now you have lots of time to think about your return journey," Hedi snapped. She stepped back, glancing at her father. "Thanks for bringing Pete."

"I didn't," he said. He pointed at one of the other strangers. "This guy works at the rehab center. At Pete's behest, he brought him down. We intercepted him on the road, and I brought Pete here myself. I figured that, if I came in, Jed would let me get close enough to drop Pete off. And that might be enough to defuse the situation."

"Maybe," she said. "But it was really Salem who put an end to it."

Pierce turned back to Pete. Salem had barely calmed down her excitement at seeing him again. She kept licking his face, trying to climb into his lap. And Pete looked like a new man. Pierce reached down, scratching Salem's forehead. She leaned into his hand, one of the happiest-looking dogs he'd ever seen. He crouched beside the two of them. "I sure hope you'll stay here now, Pete, because this girl needs you."

Pete nodded. "Like Jed will find out, it was a hard journey back, but I'm here now. And I won't leave her again." He looked at Pierce. "Are you serious about helping out?"

Pierce nodded. "I don't have a job, don't really have a home at the moment. I can go back to New Mexico and pick up my life there, but I'm more than willing to give you a hand for a couple weeks to get this house modified so it can be yours in all ways again."

Pete nodded. "I'd really appreciate it. I still have to get the accounting sorted through, but I think enough money is there to do some of the modifications."

They looked up as Hedi approached.

Pete frowned at her. "Is it true you got fired?"

She nodded, shoving her hands in her pockets. "And maybe that's a good thing," she admitted. "As you know, I can swing a hammer. If Pierce knows what to do here to update your home, then I can be a sidekick and give him an extra pair of working hands."

Several men stepped forward, and one was a spokesman for all. "We can help too. Some of us are working but have time on weekends. If we'd known that's all that was needed, we would have been here a long time ago. We're sorry, Pete."

More tears came to Pete's eyes. He brushed them away impatiently. "I can't tell you how much I appreciate this."

"We get it," Pierce said. "Or maybe they don't understand it, but I do. Because I've been there. And I know how important it is to have people help you make this last transition." He looked around the yard, seeing the cop vehicles backing out. He walked to where Jessie was. "What about the sheriff?"

"He's being relieved of his duties as we speak," Jessie said. "We're looking for someone to step in as interim sheriff, and we'll hold elections as soon as we can. It's not a job I care to do anymore." Jessie looked at Pierce, crossing his arms over his chest. "What about you? You could try it— for the interim. Then let the people decide. Why don't you sign up to be sheriff?"

Pierce's jaw dropped. When he recovered, he gave a broken laugh. "Because I'd shoot guys like Jed."

"But … because you didn't, even when he gave you lots of opportunities, means you're the right man for the job," Jessie said shrewdly.

Several of the men in the group stepped up behind him

and nodded. "You'd make a great sheriff," several of them said.

"I don't have enough money to pay people in this town to vote me in," Pierce said in disgust. "And, if that's what they want, they sure as hell don't want me because I'm not the kind of guy to turn my eye when there's cheating, lying, stealing, breaking and entering, arson and murder, not to mention making moonshine. And any person who'll abuse an animal on my watch just might feel the lash of my belt."

Jessie nodded. "Like I said, you'd make a great sheriff. We can't have you taking your belt to anyone, but just knowing you're around will kick some ass. It'll stop most people from crossing that line."

As Pierce frowned, Hedi slipped her hand into the crook of his elbow. "And, no, I didn't put them up to it. It was my dad's idea. I'd already mentioned it to you. I think you'd be a hell of a sheriff."

At that, Pierce snorted. "You don't know me very well."

"I know you well enough," she said. "And I'm hoping to get to know you better. Either way, I still think you're the right person for the town."

He looked down at her and shrugged. "I doubt anybody would elect me. I'm a stranger. The population seems to want your current sheriff, or they want your dad. I'm nobody."

"Not true," said one of the men behind Jessie. "This has already been preapproved by the townsfolk in an emergency Town Hall meeting tonight. You'll find you get more support than you expect."

"Well then, we'll see," Pierce said, tilting his head, giving a short nod. "I guess you can put my name on the ballot. Doesn't mean I'll get the job though."

Hedi and Jessie exchanged a glance that made Pierce suspicious. But their smiles were obvious.

"You guys really think I'd win?"

"Hell yeah," Jessie said. He smacked Pierce hard on the shoulder. "Welcome to town. You're already hired as the interim sheriff. Election in three months. Of course we have to get that paperwork in order." He stopped and chuckled. "Maybe I should make that *Welcome to the family*." He turned, still laughing uproariously, and walked back to his truck.

Within a few minutes, all the vehicles disappeared down the road, leaving Pierce, Hedi, Salem and Pete in the yard.

Pete looked from one to the other. "Is it that serious?"

Pierce looked at Hedi, wrapped an arm around her shoulders, tucking her close. "We haven't had two seconds to know the answer to that. I know which way I'm leaning, but I hate to rush a lady."

She chuckled. "All you've done is rush me." She reached up, kissing him on the cheek. "Let's just say, Pete, we're both looking to finding out if my dad's right."

Pete smiled, his arms looped around Salem, who looked like she'd finally found her home again. "So what's the chance some food is in the house? I'm hungry."

Salem barked in agreement.

And, on that note, everyone laughed. They headed inside to see how much of the groceries Hedi had brought they could eat right now.

CHAPTER 14

HEDI LEARNED MORE about house renovations than she thought possible. Pierce himself appeared to be always around, always helping, always building, regardless of the work being done. And, sure enough, with Hedi at his side, her father and several other volunteers had gutted the bathroom and were even now installing grab bars for Pete to use.

Tiling was about to start, and that was the finishing stage. The en suite bathroom was completely open so Pete could get a wheelchair in and out, or he could walk on his prosthetics, with or without crutches. So far the prosthetics offered to Peter were pretty ugly in appearance and fit and definitely in need of an upgrade, but a phone call from Kat, Badger's partner, had given Pete the best news ever. She was willing to take him on to get him something more advanced and which would serve him well.

Pete still had both arms, but one had been injured and was weaker. He could use it to pick up a cup and a knife and a fork, but he wasn't capable of doing much work with it. But Pierce had already devised a set of weights that would help Pete strengthen those muscles. Hedi had helped as much as she could, swinging a hammer, pounding nails, making coffee and even cooking meals, if making sandwiches counted.

Two days later her dad showed up midafternoon and told Pierce, "You've got about four days to finish up here, son. Then your days will be full."

Pierce, sitting with a cup of coffee beside Pete, looked at Jessie and said, "I need more than four days to finish this rehab, so what are you talking about?"

"This." Jessie handed over a piece of paper. Pierce looked at it, and his jaw dropped.

Hedi had some inkling of what it was because she'd heard her father and his buddies talking about it.

She herself had been reinstated to her position but had taken the week off to help out Pete and Pierce. She couldn't afford more time off now that Stephen and Roy had both been removed from office. Even the dispatcher had been replaced. A lot of court cases would be filed soon, charging the sheriff with various crimes, although she wasn't exactly sure with what. Ross, the Billy boys, and Jed wouldn't be seeing daylight for a long time. She wanted to feel sorry for them but couldn't. They were assholes of the first order. Pierce handed the piece of paper to her, and she could see the stunned look on his face.

But Pete had been looking at the page over Pierce's shoulder, and he started to laugh. He reached out and smacked Pierce on the shoulder. "Well, Interim Sheriff, how do you feel?"

Pierce shook his head. "I told you that I'm probably not any good at this," he warned.

"And I told you that we need somebody who can make decisions on the side of right," her father said quietly. "You've got three months to prove you're the right man for the job." He grinned. "I've asked to be on the committee for the election, and you can bet I'll be doing a lot of lobbying to get you in there. The town was pretty fed up with the old sheriff." He looked around at the renovations and said, "I love this. Nice job."

"So then what? You'll take over my spot here?" Pierce asked jokingly.

"Nope, you've got the rest of this week. You're supposed to show up for work on Monday," he said. "If we absolutely have to, we can push that back a week, but, considering nobody is in the station, we need you as soon as possible."

"Understood," Pierce said, frowning.

Hedi could see the wheels turning in his head. Apparently her father could too. "Think out loud, son. Think out loud," Jessie said. "We can't figure out what you're considering until you speak up."

"I'm thinking about how much work there is to be done here," he said slowly. "I don't want to leave Pete in the lurch."

"I was kind of hoping you'd live here for a bit," Pete said. "Even as the sheriff, you can stay here."

Pierce looked at him in surprise. "Are you okay with that?"

Pete grinned. "Hell yes. I'd like to see you live here for a long time, but that would entail Hedi moving in too, and I highly doubt she wants that," Pete teased.

Hedi could feel the color washing up her cheeks. "That's not fair," she said.

Her father guffawed loudly. "You're in a shitty-ass little rental now. What you guys should do is fix up someplace nearby, so you're close to Pete."

"That won't happen anytime soon," Pierce said calmly. "Pete's renos are the first priority. We have to make sure he's got a fully accessible kitchen and bathroom and properly equipped vehicle and that he can get in and out of his house on his own. We can work on the rest afterward."

"The rest?" Pete said, dazed. "What else could you possibly do?"

"Depends if you want access to the upstairs or not," Pierce said. "We could put in an elevator."

Pete looked at him, and his jaw dropped. "That would be a lot of money."

"It would be some money," Pierce said with a nod. "So that's one of those questions where you have to ask, is it worth it to you?"

"Wow." Pete looked at Pierce and said, "But you still haven't answered me."

"I guess it's a yes then," Pierce said, "but, about starting the job as sheriff, I want to make sure that bathroom is 100 percent ready and that we've opened up those double front doors and I've at least gutted this kitchen."

Pete just chuckled. "You know that usually these renos take months, right?"

Pierce shrugged and said, "For a lot of people it takes months. But for a lot of people it doesn't. I promised you full accessibility, and I'll make sure you get it."

"We'll keep working," Jessie said. "Once you're sheriff, you can be in a supervisory capacity here. Come home after work and tell us what to do the next day."

Pete clapped his hands and shouted with joy. "I can't believe this," he said. "Why the hell didn't I come home earlier?"

"Because Pierce wasn't here," Hedi said. "Remember that part."

Pete gripped Pierce's wrist. "Man, I owe you big-time."

Pierce shook his head. "We all owe you," he said firmly.

"You took a hit for our country."

Pete mumbled under his breath and then said, "I sure wish the rest of the world thought the way you do."

"You have a good group of friends around you now," Pierce said, all the others nodding. "You should be fine."

Pete looked at Pierce and asked, "And what about you? You'll accept the help being offered too?"

"What help? I don't need any help." Pierce frowned.

Hedi heard a vehicle came up the road and chuckled. She knew exactly who was coming. What she didn't know was how Pete would respond to the upcoming news.

Just then her father decided it was time to go. "Pierce, date?"

He sighed. "A week from Monday," he said. "I'd like the extra week off to make sure Pete's okay."

"I'll go in next week, Dad," Hedi said.

"Good enough. A lot of people went to bat for you, Pierce. We know you'll do a good job." And, on that note, he turned, and his cronies walked out with him.

It was already late in the afternoon, almost dinnertime. Hedi looked at Pete and Pierce and said, "Barbecued steaks for dinner?"

"I would absolutely love a barbecued steak," Pete said. "Used to love barbecuing." He looked at his prosthetics and frowned.

"Today sounds like a great day to get back into it," Pierce said. "We'll move the grill up on the deck, so you can get to it."

Pete grinned. "Wouldn't that be something?"

"Remember that your legs are injured, not your hands," Hedi said, as she'd said many times before. There seemed to be this disconnect sometimes with Pete because, being without his lower legs, he had a sense of not being able to do anything. Whereas he was capable of doing so much more. She'd even caught him swinging a hammer today with Pierce. A little weak and off center but he was helping and smiling as he did so. She smiled. "I'll take Pierce out for a walk, if you don't mind."

"Absolutely not," Pete said, waving at the backyard and beyond, grinning. "You guys need private time too. When are you moving in, Hedi?"

She shot him a look and shook her head.

He nodded. "Pierce will be living here for a while," he said. "At least I hope."

"I won't leave you in the lurch," Pierce said. "Doesn't mean somebody else might want to take my place though."

Just then a knock came at the door. Pete called out, "The door's unlocked. Come on in."

The door pushed open, followed by light footsteps. Then a soft female voice. "Pete?"

Hedi watched the color drain from Pete's face. He shook his head and said, "No. Oh, hell no."

In a firm voice Hedi said, "Yes."

He looked at her, startled.

"You are *not* disabled," she said. "You're perfectly capable of handling anything and everything life throws at you. You need to gain some strength. You need to have a mindset shift. But you're well on the way. And that means you can shift in all directions."

And just then a beautiful blonde walked into the kitchen with her eyes locked on Pete. Her gaze went to his shorts and the prosthetics on his lower legs. She swallowed hard and then looked up at him and said, "Why didn't you call me?"

Pete's jaw dropped, and he tried to answer her. He

looked at Hedi and Pierce for help.

Hedi grabbed Pierce's hand and said, "Glad you came, Lina. Pete's having second thoughts, *wiser* thoughts, about life now, and he's doing so much better. It's a perfect time for you to come and say hi to him." As she stepped outside, she said, "We'll leave you two alone to talk. We're barbequing steaks later. You're welcome to stay."

Lina looked at her and said, "I don't understand."

"Pete was trying to be the brave warrior and to let you live your life without him holding you back," she said.

A flush of anger washed over Lina's face, and she rounded on Pete. "Did you think my love was so superficial?"

Hedi and Pierce, still holding hands, dashed out the back door in the kitchen, hearing raised voices even as they continued across the backyard. And then, all of a sudden, there was silence. Pierce glanced at her and said, "That was pretty devious."

"Men like to caterwaul a lot," she said quietly. "And Pete will make a big deal out of meeting her again and about his injuries. It wasn't necessary. Pete's so much more capable than he thought."

"A lot of it is mind-set," Pierce said. "Pete mentioned her once."

"Good," she said shortly. "Pete broke Lina's heart. Maybe now they can work it out."

"So you're a little bit of a matchmaker, are you?" He wrapped his arms around her shoulders and tucked her close.

She chuckled and said, "Maybe. It's been really nice to have you around these last few days, without all the craziness when we first met."

She walked to a spot in the meadow where beautiful mossy grass grew under one of the big trees, and the stream trickled past close by. She sat down and patted the grass beside her. "Let's just sit a while and give them a chance to relax."

"I'm all for it." He lay down with his knees bent, staring up at the sky. "Did you bring me here for a reason?"

She shot him a look. "Maybe."

She hopped up, and he twisted to see her pull a blanket out from the boughs of the tree branches and spread it out. He moved onto it and opened his arms. She dropped to the ground and sagged against his chest. "There is just something about matchmaking," she said, "that makes you want a little something extra special for yourself."

He tilted her chin up and kissed her. "I meant everything I've said so far. I really don't want to lose you." He kissed her again and again. "Lina?"

"Well, Lina is a very determined woman," she said. "I wouldn't be at all surprised if she doesn't stay tonight."

Pierce's eyebrows shot up.

She nodded. "So you might be the one wanting to move out a little earlier than you thought."

"I've been wondering about staying at your place for a long time. You've never taken me there. I figured maybe it was out of bounds."

"Not at all. But it's not all that nice," she said. "And it's not big enough for two of us."

"You've brought your dog once or twice, but that's it. I have yet to meet the cat."

"My thought was maybe eventually we could move into a house together. One for both of us."

He nodded slowly. "I'd like that. I'd love to build us one. But not yet," he said slowly, holding her against his chest and gently stroking his fingers through her hair. "Not only do we have Pete to get back on his feet, but Vicky and the kids' house needs work."

"I'm sure you'll recruit the exact same guys to help out."

"Yep. I don't think there will be a problem with that," he said comfortably. "But I'm not sure there's any money for those renos."

"We can do some fund-raising for her," Hedi said, snuggling in deeper.

"You're good people, you know that?" he whispered, kissing her on the forehead.

"You're good people too," she said, chuckling. She leaned up on her elbow, rolled over on his chest again and kissed him. "We don't have much time," she whispered, dropping him another kiss. And then another one.

She sat up, straddling him and slowly pulled her T-shirt up and over her head. His hands slid up to her ribs, cupping her bra-covered breasts and murmuring, "I'm not sure there's anything quite as nice as making love outside."

She nodded. "I figured you would think so. It's not that I'm into public displays," she said, "but there's something so very elemental about being out under the wind and the sun, just the two of us." Then a bird flew over, squawking at them. She chuckled. "And Mother Nature."

Before she realized it, her bra slid down her arms. She watched the look of wonder come over his face, and she'd never felt more beautiful as she sat on his hips. "In theory," she said, "what we're doing is pretty perfect, but we still have on way-too-many clothes."

He chuckled. She straightened, stood and stepped to the side, where she kicked off her sandals and shimmied out of her jeans. There she stood in just a tiny scrap of lace and cocked an eye at him. "Like what you see?" she challenged.

He bolted to his feet, his T-shirt going in one direction, his shoes in another, and his jeans and briefs hitting the ground faster than she thought possible. And then he stood before her, his eyes feasting on her, and she chuckled.

His gaze ripped up to hers, and he asked, "What's so amusing?"

She pointed at his feet. "You still have a sock on."

He pulled it off and then pointed at the scrap of lace she still wore. "You still have clothes on too."

She took a step closer and said, "You do it."

He snatched her up into his arms and kissed her with a hot fierce passion that ignited a storm between the two of them. He'd wanted this right from the beginning, but, with everything else going on, there just hadn't been that perfect moment to explore each other. She wrapped her arms tight around his neck and half climbed his frame. Finally he picked her up, his hands under her buttocks and lifted her so he completely held her. She gasped and said, "What about your prosthetic?"

"Do you hear me complaining?" he whispered and kissed her passionately.

Finally she couldn't stand it anymore. She slid her legs back down, dropped herself to the blanket and opened her arms. He kneeled beside her, pulled off the scrap of lace and let his eyes feast on the bounty before him. He stroked her legs from her toes, over her knees and upper thighs, to gently curl in the tiny strip of hair between her legs. She moaned as his fingers delved gently between the plump folds and then slowly moved up to caress her hip bones. He spread apart her legs, with his knees planted between them, dropped a kiss right at the tip of the tiny strip of hair and dragged his lips to her belly button, where he dotted a line of kisses to one hip and then the other. His fingers were stroking, caressing, sliding under, separating her cheeks, touching spots she hadn't realized were so sensitive. She arched and moved, shifting forward and backward from his touch and then needing so much more of it. She grabbed handfuls of his hair and pulled him up, closer to her face. She whispered, "Come. I want you now."

But he resisted her orders, letting his fingers stoke the fire as he gently, reverently explored her body—the hills, the dips, the smooth skin along her ribs and over her hips. Slowly he stroked her flat belly to slide through the curls at the apex of her legs.

"Pierce," she cried out, her fingers clenching and releasing as she twisted beneath his ministrations.

"*Shhh*, I'm here," he whispered, sliding a finger between the moist skin folds to slide one finger in and then two …

She moaned, twisting her hips, rising and falling in response to the rhythm of his fingers. She reared up, tugged on his upper arms and pulled him toward her, ordering, "Come."

Chuckling, he shifted closer, supporting his weight on his elbows. He positioned his hips so he slid just inside her and stopped. He leaned over, taking her lips in a rousing kiss, his tongue sliding deep inside to war with hers. At the same time he slowly penetrated her body.

She moaned, her hips wiggling, adjusting to his unexpected size. And finally he was there, seated at the heart of her. When she could, she opened her eyes to stare up at him and whispered, "It feels so damn good."

He nodded, his voice harsh and deep, as he whispered, "Yes. But only because it's you." He kissed her again and again, but he kept his body still.

She twisted against him, her hips trying to rise up to set him in motion, but he wasn't having any of it. Finally she lay still, her body acquiescing as he slowly pulled back and then dove in again and again and again. She cried out, her body now writhing beneath him as she arched. He drove deeper and deeper, longer and harder, until finally she exploded, crying out for him.

He held her close in his arms as he drove in again and again until his body shuddered, quaking in his own release. A moment later he slowly rolled over on his side and tucked her close to him. Together, with the afternoon sun beating down on their heated bodies, they slowly recovered.

"Wow," she whispered moments later.

He nodded but didn't seem too bothered about talking.

She grinned, reached to kiss him and said, "Not into small talk, are you?"

"You did me in," he said, his voice still hoarse.

"Does that mean you're done for now then?"

His eyes flew open. "Hell no." He kissed her lightly. "We have just gotten started." He grinned and hugged her close.

"Promise?" she whispered.

He gazed deeply into her eyes and answered, "I promise."

EPILOGUE

VEN AS PIERCE stared in disbelief as the votes came in—giving him the job of the sheriff in Arrowhead, Colorado—back in New Mexico, Zane Carmichael sat down at Badger's desk and said, "I hear some dog hunting is going on."

Badger shifted back in his chair, steepled his fingers and studied Zane. "Do you have any K9 experience?"

"No," he said. "Artillery IEDs, all kinds of military experience, but nothing with dogs. On the other hand, I was raised with them, and I'd say I have a talent for them."

Badger's eyebrows pulled together. "Tell me more."

"Animals of all kinds speak to me," he said. "It's just easier for me than for a lot of people. I've had basic dog obedience training but not the high-level training of K9 handlers."

"Here's what we've got so far," Badger said and spent ten minutes sorting through what they'd done to date.

"I know Ethan and Pierce both had K9 training," Zane said. "I'd like to try though."

"We have ten files," Badger said. "The top of the pack was lost at the airport in Bangor, Maine. His last confirmed location was Stetson, Maine."

"Stetson?" Zane frowned. "How about any other place but there?"

"Why is that?"

"I've got family back in Maine, just outside of Corinna," he said. "As much as I love my family, Holly, my younger brother's widow, is somebody I'm trying to avoid."

"Why?" Badger asked.

Zane gave him a lopsided glance. "I cared too much. Brody's widow was my ex-girlfriend. After my baby brother passed away, I went home for the funeral but left as soon as I could. Holly was leaning on me too much, as if wanting me to step into my brother's shoes, and that was the last thing I wanted," Zane said bluntly. "I'd like to be loved for myself, not because I'm a reflection of another man."

"Wow," Badger said. "Sounds like you need to get back to Maine then." He picked up the file. "I've got a younger male here called Katch." He frowned at the name. "He's well-known for his ability to catch apparently." He studied the first page. "He was sent home after not following commands well enough under fire. He ended up with PTSD after one particularly bad bombing, and they couldn't get him to function properly afterward. He was returned to a training compound, then shipped out to an adopted family. He was lost at the airport, and the adopted family never got him. He showed up in Bangor, and we were alerted, but nobody could catch him. Our last notification said he was picked up by a hunter. Considering Katch is suffering from PTSD, that could be problematic. Now we're not sure where he is. Last known sighting was Stetson."

"Dammit." Zane studied the stack of files. "You sure you don't want to give me one of the others—a long way away from Maine?"

"Just for that reason alone," Badger said, leaning forward, "sounds to me like Maine it is. If you're ready …" He picked up the file and tossed it at him. "Katch."

This concludes Book 2 of The K9 Files: Pierce.
Read about Zane: The K9 Files, Book 3

THE K9 FILES: ZANE (BOOK #3)

Going home wasn't part of his plan ...

Agreeing to travel home to Maine to hunt down Ketch, a K9 dog the system had lost track of, wasn't an easy decision for Zane. It meant facing his drunk of a father, his cold older brother and, worst of all, Angela, his kid brother's widow—who used to be his girlfriend.

Finding Ketch looked to be the easiest part of this dysfunctional homecoming. Only he wasn't the only one hunting Ketch.

Angela has been through a whirlwind of emotions in the last few years. But the good thing in all of this was the hope that Zane would finally come home again. They had a history to clear up and a future to forge ... she hoped.

A call for help brings the injured shepherd to Angela's doorstep, plus a hunter looking to finish what he started. All thoughts of a future with Zane are threatened now and forever as the hunter decides two-legged prey are just as good as four-legged ones.

Book 3 is available now!

To find out more visit Dale Mayer's website.

https://geni.us/DMZaneUniversal

Author's Note

Thank you for reading The K9 Files, Books 1–2! If you enjoyed the book, please take a moment and leave a short review.

Dear reader,

I love to hear from readers, and you can contact me at my website: www.dalemayer.com or at my Facebook author page. To be informed of new releases and special offers, sign up for my newsletter or follow me on BookBub. And if you are interested in joining Dale Mayer's Reader Group, here is the Facebook sign up page.
http://geni.us/DaleMayerFBGroup

Cheers,
Dale Mayer

About the Author

Dale Mayer is a *USA Today* best-selling author, best known for her SEALs military romances, her Psychic Visions series, and her Lovely Lethal Garden cozy series. Her contemporary romances are raw and full of passion and emotion (Broken But … Mending, Hathaway House series). Her thrillers will keep you guessing (Kate Morgan, By Death series), and her romantic comedies will keep you giggling (*It's a Dog's Life*, a stand-alone novella; and the Broken Protocols series, starring Charming Marvin, the cat).

Dale honors the stories that come to her—and some of them are crazy, break all the rules and cross multiple genres!

To go with her fiction, she also writes nonfiction in many different fields, with books available on résumé writing, companion gardening, and the US mortgage system. All her books are available in print and ebook format.

Connect with Dale Mayer Online

Dale's Website – www.dalemayer.com
Twitter – @DaleMayer
Facebook Page – geni.us/DaleMayerFBFanPage
Facebook Group – geni.us/DaleMayerFBGroup
BookBub – geni.us/DaleMayerBookbub
Instagram – geni.us/DaleMayerInstagram
Goodreads – geni.us/DaleMayerGoodreads
Newsletter – geni.us/DaleNews

Also by Dale Mayer

Published Adult Books:

Hathaway House
Aaron, Book 1
Brock, Book 2
Cole, Book 3
Denton, Book 4
Elliot, Book 5
Finn, Book 6
Gregory, Book 7
Heath, Book 8
Iain, Book 9
Jaden, Book 10
Keith, Book 11
Lance, Book 12
Melissa, Book 13
Nash, Book 14
Owen, Book 15
Hathaway House, Books 1–3
Hathaway House, Books 4–6
Hathaway House, Books 7–9

The K9 Files
Ethan, Book 1
Pierce, Book 2
Zane, Book 3

Blaze, Book 4
Lucas, Book 5
Parker, Book 6
Carter, Book 7
Weston, Book 8
Greyson, Book 9
Rowan, Book 10
Caleb, Book 11
Kurt, Book 12
Tucker, Book 13
Harley, Book 14
The K9 Files, Books 1–2
The K9 Files, Books 3–4
The K9 Files, Books 5–6
The K9 Files, Books 7–8
The K9 Files, Books 9–10
The K9 Files, Books 11–12

Lovely Lethal Gardens

Arsenic in the Azaleas, Book 1
Bones in the Begonias, Book 2
Corpse in the Carnations, Book 3
Daggers in the Dahlias, Book 4
Evidence in the Echinacea, Book 5
Footprints in the Ferns, Book 6
Gun in the Gardenias, Book 7
Handcuffs in the Heather, Book 8
Ice Pick in the Ivy, Book 9
Jewels in the Juniper, Book 10
Killer in the Kiwis, Book 11
Lifeless in the Lilies, Book 12
Lovely Lethal Gardens, Books 1–2

Lovely Lethal Gardens, Books 3–4
Lovely Lethal Gardens, Books 5–6
Lovely Lethal Gardens, Books 7–8
Lovely Lethal Gardens, Books 9–10

Psychic Vision Series

Tuesday's Child
Hide 'n Go Seek
Maddy's Floor
Garden of Sorrow
Knock Knock…
Rare Find
Eyes to the Soul
Now You See Her
Shattered
Into the Abyss
Seeds of Malice
Eye of the Falcon
Itsy-Bitsy Spider
Unmasked
Deep Beneath
From the Ashes
Stroke of Death
Ice Maiden
Psychic Visions Books 1–3
Psychic Visions Books 4–6
Psychic Visions Books 7–9

By Death Series

Touched by Death
Haunted by Death
Chilled by Death

By Death Books 1–3

Broken Protocols – Romantic Comedy Series
Cat's Meow
Cat's Pajamas
Cat's Cradle
Cat's Claus
Broken Protocols 1-4

Broken and… Mending
Skin
Scars
Scales (of Justice)
Broken but… Mending 1-3

Glory
Genesis
Tori
Celeste
Glory Trilogy

Biker Blues
Morgan: Biker Blues, Volume 1
Cash: Biker Blues, Volume 2

SEALs of Honor
Mason: SEALs of Honor, Book 1
Hawk: SEALs of Honor, Book 2
Dane: SEALs of Honor, Book 3
Swede: SEALs of Honor, Book 4
Shadow: SEALs of Honor, Book 5
Cooper: SEALs of Honor, Book 6
Markus: SEALs of Honor, Book 7

Evan: SEALs of Honor, Book 8
Mason's Wish: SEALs of Honor, Book 9
Chase: SEALs of Honor, Book 10
Brett: SEALs of Honor, Book 11
Devlin: SEALs of Honor, Book 12
Easton: SEALs of Honor, Book 13
Ryder: SEALs of Honor, Book 14
Macklin: SEALs of Honor, Book 15
Corey: SEALs of Honor, Book 16
Warrick: SEALs of Honor, Book 17
Tanner: SEALs of Honor, Book 18
Jackson: SEALs of Honor, Book 19
Kanen: SEALs of Honor, Book 20
Nelson: SEALs of Honor, Book 21
Taylor: SEALs of Honor, Book 22
Colton: SEALs of Honor, Book 23
Troy: SEALs of Honor, Book 24
Axel: SEALs of Honor, Book 25
Baylor: SEALs of Honor, Book 26
SEALs of Honor, Books 1–3
SEALs of Honor, Books 4–6
SEALs of Honor, Books 7–10
SEALs of Honor, Books 11–13
SEALs of Honor, Books 14–16
SEALs of Honor, Books 17–19
SEALs of Honor, Books 20–22
SEALs of Honor, Books 23–25

Heroes for Hire

Levi's Legend: Heroes for Hire, Book 1
Stone's Surrender: Heroes for Hire, Book 2
Merk's Mistake: Heroes for Hire, Book 3

SEALs of Steel

Talon: SEALs of Steel, Book 4
Laszlo: SEALs of Steel, Book 5
Geir: SEALs of Steel, Book 6
Jager: SEALs of Steel, Book 7
The Final Reveal: SEALs of Steel, Book 8
SEALs of Steel, Books 1–4
SEALs of Steel, Books 5–8
SEALs of Steel, Books 1–8

The Mavericks

Kerrick, Book 1
Griffin, Book 2
Jax, Book 3
Beau, Book 4
Asher, Book 5
Ryker, Book 6
Miles, Book 7
Nico, Book 8
Keane, Book 9
Lennox, Book 10
Gavin, Book 11
Shane, Book 12
The Mavericks, Books 1–2
The Mavericks, Books 3–4
The Mavericks, Books 5–6
The Mavericks, Books 7–8
The Mavericks, Books 9–10
The Mavericks, Books 11–12

Bullard's Battle Series

Ryland's Reach, Book 1
Cain's Cross, Book 2

Eton's Escape, Book 3
Garret's Gambit, Book 4
Kano's Keep, Book 5
Fallon's Flaw, Book 6
Quinn's Quest, Book 7
Bullard's Beauty, Book 8

Collections
Dare to Be You…
Dare to Love…
Dare to be Strong…
RomanceX3

Standalone Novellas
It's a Dog's Life
Riana's Revenge
Second Chances

Published Young Adult Books:

Family Blood Ties Series
Vampire in Denial
Vampire in Distress
Vampire in Design
Vampire in Deceit
Vampire in Defiance
Vampire in Conflict
Vampire in Chaos
Vampire in Crisis
Vampire in Control
Vampire in Charge
Family Blood Ties Set 1–3

Family Blood Ties Set 1–5

Family Blood Ties Set 4–6

Family Blood Ties Set 7–9

Sian's Solution, A Family Blood Ties Series Prequel
Novelette

Design series

Dangerous Designs

Deadly Designs

Darkest Designs

Design Series Trilogy

Standalone

In Cassie's Corner

Gem Stone (a Gemma Stone Mystery)

Time Thieves

Published Non-Fiction Books:

Career Essentials

Career Essentials: The Résumé

Career Essentials: The Cover Letter

Career Essentials: The Interview

Career Essentials: 3 in 1

www.ingramcontent.com/pod-product-compliance
Lightning Source LLC
Chambersburg PA
CBHW060303100726
47907CB00002B/258